Praise for John Saul

"Saul has the instincts of a natural storyteller."
—*People*

"One of the masters of the genre."
—*Atlanta Journal*

"Saul can make your skin crawl."
—*St. Petersburg Times*

Midnight Voices

"CHILLING . . . Saul knows how to dish out thrills, and with a sly tribute to Levin's *Rosemary's Baby*, as well as other horror classics, this latest pulp shocker should have fans lining up."
—*Publishers Weekly*

"A gripping read . . . From the creepy doorman to the aging actress in a nearby apartment to a spooky blind matron, Saul's characters instill just what he's looking for: chills and foreboding. Saul is a master at building suspense and using small details to enhance the effect."
—*The Advocate* (Baton Rouge, LA)

"Deliciously creepy and chilling, *Midnight Voices* is definitely the scariest book I've ever read. Grand master Saul takes an everyday world and turns it—to our sheer delight—into a world of unspeakable horror. Read and enjoy!"
—*Romantic Times*

The Manhattan Hunt Club

"Nonstop action keeps the book moving at a brisk pace."
—*Library Journal*

"Thrilling . . . packed with plot twists."
—*Booklist*

Nightshade

"[Saul] hunts his shadowy realm ingeniously and persistently. . . . *Nightshade* may be his masterpiece."
—*Providence Journal*

"Gripping . . . Saul, and his unerring instincts to instill fear, returns to tap into our deepest, most closely guarded shadows and secrets."
—*Palo Alto Daily News*

The Right Hand of Evil

"[A] tale of evil that is both extreme and entertaining."
—*Chicago Tribune*

"[A] whopper of a nightmare tale . . . dazzling . . . dizzying twists."
—*Publishers Weekly*

The Presence

"A suspenseful thriller . . . provocative . . . nicely done, indeed."
—*Kirkus Reviews*

"Enough smoothly crafted suspense to keep readers turning pages long after dark."
—*The Seattle Times*

Black Lightning

"Electrifyingly scary."
—*San Jose Mercury News*

"One of Saul's best."
—*Publishers Weekly*

The Homing

"If you are a Stephen King/Dean Koontz fan, *The Homing* is a book you will only open once. You will not put it down until its last page has been absorbed. John Saul takes the psychological suspense novel to a new height."
—*The Dayton Voice*

Guardian

"Chills and thrills . . . a great hair-raiser."
—*San Diego Union Tribune*

By John Saul

Suffer the Children
Punish the Sinners
Cry for the Strangers
Comes the Blind Fury
When the Wind Blows
The God Project
Nathaniel
Brainchild
Hellfire
The Unwanted
The Unloved
Creature
Second Child
Sleepwalk
Darkness
Shadows
Guardian
The Homing
Black Lightning

The Blackstone Chronicles
PART 1: *An Eye for an Eye: The Doll*
PART 2: *Twist of Fate: The Locket*
PART 3: *Ashes to Ashes: The Dragon's Flame*
PART 4: *In the Shadow of Evil: The Handkerchief*
PART 5: *Day of Reckoning: The Stereoscope*
PART 6: *Asylum*

The Presence
The Right Hand of Evil
Nightshade
The Manhattan Hunt Club
Midnight Voices
Black Creek Crossing

BLACK
CREEK CROSSING

A NOVEL

JOHN
SAUL

BALLANTINE BOOKS • NEW YORK

2005 Ballantine Books Mass Market Edition

Copyright © 2004 by John Saul
Excerpt from *Perfect Nightmare* copyright © 2005 by John Saul

Published in the United States by Ballantine Books, an imprint of The Random House Publishing Group, a division of Random House, Inc., New York.

Ballantine and colophon are registered trademarks of Random House, Inc.

Originally published in hardcover in the United States by Ballantine Books, an imprint of The Random House Publishing Group, a division of Random House, Inc., in 2004.

This book contains an excerpt from the forthcoming edition of *Perfect Nightmare*. This excerpt has been set for this edition only and may not reflect the final content of the forthcoming edition.

ISBN 0-449-00654-9

Cover design: Carl D. Galian
Cover illustration: Phil Heffernan

Printed in the United States of America

www.ballantinebooks.com

OPM 9 8 7 6 5 4 3 2 1

For Michael—
Here we go again!

Prologue

T WAS THE COLD THAT AWAKENED HER, A COLD THAT crept first into her sleep, curling its fingers around her subconscious, making her feel as if she were walking through the woods on a winter night. Snow crunched beneath her feet, and all around her the bare limbs of trees glistened in the moonlight, every branch and twig encased in ice that sparkled with a brilliance that seemed to mirror the millions of stars that twinkled in the clear night sky. The path wound through a stand of birches, and she was striding along with the careless exhilaration of a spring afternoon rather than the sense of purposeful urgency that winter nights always brought.

Then, as the cold tightened its grip, the dream began to change.

A cloud scudded across the moon, and the stars began to fade.

The woman instinctively reached to pull her shawl tighter around her throat and shoulders, but all her fingers closed on was the thin flannel of her nightgown.

Why wasn't she dressed?

She hurried her step, and only now realized she was barefoot and the cold of the snow was numbing her toes.

She quickened her pace again, intent on reaching home

before frostbite began eating at her flesh, but now the path seemed to be vanishing from beneath her feet. She paused, peering through the darkness to find the trail once more, but suddenly everything had changed.

The moonlight had disappeared, and the stars were gone.

The trees, every branch glittering with light only a moment ago, were etched against the clouds in a black even darker than the sky itself, and their limbs, which had thrust upward in celebration, now loomed over her, their branches reaching toward her, their twigs turning to skeletal fingers straining to scratch her flesh.

Searching for the vanished path, she looked first in one direction, then in another. But everywhere she looked the snow was unbroken, as if she'd been dropped from nowhere into this dark and freezing wilderness.

Her heart pounded and she felt a wave of panic rise within her.

But why?

There was nothing to be afraid of—she'd been in the woods a hundred times and had never been frightened.

But somehow this night was different than all the others, the darkness blacker, the winter chill colder, cutting through her nightgown as if the flannel weren't there at all.

As the wave of panic built, a cry rose in her throat. She opened her mouth, but nothing came out but a gasp so faint she herself could barely hear it, and as she tried to find her voice, her throat and chest constricted until she could barely breathe.

She tried to run then, but her feet seemed mired in the snow, as if it had turned into the thick muck of the marsh behind the house.

The cold tightened its grip, and she shivered, her whole body trembling, and once again her fingers reached toward her breast to pull the flannel of her nightgown more closely around her.

The nightgown was gone! She was naked!

And she was no longer alone . . .

Somewhere in the darkness, somewhere just beyond the limits of her vision, there was something.

Something that was hunting.

Hunting for her.

Another cry rose in her throat, but this time she held it back deliberately, keeping it in check by the sheer force of her own will.

And finally, though the cold was now threatening to numb her body as the snow had numbed her feet, she began to run.

Too late. Everything was closing in on her—the cold was reaching into her bones, the snow was sucking at her feet, the blackness of the night was all but complete. And the trees themselves were reaching out, scratching at her skin, lashing at her arms, her back, her thighs, her breasts.

She sank to her knees, sobbing, and was reaching out—stretching her arms as if in supplication—when a blow from behind struck her.

Searing pain shot through her, and she pitched forward, sprawling out, and at last a scream erupted from her throat.

And she woke up.

For a moment she lay still on her stomach, gasping for breath, trying to shake the last of the nightmare from her still-reeling mind.

The memory of the forest began to fade, and the grasping limbs and twigs of the trees retreated.

The snow was gone, and she felt only the bedsheet beneath her.

Yet the cold still gripped her. And the pain in her back, instead of fading away, was growing worse. She turned her head to one side and the sense that she was not alone was stronger than ever . . .

I'm asleep, she told herself. *I'm still asleep, and this is only part of the nightmare.*

She lay perfectly still, trying to will the last vestiges of the dream away, as she had willed herself not to scream while still held in the grip of the nightmare's thrall.

Then she heard breathing.

Not the slow and steady breathing of a sleeping bedmate, nor the heavy breath of a lover.

No, this was the breath of an exultant beast, panting in rapture over its fallen prey, and as she lay on the bed trying to clear her mind and gather her wits, she knew with growing certainty that it was already too late.

The agony spreading through her body told her the predator had already struck.

Now, still lying facedown, she heard a change in the predator's breathing.

Felt it gathering itself together.

Felt it coiling, and knew it was readying itself to strike again.

She had to do something, to throw herself off the bed, to escape from the room, to escape from the house.

Escape from the predator.

Her thoughts were cut off as she felt another blow strike her back, another flash of pain sear her body.

Another scream rose in her throat and erupted into the darkness, and she threw herself over, struggling to flee from the bed and the attacker and the room and the house. But as she twisted around, her eyes locked onto the face that loomed above her.

"No!" she cried. But though she'd screamed as loud as she could, her voice was already reduced to a rattling gasp.

Then, above the face, the knife in the man's hand caught the moonlight, and for a moment that seemed an eternity, it hovered above her, glowing darkly with her own blood.

"No," she said again, the word this time no more than a weak plea, and as it died in the night, the knife began to descend.

She watched it arc toward her, her eyes following the blade as it sank into her breast. For a second she felt nothing more than the heaviness of the blow as the fist that clutched the knife struck her chest. It wasn't until the knife was yanked free of her flesh that the searing heat struck her.

"No . . ." she sighed once more as the knife rose high yet again.

This time she felt nothing as the blade plunged into her, for already her spirit had escaped her body.

For a moment the woman watched from high above, free from the pain, the cold, and the darkness of the night. Again and again the blade flashed down, slashing at the corpse that now lay still upon her bed. But the spirit hovering high above the bed was no longer concerned with the body that had once been hers. Now she thought only of another.

Her daughter . . . her little girl . . . the child she could no longer protect.

Too late . . . too late . . .

The eternal darkness swallowed her soul as her husband finished his grisly task . . .

Chapter 1

AS THE LAST BELL OF THE DAY RANG, ANGEL SULLIVAN sat quietly in her seat in the last row of Mr. English's room and waited for her classmates to disappear before she even started stowing her books in her backpack. Finally, when even the chatter in the corridor outside the room had died down, she stood up to pull on her jacket.

"You okay, Angel?" the teacher asked, peering worriedly at her from behind his desk.

Okay? she repeated silently to herself. How could she be okay after what had happened this morning? And if Mr. English didn't know what was wrong, how was she going to explain it to him? After all, it had happened right there during the first period, just before the bell sounded, when Mr. English asked the class if they wanted to sing "Happy Birthday" to her. "Happy Birthday," like it was still third grade! Didn't he know that none of her classmates even spoke to her except to say mean things? So there she'd sat, in her seat in the last row, her face burning with embarrassment as a horrible silence fell over the room and half the class turned to stare at her. The only thing that saved her from bursting into tears of humiliation was that the bell had rung. Then everyone rushed for the door.

And now Mr. English wanted to know if she was okay?

Biting her lip but saying nothing, she hurried toward the door and the safety of the corridor beyond, which with any luck would now be empty.

"Angel?"

She heard Mr. English, but was already out of the room, the door swinging shut behind her.

Angel. What kind of name was Angel?

For a long time—well, maybe not all that long, but for a while, anyway—she had thought it was a wonderful name, maybe the most wonderful name in the world. Even now, memories of phrases from when she was barely more than a baby echoed softly in her mind.

Daddy's little Angel.

Mommy's little Angel.

Grammy's perfect *little Angel.*

It had been Grammy who gave her the very first Halloween costume she could remember. It was a white dress that Angel was certain had been made of satin but her mother insisted was only cheap muslin. But it didn't matter, because it had white sequins sewn all over it that glittered even when she was standing as still as she possibly could. On the back of the dress there were two wings Grammy had made of papier-mâché and then covered with white feathers.

"I've been saving them ever since you were born," Grammy had told her as she carefully fitted the wings onto her tiny three-year-old shoulders. "Some people might tell you they're only seagull feathers, but don't you believe them."

"But if they didn't come from seagulls, where did they come from?" Angel had asked.

"Angels," Grammy told her, looking deep into her eyes. "Angels just like you. They come to me when I dream, and leave feathers on my pillow. Feathers from real angels for my own perfect little Angel."

Angel still had those wings, but they no longer hung on the wall of her room, as they once had. Now they were wrapped in tissue paper and packed away in an old hat box she'd found in the basement of the house they lived in when she was nine, and even though her mother thought they should be thrown away, Angel knew they never would be. They were all she had to remind her of Grammy, who died a little while after that wonderful Halloween when she'd worn the angel costume, and Grammy held her hand and led her up to the porches decorated with jack-o'-lanterns. Angel remembered being too shy to knock on the doors herself, and too terrified of the strangers who answered the doors to call out "Trick or treat," so Grammy had done that for her too.

Then, even before all her Halloween candy was gone, Grammy had died.

And she had been alone ever since, with only the wonderful feathered wings to remember her grandmother by.

After Grammy died, she'd still been "Mommy's little Angel" and "Daddy's little Angel" for a while, and wore an angel costume on every Halloween, but it wasn't the same. Finally, as if they understood that she wasn't anything like a "little Angel," her parents stopped calling her that.

The other kids, though—the kids her age—hadn't, and there wasn't a day that went by when someone didn't scream the dreaded phrases at her:

"Hey, Mommy's little Angel—will your wings still get you off the ground?"

"Hey, Daddy's little Angel! Why don't you use your

wings to fly to Heaven? Or don't they want you up there, either?"

The taunts had gone on and on, year after year. Her mother kept telling her it would stop, that the other kids would get tired of teasing her, but it hadn't.

A year ago today, on her fourteenth birthday, when her mother asked her what she wanted, Angel had blurted out the truth: "Another name! I don't look like an angel, and I don't feel like an angel, and I hate the way everyone always teases me." Then she told her mother what she'd been thinking about for months: "I want everyone to start calling me Angie!"

Her mother had at least tried, though no one else did.

Except Nicole Adams. Less than a week after her birthday, Nicole Adams and some of her friends had cornered her in the girls' room. "Don't you know *any*-thing?" Nicole said, as if talking to a five-year-old. "*Angie* isn't short for *Angel*. It's short for *Angela*! If you want it to be short for Angel, it should be *Ane-gey,* with a long A." Nicole's lips had twisted into a mean-looking smile. "To rhyme with 'mangy.' " Her eyes glittered with malice. "Hey, that's what we'll call you! Mangy-Angey!"

The rest of the girls had all burst out laughing, and though Angel felt like crying, she hadn't. Instead she ducked her head, pushed her way through Nicole's crowd of friends, and fled out into the sunlight of the afternoon.

And now a whole year had gone by, and it was her birthday again, and nothing was any better than it had been before. Except that wasn't quite true, Angel reminded herself. After all, it was fall—her favorite season—when the trees turned glorious colors, and the heavy humidity of the summer gave way to cool days and cold nights. It meant she could start wearing the big bulky sweaters her mom hated but that she loved, because they covered up at least some of the things that were wrong with her.

It was also that over the summer most of the kids appeared to have lost interest in calling her Mangy-Angey, and had gone back to just ignoring her completely. Or at least they had until Mr. English reminded them that it was her birthday.

But now, as she left Mr. English's room, the hall was as empty as she'd hoped it would be, and if she were lucky, she'd escape from the school before Nicole Adams or any of her friends saw her.

So that wasn't so bad either—if they didn't see her, they wouldn't tease her.

Still, it was her fifteenth birthday, and there wasn't going to be a party, and even though her mother had suggested they go to a movie tonight, she didn't think her mom could afford it, so she'd said no.

Angel was about to push the front door of the school open when she saw Nicole standing on the sidewalk with three of her friends. Quickly, she turned back into the building and ducked into the girls' room.

Empty.

Sighing with relief, she dropped her backpack to the floor, turned on the water, and washed her hands and face, so if anyone came in they'd at least see her doing something. Then, while wiping her hands, she caught a glimpse of herself in the mirror.

Angel, she silently repeated one more time, regarding her too-large features glumly.

"Don't you worry," her mother had been telling her for almost five years now. "Remember the ugly duckling who turned into a swan? You're my perfect angel, and before you know it, you'll be the most beautiful girl in town."

But now, standing in front of the mirror in the girls'

room, Angel knew it wasn't true. Her eyes bugged out and her nose was too long and her lips were too thick and too wide. Her hair was a lank and lifeless brown, and her body—

Her eyes welled with tears. *Angels are blond and thin and pretty,* she thought. *And I'm not blond, and I'm not thin, and I'm not pretty. All I am is*—

Before she could finish the thought, the door slammed open and she heard Nicole Adams's voice.

"See? Here's Mangy-Angey, hiding in the girls' room, just like she always does. What's wrong, Mangy? How come you wouldn't leave the school? It's your birthday, isn't it? How come you're not having a party? Is it because you're so ugly no one would come?"

Angel froze as Nicole's taunting words poured over her, and for a moment she wanted to grab Nicole's long blond hair and jerk her head right off her neck.

Instead, she did what she always did.

She ducked her head, grabbed her backpack, and pushed through the crowd of girls who had tumbled into the room behind Nicole. A moment later she had escaped from the girls' room, from the school, and from Nicole Adams's taunting voice.

But as she turned the corner at the end of the block and started home, she knew there was one thing she couldn't escape.

No matter how hard she tried, she couldn't escape being who she was.

It will get better, she told herself. *Someday, it will get better.*

And someday she'd have a friend—a real friend who would like her just the way she was, just like Grammy had.

Like some kind of silent mantra, she repeated the words to herself over and over again.

It will get better . . . I'll find a friend . . . it will get better . . . I'll find a friend . . .

But no matter how many times she repeated the words, Angel Sullivan knew she didn't quite believe them.

Chapter 2

MARTY SULLIVAN CAST A SIDELONG GLANCE AT THE gleaming Airstream trailer that served as an on-site office for the strip mall that was supposed to have been almost done by now. It was only last week, however, that the framework began to climb above the underground parking lot the town of Eastbury, Massachusetts, had required. Pissant regulations, as far as he was concerned—not that anybody ever listened to him. But since they'd gotten held up on the garage—one of his boss's snafus that he'd tried to blame on him, just like always—there wasn't a chance that they'd get the place framed and closed before the New England winter set in. Which, Marty knew, meant that he and the rest of the crew would be shivering in a couple of more months as much as they'd been sweltering during the summer, when they were stuck down in the pit of the parking garage, setting rebar and pounding forms without a breath of fresh air and the heat in the nineties, with humidity to match. If *he'd* been in charge . . .

But he wasn't in charge, and Jerry O'Donnell—the foreman who'd had it in for Marty since the day he'd signed on to the job last June—wasn't going to listen to anything he had to say. Marty raised the middle finger of his left hand in a sour salute toward the Airstream—

where he was pretty sure O'Donnell and the office girl were getting it on every day—then unscrewed the top of his thermos and took a long gulp. Though the liquid was only lukewarm, the warmth of the brandy he'd added to Myra's crappy coffee quickly spread through his gut. When the alcohol did nothing to brighten his mood, Marty tipped the thermos to his lips again, draining it, then dropped the lid and the bottle back into his lunch bucket.

Couple more hours and he could go home.

Couple more hours of him working his butt off while O'Donnell cooled his in the Airstream. Maybe he should just go over there and get himself a little piece of the—

"Hey, Marty," Kurt Winkowski called from the far corner of the site. He and Bud Grimes were struggling with a large piece of prefab framing. "How's about givin' us a hand over here!"

Glowering balefully at the trailer one last time, Marty heaved himself to his feet. "What's the matter? That thing too heavy for you guys?" Ambling across the newly hardened concrete, he tripped over a drainpipe that hadn't yet been trimmed, cursed under his breath, then shoved Winkowski aside. "Lemme hold it while you get a rivet in." The piece of metal framing, ten feet tall and nearly as long, tilted as Winkowski released it. It nearly twisted out of Marty's hands, but Bud Grimes reached out to steady it just before it fell.

"I can do it!" Marty growled. "Just get the damned rivet gun, Winkowski."

For a moment Kurt Winkowski seemed about to argue, but Marty's size and the look of half-drunken belligerence in his eyes made him think better of it. Picking up the pneumatic rivet gun, he moved to the point where the two pieces of framing met at a ninety-degree angle, and used his left hand to try to line up the matching holes in the two components. Bud Grimes's piece held steady, but the framing Marty Sullivan was trying to steady kept wavering back and forth.

"Jeez, Marty, how'm I s'posed to—"

"Just shoot the damn thing," Marty growled. "What kind of dumb mother—"

There was a sharp explosive sound as Winkowski pulled the trigger of the rivet gun, followed by a scream of pain as Bud Grimes let go of the framing he was holding and clutched at his left bicep. As the framing crashed against the fence that stood between the foundation and the sidewalk beyond, Marty Sullivan took a step to one side, lost his balance, then tumbled to the ground, the metal framing falling on top of him. He struggled for a moment, but the prefabricated structure was too heavy. "Someone get this damn thing off me!" he yelled as the rest of the construction crew came racing over.

"The hell with Sullivan," Winkowski shouted. "It was his fault! Someone get the first-aid kit for Bud."

Bud Grimes had sunk down onto a stack of framing, his face ashen, his left sleeve crimson with blood, despite the fact that his right hand was still clamped over the wound. Someone started toward the site office when the door of the Airstream opened and Jerry O'Donnell charged out with the first-aid kit.

"What happened?" he asked as he shouldered through the men crowded around Bud Grimes. He crouched down and opened the first-aid kit as Winkowski began to explain, then began cutting away the sleeve of Grimes's shirt.

"Get this goddamn crap offa me!" Marty Sullivan howled, and finally two men picked up the enormous piece of prefab steel and tossed it aside. "I coulda been killed!" Marty complained, starting to get up. But then he dropped back down to the concrete. "Jeez—I think my back's hurt."

Jerry O'Donnell barely glanced at him. "Someone call an ambulance," he said. "Grimes needs to go to the hospital."

"I'm okay," Grimes complained, but his pale face was damp with a sheen of sweat. "Just put a bandage on it and—" His words abruptly died as he tried to move his injured arm and an agonizing pain shot through it.

"You're not okay," O'Donnell replied. "Whatever went in there didn't come back out."

"It was a rivet," Winkowski repeated. "Just as I pulled the trigger, Sullivan—"

"It wasn't my fault," Marty bawled. "An' if anybody needs an ambulance, it's me. My back's—"

O'Donnell wheeled around to face him, his eyes hard, his expression tight. "Your back's fine, Sullivan," he said. "But if you want, I'll sure have you taken to the hospital. And I'll have 'em test your blood for alcohol while you're there."

Without thinking about it, Marty Sullivan was on his feet, towering over the foreman, his fists clenched, his face only inches from O'Donnell's.

But rather than backing away, O'Donnell was smiling at him. "Still want an ambulance?" he asked quietly. When Sullivan made no reply, he said, "The way I see it, you might just want to be quitting, Sullivan." The other man's brows furrowed uncertainly. "Or would you prefer me to fire you?"

"You can't fire me," Sullivan began, his voice still truculent, but less belligerent than a few moments earlier. "We got a union that says—"

Again, O'Donnell didn't let him finish. "You got a union that says you can drink on the job?"

"I never—" Sullivan began.

"How dumb do you think I am, Sullivan?" O'Donnell said. "You think I can't smell the stink on your breath?"

Sullivan lurched back a step, and O'Donnell moved closer.

"You think everyone on this job doesn't know what's in that thermos of yours?" He shook his head almost sadly. "It's dumb enough to be drinking on the job, but it's even dumber to think no one's going to notice. So here's the deal—you get your stuff and get off this site right now, and that'll be the end of it. And don't think anyone else in town'll be hiring you, because I'll see to it that they don't. It's way too dangerous having someone like you around."

"You can't do that," Sullivan yelped. "My union—"

"Or we can go talk to the union about it," O'Donnell said, his words silencing the other man, though he hadn't raised his voice. "Both of us. In fact, we'll take the whole crew with us." He glanced around at the dozen men who were now watching the confrontation. "How about it, guys? Want to go down to the union and defend Brother Sullivan?"

None of the men responded, and as Marty Sullivan's eyes moved from one man to another, they either shook their heads, turned away from him, or edged closer to the foreman.

"I'll have Rebecca cut your check right now, Sullivan," O'Donnell said.

But Marty Sullivan was already walking away. "Screw off, O'Donnell," he said, the alcohol in his blood fueling the anger boiling inside him. "You think I'm gonna hang around while that bitch tries to figure out how to do some real work?"

Grabbing his jacket and his lunchbox, and wondering where the nearest place to get a drink, Marty Sullivan shambled away from the site.

Chapter 3

MYRA SULLIVAN STRAIGHTENED UP, PRESSING HER left hand against the small of her own back to ease the pain. It had begun burning right after lunch, but she'd refused to give in to it until she finished the job at hand.

As the pain had spread from her back into her hips, then down her legs into her knees, she silently repeated Father Raphaello's adage: "Pain is the reward of work well done." Until today, she'd never quite understood what the seemingly self-contradictory words meant; after all, how could pain be a reward for anything? But now, as she gazed at the gleaming tile floor of the rectory's kitchen, the meaning became clear, and she nodded with satisfaction.

There was not a smear anywhere on the bright yellow glaze of the tiles, nor the faintest stain in any of the grout between them. She'd spent the last three hours on her hands and knees cleaning those crevices between the tiles with more than a dozen solvents and bleaches. Sighing, she tossed the old toothbrush she'd used to scrub every inch of grout until every speck of mildew was gone into the wastebasket at the end of the sink. Tomorrow, she would start on the counter, but at least she could stand up for that job.

As she admired her work, the pain in her body began to ease, and she recalled Father Raphaello's adage again. Though her body ached, her spirit was buoyed by the work she'd accomplished. Then, glancing at the clock, her spirits sank again. It was already five-fifteen. If she didn't hurry, she wouldn't have Marty's dinner ready on time, and then it wouldn't matter what Father Raphaello might have to say—she'd feel no satisfaction in anything for the rest of the night.

Gathering up the bottles of cleaning solvents, she packed them into the bucket and took them down to the basement. Then she left the rectory, by the outside steps, cutting across the backyard and through a gap in the hedge to the back of the duplex that faced onto the next street. Though the half of the duplex that she, Marty, and Angel lived in was cramped, at least they could afford it. Or they could afford it when Marty was working. When he wasn't—which seemed to be most of the time lately—she was able to work off the rent by taking care of the rectory.

As she fit her key into the back door, Myra silently chided herself for what she'd just been thinking about Marty. After all, he'd been working for Jerry O'Donnell for three months now, and it looked like the job would be good for at least a year, maybe even a little more.

Count your blessings, she heard Father Raphaello whisper in her head.

But as the key stuck in the lock and she heard the phone ring, words rose in her mind that had nothing to do with blessings at all. She turned away from them before they were fully formed, just as she tried to turn away from all sin, no matter how slight.

She rattled the door, then banged on it loudly. A moment later, through the window, she saw Angel appear at the door that separated the kitchen from the living room. Her daughter hesitated, as if deciding which was more important, the phone or her mother, then picked up the phone, shrugging helplessly to her. A moment later Angel put the phone down on the kitchen counter, came to the door and opened it.

"It's Aunt Joni," Angel told her as Myra worked at loosening the jammed key.

Turning the job of getting the key out over to Angel, and glancing at the clock to see how much time she had before Marty came home, Myra picked up the receiver. "Joni? Is this important, or can I call you back?"

"I've found a house for you," Joni Fletcher replied, eliciting a heavy sigh from her younger sister. "Just listen, all right? And despite what Father Raphaello might say, I'm not Satan, sent to tempt you."

"He never said you were," Myra said, opening the refrigerator to inspect its contents as she talked to Joni. "But covetousness is a sin, and how many times do I have to tell you that we can't afford a house?" Finding nothing in the refrigerator that would please her husband, she nudged it closed with her hip. "We've got next to no—"

Her eyes fell on Angel then, trying to extract the key from the lock in the back door. "Just a moment, Joni." Covering the receiver with her hand, she said, "Get the WD-40, downstairs, in the cupboard next to the washer."

As Angel disappeared down the stairs to the basement, she turned her attention back to her sister. "Sorry, I just didn't want Angel to start worrying. But we don't have any money for a house, Joni. You keep finding houses, and I keep telling you—we've got next to nothing in the bank, and—"

"But you don't need much! Not this time! And the house is *perfect!* It has three bedrooms and—" She stopped abruptly as Myra uttered a brittle laugh. "What, exactly, do you think is so funny about a three-bedroom house that's only eighty-five thousand dollars?" she asked coolly when Myra's laughter died away.

"I'm sorry I laughed," Myra said. "But do you have any idea how many houses you've described as 'perfect'? I think you need some new adjectives. Which, in our case, would be things like 'cozy'—meaning 'small'—and 'fixer-upper'—meaning 'falling-down wreck.' "

"Eighty-five thousand," Joni repeated as Angel came back up from the basement with the can of WD-40. "And I think they'll come down. Way down. And we both know Marty can fix anything he sets his mind to, as long as he—" She abruptly stopped again, but the last two words—"stays sober"—hung between the two women as clearly as if Joni had spoken them aloud.

"It's all right, Joni," Myra said as the silence threatened to get uncomfortable. "We both know what you were going to say. The sad part is, you're right—not only about what you said, but what you didn't say too. If he really wanted to, Marty could fix up the worst house you could find."

"Myra, I'm telling you, this is the house!"

Myra paused as the words sank in. Joni had been calling her about houses for almost a year now, and she had actually gone to look twice. But the houses they could afford—assuming they could qualify for any kind of mortgage at all—were even worse than the duplex they were living in now. And the ones that Joni had described as "perfect" had always been so expensive that Myra hadn't even bothered to go see them, certain they would only make her feel envious.

"It can't hurt to look," Joni said, as if sensing Myra's reluctance, and Myra wondered how many times her sister had spoken those exact words to hesitant buyers, only to sell them houses a few hours later, whether they felt they could afford them or not. It wasn't just persistence that had made Joni the most successful agent in her office; she also had an uncanny ability to sense exactly what a customer was looking for, and then find it for them.

"I don't know," she sighed. "It just seems like it's not the right time."

"It *is* the right time," Joni Fletcher assured her. "I always know these things. I have a sixth sense about them. And I know this is the right house, at the right price. And I'm telling you, this one's perfect for you. It's not huge, but—"

"I'll think about it, all right?" Myra broke in, knowing that once her sister got started, she could go on about a house for ten or twenty minutes. "I've got to get Marty's dinner ready."

"Okay," Joni agreed reluctantly. "But if you don't call me in the morning and tell me when you're coming, I warn you—I'll drive you crazy!"

"As if you don't do that already!" Myra shot back, and hung up before her sister could get in another word.

She was rummaging in the pantry for something that might pass as dinner, and wishing for once she'd ignored her conscience and splurged on some steaks for Angel's birthday, when she heard her daughter utter a frustrated yelp. "Can't get it out?" Myra asked, not turning around.

"I—I broke it off," Angel stammered, her voice quavering. "Daddy'll—"

Abandoning the pantry, Myra hurried to her daughter and took the broken end of the key from her. "Your father won't do anything at all," she promised. "I'll just call a locksmith and . . ." Her words died away as she saw that Angel's body was shaking and tears were streaming down her face. "For heaven's sake, Angel, don't cry! It's only a broken key—it's not the end of the world."

"It's not that—" Angel began, her voice catching on a choking sob. "It's just—" Her voice caught again, then she threw herself into her mother's arms and her words tumbled out in a rushing torrent. "I can't do anything right! And I don't have any friends, and I'm fat, and I'm ugly, and I hate everything about my life! I just hate it!"

"You mustn't talk that way," Myra told her, holding Angel away so she could look into her eyes. "You're not fat, and a great many people love you."

"Who?" Angel demanded, her voice muffled as she again pressed her face to her mother's breast.

"I do, and your father does, and Aunt Joni and Uncle Ed, and—"

"They're my family," Angel moaned. "They *have* to love me. But the kids—" She stopped abruptly, and Myra felt her stiffen, as if she'd suddenly decided she didn't want to say any more.

"What about your friends?" she asked. "Did something happen at school today?"

Angel pulled away from her mother, shook her head, and wiped her eyes with the sleeve of her sweater. What good would it do to try to tell her what had happened when her mother didn't understand that she didn't have any friends?

"What is it, Angel?" Myra pressed. "It's all right— you can tell me. I'm your mother."

But Angel only shook her head again. "Nothing happened," she insisted. "I just feel like—" She fell silent, then shrugged. "I'll be okay." But as they heard the front door slam, followed by Marty Sullivan's slurred voice as he shouted for Myra, Angel bit her lip. "I'll set the table," she said, and by the time her father staggered into the room a moment later, she was already pulling the silverware out of the drawer next to the sink.

"I quit," Marty Sullivan announced, his face red and

his voice thick from the half-dozen drinks he'd had before he came home. "Won't work for that son of a bitch O'Donnell anymore!"

As her husband's words echoed in the kitchen, Myra Sullivan's heart sank.

Once again, her husband was drunk.

Once again, her husband had been fired.

And this time she doubted there would be a new job, because she was fairly sure Jerry O'Donnell was the last man left in Eastbury who would give Marty Sullivan a chance.

Maybe, after all, it was time to go talk to Joni.

Chapter 4

ETH BAKER WAS SO FOCUSED ON THE COMPUTER screen that he didn't hear his father's first rap on his bedroom door. The image that had captured his attention for the last ten minutes was one of almost a hundred photographs he'd taken that day, wandering around Roundtree after school with the digital camera his mother had given him for his birthday last week.

"A camera?" his father had groused when Seth ripped the paper off the box. "For God's sake, Jane—he's fifteen! What does he want with a camera?"

"All I know is that he said he wanted one," his mother had replied. "I didn't ask him *why* he wanted one." Then she turned and smiled at him, but it was the same kind of smile he'd seen her put on a million times before, when she was pretending to be interested in something but really wasn't. "Did I get the right one? It was the most expensive one I could find without going all the way to Boston."

Seth had given her the nod he knew was expected. "It's cool," he'd said, though he hadn't even looked at it yet.

But that night, he read the instruction manual and decided that the camera was, indeed, very cool. The biggest problem was that though it would take pictures at very high resolution, the memory card it came with wasn't big enough to hold more than eight pictures at full resolution. And ever since taking a class in photography at summer school, he'd been taking dozens of pictures a day.

His father had been grumbling about that too. "For God's sake, Jane," he'd said when Seth's mother told him about the class. "What's he want to spend the summer in a darkroom for? He should be out playing baseball with his friends."

Seth had said nothing, knowing there wasn't any point in trying to explain that not only did he hate baseball, but nobody wanted him to play anyway. That was one of the things he loved about photography—in the darkroom, nobody paid any attention to what anybody else was doing, and no one was choosing up sides, and no one was yelling at him because he wasn't very good at sports, which was about all anyone else seemed to care about. For as long as he could remember, he'd always been the last one picked when they chose up sides for football or baseball, and though he could sort of swim, he wasn't good at it, and though he could dive off the low board, the high board terrified him so much he couldn't even bring himself to climb up the ladder. It seemed he managed to fumble every time someone threw a football at him, and strike out every time at bat in baseball.

But in the darkroom, he was alone with the pictures he'd taken, with no one waiting for him to mess up. Ever since he'd developed his first roll of 35mm film last June, and the teacher had looked over the pictures and pronounced them "not bad—not bad at all," he had been hooked. All through the summer, he'd used whatever money he had to buy film, and he spent hours every week in the darkroom in the basement of the high school, developing pictures, experimenting with printing them, enlarging them and cropping them, playing with exposures, as he did with the camera as well.

The funny thing was, the more pictures he took, the more he discovered he liked looking at the world through a viewfinder and then bending its reality in the darkroom. But the amount of film he had to buy had become a problem. Then, a month before his birthday, his teacher gave him the solution. As they were looking over the three rolls of film Seth had burned over a weekend, Mr. Feinberg shook his head and said, "You'd better get a digital camera, Seth. At the rate you're taking pictures, you're going to need a student loan just for film."

So when his birthday came around, all he'd asked for was a digital camera, and his mother had come through.

His only problem then was the small memory in the camera, which he'd dealt with by setting the resolution as low as possible, so he could take as many pictures as he wanted, and reshoot the good ones at a higher resolution.

Until today, it had been working out pretty well. But on his way home from school, he took pictures of some of the oldest houses in Roundtree, and when he got home and looked them over on his computer, he saw that most of them weren't good, that the lighting hadn't been right. But he expected that and knew he could go back another day and take the good ones at a higher resolution. It was the shot of the old house at Black Creek Crossing that presented a problem he couldn't resolve.

When he brought it up on the screen, there was something wrong with one of the upstairs windows. It looked out of focus, though the rest of the picture was in focus. How could one window on the second floor not be? As he looked closer, he wasn't sure. Maybe it wasn't out of focus; maybe it was just a shadow, or a reflection. But the sun wasn't shining on the front of the house, and even if it was, where would a shadow have come from? And if it was a reflection, it should have been mirroring something outside the house. But what?

Seth fiddled with the picture, using the controls in the program first to zoom in on the window, then to try to sharpen the image and increase the contrast. But no matter what he did, the area of the window wouldn't come into focus, wouldn't sharpen up like the rest of the picture. Not that the rest of the picture was all that sharp once he'd blown it up, because of the low resolution, which was fine if he was just going to look at the pictures on the computer screen. They might even print okay, if he didn't try to make them much bigger than three-by-five; they weren't much different, after all, from the contact prints he'd made from the innumerable rolls of 35mm film he shot before he got the digital camera, most of which he'd never bothered to blow up at all. But with film, if he'd found something like he was now seeing in the photo of the house on Black Creek Road, he'd have been able to enlarge it until he knew exactly what it was, instead of having it turn into a bunch of pixels that didn't form into anything at all.

Seth began experimenting with the color controls, thinking the image might be clearer in black and white, when his father's second rap on the door—much louder than the first—broke his concentration. Then the door opened and his father came in.

Blake Baker's eyes darkened. "What the hell are you doing?" he demanded.

"Just working on some pictures."

" 'Just working on some pictures,' " his father repeated mockingly. "What kind of pictures?" He moved closer to the computer, and Seth could see the suspicion in his eyes.

"Just some houses," he said.

"Houses? For God's sake, Seth! You're fifteen! What are you doing taking pictures of houses?"

Seth said nothing, knowing that whatever he said would be wrong.

"Chad Jackson and a bunch of his buddies are out in the street playing softball. How come you're not down there with them?"

"I was just working on my pictures—" Seth began, but his father didn't let him finish.

"Not anymore you're not," he said, reaching out and switching off the computer. As Seth helplessly watched his unsaved images vanish from the monitor, his father said, "You're going to go down there and play ball with your friends like a normal kid, understand?" Seth felt his eyes begin to burn, and he bit his lip. "Understand?" his father repeated.

Knowing there was nothing to be gained by arguing with his father, Seth stood up and started downstairs, his father's words echoing in his mind.

. . . *play ball with your friends* . . .

Didn't his father know he didn't have any friends?

. . . *like a normal kid* . . .

Was that what his father thought? That he wasn't normal? Just because he wasn't like the rest of the kids, did that mean he wasn't normal?

Seth grabbed a jacket off the hook by the front door, pulled the door open, and went out into the fall afternoon. But instead of trying to join the game in front of the Jacksons' house down the block, he turned the other way.

If he hurried, there might be just enough light to see whatever it was his camera had caught in the upstairs window of the old house at Black Creek Crossing.

* * *

"Tell me you're kidding," Zack Fletcher groaned, his dark eyes fixing on his mother, the Kentucky Fried drumstick in his hand quivering at the halfway point between the plate and his mouth. His expression was a combination of disbelief and something that resembled panic. "Please, Mom, tell me you're kidding."

"Why would I be kidding?" Joni Fletcher countered. At the far end of the table, Ed had also stopped eating, and though his face was impassive, there was a flatness in his eyes that told her he shared their son's lack of enthusiasm for the news she'd just given them. "I don't see why you're so surprised," she went on, deciding to concentrate on Zack first. "It's not like your aunt Myra and I haven't been talking about them moving here for years. And the house is perfect for them—absolutely what they've been looking for."

Zack rolled his eyes with the disdain typical of a sixteen-year-old who has recently discovered that his parents know nothing about anything. Shaking his head in disgust, he returned his attention to the chicken.

Ed, on the other hand, chose to respond on behalf of both the males in the house:

"As far as I know, *they* haven't been looking for a house at all," he said. "Seems to me it's been you who's been doing all the looking."

"I'm a real estate broker, remember?" Joni reminded him. "It's my job to look at houses and match them up with people."

"Couldn't you match them up with people who are actually looking for a house?" Ed replied. "And can afford one?"

Joni decided to ignore the first question. "They can afford the one I found today."

"Must be some house," Zack observed darkly. "Does Uncle Marty even have a job?"

"Do you?" Joni shot back, fixing her son with the kind of look that up until a year ago would have silenced him. Now he only shrugged.

"I'm only sixteen, remember, Mom? What do you want me to do, drop out of school?"

"When your father and I were your age—" Joni began, but Ed didn't let her finish.

"When we were his age, your folks didn't have a pot to pee in, and neither did mine. That's why we worked, remember? If we wanted any money, we had to earn it ourselves."

"Which didn't hurt either one of us," Joni replied.

Ed's brows arched. "And we *both* decided that we'd never put our own kid in the same position."

There was just enough emphasis on the word *both* to make Joni squirm. "Maybe we were wrong," she suggested.

"Maybe we were," Ed agreed in a tone far more affable than the expression on his face. "But it's not what we were talking about. So why don't you tell us just which house it is you think would make such a perfect home for your sister and—" He hesitated a moment, his eyes darting toward Zack, and Joni could see him censoring whatever phrase he'd been about to utter. "—your brother-in-law," he finally finished.

"Gee, Dad," Zack said, a broad grin spreading across his features. "That's not what you called him when we were out fishing last week."

Joni cocked her head, eyeing her son. "Really? And just what *did* your father call him?"

"A shiftless son of a—" he began, but his mother cut him off.

"That's enough, Zack!"

"Jeez, Mom," the boy complained. "I didn't say anything Dad didn't say! How come you're not picking on him?"

"Because he's not sixteen," Joni retorted. Her gaze shifted to her husband. "And I suggest you be a little more careful of your language." Ed Fletcher rolled his eyes, and Joni felt a twinge of anger rise inside her. "If I talked about your sister and brother-in-law the way you talk about mine, you wouldn't put up with it for a moment."

"My sister is a nurse, and her husband is a doctor," Ed shot back. "Which puts them a little further up on the winners' list than the scullery maid at the rectory and her shiftless drunk of a husband."

"That's a very mean thing to say," Joni said, her anger coalescing into a hard knot in her stomach. She pushed her chair back from the table, suddenly no longer hungry. "If they decide to move to Roundtree and buy the house at Black Creek Crossing, I expect that you'll keep a civil tongue in your head." She shifted her attention back to Zack. "And I'll expect you to take care of your cousin Angel and make sure she meets all your friends."

Now Zack shoved his chair back and stood up, his face stormy. At six feet tall—a height to which he'd grown seemingly overnight—he loomed over her. "Angel?" he yelled, his handsome features contorting in sudden anger. "Why do I have to take care of her? She's a—"

"Don't!" Joni commanded, holding up a hand as if to physically block whatever words Zack had been about to utter. Her eyes darted between her husband and her son. "I think it's time both of you started getting into the habit of speaking as nicely about other people as you'd like them to speak about you."

"Aw, Jeez," Zack groaned. "I'm gonna go get a pizza," he declared, and started out of the dining room.

Joni rose to her feet. "You have not been excused from this table, young man!" Zack ignored her, and a moment later she heard the front door slam. "Are you just going to let him go?" she demanded, wheeling on her husband.

"Oh, come on, Joni, calm down," Ed Fletcher said, reaching for the box of Kentucky Fried and helping himself to another piece. "He'll be back when he cools off."

"And you're just going to let him speak to me that way?"

Ed shrugged. "What do you want me to do? Hit him the way my dad always hit me?"

Joni was about to respond, then changed her mind and dropped back onto her chair. "Of course I don't expect you to hit him," she replied. "But am I the only one that thinks he's getting a little big for his britches?"

"Well, you've got to admit, he's got pretty big britches," Ed drawled, and Joni, caught off guard, found her anger giving way to a laugh.

"I swear to God," she sighed, "the two of you are going to drive me to an early grave."

"If your sister really does wind up moving here, the men in this house aren't the only ones who will have to clean up their language," Ed observed. "As I recall, Sister Myra doesn't take kindly to taking the name of the Lord in vain."

"Don't call her 'Sister Myra,' " Joni grumbled. "It makes her sound like a nun."

"No nun would be married to Marty Sullivan. He'd be more likely to drive a woman into a convent than make one leave." Rising from his chair, Ed came around to Joni's end of the table, bent over and nuzzled his wife's neck. "You know, there's a good chance Zack won't be back for a couple of hours," he whispered huskily. "If you're not still mad at me . . ." He let his voice trail off suggestively, then nibbled Joni's ear in the way that always drove her crazy. He felt her resisting, but then a shiver ran through her. "Let's go upstairs," he whispered.

An hour later they lay curled in each other's arms, with Joni's head resting on Ed's broad chest. As his fingers idly twisted her hair and stroked her ear just the way she liked it, she said, "You do remember that you promised to give Marty a job if they ever moved here, don't you?"

"Oh, Christ," Ed groaned, but it was a far more exaggerated groan than he would have uttered if he was really angry. "That was years ago! You're not going to hold me to that, are you?"

"A promise is a promise," Joni said, snuggling closer and running her fingers down her husband's naked thigh.

"Not fair," Ed protested. "Not fair at all." But as she rolled over and kissed him, he knew it didn't matter if it was fair or not.

Chapter 5

ETH BAKER GAZED AT THE HOUSE THAT HAD STOOD at Black Creek Crossing for more than three hundred years, his eyes fixed on the second story window that had shown up blurred in the photograph he'd taken only a few hours ago. But now, in the fading light of the early evening, it looked perfectly normal; just an ordinary window in a house that, though one of the oldest in Roundtree, didn't look that much different from any of its neighbors.

Not that it had many neighbors. Even though the actual address was 122 Black Creek Road, there weren't many other houses this far out. Everyone in town merely called this one the house at Black Creek Crossing because it was supposed to be the house where the man who ran the ferry lived back when the stream was wide enough and deep enough that horses and wagons couldn't just ford it. An overgrown path behind it still led through the forest to the old crossing spot, and there were even a few rotting timbers near the stream that could have been the remains of an old ferry landing.

Black Creek Road itself was a narrow lane that had never been completely developed, even after more than three centuries, which was one reason it had always been one of Seth Baker's favorite places. There was natural beauty to the area, with the dense forest and the meandering stream that ran through it. But even more important to Seth was that few people lived in the area and there were no families at all with children his age. When he was playing along the banks of the stream, or exploring the thick undergrowth of the maple forest, he didn't feel lonely. Ever since kindergarten—maybe even longer—Seth had always felt like he wasn't part of the crowd, that somehow he was set apart from the rest of the kids.

It hadn't helped that he'd always been so shy he could barely bring himself to talk to anyone who didn't speak to him first.

Or that he'd always been small—even most of the girls in his class were taller than he was.

Or that he'd hated sports.

So while the rest of the boys played soccer, softball, football, and hockey, first in the Pee Wee League, then Little League, then on school teams, he had played alone. During the winter months, he lost himself in the books in the old Carnegie Library, which had dominated the north side of the town commons for more than a hundred years; when the weather was good, he'd explore the woods that surrounded the little town.

But no matter how much exploring he did, he always found himself coming back to Black Creek and the Crossing. He knew almost every inch of the area—where the best swimming hole was, in which pools trout were most likely to be lurking, which rocks were the turtles' favorites for sunning on summer days. He'd caught turtles and frogs and polliwogs, and every variety of fish that lived in the stream, and taken them home to put in aquariums and terrariums. Once, he'd taken an old enamel bowl and put it in the backyard, filled it with stream water and grasses he'd pulled from the stream bed, then stocked it with polliwogs and waited for them to metamorphose into frogs. He hadn't thought it would take long, since they'd already been sprouting legs when he caught them, but two months later, as summer was fading into fall, they hadn't changed at all, and deciding the bowl was just too small for them, he took them back to the stream.

Of course, he knew about the murder that had occurred in the old house at the Crossing—everyone in town did. He'd heard the stories about why the man had killed his wife and child, but he knew they were just stories. When Chad Jackson had first told him that the man had gone crazy and killed his wife, and that everybody who ever lived in that house afterward went crazy too, Seth had asked his mother about it.

She'd laughed when he repeated Chad's tale, and told Seth that people had been telling stories about that house for as long as anyone could remember, and he should just ignore them.

Instead, he'd gone out to Black Creek Road the next day and stood exactly where he was now, gazing at the house across the street.

Though the lot it stood on wasn't particularly large— maybe half an acre—there weren't any houses on the lots next to it, or the lots next to those. Nor were there any houses at all on the side of the street where he stood. In fact, there weren't more than five houses on the whole stretch of Black Creek Road that lay between there and town.

All of them were old, but Seth knew the one at the Crossing was the oldest. It was small, and practically square, and had no front porch—only a stoop with an ugly metal awning over it. There were shutters at the windows, but they were all sagging and didn't look like they'd close even if anyone wanted them to. There was nothing particularly special about it. It was just an old house, lacking even the smallest interesting design detail. Not like the wonderful big Colonial, Georgian, and Victorian mansions strung along Prospect Street, or the smaller versions with the same kind of architecture that filled Roundtree's side streets.

But this house—and what had happened within its walls—held a strange fascination for Seth, and time after time, year after year, he found himself coming back to gaze at the nondescript building as if something in the structure might explain the terrible events that had taken place inside. It was as if the house itself didn't look very happy—if a house could look happy—and now, with the FOR SALE sign stuck in the unkempt front yard yet again, Seth thought it actually looked sad.

Sad, but no different than it looked earlier in the day.

And there was nothing unusual about the second story window. *Nothing except the killing of the little girl who had once lived behind it.*

Taking his camera out of the pocket of his jacket, he took a few more shots in the fading light. In one of them, a glimmer of the setting sun found its way through the branches of the maple forest and caught the second story window perfectly. If he'd caught the moment, and the picture came out right, the upper window should contain at least a partial reflection of the setting sun.

As dusk began to settle, Seth finally started back toward the center of town, silently praying that his father wouldn't notice that he hadn't tried to join Chad Jackson's softball game.

As he approached the pizza parlor, he saw Zack Fletcher and some of his friends crowded around one of the outside tables, and he crossed the street before any of them saw him.

Better to turn away and pretend he didn't see them than walk right by and have *them* pretend they didn't see him.

Two blocks later he turned on Church Street, and a couple of minutes after that he was in front of his own house. He was about to climb the steps to the front porch when he looked up at the house and cocked his head. Then, instead of going in, he crossed the street and turned around to look at it from farther away.

If he pretended the houses next door weren't there, and the big oak tree in the front yard was gone, and took away the front porch, his house looked almost like the one out on Black Creek Road.

His was bigger—much bigger—and newer, and its shutters weren't sagging, and it had a front porch instead of just three steps to a stoop, but otherwise they didn't seem much different.

Maybe that was why he'd always been so intrigued by the house near the stream, he thought. It looked like a smaller, worn-out version of his own home.

The last light of evening faded away, and as darkness gathered around him, Seth hurried back across the street.

That night, just before he went to bed, Seth slid the memory card from the camera into his computer and opened the file containing the pictures he'd taken that afternoon. A moment later the monitor was filled with the image of the house at Black Creek Crossing, with the reflection of the setting sun caught in the second story window.

Except that in the picture, it didn't look like the setting sun at all.

Nor did it look like a flame was coming from the window.

Instead, it looked exactly as if the entire house were on fire, its upper floor engulfed in flames.

Chapter 6

MYRA SULLIVAN ROSE STIFFLY TO HER FEET. HER rosary beads still twined through the fingers of her left hand, she silently repeated the last of the prayers one more time as she moved from the pew out into the aisle and toward the main door. She was halfway up the aisle when she abruptly changed her mind, and crossed over to the left side of the church and the statue of St. Joseph. Lighting a candle, she dropped once more to her knees, and though the rosary beads were still in her hands, it wasn't the rosary prayers that tumbled softly from her barely moving lips.

"Please," she pleaded. "Make it work. Make this be the right one."

Getting to her feet once more, she hurried on out the main door of the church. Father Raphaello had told her she could cut through the chancery behind the altar and use the back door to make it easier to cut through the hedge to her house, but she never had. Taking the short-cut from the rectory was one thing. Taking it from the church was quite another.

She thought that would be disrespectful, and she was certain that if she showed any form of disrespect at all, none of the saints would ever answer her prayers.

This morning, though, it seemed that things were going to be different. Marty hadn't awakened by the time she got home, and when he finally came downstairs half an hour later, the smell of bacon and fresh coffee filled the kitchen, and she put his oatmeal in front of him even before he asked for it.

Nor did he seem to be quite as hung over as he should have been, given his condition when he came home the night before. In fact, he'd come home drunk every night since he'd been fired, and then gotten up each morning with bloodshot eyes, foul breath, and an even fouler temper. She'd been praying about it all week, though, and this morning the Holy Mother finally seemed to be answering her prayers. *Now, if St. Joseph would only come through too—*

She cut the thought short, reminding herself that all she could do was open her heart to the saints, and then leave it to the Holy Spirit to know what was best for her. "Prayers are never unanswered," Father Raphaello had told her. "It's just that sometimes the answer is no." Myra had listened carefully as he explained that it was a sin of pride to think that either God or the Holy Mother, or even the saints, were bound to give her something merely because she had asked for it. "Virtue takes many forms," he said, "and often the gift of grace is given to those whose burdens seem otherwise too heavy to bear." The priest had been talking about Marty then, and how God would grant her the grace to please the man she'd married, no matter how hard it might sometimes get. But she was pretty sure Father Raphaello would give her the same advice about the house too. Whatever happened with the house they were going to see today, she would understand that it was God's will.

Still, when Angel came in for breakfast and Marty didn't start in with his usual carping at her, Myra couldn't help but let a little ray of optimism touch her soul; perhaps today was going to be the day when things began to get better for all of them.

Marty Sullivan pulled the battered Chevelle that had served as the family car since before Angel had been born to a rattling stop in front of 122 Black Creek Road. Joni Fletcher's brand new Volvo was already there, and Marty's lips twisted into a sneer as he eyed it. "Don't see why people think those are so hot," he observed. "Bet it won't hold up anywhere near as good as old Gracie, here."

Myra, already getting out of the car to greet her sister, ignored the remark. Joni was coming down the front steps of the house.

Angel, still sitting in the backseat of the Chevelle, barely heard her father. *A house,* she thought. *It's a real house—not even a duplex.* And even better, it was all by itself in the middle of a small lawn surrounded by a forest of maple trees, with the nearest neighbors so far away you couldn't even see them. Well, maybe you could see them, but you wouldn't hear them at all, which meant that for the first time in her life she wouldn't have to worry that no matter how low she turned the volume on her radio, the neighbors were going to complain.

And then her father would yell at her, and then—

She shut down the next thought before it could form in her mind and forced her attention back to the house. *There were some things it was better just not to think about.*

"Well, don't just sit there," her father growled. "Might as well see what it is got her prayin' so early this morning." Getting out of the car he eyed the structure balefully, and as Angel scrambled out of the backseat, she could almost hear him thinking up arguments against the house.

"I think it's beautiful," she declared, believing that even though it wasn't true, the house she saw in her mind's eye existed somewhere beneath the tired facade she now beheld. All it needed was a straight roof beam, a fresh coat of paint, and new shutters, and it could be even prettier than she imagined.

"You think lots of stuff," Marty Sullivan growled. "Thinkin' it don't make it so."

By the time Angel and her father got to the front door, Myra and Joni were already inside.

"It's not big," Angel heard her aunt saying. "But it's certainly big enough for the three of you."

"And it's a lot bigger than what we have now," Myra said, her sharp eyes taking in the empty living room. It echoed the simple rectangular form of the house itself, with a fieldstone-faced fireplace in the southern wall. The firebox was small, the bricks that lined it blackened by decades of flames, and above it, set into the stone facade, there was a rough-hewn oak mantel.

"I'm told it's original," Joni Fletcher said, crossing to the mantel and stroking its ancient patina with gentle fingers, almost as if she were stroking the soft fur of a mink coat. "I can't swear to it, of course—the house has changed hands so many times and had so much done to it that it's hard to tell what's original."

"That's the real thing," Marty Sullivan declared, striking the mantel with enough force to make Joni snatch her hand away. "Can't get oak like that anymore. And you can believe it's twice as big as it looks—there's gotta be more'n half of it buried in that stone."

Angel saw her mother and aunt glance at each other. Her aunt winked, and when her mother crossed her fingers, Angel did too.

They went through the rest of the house, which consisted of the living room in front downstairs, a dining room and kitchen at the back, and three bedrooms and a bathroom upstairs. There was a basement below the house, which was a single cavernous chamber walled with concrete, and the huge oaken timbers were clearly visible above, timbers that Marty was certain were as ancient as the one that formed the mantel.

"Probably came from the same tree," he declared, prodding at one of them with the tip of his jackknife. "But the concrete's starting to rot. Gonna cost a bundle to fix that." He fell silent for a moment, then shrugged. " 'Course, I could build the forms myself, and maybe even mix the concrete."

While her parents and aunt fell into a discussion of just how much work the house might require and what it might cost to accomplish it, Angel went back up to the second floor. The stairs, built in a narrow well between the kitchen and the dining room, led straight up to the second floor landing. The three bedrooms were of varying size, with the largest one occupying the southern wall. It was long and narrow, with a second fireplace to give it heat, and Angel could see by the worn areas on the pine floor that the bed had stood at the back, leaving enough room at the front for a table and a pair of chairs.

The other two rooms were smaller, separated by the bathroom, and Angel went first into the one at the back of the house. Its windows faced north and east, which meant the sun would pour into it every morning just like it did in her room in Eastbury. But even though she had always loved the morning sun, she kept thinking about the other room.

The one at the front of the house.

It was the smallest of the three bedrooms, and shared a wall with the big room that would be her parents', and the front window faced west, so she'd never get to see the sunrise or have her room flooded with light when she woke up. But there was still something about the room that tugged at her.

But what?

There was nothing special about it, really. In fact, as she looked at it more closely, it was easily the ugliest room in the house. Its walls were covered with faded wallpaper with a floral pattern Angel thought must have looked worse when new than it did now. There were cheap lace curtains hanging at the windows, and they were dirty, and most of them were torn too.

There was one little closet that didn't even have a light inside.

Frowning, she went back to the other room, which was larger, and brighter, and had a bigger closet.

A much better room.

So why did she like the other one so much?

Her frown deepening, she went back to the smaller room, closed the door, moved slowly around to look at it from every angle. Finally, she sank down to sit on the floor, her back to the wall, her knees drawn up against her chest with her arms wrapped around them.

And all at once she knew why she liked the little room. *Because it's just like me,* she thought. *It's ugly, and it's gawky, and nobody else will ever like it.* But she would. It would be her room, and she'd love it. And it would love her.

"Well, you certainly were right," Angel heard her mother saying as she came back down from the second floor. "It would do just fine for us." Angel paused at the bottom of the stairs as she felt a tingle of anticipation, then her mother spoke again, with a wistful tone that made her excitement fade as quickly as it had come. "But I just don't see how we can afford it."

"For heaven's sakes, Myra," Joni Fletcher replied, her tone that of a big sister patiently explaining something to a deliberately dense younger sibling. "Don't be a defeatist—where there's a will, there's a way."

Myra sighed. "I wish I could see how. I suppose the price might be fine for someone else, but I don't see how we can swing it with Marty out of work and—" Her words died on her lips as Angel entered the room. "Maybe we should talk about this later," she suggested, her eyes darting pointedly toward her daughter.

"I'm not a baby, Mom," Angel said, flushing. "I know Dad doesn't have a job right now."

"I can get a job," Marty Sullivan said, his eyes fixing on his daughter almost as if he thought it was her fault that he wasn't working. "But I'm not gonna work for some ass—"

"Marty!" Myra broke in, her lips compressing in disapproval.

"Jeez, Myra—" Marty began, but seeing his wife's expression turn even cooler, he quickly changed the subject. "This is a good house," he declared, reaching out to gently touch the oak of the mantel, much as Joni Fletcher had earlier. "And a hell of a price."

For a moment Myra seemed about to complain about her husband's language yet again, but then decided there was a more pressing problem at hand. "But it's still too much for us," she reminded him.

"I told you, the price isn't fixed," Joni said, a little too quickly.

Myra eyed her sister suspiciously. "Why would that be? It's already so far below anything else on the market . . ." Her voice trailed off as she tried to read her sister's face, and realized it was the same expression she'd had when they were kids and there was something Joni didn't want to tell their parents. "What is it, Joni?" she asked. "You might as well tell me what's going on now—I can see by your face you're going to have to do it sooner or later anyway."

Joni Fletcher licked her lips nervously, then took a deep breath. "You're right—I do have to tell you. It seems that—well, something happened here a few years ago, and—"

"What?" Myra interrupted. "The way you look, someone must have gotten killed, or—" Her voice died abruptly as she realized she'd come very close to the truth. "Holy Mary, Mother of God," she whispered, her right hand quickly tracing the four points of the cross on herself. "What happened?"

Joni Fletcher bit her lower lip, searching for the right words, but knowing there really weren't any. Still, there was no way she could legally avoid telling any prospective buyer what had happened in this house, and sooner or later they would hear it anyway. "It was actually quite some time ago," she began, the fingers of her right hand toying nervously with the tab on the zipper of her shoulder bag. "One of those domestic things."

Myra's expression tightened. " 'One of those domestic things,' " she repeated. "I think you're going to have to be a little clearer, Joni."

Joni took a deep breath, and then her words came in a rush. "A man went crazy, Myra. No one really knows exactly what happened, but—well, apparently he killed his wife and daughter while they were asleep."

Myra Sullivan gaped at her sister, the words stunning her into complete immobility. As their meaning slowly sank in, she turned to her daughter. But instead of looking as horrified as her mother felt, Angel was looking at her aunt as if waiting for the story to go on. It left Myra feeling disoriented, and as she looked once more around the living room of the house on Black Creek Road, she was certain that somehow—in the light of what she'd just heard—it would look different.

But it didn't.

It looked exactly the same.

Yet how could it? After what had happened here, shouldn't the house look like someplace a murder would have occurred?

Shouldn't it reflect the horror that had taken place within its walls?

Then she thought: *Why would it look any different? After all, it was just a house. Only in movies did they make places where terrible crimes had occurred look foreboding.*

Stupid, Myra told herself. *Just find out what happened, and don't read anything into it.* In an unconscious imitation of her sister, she took a deep breath to steady her nerves. "Maybe you'd better tell us exactly what you do know about it," she said. When Joni's eyes flicked warningly toward Angel, Myra shook her head. "If we should happen to buy this place—which I seriously doubt—Angel's going to be living here too. So I think she has a right to know what happened, at least if she wants to." She smiled thinly at her daughter. "Do you want to hear, Angel? If you don't want to, you certainly don't have to. In fact," she added, shuddering and glancing around the room one more time, as if searching for ghosts, "we can leave right now and just forget this place."

Angel's eyes too, prowled the room for a moment. Then she shook her head. "It's okay—it's not like I've never seen people get murdered on TV."

"The thing is, we don't actually know it was a murder," Joni said.

"Seems to me like it couldn't have been much else,"

Marty Sullivan grumbled. "You don't kill your wife and kid by accident."

"It's hardly that simple, Marty," Joni went on. "There were only the three of them living here when it happened—a couple in their thirties, who'd only moved to town a few months earlier, and their daughter. She was about eleven, I think. Anyway, they'd barely had a chance to get to know anyone yet, and then . . ." Her voice trailed off and she shook her head, shrugging helplessly. "He called the police one night—actually, early one morning—and told them something terrible had happened. When they got here, they found him sitting upstairs with his wife." She bit her lower lip, then went on. "She'd been stabbed several times—I don't really know how many—and he was covered with blood. And the knife was on the floor, right by the chair he was sitting on. The little girl was in the next room. She was—" Joni choked on her own words, tried to speak again, but couldn't.

A silence fell over the little group, and then Myra said, "Show me," her voice little more than a whisper. "I think I need to see where it happened."

Joni hesitated, then led them up to the second floor and into the large room that occupied the entire south side of the house. "The bed was at the back," she explained, nodding to the spot where Angel had placed it in her mind earlier. "There was a table and two chairs, I think. Anyway, Nate Rogers—that was his name—was sitting in one of them, and the knife was lying on the floor next to him."

"Nate Rogers," Myra breathed softly. "I remember hearing about him." She turned and looked directly at her sister. "Wasn't there something about him saying he couldn't remember what happened?"

Joni nodded, and Marty Sullivan snorted in derision.

"Yeah, right—'couldn't remember.' Amazing how these guys kill their wives and kids and 'can't remember.' Like it means they didn't do it or something."

"Nate Rogers never said he didn't do it," Joni said. "That's the strange thing—he always said he must have done it but he just couldn't remember. All he could recall was a voice whispering to him, but he couldn't even remember what the voice said. He went through hypnosis and those truth drugs—lie detectors and everything else—and nobody could ever get anything else out of him. Even the doctors finally said that if he did it, he'd blotted the memory out so completely that they doubted it would ever come back to him."

"Maybe he really *didn't* do it," Angel suggested. "Maybe—"

But before she could even formulate what might have happened, her aunt shook her head. "Oh, he did it, all right. They got enough experts in here to make sure, and by the time they were done, there wasn't any question at all." She frowned, recalling the reports she'd read that were in the papers at the time of the trial. "They found blood spatters on his face and clothes and hands that were only consistent with what would have happened if he'd—" Again she hesitated, but forced herself to go on. "Well, if he'd done it all himself. And there was a lot else—I can't really remember it all. But there wasn't any sign of anyone else having been in the house—I mean, not since the day they'd moved in."

Myra Sullivan said nothing, scanning the bedroom, trying to picture it as it must have been the day its last occupant died. Her eyes roved over the floor, searching for bloodstains.

She looked at the walls as if seeking something—anything—that might give some physical sign of what had happened here. But there was nothing. "Did they ever find out why he did it?" she finally asked.

Joni Fletcher shook her head. "That was another of the weird things—there didn't seem to be a motive. Everyone who knew them—their families, their friends from before they came here—said they were crazy about each other and had a terrific kid. No problems. But I guess you never know, do you?"

"So what happened to him?" Marty Sullivan asked. "They burn him?"

Joni chose to ignore the callousness of her brother-in-law's tone. "In the end they sent him to a hospital for the criminally insane. I guess he'll be there for the rest of his life." She fell silent, then tugged at her sleeve and fingered the top button of the blue blazer she always wore when she was working.

"At any rate, that's the story, and it's why the price is negotiable. The bank took it over after Nate Rogers went into default on the mortgage, and the thing is, it appears that nobody wants to live in it. The bank keeps dropping the price, but it doesn't seem to matter. So here it sits, and I think if you can deal with what happened, you can pretty much name your price—the bank just wants to get rid of it."

"How come no one's just bought it and torn it down?" Marty asked.

"Someone already tried," Joni told him. "But as you saw from the beams downstairs and the fireplace and mantel, this is one of the oldest houses in the area— parts of it might date from the seventeenth century. So the Historical Society made sure it was protected years ago."

Marty was quiet, as if turning it all over in his mind. Finally, he turned to Myra. "What do you think? If we really go in low and wind up getting it for next to nothing . . ." He let his voice trail off, leaving temptation hanging in the air.

No, Myra thought. *It's too awful.* But even as she thought it, her eyes were again wandering over the room, examining every corner, searching the walls and ceiling, trying to find any trace of what had taken place here.

And then, in one of the filthy windows, she saw something. *A face . . . the face of the Holy Mother . . . the Holy Mother smiling at her . . .* As quickly as the fleeting vision came, it was gone, but it was enough for Myra. She'd seen the Holy Mother before—not often, but enough times—and knew that whenever the Virgin appeared to her, it was a sign of something good.

Something good. But what was it? Why had she appeared here, in this house?

A second later, when her husband spoke, she knew.

"Come on, Myra," Marty said as they went back downstairs. "You've been talking about wanting a house for years, and maybe it's just what we both need."

With the vision of the Holy Mother still in her memory, Myra looked into her husband's eyes, and for the first time in years saw the warm, gentle look he used to give her when they were dating and he could never do enough for her.

"A place of our own—a new beginning," he said. "Maybe it's what we all need. I can do most of the fix-up myself. You know I can."

You can if you will, Myra thought, and instantly regretted the unspoken words. "Charity begins at home," Father Raphaello had admonished her only a week ago. "You must be as charitable and forgiving toward your husband as God is toward you." That must have been why the Virgin had appeared—to give her a new beginning.

"But how will we qualify for a loan?" Myra asked. "With you not working—"

"Ed's very busy right now," Joni Fletcher broke in. "He can use Marty. I know he can."

Myra saw her husband's expression darken, but then he shrugged. "If he's got a job, I'll take it. I say we go for it."

Angel, her heart suddenly racing, turned to her mother, waiting.

Once again Myra moved through the rooms of the house, even going upstairs for one more look at the rooms on the second floor. At last she came back down and spread her arms in submission. "Okay," she said. "If we can figure a way to swing it, I don't suppose I should object. It's not like we have anything to lose, is it?"

Five minutes later they were back in the old Chevelle, getting ready to follow Joni Fletcher back to her office to work out the details of making an offer. Angel, alone in the backseat, peered out the window at the little house at 122 Black Creek Road. Now that it might actually be theirs, it seemed to look different—as if it knew someone was coming to live in it again.

Just as her father pulled away from the curb, she looked up at the window of the room that would be her own. And for just an instant she thought she saw someone looking back at her.

So distracted was she by what she thought she'd seen in the window that Angel didn't notice Seth Baker, standing in the shelter of the tree across the street from the house, taking pictures.

Chapter 7

"SETH?" JANE BAKER CALLED, KNOCKING SHARPLY ON her son's closed bedroom door. As she waited for a response she glanced at her watch, then tapped her foot nervously on the floor. They were due at the country club in twenty minutes, and it was a ten-minute drive.

And she'd told Seth to be ready ten minutes ago.

When he didn't answer, she rapped again, harder this time, then turned the knob and pushed the door open. "Seth, we have to—" she began, and abruptly fell silent.

Seth was sitting at his desk, staring at the computer screen, still dressed in the same ratty jeans and stained shirt she'd told him to change when he came downstairs that morning. Not that he ever listened to her, which Jane supposed was her penance for having given birth to a boy, instead of the girl she'd been counting on.

"Really, Seth," she said, making no attempt to hide her annoyance. "Didn't I tell you what time we had to leave? And you haven't even started getting ready yet!" Quickly turning off the monitor, Seth turned to look at her, and Jane could see by his expression that there was going to be an argument.

An argument she was in no mood for, given how badly her day had gone so far. First, she'd been late getting to the Gardening Club luncheon, and was certain from the moment she walked into the restaurant that the other women had been talking about her. Then the lunch itself had run late, and as the last to arrive, she hadn't dared be the first to leave.

This, in turn, made her late to the Junior League Membership Committee meeting, which was to have been her first as chair of the committee. But when she arrived, LuciAnne Harmon had already begun conducting the meeting, and instead of sitting at the head of the table, Jane had to content herself with the only chair left—at the foot of the table.

And now she was going to have to contend with Seth.

"Why did you turn off the monitor?" she asked, her eyes narrowing. "Were you looking at something you shouldn't have been?"

"I don't—" Seth began, but his mother didn't let him finish.

"Turn it back on," she said. "Now. And don't look at me that way, young man," she added as Seth's brows knit into a deep scowl.

Sighing heavily, he pushed the power button on the monitor, and a few seconds later the screen lit up. On it was a picture of the old house out on Black Creek Road by the Crossing where that man—Jane couldn't remember his name—had murdered his wife and daughter.

"Where on earth did you get that?" she asked.

"I took it, Mom," Seth said, closing the program with a quick mouse click.

Jane gazed at her son in puzzlement. Why couldn't he be like the rest of the boys; why couldn't he at least play tennis? There was a wonderful pro at the country club— she'd seen to that when she was on the Tennis Committee three years ago, and it was one of the few things the new members on the committee hadn't tried to change.

But even Rick Stacey hadn't been able to get Seth to pick up a racket. "Can't you find something better to do with your time?" she finally said. Before Seth could reply, she plunged on. "I want you to shut that computer off and change your clothes—you won't have time to take a shower. We have to leave in—" She glanced at her watch. "—seven minutes, exactly."

"Why do I have to go at all?" Seth asked. "Why can't I just stay home?"

Jane felt another surge of annoyance. "Because it's Saturday afternoon, and that's when families get together at the club. You know that perfectly well!"

"But it's just the Dunnes, isn't it?" Seth complained.

"And Mel Dunne is *just* one of your father's most important clients, isn't he?" Jane countered, mimicking her son's complaining tone almost perfectly.

"Mr. and Mrs. Dunne won't care if I'm there or not."

Jane lifted one of her carefully plucked eyebrows. "And what about Heather?"

Seth felt himself flushing, but could do nothing to stop it, and when he spoke, his voice was an unintelligible mumble.

"For heaven's sake, Seth! Speak clearly!"

"I said, Heather doesn't even like me!" Seth replied, his face burning now. "And none of her friends like me either."

"And whose fault is that?" Jane shot back. "If you'd just make a little bit of an effort to—" Her words were cut off by her husband's appearance at Seth's door. Jane could see that Blake was even more annoyed than she was.

"What the hell is going on in here?" Blake Baker demanded. "Do either of you know what time it is? The last thing I need is—" Seeing how his son was dressed, his face darkened. "Goddamit, didn't I tell you to be dressed and ready to go by three?"

Seth paled in the face of his father's anger, but said nothing.

"Didn't I?" Blake repeated, taking a step closer to Seth, who shrank back in his chair. When he still didn't answer, Blake glanced at his wife. "Leave us alone, Jane," he said in a tone that made Seth's eyes widen.

He turned to his mother. "I'll be ready in just a minute," he said, finally getting up.

Jane shook her head. "Too late," she said. "Maybe next time you'll learn to keep track of time and do as you're told." Turning her back on her son, Jane left the room, pulling the door closed behind her. She didn't want to know about her husband's disciplinary methods. She'd turned her back on them before, and she knew she'd do it again.

"Turn around and drop your pants, Seth," Blake Baker said. Though he spoke quietly, Seth began to tremble, and when his father unbuckled his belt, Seth's eyes glistened with tears. "And don't cry," Blake added coldly. "For once in your life, be a man."

Silently, Seth turned around, dropped his jeans and underwear around his ankles, and bent over.

A moment later he heard his father's belt whistle as it lashed through the air, and felt the sting of the thick leather against his bare flesh. He clamped his jaw shut, stifling the scream of agony and allowing only a low grunt to betray the pain he was feeling.

Twice more his father's belt lashed his backside, and though each lash sent a spasm of pain through him, Seth bore it in near silence, and let only a single tear slide down his cheek.

"Two minutes," Blake Baker said as he slid his belt back through the loops of his pants. "Be dressed and downstairs, or we'll go without you. And believe me when I tell you that you don't want that to happen."

Exactly 115 seconds later, Seth appeared at the bottom of the stairs, wearing a clean blue shirt stuffed into equally clean khaki pants. His bare feet had been shoved into the loafers he hated, but that his mother always insisted he wear when they went to the country club. The welts on his buttocks still stung and had already begun to swell, but at least they weren't bleeding. In silence, he followed his parents out to the Lexus. He hesitated before getting into the backseat, but knew better than to stall too long.

Better to just get it over with.

Climbing into the car, he lowered himself gingerly onto the seat, and thought he would scream out loud as the pain radiated from his bruises. But no sound escaped his lips, and he held back his tears through the sheer force of his will. *Ten minutes,* he thought. *I'll just think about something else, and when we get there, I won't have to sit down anymore at all.*

Turning his mind away from the sting of the whipping his father had given him, he summoned up the image that had been on his computer screen.

The image of the house at Black Creek Crossing.

The image of the window on the second floor.

And the face—or at least something that looked like a face—that seemed to be peering out the window, watching as Mrs. Fletcher and the people she'd shown the house to drove away.

The face that had seemed so clear when he'd seen it in person that afternoon, yet showed up on his camera as nothing more than an indistinct blur, almost as if there was nothing there at all.

Chapter 8

T WAS GOING TO HAPPEN, ANGEL TOLD HERSELF. IT was really going to happen. All afternoon, ever since they'd arrived at Aunt Joni's house and her parents had begun filling out the forms to buy the house on Black Creek Road, she'd been certain that something was going to go wrong. And there were so many things that could go wrong.

Her parents could suddenly get in a fight.

Or her father could suddenly change his mind for no reason at all. She couldn't remember how many times that had happened—how many times they'd been planning to go to a movie, or go to the lake for a picnic, or just to McDonald's for lunch on Saturday, and all of a sudden, for no reason at all, her father would decide they weren't going to do it. When she was younger, she'd always thought it was her fault, that she had done something to make her father angry, and finally one day she burst into tears and told her mother she was sorry, that she didn't know what she'd done.

Her mother assured her that she hadn't done anything at all, that it was just something about her father she would have to get used to. "It doesn't mean a thing," her mother had said, her voice sounding even more tired than usual. "It's just the way he is."

But he hadn't changed his mind about the house on Black Creek Road, even when her uncle Ed didn't look happy about giving her father a job. In fact, that had been the worst moment of the whole day, and she found herself holding her breath as she waited to see what Uncle Ed would say when her father asked him about a job.

There was a long silence before her uncle responded. Finally, he said, "I'm not sure hiring family is a good idea," and Angel's heart had sunk. Her eyes shifted from her uncle to her aunt, but her aunt hadn't said anything. "On the other hand," Uncle Ed went on—and she felt a twinge of hope—"I gave Joni and Myra my word, and I won't go back on that." Angel started to relax, but then her uncle added, "But there are a couple of things you'd better understand, Marty. You're going to be working for me, not with me, and I'm going to be giving the orders, not you."

Angel had waited, once more holding her breath. Her father's jaw tightened the way it did when he got mad, and her mother shot her father a look of warning. "I guess I can live with that," her father replied. "At least till you see what I can do."

Her uncle's eyes had narrowed, and Angel was afraid he would change his mind, but he'd only shrugged. "Then I guess we'll see what you can do, won't we?" he said, and smiled. But Angel could see he didn't really mean it. "Want a drink, Marty?" he asked, and Angel saw her mother shoot her father another warning.

To Angel's relief, her father shook his head, picked up a pen, and signed all the papers her aunt had spread out on the table. Aunt Joni then went into another room for a few minutes, and when she came back, she was smiling.

"That's that," she said. "You've bought a house."

Her mother had looked stunned. "Just like that?"

"Just like that," her aunt replied. "I told the bank's rep I might have an offer over the weekend, and he gave me his home number. It's done."

Her aunt invited them to go to a party at the country club with them, but her mother declined. "We're not dressed for a country club," she said, "and we wouldn't fit in, anyway."

"But it would be such a wonderful opportunity for Zack to introduce Angel to his friends," her aunt said, though Angel had seen Zack glaring at her. Not that it mattered to her if Zack didn't want her to meet his friends, because he was a year older and she wouldn't be in his class anyway.

Afterward, in the backseat of the car as they drove back through the center of Roundtree on their way home, the scenery looked different to Angel.

She was going to live here, she thought, gazing out at the little town. If it had had horses and carriages instead of cars, it would look as if it came out of another century. There was a small square in the center of town, a black wrought-iron fence surrounding it, and neatly trimmed hedges lining the paths that wound through it. There was a bandstand in the center, and an old wooden teeter-totter stood near a swing hung from a branch of an enormous maple that spread its limbs over a quarter of the square.

At one end of the square was the library, a wonderful old stone building that was nothing at all like the ugly modern Eastbury Library, and at the other end was a large church with what looked like a cemetery behind it, and all the shops around the square were in buildings that looked at least as old as the library.

It would be wonderful, Angel told herself as they left town on the long drive back to Eastbury. They were going to live in their own house, and she would have friends, and she'd be in a new school, and everything was going to be perfect.

Chapter 9

THE ROUNDTREE COUNTRY CLUB WAS SPRAWLED OVER more than two hundred acres on the south side of the town. As Ed Fletcher turned his Mercedes through the gates and started up the long drive that wound through the maple forest toward the clubhouse that generations ago had been the home of his great-great-grandfather, he heard a small sigh of happiness escape his wife's lips.

"Aren't they glorious?" she asked, gazing at the trees with the same wonder he'd seen in her eyes the first time he brought her to the club, when they were still teenagers. And it was true—the maples were glorious, their foliage just beginning to take on the blaze of color that would build steadily for the next few weeks. On the day of the annual Maple Cup father-son golf tournament—which Ed and Zack had won last year— the area around the club would shimmer with the golden light reflecting off the leaves of the ancient trees. "It's just so wonderful that your family never cut them down."

"They cut enough others down that they could afford to save these," Ed observed dryly. "And it didn't hurt that they put the whole thing in a trust for the club either." He shook his head as he scanned the forest, and though he said nothing, both his wife and son knew exactly what he was thinking: how many houses he could have put on the property, if only his great-grandfather hadn't been so shortsighted as to turn the property over to what had then been the Roundtree Golf, Croquet, and Lawn Tennis Club. Ed suspected that his great-grandfather had founded the organization not so much out of love for any of those three games, but because he wanted his property preserved in the condition in which he'd inherited it, even though he could no longer afford to maintain it. Thus the trust, allowing what was now the Roundtree Country Club to hold the land and every structure on it in perpetuity, so long as they preserved certain acreage—including the Maple Grove—as wilderness.

Or, at least, his great-grandfather's definition of wilderness, which wasn't exactly the kind of untamed forest most people associated with that word. The Maple Grove—which had come to be capitalized at least in the members' minds, if not in any of the legal documents that pertained to the small forest—was kept free of anything that might distract from the magnificence of the trees themselves. No undergrowth was allowed to sprout from the soil around their roots, no twig or branch was allowed to lie where it fell for more than a day or two. Only the leaves could stay on the ground, for one of old Thaddeus Fletcher's few pleasures in life had come from scuffling through them in the fall, listening to them rustle around his feet.

Given the hard-eyed, angry scowl that adorned the portrait of Thaddeus that hung over the fireplace in the club's main dining room, Ed Fletcher suspected it more likely that he liked crushing the leaves under his boots. Still, whatever his great-grandfather's motivations, the

Roundtree Country Club was a magnificent place that was open to everyone in Roundtree, assuming, of course, that they could afford the initiation fee and the annual dues. The irony was not lost on Ed that Thaddeus Fletcher himself probably wouldn't have been able to afford the fee and dues had he not managed to unload the property onto the club in the first place, but it wasn't something either he or any of the other members ever talked about.

He pulled the Mercedes up to the front door, turned it over to the valet, and followed Joni and Zack into the clubhouse. At least a hundred people had already gathered there, the men dressed in perfectly pressed khaki pants and Ralph Lauren shirts, the women in the kind of peasant skirts that real peasants never would have been able to afford.

"I'm going to go find Heather Dunne and Chad Jackson," Zack announced, heading for the French doors that led out to the terrace and the swimming pool beyond.

"You and Heather stay out of the bushes," his father said with a wink that earned him a warning look from his wife. "Hey, you can't stop them from growing up," he said when Zack was gone.

"Why don't I think that 'growing up' and 'seducing innocent girls in the bushes behind the pool house' are synonymous?"

"It worked with you," Ed teased. "Wouldn't you say you grew up that night?"

Joni lifted an eyebrow. "Me?" she countered. "As I recall, exploring those bushes was my idea, not yours." Glancing around to see if anyone was watching them, she licked her lips lasciviously. "And I wasn't any more innocent then than I am now. Myra was always the religious one. Want to go back there again?" She reached out and stroked his chest, slipping her finger between the buttons to touch his bare flesh. "Just for old times' sake? Let yourself be seduced by the poor girl from the wrong side of the tracks one more time?"

"I think we'd better leave it to the kids," Ed replied. "Let's go get a drink and see who's here." He'd started toward the bar when Joni put a hand on his arm, stopping him. When he turned back to her, the mischief of a moment ago had vanished.

"I know you didn't really want to hire Marty," she said quietly.

Ed shrugged. "Hey, I promised, didn't I?" His expression clouded. "But if it doesn't work out, I'm not promising to keep him on."

"It'll work out," Joni said. "Myra's the only family I have left, and . . ." Her voice trailed off, then she added, "I just want her closer to me, that's all. Everything's going to be perfect—I can just feel it."

Ed turned away, but not quickly enough to keep his wife from seeing the doubt in his eyes.

Seth Baker saw Zack Fletcher coming out of the clubhouse, and in response he found himself moving toward the shelter of the pool house before he even realized it. Then, his skin prickling with the sensation of someone watching him, he stopped short. But when he turned around, Zack was talking to Heather Dunne and Chad Jackson, and most of the rest of the kids seemed to be gathering around them like iron filings drawn to a magnet. And no one was looking at him.

Then he spotted his father standing on the terrace about thirty yards away. Though he was talking to Mel

Dunne, Seth knew that his father was also keeping an eye on him.

If he didn't at least try to mix into the crowd around Zack and Heather, he didn't even want to think about what his father might do to him when they got home.

Feeling his father watching every move he made—and feeling the sting on his backside—Seth edged closer to the group of teenagers. There were almost a dozen of them, all of whom he'd known all his life. But even when he was only a few feet away, not one of them spoke to him.

Not one of them even looked at him.

And they certainly didn't make room for him in the circle around Zack and Heather. In fact, he thought Chad Jackson and Josh Harmon moved closer together so there would be no room for him, and once more he was seized by the urge to disappear into the pool house, where he could just sit by himself until it was time to go home. He stole a glance at the clubhouse, and his father was still there, still watching him. Then, as he saw his father finally turning away, he heard Heather Dunne say something that stopped him from slipping away to the sanctuary of the pool house.

"Get *out!* Your mom actually *sold* that awful house? To who?"

"My aunt and uncle," Zack replied.

"And they're actually going to live in it?" Heather asked, shaking her head when Zack nodded. "Oh, God—I could never do that! It creeps me out just thinking about it. I mean, isn't there blood all over the place?"

"Jeez, Heather," someone groaned. "They didn't just leave it there."

Heather Dunne shot the groaner a dirty look. "Well,

even if they didn't, it's still too gross!" Then, abruptly, she changed the subject. "So what's your cousin like?" she asked.

Zack rolled his eyes. "You won't believe. She's—" He hesitated a moment, and as he searched for the right words to describe Angel Sullivan, his eyes fell on Seth Baker and his lips twisted into a smirk. "She's the kind of girl who'd go out with Seth," he said.

Seth felt his face burning as the rest of the kids burst into laughter, and then, with his father mercifully gone from the terrace, he turned and fled into the pool house.

He was still there an hour later when his father came to find him.

"What the hell kind of kid are you?" Blake Baker demanded. "You think you're going to get anywhere in this world by hiding?" Seth bit his lip, knowing better than to say anything. "You think I didn't see what was going on earlier? You think I didn't know what you were doing, pussy-footing around the rest of the kids? It was just a show, Seth. I knew it, and they knew it. You know why they didn't let you into their little group? Because you didn't make them, that's why! And guess what? Your little show didn't impress me any more than it did them. So here's what's going to happen: You and I are going to enter the father-son golf tournament, and we're going to win."

"I don't even know how—" Seth began, but his father cut him off with a look so icy it made Seth's blood run cold.

"You're going to learn," he said. "You're going to play golf, or I'm going to know the reason why. Understand?"

Seth nodded, afraid to utter even a single syllable.

"Good," Blake Baker said. "Now let's go home."

Seth could tell by both the tone of his father's voice and the look in his eyes that when they got home he was going to be hurt even more by his father than Zack Fletcher's words and Zack's friends' laughter had hurt.

Chapter 10

IS IT REALLY OURS, MOM?" ANGEL SULLIVAN ASKED AS her mother pulled the Chevelle to a stop well behind the big yellow truck Marty had rented the day before. All three of them had been up until past midnight, packing everything into the truck except the blankets in which they caught a few hours of rest before getting up with the sun to make the drive to Roundtree.

"Why don't we go right now?" Angel had suggested when the last box had been stuffed into the truck. "I'm not going to be able to sleep, anyway."

"And do what when we get there?" her mother replied. "Haul everything inside in the middle of the night? What would people think?"

When her father had been no more enthusiastic than her mother, Angel wrapped herself up in a blanket and tried to go to sleep. But between the hardness of the floor and the excitement of moving in the morning, she hadn't slept at all.

Or at least not for more than a few minutes.

But now the night was over, and the drive was finished, and the house at Black Creek Crossing was standing before her, looking even more wonderful than she remembered.

"It's really ours," Myra Sullivan replied, shutting off the engine. She got out of the car as Marty emerged from the cab of the truck. *At least for now,* she added silently to herself. She hadn't slept much last night either, but it wasn't out of excitement as much as worry. Until she got the closing papers, she hadn't realized just how much the mortgage payments would be—almost twice what the rent on the duplex behind the rectory in Eastbury had been—and there were so many times over the last few years when she'd wondered how they were going to make the rent that the idea of a mortgage terrified her. Falling behind in the rent was one thing; falling behind on the mortgage could cost them the house.

"Will you for Christ's sake stop worrying?" Marty had told her over and over again. "You think Ed Fletcher's ever going to fire me? He's family, for Christ's sake!"

Myra had known better than to remind him that his sister-in-law's husband was among the thirteenth generation of Fletchers in Massachusetts, while Marty's family had arrived in Boston as servants—perhaps to cousins of Ed Fletcher—only four generations back. There wasn't much likelihood that Edward Arlington Fletcher was going to claim close kinship to Martin O'Boyle Sullivan, the fact that they had married sisters notwithstanding. And if the chips were ever down, Myra was fairly certain that Joni Fletcher would stand with her husband rather than Marty.

Still, Marty hadn't been drinking as much the last few weeks, which was a good sign, and maybe after getting fired by Jerry O'Donnell—who was a lot closer to being "family" to Marty than Ed Fletcher would ever be— he'd learned his lesson.

And maybe actually owning the house would give him the motivation that having nothing never had.

Marty pulled open the back doors of the truck, climbed in, and began handing boxes down to Myra, who passed them on to Angel. "Shall I start taking them in?" Angel asked as the pile on the lawn began to grow.

"Maybe we'd better all take them in," Myra replied, glancing at the sky, which was rapidly clouding over.

"It's not gonna rain," Marty declared. "Let's just keep going."

The three of them unloaded the truck as fast as they could, and moved the furniture into the house so it wouldn't get ruined if it rained. In less than an hour they'd hauled in the beds, and in another hour Marty had gotten them set up. The table was in the kitchen, and most of the rest of the furniture was in the living room.

They were only half done when there was a flash of lightning and a crack of thunder. A moment later the first drops of rain splattered onto the pile of packing boxes Marty had left on the lawn. "Goddammit, how come it always happens to me?" he complained, climbing out of the truck. He slammed the doors shut and picked up one of the boxes. "Well, don't just stand there," he called back as he headed for the front door. "You want everything to get wrecked before we get it inside?"

Another bolt of lightning slashed across the sky and the rain increased as both Angel and Myra snatched up boxes and ran for the house, ducking through the front door just as the thunderclap crashed over the house, rattling its windows. Setting her box down, Myra quickly crossed herself and uttered a silent prayer to St. Peter and St. Swithin that the violent storm that had blown up out of nowhere was nothing more than a freak weather system.

Angel's clothes were soaked through and she was shivering with cold.

"Go up and put on something dry," Myra told her.

"I don't have anything," Angel replied through chattering teeth.

"That box," her mother told her, pointing to a stack in the corner of the living room. "The one next to the top that's marked 'A.R. Clothes.' 'A.R.' stands for Angel's room."

A minute later Angel pushed her way into the little bedroom at the front of the house that had fascinated her from the first moment she set foot in it, using her hip to close the door behind her and lowering the box to the floor. She was just starting to pull its flaps open when she heard a noise.

A soft noise, barely audible. A moment later it came again, but this time she was listening for it, and she recognized it instantly.

A cat!

It mewed a third time, its voice muffled but insistent, as if it had been locked outside and now wanted to come back in.

Angel went to the window and looked out. The storm was still raging, the glass so streaked with rain that she could barely see. Despite the rain, she lifted the window, and peered outside.

Nothing.

In fact, the ledge was so narrow, she couldn't see how even a cat could cling to it, and the only other place it could be was on the little roof that sheltered the front stoop. But even if there had been a cat on it, how could she have heard it through the window and the storm?

She slid the window down again, and just as the sash dropped onto the sill, the sound came again. But this time it came from behind her.

Turning, she scanned the room, but saw nothing. Then, when the cat mewed yet again, this time accompanying its mewl with a scratching sound, she knew. She crossed the room and slowly pulled the closet door open. The gap was no more than three inches wide when the cat's nose appeared, followed by its head and body. The moment it was out of the closet, it wound back and forth between Angel's legs, rubbing first one side against her, then the other. Angel gazed down at it. "Where did you come from?"

The cat—pure black, except for a tiny white blaze in the exact center of its chest—looked up at her, then bounded up onto the bare mattress that Angel and her father had set up only an hour ago.

As it began licking itself, Angel pulled the closet door all the way open. Except for a single shelf and a bar for hanging clothes, it was empty. She searched the baseboard, looking for a hole the cat could have crept through, then searched the ceiling as well.

Nothing. Not even a hatch to get to the attic.

"How did you get in?" Angel asked, sitting on the bed next to the cat. The cat stopped grooming itself to creep onto her lap, its sinuous body shivering as Angel began to pet it. Rolling over to get its stomach scratched, it began licking Angel's hand. Then it rolled over again, curled up, and began purring.

Though it wore no collar, it didn't look like a stray to Angel. She could feel its muscles rippling beneath its skin, and the cat neither looked nor felt underfed. In fact, its coat was thick and clean, as if someone had been looking after it all its life. But how long had it been in the closet? If it had been more than a day or two, why didn't it seem either hungry or thirsty?

Maybe she should change her clothes, she thought, and go down and see if she could find something for it to eat, and a bowl for it to drink out of. Easing the cat off her lap, Angel went back to the box she'd just opened when she first heard the cat, and burrowed through it. She found clean underwear, a pair of sweatpants, and a thick sweater, and stripped off her wet clothes. As she used a second pair of sweatpants to dry her skin, she heard the cat hissing. Turning, she saw that it was standing straight up, its back arched, staring at the bedroom door. As the cat hissed again, Angel heard the door open behind her. Whirling around and clutching the sweatpants over her naked torso, she saw her father standing in the doorway.

"Daddy!" she cried. "What are you doing in here? I'm not even dressed!" For a moment her father's eyes remained fixed on her, and then he backed out and pulled the door closed.

"Sorry," he called out. "I—I thought you were in the other room."

Still clutching the sweatpants against her body, Angel went to the door and locked it. But even knowing it was locked, she couldn't get the image of her father out of her mind, of him looking at her before he left the room. There had been something strange in his expression, something she'd never seen before as he gazed at her.

Gazed at her nakedness, with a look in his eyes—

But that was crazy! He was her father! He'd never looked at her like that before. He *wouldn't!*

She was wrong. She had to be!

Suddenly, the room was filled with a blinding light, and Angel whirled around as an explosion of thunder shook the house. Angel shrank back against the closed door as the storm howled outside. Another bolt of lightning flashed, and the house trembled again as the second thunderclap struck. As it died away, Angel remembered the cat.

It was no longer there.

"Kitty?" she called, as she pulled on her dry clothes and scanned the corners of the room.

Nothing.

Crouching down, Angel peered under the bed.

Nothing.

The closet?

The door was still ajar, and Angel pulled it wide.

No sign of the cat at all.

Angel searched the room again, then gave up. However the cat had gotten in, it must have gotten out the same way. "Houdini," she said softly, as rain slashed against the window. "If you ever show up again, that's going to be your name." With one last glance around the room, she went back downstairs.

Her mother was unpacking boxes in the kitchen, a kettle of water was coming to a boil on the stove, and there were three mugs on the table, along with a box of hot chocolate mix.

"I thought a cup of cocoa might do us all some good," Myra said, offering Angel a wan smile that didn't quite cover the nervousness the storm was causing her. She glanced out the window. "They certainly didn't say anything like this was going to happen on the weather reports." Another bolt of lightning struck, and Myra winced as the thunderclap immediately followed. "Go tell your father his hot chocolate will be ready in another couple of minutes."

The memory of what had happened upstairs flooded back to Angel, and she hesitated. Should she tell her mother? But what *had* happened, really? Her father thought she was in the other room, that's all.

And nothing had happened.

So there was nothing to tell her mother.

Nothing at all.

Chapter 11

HE SOUND WAS SO LOW THAT AT FIRST ANGEL WASN'T sure she heard it at all. She was sitting in her bedroom in the new house, looking out the window. Across the road she saw a tree, a huge maple, whose limbs seemed to be reaching toward the house—toward Angel herself. At first the branches appeared friendly, as if they wanted to cradle her, and she felt an urge to go out into the night and climb the tree, disappearing into its foliage—able to see out, but knowing that no one could see in. But then the branches took on a threatening look, as if the giant maple wanted to reach across the road and through the window and pluck her from the safety of her room. Though she told herself that it was only a tree— that it couldn't hurt her—she'd still been unable to tear her eyes away from it.

Until the sound came.

Its first faint whisper wasn't enough to penetrate Angel's consciousness. The sound grew, though, almost imperceptibly, so that when she finally became conscious of it, it didn't seem out of place.

Rather, it seemed just one more of the sounds that filled the night—the chirping and whirring noises of insects, the soft croaking of frogs, and the muted hooting of owls. Yet as the sound crept out of the background and grew, it began to take on form as well.

By the time Angel recognized it as being apart from the rest of the sounds of the night, she also realized what it sounded like.

A girl.

A girl her age.

A girl crying.

Her attention torn from the tree beyond the window, Angel turned, half expecting to see the crying girl behind her. But except for herself, the room was empty.

Herself and the shadows, deep and dark, that filled the corners, for there was barely a moon tonight, and even its faint light kept fading as clouds scudded across it.

Yet she could still hear the crying, and she no longer felt alone in the room.

She squinted, straining her eyes to see where the girl might be hidden.

The crying grew louder, and finally Angel left the window and moved into the center of the room. At first the crying seemed to be coming from everywhere, echoing off the walls and ceiling and even the bare floor. It grew louder, until Angel was certain her mother or father would wake up and hear it.

Then she realized that it wasn't coming from inside the room at all.

It was coming from the closet.

The crying became harsher, as if the girl was in some kind of pain.

A ray of light, barely visible, crept from under the closet door, then brightened, turning from a faint orange to a brighter yellow. Angel stared at the light, and it began pulsating, mesmerizing her.

Meanwhile, the sound grew, until Angel could feel it as well as hear it.

Yet somehow she didn't feel frightened.

Instead, she felt herself being drawn toward the closet door.

Slowly, she moved toward it, her eyes fixed on the yellow light pulsing from the gap beneath the closet door, her ears filled with the now-howling sound of the girl's cries.

She reached for the door. Heat seemed to radiate from it, yet still Angel felt no fear.

Her fingers tightened on the knob, and she turned it and pulled the door open.

To her amazement, the closet was filled with flames, and in the midst of the flames stood a figure, its back to her. As Angel stood rooted to the spot, the figure turned.

The face of the girl was gone, its flesh burned away. But the empty sockets where the girl's eyes had been stared straight at Angel.

The girl raised her right arm and reached toward Angel in eerie imitation of the branches of the tree she'd been staring at moments earlier.

Just before the fingers touched her face, Angel stepped back and slammed the closet door.

And as the door slammed shut, she jerked awake, sitting bolt upright in her bed.

Her heart was pounding and she was covered with a sheen of sweat that felt hot but quickly turned cold and clammy. She was gasping for breath and her lungs hurt.

Hurt almost as if they'd been burned.

Angel sat perfectly still, waiting for the terror of the nightmare to pass, but even as her breathing returned to normal and her heartbeat calmed, the image of the girl, her flesh burned away by the raging flames, remained vivid in her mind. Finally, when even the sweat that covered her skin had dried, she lay back down and pulled the covers up until they were snug around her throat.

A nightmare, she told herself. *That's all it was.*

She turned over, wrapped her arms around the pillow, and closed her eyes. But the vision still hung in the darkness, and a moment later she rolled over again, this time opening her eyes to look at the dimly glowing hands of the alarm clock that sat on the scarred table next to the bed.

Just a little after midnight.

Though she felt so tired from unpacking boxes all day that her whole body ached, she knew she wouldn't be able to sleep until she banished the terrible image of her dream from her mind.

Throwing back the covers, she got up, pulling the blanket off the bed and wrapping it around her shoulders. She moved toward the closet, intending to open the door to prove to herself that nothing was inside except the clothes she'd hung there herself. Yet when she reached out to turn the knob, her hand hovered in the air a few inches from it, and she found herself unable to close her fingers on the brass.

She went to the window then and gazed out at the huge maple across the street, and slowly the vision of the horror inside the closet began to fade as the memory of the tree's branches reaching out to her rose in her mind once more.

But in the dream, the tree had been covered with the bright green foliage of summer, and now, as she gazed out into the autumn night, she could see that its leaves had shriveled and fallen, until now its branches were almost bare.

It didn't look at all as it had in the dream.

Turning away from the window, Angel gazed again at the closed door of the closet. *There's nothing in it,* she told herself. *Nothing but my clothes and a bunch of other junk.* Yet even as she steeled herself and started toward the closet again, her heart began to race, and a clammy sheen of cold sweat once more broke out on her body. But she didn't stop. She forced herself to keep going until she once more stood before the door.

This time she closed her fingers on the cold brass, she turned the knob, and pulled the door open.

Just as she had told herself, there was nothing inside the closet except the clothes she'd hung up this afternoon.

On the floor were her three pairs of shoes.

On the shelves were some boxes filled with stuff she hadn't been able to bring herself to throw away.

And nothing else, except for a strange odor.

The odor of something burning . . .

"Angel?" Myra Sullivan said as her daughter came into the kitchen the next morning. "Are you all right?"

"I guess I didn't sleep very well," Angel replied, rubbing her eyes with the sleeve of her bathrobe. "I had a bad dream—"

"Well, that's hardly a good sign, is it? You should have had wonderful dreams on your first night in our new house. What was it?"

As Angel tried to recall and relate the strange dream she'd had, Myra found the box she'd packed especially for this morning—buried, of course, under half a dozen other boxes, all of them heavier than the one she was after—opened it, and began taking out cereal bowls, glasses, and plates. "Rinse these for me while we talk," she told Angel, stacking them on the counter next to the sink. "Everything gets so dirty when you pack it up."

Angel ran the hot water and began rinsing and drying the dishes and silverware as she began once more to re-construct the strange dream she'd had the night before, but already some of the details were starting to slip away.

"But the weirdest thing was that when I finally woke up, the whole thing still seemed so real that I got up and looked in the closet."

Her mother smiled thinly. "Just like when you were little, remember? You always made me open the closet door in your room to prove that there were no monsters inside." She looked up from the oatmeal she was stirring. "And you didn't find anything, did you?" she asked, her voice taking on an edge. "It was just a nightmare then, and it was just a nightmare last night. You didn't actually hear anything, or see anything, did you?" Angel shook her head. Yet the look on her face told Myra there was something her daughter hadn't yet told her. "What is it?" she pressed. "There's something you're holding back."

"I—I don't know," Angel stammered. "It's just—well, it sounds sort of crazy. . . ."

Myra stopped stirring the oatmeal. "I think I can be the judge of that. Why don't you just tell me what you think happened, and maybe I can figure it out."

Angel hesitated, and then blurted it out: "I smelled smoke."

Myra frowned. "Smoke? You mean like wood smoke?"

Again Angel hesitated. "Well, sort of, but not really— I mean, it sort of smelled like burning wood, but there was something else too."

"Something else?" Myra prodded when Angel fell silent. "Am I supposed to figure it out myself, or are you going to tell me?"

"Well, it was weird," Angel said. "Remember when you burned yourself with the iron?"

Myra winced at the memory, and her eyes went to the scar that still showed clearly on the back of her left hand. It had happened five years ago, when she'd been talking to Angel while pressing Father Raphaello's vestments and accidentally placed the scorching steam iron on her own hand.

"It smelled like that," Angel said. "And like the time I scorched my hair trying to blow out the candles on my birthday cake."

"Good heavens! I thought you would have forgotten about that years ago. You were only two."

"Forget it?" Angel echoed. "I'll never forget it— I thought I was going to burn up!"

"Well, there you are, then," Myra told her. "That's probably where the dream came from—maybe moving into our own house made your subconscious decide to start clearing out a bunch of old memories. And if lighting your head on fire scared you as much as it scared me, I'm amazed you haven't had nightmares about it for years." She moved the oatmeal off the stove and started scooping it into the three bowls Angel had rinsed and dried. "But if it scared you that much, how come you never told me? We could have talked about it."

"I didn't want you to think I was a baby."

Myra laughed out loud. "But you *were* a baby! And I don't know why I didn't understand that you must have been even more scared than I was." Abandoning the oatmeal, she put her arms around Angel. "I'm sorry, honey. Really I am."

"Come on, Mom," Angel groaned, pulling away from the embrace. "I hardly even remember it. Maybe I don't—maybe I only remember Daddy talking about it on every birthday I've ever had, and I just feel like I remember."

"If you didn't really remember, I don't think you would have had that nightmare. And if you thought you smelled smoke, why didn't you wake me up? Or wake your father up?"

At the mention of her father, the memory of him walking in on her when she'd been changing her clothes yesterday rose in her mind.

Walking in on her and looking at her and—

The image of her father framed in the doorway of her room was abruptly replaced by the reality of his figure framed in the kitchen door.

"Wake me up?" he asked. "I'm awake—what's going on?"

"It's Angel," Myra explained. "She had a nightmare last night."

"About me?" Marty Sullivan asked, his eyes fixing on Angel with an intensity that made her pull the bathrobe more tightly around her. "Why would she have a nightmare about me?" he asked, speaking to his wife, but his eyes remaining fastened on Angel.

"It wasn't about you," Myra said, barely glancing at her husband as she put the dishes of oatmeal on the table. "She had a nightmare about a fire, and when she woke up, she thought she still smelled smoke."

"In the house?"

"Well, of course in the house," Myra replied. "She wasn't sleeping in the backyard, was she?" She glanced at her watch, then shifted her gaze to her husband and daughter. "You've got half an hour before we have to leave for church."

"Today?" Marty groaned. "You gotta be kiddin' me! We got all this stuff to unpack, and there's a game on, and I haven't even got the TV hooked up yet. How about you go, and me and Angel'll stay here and take care of some of this mess?"

Feeling the same strange knot in her stomach that she'd felt a moment ago, Angel shook her head. "I— I want to go to church," she said. "And I better go up and get dressed." She started toward the door and the stairwell beyond, but her father blocked her way.

"Hey," he said. "Doesn't daddy still get a kiss from his little Angel?"

Angel froze, but rather than run the risk of getting into a fight with him, she gave her father a quick peck on the cheek.

"I've just got to take a shower and get dressed, Mom," she said as she slipped through the door and started up the stairs. "I'll be as fast as I can."

"All right," her mother called back. "But be quick—if you take too long, I'll have to leave you here."

Hurrying upstairs, Angel turned on the hot water in the combination shower and bathtub, took off her bathrobe and hung it on the hook on the door, and started to step into the tub.

But before she did, she locked the bathroom door.

"Are you sure you're all right?" Myra asked as she and Angel left the house twenty minutes later.

"I—I guess," Angel stammered.

The note of uncertainty in her daughter's voice made Myra turn to look at her. "Angel, it was only a nightmare. Nothing to worry about."

What about Daddy? Angel thought. *Should I worry about him?*

"Is there something else?" Myra asked. "Did something happen that you haven't told me about?"

Maybe I should tell her, Angel thought. *Maybe—* A flicker of movement distracted her, and she turned to see a cat coming out of the woods.

A black cat.

A black cat with a single blaze of white in the exact center of its chest.

"Houdini?" Angel blurted as the cat ran across the patch of lawn surrounding the house. It came right to Angel and began rubbing up against her legs.

Myra looked disapprovingly down at the cat. "Houdini?" she repeated. "How on earth would you know its name?"

"I don't," Angel said, leaning down to scratch the cat's ears, then picking it up. "It's just what I call him." She nuzzled the cat's neck. "Where'd you go?" she whispered into its ear. "How'd you just disappear like that?"

"What do you mean, it's what you call him? Where did you even see him before?"

"He was in my closet," Angel replied. "Remember when I went up to change my clothes yesterday? He was up there, meowing to get out of the closet."

"And how did he get *in* the closet?" Myra asked.

Angel shrugged. "I don't know—that's why I call him Houdini. He came out of the closet, and then, when it started thundering again, he disappeared."

"Cats don't just disappear," Myra told her.

"Houdini did. Just like that magician I read about— the one who got out of jail cells and locked trunks and everything." She scratched the cat again. "Can I keep him?" she asked. "I mean, he doesn't have a collar or anything, and he likes me."

"No, you can't keep him," Myra said. "Your father's allergic to cats."

Angel remembered, then, how Houdini had hissed yesterday, just before her father walked in on her. Again, Angel wondered if she should tell her mother, but the words died in her throat long before they reached her lips. What was she supposed to say? That her father had walked in on her while she was changing her clothes? That he'd looked at her funny?

And even if she told her mother, what would happen?

If her mom told her dad, then he'd get mad at her, and she'd seen him mad enough times that she didn't want that to happen.

"Houdini could live in my room," she finally said. "Then Dad would never even have to see him."

"Cats don't stay in one room," Myra told her. "Now put it down and forget about it. The longer you hold it and pet it, the more you'll want to keep it."

Reluctantly, Angel put the cat back on the ground. As if understanding exactly what had happened, the cat sat down, curled its tail around its feet, and glared up at Myra.

"I don't like you much either," Myra said, reading the cat's expression as clearly as if it had spoken out loud. "Shoo!"

The cat ignored her, and began licking its forepaw.

They walked on into the village in silence, but Angel glanced back several times when she thought her mother wasn't looking.

The cat was behind them, keeping pace.

They were near the church when Myra felt a sudden chill in the air. As she buttoned the collar of her thin wool coat, she looked up at the sky, where fast-scudding clouds were quickly graying the crisp blue the sky had been only a moment earlier. Beside her, Angel seemed oblivious to the sudden cold, and when Myra told her to button up her jacket, her daughter ignored her. They turned the corner, and Myra found herself facing the small white clapboard structure that was the only Catholic church in Roundtree and stopped short, feeling a twinge of something almost like anger.

The tiny Church of the Holy Mother stood kitty-corner from the far larger Congregational church that dominated the east side of the Roundtree common. It didn't seem right to Myra that a church named for the

Blessed Virgin who had actually given birth to the Lord Jesus—who was the true Mother of God, for heaven's sake—should be completely overshadowed by a temple built by heathen apostates whom Myra knew deep in her heart were condemned to spend eternity in the fires of Hell for having turned their back on the one true Church.

Her anger gave way to sadness as she gazed at the little church, its white paint peeling from the graying clapboard, the shutters at its windows no longer quite straight, the small stained-glass windows themselves coated with grime. The church seemed to huddle beneath the heavy gray sky as if it weren't certain how much longer it could continue even to stand. And then, as the clouds suddenly parted to let the sun shine through, Myra gasped as the stark silhouette of a cross slashed across the church's front doors like some mighty sword cleaving the very foundation of her faith. She crossed herself and began a prayer for salvation, and when a voice murmured at her side, she didn't hear it for a moment. Then, peripherally, she saw the black material of a priest's cassock, and looked up to see a gentle face with twinkling eyes that transported her back to the day when she was only eight years old . . .

She'd gone to visit her grandfather, who lay dying in the hospital. She'd been terrified, but her grandfather, even in the last hours of his life, saw her fear and did his best to reassure her. "It's all right, lassie," he'd told her, smiling at her as if they were about to be off on some great adventure together. "Soon I'll be returnin' to the blessed Isle."

"Can't I go with you?" Myra had asked.

Her grandfather shook his head. "This is a trip I have to take by meself," he'd said. "But not to worry," he added, his eyes twinkling brightly. "I'll still be lookin' after you."

A few seconds later, his eyes had closed, and until this moment Myra had never seen such a twinkle again.

"I think they did it on purpose," she heard the priest saying now, a smile playing around the corners of his lips.

"Did what?" Myra asked, coming out of her reverie.

"That," the priest said, his smile broadening, his right hand sweeping upward. "Now you can't tell me that's a coincidence." He was pointing up to the steeple that towered above the Congregational church across the street. Unlike the humble wood-frame building that was the Church of the Holy Mother, Roundtree First Congregational was built of huge blocks of granite hewn from a quarry a mile from the center of town. Its style was Gothic, with a steep slate roof from which the steeple soared another fifty feet toward the sky.

The priest was pointing at the cross that surmounted the steeple. "I can't prove it," he said, "but I suspect an engineer spent weeks figuring out exactly where that steeple had to be, and exactly how high, in order for the shadow of their cross to fall across our door. Now of course," he went on, "it only happens a couple of times a year, you understand, so I suppose it could be only the coincidence they claim it is. But if you ask me, it is just another way for those Protestants to try to stick it to us!"

"Father!" Myra breathed, shocked by the priest's words. Her eyes flicked toward Angel, who didn't seem as shocked by what the priest had said as she was.

"It's a joke, my child," the priest quickly assured her, his smile fading as he saw the look on Myra's face. "I'm sure they meant no harm at all." He held out his hand.

"I'm Father Michael Mulroney, but everyone calls me Father Mike," he offered.

Myra took his hand for only the briefest of moments, introducing herself and Angel as she did so. "We just moved here from Eastbury."

Father Mike nodded. "Ah, the very ones Father Raphaello wrote me about," he said. "It will be wonderful to have you as part of our parish. Not as many of us as there are in Eastbury, I'm afraid." The mischievous twinkle came back into his eyes. "Maybe we just didn't get here in time." He nodded toward the huge stone edifice across the street. "If we'd come in 1632, the way they did, maybe we'd have a building like that too." Now he sighed heavily. "Not that we could fill it, even if we did. These days . . ." He let his voice trail off, but Myra knew exactly what he meant. The last few years, donations even to the church in Eastbury—where there hadn't been even a breath of scandal—had dropped so low that she'd been the last person Father Raphaello had been able to pay to take care of the rectory.

"Well, now you've got us, and I have a husband too, so that's three," Myra said.

"And I can't tell you how much I appreciate it," Father Mike told her. Then his voice and expression took on a note of regret. "But I'm afraid I'm not going to be able to give you the work you had with Father Raphaello. We're just too—well, I'm sure you know as well as I do what the last few years have been like." Taking Myra's arm, he led her up the steps toward the front door of the church, with Angel following. "And where might you be living?"

"On Black Creek Road," Myra told him. "It's a small house, and it needs some work, but I understand it's one of the oldest houses in town."

The priest's eyes clouded. "The house at the Crossing?" he asked. "Where all those terrible—" He stopped abruptly, then said, "Oh, dear—what am I saying? I—"

"It's all right," Myra said stiffly. "We know what happened in the house."

More people were coming up the steps now, and Father Mike began introducing Myra and Angel, then excused himself to go prepare for the mass.

Just before she followed her mother into the church, Angel looked around for Houdini one more time.

The cat was sitting across the street, its tail neatly curled around its feet.

An hour later, as they were leaving the church and saying good-bye, Father Mike took Myra's hand in both of his. "I've been thinking," he said. "And it occurs to me that maybe I can find some work for you. Not in the rectory, but here in the church itself."

"But you said—" Myra began.

"I know what I said," the priest cut in. "But I'll find the money someway." His eyes shifted over to Angel, then returned to Myra. "It's a good place to be," he said. "The church can shelter you from many, many things. So I'll just find the money, and that's all we'll say about that."

A few minutes later they started the walk home, Father Mike's words echoing in Myra's thoughts.

The church can shelter you from many, many things.

What had he meant by that?

Did he think there was something she needed sheltering from? Maybe she should have told him that the Holy Mother had been looking after her for years already, coming to her in visions when her problems were the worst.

And why had he looked at Angel just before he said those words?

The questions so completely occupied her that Myra Sullivan never noticed the black cat following them home.

Chapter 12

ANGEL SULLIVAN TURNED THE CORNER ONTO PROSpect Street and saw the old brick building that had once been all of Roundtree High School and now served as the main building. It sat in the middle of a large lawn studded with huge pines that looked even older than the building itself. Behind it were the newer buildings, scattered over the four full blocks the school now occupied, but none of them had the warm and friendly look of the old original building. White shutters flanked its windows, tall columns rose a full three floors to support the roof in front, and the roof itself was ornately peaked and dormered. There was even a widow's walk high on the main peak, though Roundtree was nowhere near the coast, so there would have been no captains' wives waiting for their husbands to return from the sea.

Angel paused across the street from the school, just to enjoy the warm feeling running through her. It was a completely different feeling than the one that had gripped her in Eastbury every morning, and she was certain it wasn't just because the school in Roundtree was so much prettier than the drab block of grime-covered bricks that was Eastbury High. No, this was something more.

This was a whole new beginning, in a town where no one knew her except for her cousin.

Where no one had ever heard of Mangy-Angey, or Daddy's little Angel, or any of the other things she'd been called ever since kindergarten.

As she started across the street, she found herself smiling, wondering who Nicole Adams would start in on now that she was gone. But she banished the thought as it came into her head—nobody should be treated the way Nicole and everyone else had treated her.

But that was all behind her now, and when she got up that morning to see a bright and sunny sky, Angel wished she had clothes just as bright as the morning. But there was nothing in her dresser or closet, and in the end she'd dressed in her usual drab sweatpants and a blouse with a bulky sweater over it. Still, she felt different, and that was what counted.

At her feet, Houdini rubbed up against her leg. Just as he had yesterday when she and her mother had gone to church, the cat had appeared this morning—seemingly out of nowhere—and walked along with Angel all the way to school. The only difference was that with her mother not there to shoo him away, the cat had never been more than a foot from her. Now, across the street from the school, Angel bent down to scratch his ears. "See you later."

Crossing the street and starting up the steps toward the front door, she smiled at two girls who were talking to a wavy-haired boy with eyes that were the same blue as the clear autumn sky.

Neither of the girls nodded back, and the boy didn't seem to notice her.

They were busy talking, Angel told herself. *They probably didn't even see her.*

She found the principal's office, got registered, and was given her class schedule and a locker assignment. "Here's your combination," the secretary told her, handing her a slip of paper with four numbers written on it and instructions on how many times to turn the lock in each direction. Angel gazed glumly at the combination—she'd just barely learned the one in Eastbury, and now she had to learn a brand-new one.

Her homeroom was here in the main building, and so was her locker, and with a half hour before the first class started, she had plenty of time to find all her other classrooms, so at least she wouldn't have to suffer the embarrassment of being late and having everyone stare at her. She even got to her first period classroom early enough so she was the first one there.

" 'Angel,' " the teacher said, reading her name off the registration form. "That's a pretty name. I'm Mrs. Brink."

Angel was about to say that her name was Angie, then realized that Zack Fletcher knew what people called her and might make fun of her.

She decided to say nothing at all, and after the first bell rang, Mrs. Brink introduced her to the rest of the class. A few people turned to look curiously at her, and a couple of people actually nodded to her, but within a couple of minutes the teacher had begun a lesson on diagramming sentences, and for the rest of the hour no one even looked at Angel.

Nor did anyone speak to her after class, but Angel told herself it was only because everyone was hurrying to their next classes and they only had ten minutes.

The morning raced by, and when the bell for lunch rang, Angel could barely believe the day was half over. And though no one had exactly gone out of their way to talk to her, no one had turned their back on her either.

Nor had she heard people whispering among themselves as she came down the hall, only to fall silent when she came close, turn away as if even looking at her would somehow be wrong, then start giggling as soon as she'd passed.

Stowing her books in her locker, she found her way to the cafeteria, picked up a tray, and got in line. Five minutes later, with her tray laden only with cottage cheese and a fruit salad that didn't look very good, but at least didn't look as fattening as the macaroni and cheese, she looked around for a place to sit.

And saw Zack Fletcher sitting at a table on the far side of the cafeteria with a still-empty chair right across from him. When he looked up and beckoned to her, a great wave of relief flooded over her—she wasn't going to have to sit by herself, even on the first day of school. She started making her way toward his table, threading between tables and chairs set so close together that half a dozen people had to squeeze up against a table in order to let her by. And then, when she was only a yard from the empty chair at Zack's table, a girl with exactly the kind of long, straight blond hair that Angel had always envied but knew she would never have—any more than she would have the blond girl's small features and slim figure—came from the other direction, set her tray down, and slipped into the chair opposite Zack.

Angel stared at the girl, but she gave no sign that she'd even seen Angel moving toward the chair.

Angel waited for Zack to say something, to tell the blonde that he'd been saving the seat for his cousin.

But Zack wasn't even looking at her—he was staring at the blonde with the kind of stupid grin on his face that boys in Eastbury always had when Nicole Adams was around.

Zack hadn't been saving her seat at all! In fact, he probably hadn't even been waving to her—he'd probably been waving to someone behind her.

Someone like the blonde who was now smiling at

Zack the way Nicole Adams had smiled at the boys who were always fawning over her. "I'm so late," she said. "I couldn't get my locker open, and then I got stuck talking to Seth Baker, and then—"

"Hey, chill, Heather," Zack broke in. "Would I let anyone else sit there?"

Heather, Angel thought as she quickly turned away, scanned the room for another chair, and started working her way toward an almost empty table on the far side of the cafeteria. *Of course her name is Heather. And of course she's pretty, and of course she's Zack's girlfriend.* As she pushed her way between the tables, she heard someone grumble about her going some other way next time, and she was sure two other people shoved their chairs backward when she was trying to get past.

By the time she got to the nearly empty table, she was certain that everyone in the cafeteria was watching her, and she didn't even ask the one boy who was sitting at the table if she could join him. Instead, she simply set her tray down at the other end of the table, sat down with her back to the room, and started poking at her fruit salad.

The boy at the other end of the table was eating a heaping plate of macaroni and cheese.

Angel poked at the fruit salad again, and finally put a piece of grapefruit in her mouth.

"That stuff any better than it looks?"

For a moment, she didn't realize the words were directed at her.

"I mean, I like fresh fruit, but when it's out of a can, it always tastes tinny to me."

Angel finally looked up to find the boy on the other side of the table looking at her, his head slightly cocked. "You should've gotten this," he said, pointing at his heaping plate. "It's really good."

"It looks good," Angel agreed. "But—"

"So I'll get another plate, and you can have some of mine. I got way too much anyway."

Before she could protest, the boy was gone, and a minute later he was back, an empty plate in one hand, and a knife and soup spoon in the other. Sliding his tray down the table until it was across from Angel's, he used the soup spoon and knife to move half his macaroni and cheese onto the empty plate, then set the now half-full plate in front of Angel. "There—now you don't have to eat that crappy fruit salad. Unless you want to, of course," he added, flushing. "I mean, you can eat anything you want, but—" His flush deepened, and he started to get up again. "Look, if you want, I'll go sit somewhere else."

"No!" Angel said, and felt herself flushing as she realized how loudly she'd spoken. "It's okay." As the boy sank back into his chair, still looking uncertain, Angel smiled at him. "You're right—the fruit salad sucks. But I shouldn't eat the macaroni and cheese. I'm trying to . . ." Her words trailed off and she shrugged, certain she didn't have to finish the sentence.

"So who cares if you don't look like Heather Dunne?" the boy asked. "If you ask me, I think she's bulimic—probably pukes her brains out right after lunch every day." The boy leaned forward and dropped his voice. "S'pose your cousin can taste it when he kisses her?"

Angel's eyes widened as she stared at the boy, and though she tried to suppress the giggle that rose in her throat, she couldn't. "That is so gross!" she finally managed to get out between giggles.

"Not as gross as kissing someone who's been hurling lunch," the boy said.

"How do you know he does that?" Angel asked.

The boy rolled his eyes. "It's hard not to know when

they're doing it right in front of you," he said. "Right after fifth period. They're both in my math class, and they practically get it on in the hall before the bell rings."

"How do you know she barfs up her lunch?" Angel asked.

"You saw her, didn't you? And did you see her plate? An elephant couldn't eat that much. Believe me—she's barfing."

"So how'd you know Zack's my cousin?"

"Everybody knows," the boy said. "He's been moaning about—"

The boy cut his words short as he realized what he'd been about to say, but it was too late. Angel felt her eyes stinging with tears, and she struggled not to let them overflow. Wishing she could sink through the floor and vanish forever, but knowing she couldn't, she started to stand up, intent on getting far from the cafeteria as quickly as she could.

But before she was even out of her chair, the boy said, "Don't do it." He said it softly enough so no one but Angel could hear him. "Don't give them the satisfaction." As she hesitated, he explained: "Hey, I saw what happened over there. You think Zack didn't make sure there wasn't going to be enough room for you at his table before you even came in? I know he's your cousin, but that doesn't mean he's not a jerk."

He fell silent for a moment, his eyes scanning the room, then went on. "There's a lot of jerks around here," he said, then shrugged helplessly. "I guess maybe I'm a jerk sometimes too. My name's Seth Baker."

"I'm—" Angel began, but cut herself off before blurting out her true name. "—Angie," she finished.

Seth frowned. "I thought it was 'Angel,' " he said uncertainly.

Angel felt her face burn. "I hate it," she blurted before she even thought about it.

"Well, you're wrong," Seth said. "It's a beautiful name."

"It is not," Angel shot back.

"It is too. You just hate it because it's yours. Everybody hates their own name."

Angel stared at him. "How can you hate 'Seth'? It's a good name."

"Even if it were, it's not what they call me."

Now it was Angel's turn to frown. "What do they call you?" she asked. Seth said nothing, but his face reddened, and now it was Angel who cocked her head. "Come on, what do they call you?" Without thinking about it, she began blurting out the taunts she'd heard all her life. "They always used to call me 'Daddy's little Angel,' and 'Mommy's little Angel.' "

"That's not so terrible," Seth countered.

Angel raised her eyebrows. "Then try 'Mangy-Angey'!" she added, again speaking before thinking.

Seth winced. "That's pretty harsh," he admitted. "But it's still not as bad as what I get."

"I bet it is," Angel said. "So tell me what they call you."

Seth was silent for several long seconds, but finally his eyes met Angel's. "Maybe I will," he said softly, and Angel saw all the pain she'd ever felt reflected in Seth Baker's eyes.

All of it, and more.

Chapter 13

HEY, SULLIVAN! YOU GONNA GIVE ME A HAND WITH this or just sit on your ass all day?"

Marty Sullivan flicked his cigarette butt into the puddle that had formed under the cement mixer, then ambled over to the spot where Jack Varney was readying the huge header that would span the double front door of the house they were working on. In the five hours since Ed Fletcher had brought Marty to the site of the half-dozen new houses he was building on a cul-de-sac a mile east of the village's center, Marty had figured out exactly what was wrong not only with the house he was working on, but the whole project as well.

And the problems all started with Jack Varney, who was supposed to be the foreman of the job.

For the first couple of hours this morning, Marty had tried to do pretty much what Varney wanted him to, but it hadn't taken long before he figured out that Varney was giving him all the crap jobs because he was the boss's brother-in-law.

First it had been building forms for the bases of the columns that would eventually support the roof of the Colonial-style house, and no matter what Marty had done, Varney found something to bitch about. Initially, it had been the forms themselves, which Varney insisted weren't squared perfectly. "What the hell does it matter?" Marty argued as Varney had shown him that the form was a quarter of an inch wider on one side than the other. "The thing's going to be buried in dirt anyway!"

"Ed's got a reputation, and I got a reputation," Varney replied. "We build things right, whether you can see them or not."

"And piss away half your profit," Marty muttered.

Varney had acted like he didn't even hear him, and made him knock the form apart and start over again. Marty had done it, though he knew it was a waste of time.

Then Varney started in about the way he'd put the rebar in the forms. "You need twice as much—I don't want that thing breaking when we put the columns on them."

"They're not gonna break," Marty countered. "I used plenty."

"You got a degree in engineering?" Varney asked, loud enough for three of the other guys on the job to hear him.

Once again Marty had seethed, and once again he'd done what he was told. But as the morning wore on, he'd come to the conclusion that Varney had it in for him.

All morning long Varney made him do everything over again, always claiming there was something wrong, when Marty knew damned well there wasn't. But what really pissed him off was that Jack Varney was at least ten years younger than he was. What the hell was Ed Fletcher thinking of, putting a kid like Varney in charge of the whole project, then making his own brother-in-law work for the kid?

What Ed should have done, Marty thought, *was put him in charge.* If he was running the job, these crappy houses would get put up in half the time, and they'd make twice the profit. Everywhere he looked he saw guys using screws where nails would have done just as well, and measuring over and over to get the studs just the right length when any idiot knew you could shim up the headers to fill the gaps where the studs were too short. If it all looked okay when it was finished, who cared if a few things didn't fit perfectly under the siding and plasterboard?

And the frosting on the cake was that everybody else seemed to just go along with Varney.

Now Varney was yelling at him again, just because he'd taken a couple of minutes to have a smoke. "Can't a guy even take a break around here?" he grumbled as he started to pick up one end of the twelve-foot beam that would form a header strong enough to support three times the weight that would be put on it.

More stupidity.

Less profit.

If Ed put him in charge—

"You put on a brace?" Varney asked just as he was about to lift the end of the beam.

Marty glowered at him. "What kind of sissy wears a brace just to pick up a piece of wood?"

"I do," Varney replied, tapping the thick leather device strapped around his waist to give his back extra support.

"What are you, some kinda pussy?" Marty shot back. Twenty feet away, Ritchie Henderson looked up from the stud he'd been about to cut, his Skilsaw hovering in the air.

Varney's eyes narrowed. "Why don't you try not arguing with me just once, okay?"

"If you had any brains, I wouldn't have to argue with

you," Marty countered, clenching his fists and feeling a rush of pleasure as he saw the foreman's face redden.

Varney took a deep breath. "If you're looking for a fight, go somewhere else, okay? And I'm tired of arguing with you—we've got work to do here." He raised his voice. "Hey, Henderson! You want to give me a hand with this beam?"

"Be right with you," Ritchie Henderson replied.

But before the other man could get there, Marty Sullivan bent down, tipped the beam enough to get his fingers under it, then lifted it into the air, hoisting it above his head and getting his other hand under it just before it toppled back to the ground. "Where do you want it?" he growled. Without waiting for a response, he started toward the upright studs that flanked the doorway, staggering under the weight of the beam.

"Jesus, Sullivan!" Varney yelled, moving quickly toward one end of the beam, which was now starting to twist in Marty's grip. "What are you trying to—"

But it was too late. A spasm of pain in Marty Sullivan's back made him suddenly jerk around, and one end of the beam clipped Varney's chin, cutting off his words and knocking him to the ground. At the same instant, Marty let out a howl of agony and dropped the beam, which missed Varney's head by a fraction of an inch as it crashed down.

Swearing, Ritchie Henderson knelt down next to Jack Varney. "You okay, boss?"

Varney reached up to rub his jaw, then sat up. "Yeah, I'm fine."

Now Henderson stood up, his fists clenched as he glowered at Marty Sullivan. "Are you nuts? You coulda killed him!"

"It was his fault," Marty yelled. "If he hadn't made me lose my balance—"

"His fault? He wasn't the one who—"

Jack Varney was back on his feet, stepping between the two angry men. "Okay, okay, let's all calm down," he said. His jaw was throbbing and he could taste blood in his mouth from where his teeth had cut into his cheek when the beam had smashed into him. "Nobody's dead, and my jaw's not broken."

"You coulda broken my back, throwing me off balance that way," Marty said, rubbing at the cramped muscle in his lower back. "I should—"

"You should take the rest of the day off," Varney told him. When Marty started to say something else, he shook his head. "Just leave it alone, Sullivan, okay? Maybe it was your fault and maybe it was my fault, but either way, it's over. Just go home, take it easy, and we'll start fresh tomorrow."

Two minutes later Marty Sullivan was gone, but as he left the job site, he knew he wasn't about to go home.

Not right now anyway.

Right now he was going to have a drink.

Chapter 14

$\mathcal{A}$S THE CLOCK ON THE WALL TICKED TO EXACTLY three o'clock, Angel checked her work one last time. When Mrs. Holt had first announced the pop quiz, a sinking feeling had come over her, and it only got worse when the algebra teacher went on to say that since it was her first day in class, Angel didn't need to take the quiz. She unconsciously sank a little lower at her desk as she felt the rest of the class staring enviously at her. But a minute later, when Mrs. Holt began writing the five equations on the blackboard, Angel relaxed. She'd solved the first equation in her head before Mrs. Holt had even finished writing the other four on the board, and five minutes after the quiz began, Angel was finished, the equations and their solutions neatly laid out on a single sheet of paper, while all around her the rest of the class seemed to be going through page after page.

Twice Mrs. Holt warned the two girls behind Angel that if they kept talking she would fail both of them, but even as the minute hand ticked closer to three o'clock, Angel could still hear them comparing answers and knew why they hadn't stopped talking: neither of them had any idea of how to solve the problems.

"Time," Mrs. Holt said. "Pass your papers forward."

As Angel took the stack from the girl behind her and added her own, the teacher spoke again. "I thought I told you that you didn't need to take the quiz, Angel."

Angel shrugged and passed the stack of quizzes to the boy in front of her, who put his own on the bottom, then handed them to Mrs. Holt. A moment later, as she saw the teacher glance at her test, then look up at her, Angel wished she hadn't taken the quiz after all.

Or at least hadn't turned it in.

But now it was too late.

"It seems Angel has set the standard for the rest of you," Mrs. Holt said, holding her single sheet up for the rest of the class to see. "This is what a math quiz should look like. Every equation solved, and every step shown." She smiled at Angel, and Angel slunk lower in her chair. "Thank you, Angel. Well done."

All around her Angel could feel the envy the class had felt for her a few minutes ago hardening into resentment, and she knew she'd made a mistake.

Why did she have to write down the answers? Why couldn't she have just solved the problems in her head, then taken a book out of her bag and spent the last ten minutes reading? But now it was too late, and everyone was staring at her, and—

The clock ticked one more time, and then the clanging of the last bell erupted through the school. As the rest of the class began picking up their backpacks and heading toward the door, Angel stayed where she was, deliberately slowing the process of putting her books in her pack so that by the time she left the room the rest of the class would be gone. But even hanging back didn't keep her from hearing what the rest of the kids were saying.

"Of course she's a suck-up—her name's Angel, isn't it?"

"Who cares if she's smart—just look at her! Yuck!"

Her face burning and her eyes stinging, Angel sat at

her desk waiting for the room to empty. After two minutes that seemed to take forever, the door swung closed
for the last time and silence fell over the room. At last
Angel stood up from her desk, picked up her backpack,
and started toward the door. She was just starting to
push it open when Mrs. Holt spoke to her.

"Angel? Is something wrong?"

She froze, her hand still on the doorknob. How could
Mrs. Holt not know what was wrong? Couldn't she see
what had happened? Hadn't she heard what everyone
was saying? *But it wasn't her fault,* Angel told herself. *It
was my fault.* Mrs. Holt had said she didn't have to take
the quiz, but she did it anyway. Shaking her head but
saying nothing, Angel fled from the classroom.

The corridor was even worse. All around her, kids were
laughing and talking; lockers were slamming. Angel
worked her way through the throng toward the foot of
the stairs that would take her to her own locker on the
second floor. Keeping her head down, she did her best to
look at no one and be deaf to anything the other kids
might be saying about her. By the time she reached the
head of the stairs, the corridor was almost empty. Hurrying to her locker, Angel began working the combination, but the metal door didn't open until the third try.
She was reaching for the jacket she'd hung on the
locker's single hook when she felt someone behind her.

Felt eyes looking at her.

Go away, she thought. *Just leave me alone.*

Then she heard a voice.

A soft voice that sounded just as apprehensive as
Angel felt.

"I thought—well, if you want to, maybe we could
go get a Coke or something." Turning away from her
locker, Angel saw Seth Baker standing a few feet away,
his backpack slung over one shoulder. Angel felt a lump

forming in her throat as he gazed at her, and then her eyes began to sting once more as the tears she'd been struggling to control threatened to overwhelm her. The silence lengthened, then Seth started to turn away. Angel reached out toward him, trying to force something— anything—from her constricted throat, when he spoke again. "Come on—let's just get out of here, okay? Then you can tell me what happened."

Still without having spoken a word, Angel followed him down the stairs and out of the building.

Houdini was sitting on the sidewalk across the street, exactly where she'd left him this morning, and Angel wondered if the cat could possibly have been sitting there all day. As she and Seth crossed the street, the cat stood up, stretched, and gazed suspiciously at Seth. His tail twitched slightly, but when Angel introduced them, Seth squatted down and looked the cat squarely in the eye.

"Very nice to meet you," he said, extending his hand, as if Angel had introduced him to another human being.

Houdini's tail stopped twitching and he licked Seth's hand, and when Seth and Angel started down the street toward the center of the village, he followed, walking between them.

"You really want to go in there?" Angel asked ten minutes later as she and Seth stood in front of the Roundtree drugstore, which still had the kind of old-fashioned soda fountain that had disappeared from most drugstores nearly fifty years earlier. All the booths were occupied, as were all but two of the stools. And every face was familiar, though Angel could put names to only two or three of them. As she and Seth gazed through the window, she saw her cousin Zack look up, glance toward them, then lean across the table to whisper something to Heather Dunne. Though they could hear nothing through the thick plate glass, both Angel and Seth could see Heather—and everyone else—first laughing at whatever Zack Fletcher had said, then turning to look at the two of them.

"You want to go to my house?" Angel asked, and saw Seth hesitate. But then he nodded.

"Sure."

Turning away from the drugstore, they continued along the sidewalk toward the corner, where they would turn right to follow Black Creek Road out of town. "I guess it was stupid to think anything would be any different here," Angel said. As they'd walked from the school to the drugstore, she'd told Seth what had happened at the end of the last period.

"How come teachers do things like that?" Seth asked. "Seems like she didn't have to tell the whole class what you did."

"It's not like she was trying to be mean or anything. And it was my fault. If I'd—"

"It *wasn't* your fault!" Seth broke in, the words bursting from his lips with enough force that Angel jumped almost as if something had struck her. Seth barely seemed to notice. "So you could do the stuff in your head—how does that make you wrong? And how could Mrs. Holt not know what was going to happen when she started telling everyone what you did? Come on, Angel—it wasn't your fault at all."

"Then how come it felt like it was my fault?" Angel asked.

Seth shrugged. "How come it always feels like it's my fault when my dad—"

Abruptly, he fell silent, and Angel stopped and looked at him. "When your dad does what?"

A shadow seemed to pass over Seth's face. "Nothing," he said. "Sometimes he just gets mad at me, that's all."

That's not all, Angel thought. But there was something in Seth's expression that told her not to push, so she didn't press him, and for the rest of the walk out to the Crossing, neither of them said another word. But when they finally came around the last bend and stood across the road from Angel's house, Seth paused, cocking his head as he gazed at the structure on the other side of the road.

"Seth? What is it?" Angel asked. "Do you see something?"

Seth hesitated, remembering the strange image he'd seen on his computer—an image he'd been unable to duplicate, even though he'd come back out here half a dozen times since, taking pictures of the house in all kinds of light. But none of the pictures had shown the strange flames bursting from the second story window or the faint shadow, as if someone—or something—might have been inside the house.

Now it looked perfectly normal.

Perfectly normal, and perfectly ordinary.

Seth finally shook his head in answer to Angel's question. "I was just wondering," he said. "I mean—is it weird living in there, knowing what happened?"

Angel wondered if she should tell Seth what had happened on her very first night in the house. *Yeah, right. And have him think I'm crazy.* "It's just a house," she said, not quite answering his question. "Come on."

As they went inside, the cat that had followed them all the way from town darted off into the woods.

They were in Angel's room, their backpacks on the floor, the two of them sitting side by side on the bed, leaning against the wall. Seth glanced uneasily around the room. "This was the girl's room."

Angel shrugged. "I guess."

"I don't need to guess—this was the room they found her in. Doesn't it bother you, sleeping in here?"

"Why should it?" Angel countered, a little too quickly, her voice sharper than she'd meant it to be. "I mean, it's not like there's—" She hesitated, then went on. "—not like there's a ghost or something."

Seth cocked his head as he gazed at her, just like he had when he'd been looking at the house earlier, and Angel felt herself reddening. "What?" he asked. "What is it?"

"Nothing," Angel said, again too quickly.

"I don't believe you." For an instant he thought Angel was going to say something, but then he could see her changing her mind. "Come on," he pressed. "Tell me. Did something happen?" Now he could see by the look in her eyes that he was right—there was something she didn't want to tell him. "What is it? You might as well tell me, 'cause I'm going to keep bugging you till you do."

"It wasn't anything," Angel protested. "It was only a dream!"

"So if it was only a dream, what's the big deal?"

"It isn't a big deal," Angel countered. "It was just a nightmare, that's all. Can't we just talk about something else?" But when she saw that Seth wasn't going to talk about anything else, she finally told him about the strange dream in which she'd seen a girl burning in the closet, and what had happened when she finally woke up, when she was certain she could still smell smoke in the closet, even though the fire had only been a dream.

Seth listened in silence until she finished. "See?" she said. "I told you it was just a dream, didn't I?"

Instead of replying to her question, Seth opened his

backpack and pulled out a notebook. From the pocket in the back cover he took an envelope, which he wordlessly handed to Angel.

"What is it?" she asked, holding the envelope gingerly, as if it were hot.

"A photograph," Seth said, his voice sounding oddly hollow. "I took it a while ago, the day you and your folks came to look at this place. There's something in the window—something like . . ."

He spread his hands helplessly. "I don't know—it doesn't show up real well. Even when I blew it up, I couldn't really see anything."

Angel pulled the photo out of the envelope. "How did you know we were looking at the house?" she asked as she studied it. The photo showed the house exactly as it had been the day she and her parents first came to see it. But one window on the second floor—her window— looked strange. Fuzzy, and slightly out of focus. But there seemed to be something behind the glass, something she couldn't quite make out.

"I saw you. I was across the street when you left."

And then Angel remembered. It had been just as they were driving away from the house. She'd looked back at the house and seen something—something that looked like the face of a girl looking out the window of her room. Was it possible that Seth had actually taken a picture of it? "Are there any more?" she asked.

Seth nodded, and handed her another envelope. Her pulse suddenly quickening and her fingers trembling, Angel opened the envelope and pulled out another photograph, also of the house, but in this one flames were pouring out the second story window.

Her window.

She stared at it silently for almost a full minute, then

tore her eyes away to gaze at Seth. "I don't understand. If the house was on fire—"

"It wasn't," Seth broke in. "It was sunset, and the sun was sort of reflecting in the window, but when I looked at the picture on my computer . . ." His voice died away and he shook his head. "It's weird, isn't it? I mean, doesn't it look exactly like flames?"

Angel's eyes narrowed, and she was suddenly certain she knew what had happened. "You used one of those programs like Photoshop, didn't you?" But as soon as she uttered the words, she could see by the expression in his eyes that she was wrong. "But if you didn't do it . . ." Now it was her voice that died away, and when she spoke again, her voice held the same hollow note she'd heard in Seth's a few minutes ago. "So how come you're taking so many pictures of my house?" she asked, looking once more at the strange image of flames seeming to billow from her window.

Seth shrugged. "I like it. I mean, it's not like it's huge or anything, but it's really old, and—" His eyes shifted away from her. "Maybe part of it is that nobody else usually comes out here."

"Why not?"

"All the stories," Seth replied. He glanced around the room, which appeared utterly ordinary with the afternoon sunlight pouring in.

"You mean about the murders?"

Seth nodded. "But there's other stuff too." He fell silent again, but looked at her. "You know how kids tell stories about haunted houses?" Angel nodded. "Well, around here, this is the haunted house. I mean, even before that guy killed his family, everyone talked about it."

"About what?" Angel pressed. When Seth still hesitated, she reminded him that she'd told him about her dream.

"There's stories about all kinds of stuff," he finally said. "You know—ghosts and witches."

"I don't believe in that kind of stuff," Angel replied, but even as she said it, her gaze drifted to the photo that still lay on her lap. Was it possible that whatever was behind the window was the strange apparition she'd seen that day they'd come to see the house? She decided then that she didn't want to talk about it anymore. Getting up, she went to the dresser, turning her back on Seth. But she could still see him reflected in the mirror, staring at her.

"Don't do that," she said.

"Do what?"

"Don't stare at me—I hate it when people stare at me."

"I wasn't staring at you," Seth protested as he put the pictures in his backpack. "But even if I was looking at you, so what?"

Now it was the memory of the kids in Mrs. Holt's class that rose in her mind: *Who cares if she's smart— just look at her! Yuck!* The stinging words made her eyes well with tears again. "Because I'm not pretty," she blurted, wheeling around to face Seth. "I mean, just look at me!" When Seth said nothing, Angel said, "See? Everyone's right! I'm just *yuck!*"

Now Seth was truly staring at her. "What are you talking about?" he asked.

Finally giving in to the tears she'd been struggling against all day, she said, "What does it matter if I'm smart? All anyone cares about is how I look! And I look awful!"

"You don't look awful," Seth protested. "You look—" He stopped, seeing in her eyes that if he said she was pretty, she wouldn't believe him. "You look interesting," he said. "So your face isn't like Heather Dunne's. Who cares?"

"I care," Angel wailed. "I don't want to be 'interesting.' I want to be pretty." She turned around again and was staring at herself in the mirror when Seth appeared next to her. For a long minute the two of them stared at her reflection in the mirror, and then Seth cocked his head slightly and a little smile played around his lips.

"What?" Angel asked, still truculent. "Are you going to try to convince me I *am* pretty? Because if you are, don't bother—my eyes are too big, and my lips are too big, and my eyebrows—"

"Will you be quiet for a minute?" Seth broke in. "I was just thinking—have you got any makeup?"

"You mean like lipstick and eyeliner and that kind of stuff?" When Seth nodded, Angel shook her head. "My mom won't let me wear any, except on Halloween. Last year I was going to be a vampire, but—"

"But what?" Seth pressed. Angel said nothing, but Seth thought he knew the answer to his question. "Nobody invited you to a party, did they?" The tightening of Angel's expression told him he was right. "Nobody invited me to any parties either," he went on. "So, you still got the vampire stuff?"

"It's just junk!" Angel protested. "It's not makeup."

"Sure it is," Seth told her. "I bet it's the same stuff they sell in the cosmetics section of the drugstore in a different package. Get it out." Angel didn't move. "Oh, come on—it can't hurt just to try something, can it?"

Still not sure what Seth was up to, Angel rummaged around in the bottom drawer of her dresser until she found the unopened package that contained not only the makeup kit for the vampire, but the teeth and a black cape as well. "This is stupid—" she began, but Seth had already taken the package out of her hand and began ripping it open.

"Cool!" he said, shaking out the cape and throwing it

around his shoulders, then gazing at himself in the mirror over Angel's dresser. Then he opened the box that contained the makeup. " 'Dead white,' " he read off one of the labels. "And they have 'bloodred,' 'bruise purple,' and a bunch of other stuff. Put it on," he told her.

Angel reddened. "I—I don't know how," she finally admitted. "I've never put on makeup before."

Seth rolled his eyes. "Then I'll do it," he said. "Come here." He pulled her over so she was standing in front of him. "This is going to be fun," he said. "Like painting a picture on your face."

Angel glanced sourly at her reflection in the mirror. "You can't fix my face with makeup," she told him.

"Bet I can," Seth retorted. "Besides, I don't want to fix anything—I'm going to make everything bigger."

Angel's eyes widened. "Are you crazy?"

"Be quiet," Seth told her. "I'm just going to try it, okay? I mean, what can it hurt? No one's here but me, and if it doesn't work, we can just take it off." He held up a small jar of cold cream. "See? They even put it in the kit, in case the sight of blood makes you sick."

Angel made a face. "That's disgusting. And besides—"

"Stop arguing," Seth said. "Let's see what happens."

Angel reluctantly turned back to Seth, but still couldn't believe he was actually going to try to make her features even bigger. Everything was already so large!

"First we'll do your eyes," Seth said. Opening the purple eye shadow, he began carefully applying it, first to her eyelids, then below her eyes.

"How'd you learn to do this?" Angel asked.

"I was in a play last year—Mr. DeBerg showed us. Now be quiet—every time you say something, your whole face moves." Finished with the shadow, he found the black eyeliner and began outlining her eyes, pulling the line outward on both sides so her eyes seemed to be a little farther apart, just like the drama teacher had showed him.

When he was done with the eyeliner, Angel turned to look at herself in the mirror. Her eyes actually did look even bigger, but somehow, with the color Seth had added, they looked deeper too.

"Is that so terrible?" Seth asked.

Angel shook her head.

"Then let me do the rest." Seth set to work, accentuating every feature Angel had spent her life hating, making her cheekbones look higher and more pronounced, her nose longer, and finally applying "bloodred" to her lips. "Cool," Seth pronounced when he was finally finished. Turning Angel toward the mirror, he stood beside her as they gazed at his work. "Nobody's going to say 'yuck' when they see that!"

Angel stared silently at her own reflection, and as she slowly got used to what Seth had done, she found herself thinking that maybe she actually *did* look a little better.

And then the bedroom door suddenly opened, and Angel turned to see her father framed in the doorway. His eyes fixed on her, shifted to Seth for a moment, then came back to her. "What the hell's goin' on in here?" he demanded, his slurred words telling Angel that he'd been drinking.

"Nothing, Dad," she began. "Seth and I were just—"

"Nothing?" Marty Sullivan repeated. "I come home and find my little Angel painted up like some whore, with a boy in her bedroom? Don' tell me nothin's going on." His malevolent gaze swung back to Seth Baker. "Get out, you little punk." Abruptly, he lunged forward, grabbed Seth by the shirt, jerked the vampire cape off his shoulders, and began propelling him toward the door. Seth barely had time to grab his backpack before Marty pulled him out of the room.

"Dad!" Angel cried out, but Marty Sullivan didn't even hear her. He was already half dragging Seth down the stairs.

A moment later Angel watched from the window as her father shoved Seth off the front porch. "You stay away from my girl, you hear?" she heard him yell. Then the front door slammed shut, and she saw Seth run across the yard and disappear down the street.

Hearing her father coming back up the stairs, Angel ran to the bedroom door, closed it, and twisted the key in the lock.

"Let me in," her father called a moment later as he began pounding on her door. "Don't you think you can lock me out! This is my house, and you're my daughter, and you'll by God do what I tell you to do. Now open this door!"

But instead of opening the door, Angel backed away from it, praying that her mother would come home before her father broke it down.

Chapter 15

ETH BAKER STOPPED SHORT AS HE TURNED THE corner onto Elm Street. A quarter of the way down the block Chad Jackson and Jared Woods were throwing a football back and forth across the street between the Jacksons' and the Woodses' front yards. Chad and Jared had been best friends for as long as Seth had known them, which was ever since kindergarten, but he hadn't paid much attention to them until the day eight years ago when his parents bought the house on Elm Street—and suddenly Chad and Jared's favorite thing to do had become the torturing of Seth Baker.

Or that was the way it seemed to Seth.

He'd tried to be friends with them, or at least tried to get along with them, even though the two things they seemed to like best—baseball and football—were the things Seth hated most. Still, he'd done his best, knowing better than to argue the first time his father had sent him out into the street to join in the softball game Chad and Jared had organized. They'd let him play just long enough to find out he wasn't any good at it, and then, when it got too dark to play any longer and everyone but Chad and Jared had gone home, they'd "pantsed" him and thrown his jeans up into the big oak tree in front of the Jacksons' house. He'd tried to climb the tree, but only succeeded in skinning his legs, and finally went home in his underwear and T-shirt.

His father only wanted to know why he'd let it happen, and told him that the next time they tried it, he should fight back.

Seth had tried that only once, and all he'd gotten for his trouble was a black eye to go with the pantsing. After that, he'd decided it was better not to tell his father what Chad and Jared did to him and just do his best to avoid the two of them, especially when they were alone. Now, as he watched Chad toss the football to Jared, he wondered if he shouldn't just go around the block and get to his house from the opposite direction.

He was just about to turn away when Chad called out to him. "Hey, Beth! Want to throw a few?"

Beth! The nickname stung just as badly now as it had the day they'd thought it up.

The day they'd pantsed him for the first time.

"Come on, Beth," Jared chimed in. "Don't you want to come and play with us?"

It was too late to turn away. It was better just to ignore them.

Steeling himself, Seth started down the sidewalk.

Chad Jackson began making sucking noises.

Jared Woods grabbed his crotch. "Come on, Beth— isn't this what you want?"

Seth felt his face begin to burn, but he kept on walking, moving steadily down the sidewalk.

The taunts grew louder, then Jared darted off his front lawn to stand directly in front of him, his hand still on his crotch, his lips twisted into a cruel sneer. "You want it, Beth? Huh?"

Seth kept walking, staring straight ahead, and finally Jared Woods turned away, laughing loudly.

Then the football slammed into Seth's back.

He'd been expecting it—even braced himself for it—but when it happened, it still almost knocked him off his feet.

"Jeez, Beth!" Chad Jackson yelled. "Can't you catch anything?"

Seth clenched his jaw, resisted the almost overpowering urge to break into a run, and kept walking at exactly the pace he'd set when he decided to face Chad and Jared rather than go around the block.

Slowly, the taunts died away behind him.

Safe.

Then, as he cut across the lawn toward his own house, he saw his father framed in the open front door, and the notion of safety—along with the feeling of victory that had swelled inside him—faded away.

"Where were you?" Blake Baker asked as his son stepped onto the porch.

For a moment Seth's mind went blank, but then it came back to him.

Golf.

This was the afternoon his father was going to pick him up after school so they could practice for the golf tournament.

He'd completely forgotten.

But he could tell from the look in his father's eyes and the coldness in his voice that he wouldn't forget what was going to happen next.

"Go upstairs and wait in your room," his father said. "I'll be up in a minute."

As he began climbing the stairs, Seth could almost feel the sting of his father's belt.

Chapter 16

WHORE!

The word reverberated in Angel's mind. When she first heard it, it had slashed into her like a knife, cutting so deep it penetrated her very soul.

My father called me a whore!

She told herself that he was drunk, and tried to shut out his words as he pounded on her door, railing at her. After what seemed hours but couldn't have been more than a few minutes, his voice finally died away into an unintelligible mutter, and then she heard him go back downstairs.

She stayed in her room, kept her door locked, prayed for her mother to come home, and tried to silence the echoes of her father's voice.

Her mother at last came home, but Angel didn't unlock her door until she was upstairs and rapped sharply, asking if she was all right.

Only then did Angel finally twist the key in the lock and open the door, letting her mother in. By then she'd wiped off the last vestiges of the makeup.

Her mother knew in an instant that something was wrong, though Angel insisted that she was fine.

And the word echoed once more in her head.

Whore!

Somehow she got through dinner. All through the meal she felt her father's baleful glare boring into her as he washed down the spaghetti her mother had made with one beer after another. When he abruptly left the table while she was clearing off the dinner dishes and her mother was serving ice cream for dessert, Angel felt a few short moments of relief. Then her father returned, and there was a look in his eye—a dark gleam—that brought her fears flooding back.

After dinner she went back upstairs to do her homework, and it was only then that she fully understood the glimmer in her father's eyes when he'd returned to the table.

The key was gone from the door of her room.

She had no idea how long she stared at the empty keyhole, willing the key to somehow magically reappear, until she finally turned away, pulled her books from her backpack, and started on her homework.

It was impossible to concentrate, though, with her father's voice ringing in her head and the empty keyhole drawing her eyes away from the textbooks so often that she couldn't follow the simplest paragraphs.

Her mother came in at ten. "What is it, Angel?" she asked. "What's wrong? Did something happen before I got home?"

And finally Angel blurted it out, telling her mother everything. "He called me a whore, Mommy," she finished, and began crying again.

Her mother held her stiffly for a moment, then eased her away and looked into her eyes. "Why did you have a boy in your room?" she asked.

"We weren't doing anything," Angel protested. "We were just goofing around with that old vampire stuff I had for Halloween last year."

"You're sure?" Myra pressed, searching deep in Angel's

eyes for the truth. "All you were doing with this Seth person was putting on makeup?"

Angel nodded. "I swear to God," she said. "That's all we were doing. Seth just wanted me to—"

Her mother put a finger over Angel's lips to silence her. "We don't swear to God," Myra Sullivan said. "We pray to Him for guidance. And I'm sure your father didn't mean what he said, at least not the way it sounded. He loves you, Angel. He loves you more than anything, and I'm sure he was just worried about you."

"But—" Angel began, but once again her mother's finger pressed against her lips.

"He loves you," she repeated. "And he'd never do anything to hurt you. Never forget that. He's not always the easiest man, but he's my husband, and he's your father, and we must respect him. Now it's time to put away your books, say your prayers, and go to bed."

Then her mother was gone and Angel went back to her books, but she still couldn't concentrate. Finally giving up, she returned them to the backpack and went to bed.

Whore!

The word still echoed in her mind. Why had he said it? She and Seth hadn't been doing anything at all— she'd just put on some makeup, and that was only to see what she'd look like.

She tossed restlessly in her bed, turning first one way and then another, but no matter how she twisted around or pummeled the pillow or tugged at the covers, she couldn't get comfortable. Finally she gave up, rolled over on her back, and gazed out through the window at the moon that hung just behind the treetops, its silvery light casting dark shadows on the wall of her room.

The wind came up, and the shadows on the wall began to dance, taking on a strange rhythm that at last calmed her, and finally she drifted into a fitful sleep.

Blood.

It was everywhere, on his hands and on his shirt, and on his pants and on the walls and the rug and everywhere else he looked. But mostly it was on the bed.

The sheets were crimson with it, and the hair of the still form that lay beneath the sheet was matted with it, and it was smeared on the headboard and the pillows and the blanket that lay at the foot of the bed.

Marty rose from the chair in front of the fireplace and walked slowly toward the bed. It was almost as if he was floating, for he felt nothing under his feet.

Nor could he hear anything. The silence around him was complete—not a creaking floorboard, or a whisper of wind from beyond the house, nor any of the other sounds of the night.

No insects or frogs chirruping in the darkness.

No low murmuring of birds roosting in the trees.

And no breathing from the form on the bed.

It lay facedown, the flesh of the back lacerated by the knife he'd wielded, slashed in every direction, the skin and flesh laid back so he could clearly see the unmoving ribs that had failed to protect the lungs or the heart.

He reached down and turned it over. It seemed utterly weightless, moving as if it were somehow floating above the bed rather than lying deep in the blood-soaked sheets. And as it rolled over, the sticky matted hair fell away from the face, and Marty gazed at the visage of death that was smiling up at him, the lips drawn back in a rictus around stained teeth, the deep-sunk eyes gazing sightlessly up at him, but seeming to peer directly into his soul.

As he gazed down into the face of his wife, the silence was finally pierced by a whispering voice, so faint at first that Marty barely heard it at all. But as the seconds slipped by—seconds that seemed to stretch out into eternities—the faint whispers coalesced into words.

"The other one . . ."

"Not done . . ."

"The other . . ."

"You want to . . . you know you want to. . . ."

As the voice kept whispering, the still form on the bed slowly began to sit up. The bloody sheets fell away, revealing the carnage beneath. His wife's throat was slashed open, the already shrinking skin pulling back to expose the torn flesh and ligaments. Her breasts had been slashed away too, and her chest laid open to reveal her heart.

But it wasn't any kind of heart that Marty Sullivan had ever seen—not even in the worst horror movie he'd ever gone to.

This was a black mass of muscle, crawling with worms and maggots.

And it was beating—throbbing in a slow rhythm that spewed a stream of maggots from its puncture wounds with every beat.

Transfixed, Marty Sullivan stood still as the right arm of the living corpse began to rise.

The hand reached out, as if to seize him.

He shrank away, but it didn't matter.

The forefinger, its nail torn away and hanging only by a thread of cuticle, pointed directly at him, and he felt his flesh begin to crawl as if he himself had just felt the touch of death.

The mouth opened and a croaking voice erupted from the mangled throat.

"You have to," the voice said. *"You want to!"*

The finger came closer, and as he felt its touch, a convulsion seized Marty.

An instant later he was wide awake.

His heart was pounding, and the echo of the voice was still in his head: *You have to . . . you want to. . . .*

He lay still, and the images of the dream began to fade. He could hear Myra breathing next to him—the long, slow, even rhythms of sleep.

She wasn't dead. He hadn't killed her. It was only a dream.

"You want to, Marty," the voice whispered again. *"You need to. Go on, Marty . . . do it. Do it now."*

Listening to the voice in his head, knowing what it was telling him to do, Marty Sullivan rose silently from the bed and slipped out of the room, leaving his wife's sleep undisturbed.

A moment later he stood at the door to Angel's room, his hand on the knob.

"Go on, Marty," the voice whispered. *"You know what you want . . . go on . . . she wants it too . . . she's a whore, Marty. She's only a whore . . .*

"She's your whore. . . ."

Listening to the voice, Marty turned the knob of Angel's bedroom door and let himself in.

The moon had set when Angel awoke, and the shadows on the wall had vanished into nearly total blackness. Even the sounds of the night had fallen silent.

But what had awakened her?

She lay still, listening.

Nothing.

But then she heard a sound—the creak of a loose floorboard.

Now she could feel something—a presence in the room, close by her bed.

Then she heard a single word, uttered in a whisper so low she almost thought she was imagining it: "Whore."

Another floorboard squeaked, and she felt the presence in the room draw closer.

The voice whispered again, repeating the loathesome word once more.

Angel felt her heart pound, and she began repeating the words her mother had spoken only a few hours ago: "He loves you, and he'd never do anything to hurt you . . . he loves you and he'd never do—"

"Whore!"

The word struck her with a force that was almost physical, and at the exact moment the word was uttered, she felt a hand touching her.

Touching her chest at exactly the spot where her breasts were beginning to grow.

Terrified, too frightened even to scream, she lay perfectly still, praying that if she didn't move, didn't speak, didn't cry—not so much as a whimper—it would stop.

He would go away, and the sounds of the night would begin again, and moonlight would stream in the window, and she would be safe.

Instead, the hand on her chest pressed harder, then moved away. For an instant Angel felt a glimmer of hope. But then the hand was back, this time gently pulling the covers away so that all that covered her budding breasts was the thin cotton of her pajama tops.

Fingers reached out of the darkness and began unfastening the buttons of her pajama tops.

Angel clenched her jaw against the scream rising in her throat, and her body stiffened as she tried to prepare herself for the terrible thing that was about to happen.

She felt the heat of the hand poised just above her left breast.

Then, just as she felt the rough skin of a heavily callused hand brush against her nipple, Angel heard a hissing sound.

The hand on her breast was jerked away.

For a few interminably long seconds there was an eerie stillness in the room.

Angel lay perfectly still, too frightened even to breathe now.

More seconds passed—more eternities—but still she didn't take a breath. And in the stillness and the darkness, she felt the unseen hand moving toward her once again, like a viper slithering silently through deep grass, moving invisibly toward its prey.

Her skin crawled as she felt the hand grow nearer.

Then, out of the darkness, the hissing sound came again, followed by a crash and a brief grunt of pain. A moment later she heard the sound of her bedroom door opening and closing.

Angel lay still for a moment, her heart pounding.

The house had gone silent, but from outside she could once more hear the faint sounds of the night—the hooting of an owl.

She switched on the lamp that stood on her night table, the bright glare momentarily blinding her. As her eyes slowly adjusted to the light, she looked around, at first seeing nothing. Then, on the floor next to her dresser, she saw her piggy bank—a heavy bronze one that she'd been given on her first birthday, and into which she always deposited a little bit of her allowance, even if it was only a penny. How had it gotten there? It was always on top of her dresser, watched over by her teddy bear, who was still leaning against the mirror, just where she'd put him.

But now the piggy bank was lying on its side on the floor.

For several long seconds she stayed in her bed, staring at the object on the floor.

How had it gotten there?

Then, as she tried to remember exactly what had happened, she understood.

Houdini!

Somehow, the cat must have gotten into the room and been on the dresser. And when her father came in—

The cat had leaped at him! Leaped off the dresser, knocking the piggy bank off.

Getting out of bed, she picked up the piggy bank and put it back on the dresser where it belonged. She was about to go back to bed when something in the mirror caught her eye. Her heart suddenly racing again, she whirled around to face whatever was behind her.

And saw nothing.

But there had been something in the mirror—she knew there had!

The cat?

Once again she scanned the room, searching for some sign of the black animal that had appeared the day they moved into the house. "Houdini?" she called out, keeping her voice low enough so it wouldn't carry beyond the walls of her room. "Here, kitty, kitty. Come on, Houdini—I know you're in here somewhere."

Nothing.

She crouched down and looked under the bed, then behind her desk.

Finally she went to the closet and pulled the door open.

The smell of smoke almost overwhelmed her. Gasping, she staggered back and turned away.

Her eyes fell once more on the mirror, and once again

she froze. For right behind her, clearly reflected in the mirror, she saw it.

A face.

The face of a girl, about her own age.

Her heart racing, she whirled around again.

And found herself staring into the empty closet.

The smell of smoke was gone.

No, she told herself. *I didn't imagine it! I smelled smoke, and I saw a face!*

Steeling herself, Angel stepped into the closet. Except for her clothes and a few boxes on the shelf, it was empty.

And the smell of smoke—the acrid aroma so strong a moment ago that it had almost choked her— was completely gone.

Now she smelled nothing except the faint aroma of the cedar that lined one wall of the closet.

Closing the closet door, she leaned against it for a moment, staring across the room at her teddy bear and piggy bank. They were sitting on her dresser, the bear seemingly watching over the piggy bank, just as they had always been.

Her head swimming with confusion, Angel went back to her bed, sat down, and stared for a long time at the teddy bear and the piggy bank.

The cat.

It had to have been the cat!

But where was it?

And what had she smelled, and seen?

What if she'd simply dreamed the whole thing, like she dreamed about the house being on fire the other night?

Wrestling with the confusion, she slid back into the bed and pulled the covers tight around her neck.

Resolutely, Angel turned off the light; the room plunged

back into darkness. For a long time she lay awake, staring into the darkness, trying to decide whether any of it had been real or if she had simply dreamed it. *It was a dream,* she told herself. *It was just a dream, and Daddy wasn't in here at all, and nothing happened, and I'm all right.* Soon, with the night holding her in its embrace, she drifted once again into the same fitful sleep from which she had awakened so short a time ago.

Chapter 17

"ANGEL?" MYRA SAID. "ARE YOU ALL RIGHT?"

Angel nodded automatically, though she barely heard the question.

"You're sure?" her mother fretted, eyeing her critically. "You look a little peaked. Do you feel like you have a temperature?"

"I'm fine, Mom," Angel said, digging resolutely into the almost untouched bowl of fast-cooling oatmeal her mother had put in front of her five minutes ago. But despite her words, she wasn't fine at all, and hadn't been fine since she'd awakened. Almost as soon as she opened her eyes, the memories of last night came streaming back.

The creaking of the floorboards.

Her father coming into her room.

The touch of his hands on—

She'd shuddered as that memory came flooding back, tried to shut it out, and failed.

Then, as the rest of it came back, she decided that nothing had happened—it had been nothing more than a dream. It had to be, didn't it? Her piggy bank hadn't flown off the dresser all by itself, and she hadn't seen anything in the closet. She couldn't have smelled the acrid aroma of smoke, since there hadn't been a fire in the fireplace last night, and the house certainly hadn't caught on fire.

So if all that had been a dream, her father coming into the room must have been a dream too.

But then as she got out of bed it all changed.

First she saw the marks on the mirror—a drawing, scrawled smearily in what looked like blood.

There was a stick figure, like one she might have drawn in kindergarten, and a jagged line that almost looked like stairs. In fact, it almost looked like the stick figure was going down the stairs.

And under the jagged line was something else—something that looked like a small square.

For several long minutes Angel had stared at the strange marks, her heart racing. Where could they have come from? Then, as she started to get out of bed, she saw that it wasn't just the mirror that bore the bloodred smears.

Her sheets were stained as well.

And the forefinger of her right hand! She instinctively put the finger to her mouth, as if she'd cut it. But instead of the almost coppery taste of blood, she felt something else on her tongue.

Lipstick!

She'd pulled her finger out of her mouth and stared at it for a moment. How . . . ? Then, out of the corner of her eye, she saw something lying on the table by her bed.

The lipstick from the vampire kit—the same one she and Seth were experimenting with yesterday afternoon! Its cap was off and most of it was gone. She felt almost dizzy now as her eyes moved from the ruined lipstick to the marks on the mirror to the stains on her sheets and on her finger.

Had she done it herself? She must have! Then why didn't she remember?

A wave of panic rose inside her, and she almost called out for her mother. But what would she say to her mother? She had no idea how the markings had gotten on the mirror. And what about everything else? The things that seemed like memories but must have been dreams?

The memories, or dreams, or whatever they were, began churning in her mind, mixing in with the images on the mirror.

She turned to the dresser. The piggy bank was exactly where it should have been.

But the teddy bear was no longer in its regular spot, leaning against the mirror, watching over the piggy bank. Now it was at the end of the dresser, lying face-down.

She was mired in confusion again, and all she wanted was for things to look right—to look the way they had last night, when she'd gone to bed.

She moved the teddy bear back to its regular place, then grabbed some Kleenex from the box on the dresser and began rubbing at the markings on the mirror.

A moment later the stick figure and the other markings had vanished, leaving only a reddish smudge.

A second handful of Kleenex wiped even that away.

Wadding up the tissues, Angel was about to throw them in the wastebasket when she changed her mind. Taking them into the bathroom, she flushed the whole mess down the toilet. Then she scrubbed her hands until every trace of lipstick was gone.

Back in her room, she stared at the lipstick-smeared sheets and pillowcase. A moment later it all vanished beneath the bedspread—this afternoon, when she got home from school, she would wash them. By the time she was dressed, everything was almost as it had been when she went to bed last night.

Except that everything had changed, and the minute she'd come downstairs, her mother knew that something was wrong. And now, even though she'd already said she was fine, her mother was giving her one of those penetrating looks that always made Angel feel as if she couldn't hide anything, no matter how hard she tried.

Then her father came into the room, and Angel felt a terrible chill pass over her. There was a bandage on his left cheek, high up near the temple. Though she wanted to look away—look anywhere but at the bandage—she couldn't tear her eyes from it. As the seconds ticked slowly away, her father's eyes finally fixed on her, and when he spoke, his voice was as dark as his expression.

"What you looking at?"

"N-Nothing," Angel stammered, at last managing to pull her eyes away from the bandage. But even as she looked back down at her oatmeal, she could feel her father's eyes still fixed on her, and felt her skin begin to crawl as it had last night when she'd felt the presence of someone in her room and heard the floorboards creak as he came close to the bed.

Came close, and bent down, and—

"Gotta go." Her father's voice jerked Angel back into the present, and a second later she reflexively jerked away as his lips brushed her cheek. "What's with you? Too old to kiss your daddy?"

Then he was gone, but it wasn't until she heard the old Chevelle roar away that Angel finally tried to eat again.

Tried, and failed.

"Maybe you'd better not go to school today," her mother fretted. "You look tired."

"I'm okay," Angel insisted. "I—I just had a lot of homework to do."

Her mother frowned. "There's something you're not telling me."

Angel looked up at her mother, and once more her mother's words from yesterday echoed in her head: *He loves you . . . he'd never do anything to hurt you.* And he hadn't hurt her, really. He'd scared her, and she was terrified of what might happen if he came into her room again, but he hadn't really hurt her. And after he got cut, maybe he wouldn't come back at all.

"Well?" her mother pressed. "What is it? You'd better tell me."

Angel felt her resolve to say nothing about what had happened last night weaken. But even if she told her mother, how would she start? The answer rose as quickly as the question: "D-Did Dad tell you how he cut himself?"

Myra, caught off guard by the question, cocked her head. "What does that have to do with anything?" she asked.

"Did he?" Angel pressed.

"He cut himself shaving." Now Myra lowered herself into the chair across from Angel. "What's going on?" she asked. "Why are you so interested in a shaving cut?"

Suddenly, her fear and the exhaustion from the nearly sleepless night overwhelmed Angel, and the whole strange story—everything except the marks she'd found on the mirror this morning—came pouring out. She tried to make sense of it as she told it, but even as she spoke, she knew it sounded even stranger out loud than it had when she'd pieced it together this morning.

And when she saw her mother's expression, she knew she'd made a mistake telling her anything at all.

"How dare you?" Myra Sullivan said, her voice hard. "Your father loves you, and takes care of you, and would never do anything to hurt you! And what are his thanks? To have you come to me with terrible stories?

You must have been dreaming! How could you even *make up* such vile things?"

Angel's mouth opened as if to say something, but before she could utter even a single word, Myra's hand snaked across the table and slapped her hard across the cheek.

"Filth!" her mother shouted. "That's all it is! Filth! And you will not speak it in my house! After school today you will go to church, and you will confess your sins to Father Mike! All of them!" Myra's eyes narrowed to angry slits. "It's that boy you had in the house yesterday, isn't it? That's really what this is about. Your guilty conscience!"

Seeing the fury in her mother's eyes, Angel knew better than to argue. The house felt like it was closing in around her, and all she wanted was to escape, to get away both from the terrors of the night and her mother's rage. Leaving her oatmeal half finished, she stood up. "I better hurry," she said softly. "I'll be late."

"Yes," Myra Sullivan said coldly. "You'd better hurry. And you'd better think twice before you tell me any more lies about your father!" As Angel picked up her backpack, Myra said, "Aren't you going to give me a kiss?"

Angel hesitated, then gave her mother a quick peck on the cheek and fled from the house into the crisp sunshine of the fall morning.

Skirting around the house, she cut across the front yard and headed along the road toward town, but before she went around the curve that would cut the house off from her view, she turned to look back at it once more. In the bright morning light it looked just as it had the first time she'd seen it—a small white house with a peaked roof, nothing out of the ordinary.

And there was no sign at all of the black cat.

So her mother must be right—she must have dreamed it all.

But then she remembered the pictures Seth Baker had showed her yesterday, with flames billowing from her window in one of them, and something that looked like it might be the shadowed image of a face peering out of another.

Chapter 18

WITH THE MEMORIES OF THE NIGHT DOGGING HER every step, Angel dragged herself through the morning. By the time the bell signaling the lunch break rang, she wasn't sure she could get through the rest of the day. She made her way to the cafeteria, looked around until she spotted Seth Baker sitting alone at the same table as yesterday, and bringing her lunch over, sank into the chair opposite him. He looked up, a smile starting to spread across his face, but as he gazed at Angel, his smile faded.

"What's wrong?" he asked.

Her eyes darted nervously around the cafeteria. Zack Fletcher and Heather Dunne were sitting at the same table as yesterday. Angel hesitated about saying anything, then couldn't keep it inside any longer, and words began tumbling from her mouth. She poured out every detail about what had happened—or what she thought had happened—and Seth listened to it all, not interrupting. He was so engrossed in what she was saying that he didn't even notice Chad Jackson and Jared Woods ease themselves into two chairs at the table directly behind him, their backs to the table at which Angel and he were sitting.

"And the worst part of it is I don't even know how

much of it was a dream and how much of it was real! I mean, things don't just fly off the dresser! And how could I have made a drawing on the mirror and not even remember it?"

When Angel at last fell silent, Seth sat quietly for a while, trying to sort it all out in his mind. But none of it made any more sense to him than it had to Angel. Unless . . .

"What if you *didn't* draw on the mirror?" he finally suggested. "What if it all happened just like you remember it? And what if you don't remember some of the stuff because you didn't do it?"

Angel stared at him. "But if I didn't do it, who did?"

Before Seth could respond, a sound erupted from the table behind him—the same loud, mock sucking and kissing sounds he'd heard yesterday afternoon as he passed Chad and Jared on his way home. His jaw clenching, Seth tried to shut the sounds out.

Then, while Jared kept making the kissing sounds, Chad stood up and turned around, his eyes glittering with malice. "Maybe it was Beth," he said, his voice as scornful as the sneer on his lips. "Maybe Beth sneaked into your room last night to play with your lipstick!"

Angel gazed uncertainly at Chad. *Beth? Who was Beth? What was he talking about?* But a second later, as she saw Seth's face paling, she understood.

Chad shifted his attack. "Except who would want to sneak into your room in the middle of the night?" he said to Angel. "Even Beth can't be that hard-up!"

Jared Woods, bursting into laughter that was even uglier than the sounds he'd been making, stood up too. "Come on," he told Chad. "Let's get out of here before we catch whatever they've got!"

Picking up his tray, Chad shoved hard on Seth's chair. Seth winced as the table dug deep into his stomach, but he managed to stifle the yelp of pain that rose in his throat. Neither he nor Angel said a word until they saw Chad and Jared drop into a couple of chairs at the table next to the one across the cafeteria where Zack and Heather were sitting.

"What was that all about?" Angel finally asked.

Seth shrugged and tried to look nonchalant. "They live down the street from me." He picked up his fork and poked at the food on the plate in front of him.

"But how come they called you Beth?" Angel pressed.

Seth's face flushed again. "How should I know?" he asked. "Maybe it's just because I'm not very good at sports."

Angel frowned. "That's the name, isn't it?" she asked. "The one you wouldn't tell me yesterday."

Seth nodded but said nothing.

"It isn't any worse than 'Mangy—' " Angel began, but Seth didn't let her finish.

"Can we just talk about something else?"

"Like what?" Angel challenged.

"Like how that stuff got on your mirror last night," Seth replied. "'Cause I know it wasn't me." He pulled a piece of paper from his notebook and pushed it across the table. "Draw what was on the mirror."

Angel sat perfectly still, gazing at Seth, but when he said nothing else, and wouldn't even meet her gaze, she finally fished around in her backpack, found a pen, and began to draw, doing her best to recreate the image she'd found on the mirror this morning. When she was done, she pushed it toward him.

Seth gazed at the drawing for a long time. "It looks like someone going down stairs," he said at last. "But what's that square under the stairs?"

Angel gazed at him in exasperation. "How should I

know? I don't even know if the jagged line is supposed to be stairs!"

"Well, what else could it be?" Seth argued.

"I don't know! Maybe it's supposed to be lightning or something?"

"That's not what lightning looks like," Seth shot back. Picking up the pen, he drew the kind of zigzag line that depicted lightning in every comic strip he'd ever seen. "Does that look like what was on your mirror?"

Angel shook her head. "But it doesn't matter anyway, because it had to have been me that made the marks. I mean, the lipstick was all over my fingers, and my sheets and pillowcase, and everything."

"Well, it won't hurt for us to at least look, will it? And with all the stories about your house . . ." His voice trailed off. Then: "It just seems like we should try to find out, that's all."

There was a burst of laughter from Zack and Heather's table, and a moment later Jared Woods was once again making the ugly sucking and kissing sounds. Then Chad Jackson joined in, and then Zack and the rest of the boys at his table took up the chorus. As the mocking sounds echoed through the cafeteria, Seth's face turned crimson.

"Let's just leave," Angel said, putting the pen back in her backpack.

Seth shook his head. "That's what they want."

"So what are we supposed to do, just sit here and pretend it isn't happening?"

Seth looked directly into her eyes. "Isn't that what you did back in Eastbury?"

Angel wanted to shake her head but knew she couldn't, because back in Eastbury it had been the same as it was here and there had never been anything she could do about it except pretend it wasn't happening.

Just like Seth was pretending the laughter that was steadily building around them wasn't directed at him.

"Why won't they just leave us alone?" she finally asked. "What did we ever do to them?"

Seth said nothing, because he knew the answer as well as Angel did.

Neither of them had done anything at all.

They just had to deal with it.

Or figure out a way to make it stop.

Chapter 19

WELL? WAS I RIGHT? AREN'T YOU JUST LOVING YOUR house?" Joni Fletcher asked, fixing Myra Sullivan with a look of such utter triumph that Myra half wished she hadn't agreed to have lunch with her sister. "I'm telling you," Joni plunged on, "it was an absolute steal!"

The dining room of the Roundtree Country Club had barely begun to fill, and Joni's final word seemed to bounce off the walls, echoing through the room like a gunshot. Three women at the next table—women Myra had never seen before—turned to look at them, and Myra felt her face flush with embarrassment. She'd known it was a mistake to come here; she'd never felt comfortable with Joni's country club friends. And it wasn't just because she had nothing to wear, though she was honest enough to admit that her wardrobe—or the lack of it—was at least a factor. Nor was it the fact that she knew there was no chance at all that she and Marty would ever be members here. For Myra Sullivan, the biggest problem was the people who *were* members here.

At the moment, that applied to the three women who had looked at her just long enough to make her uncomfortable, then pointedly looked away again without even acknowledging her presence when she nodded to them. *They could have at least nodded back,* she thought, but she rejected her own notion. "We must always be charitable to others," Father Raphaello had always said, "even when others are uncharitable to us." *I'm sure they're very nice women,* she told herself, shifting her attention back to her sister, who seemed not to have noticed the other women at all.

"I'm telling you, Myra—you owe me big-time for this one, if I do say so myself."

"And don't you always say so?" a new voice said. Myra looked up to see two more women standing just behind her, both of them as perfectly dressed as Joni Fletcher. One was a pretty blonde whose hair was cut in the kind of pageboy that never seemed to go out of style for the kind of women who always fit perfectly into places like the Roundtree Country Club. The other woman had glowing auburn hair drawn up into a severe twist. A square-cut emerald hung from a simple gold chain around her neck, and she wore a smile that looked no more real than the color of her hair. It was the second woman who had just spoken. "I'm Gloria Dunne, and this is Jane Baker."

"I'm My—" Myra began, but Jane Baker didn't let her finish.

"Oh, you don't have to tell us who you are—Joni's been an absolute *bore* on the subject for simply weeks now! And I want you to know how much I admire you for buying the house out at the Crossing!"

"We all do," Gloria Dunne added as she and Jane Baker took the two vacant chairs at the table. "Although frankly, I can't imagine living there. If even half the stories are true—"

"For heaven's sake, Gloria," Jane Baker cut in. "We were all children!"

"I'm not saying I believe all of them," Gloria Dunne said. "But you know what they say—where there's smoke there's fire."

"Now there's an unfortunate choice of words," Jane remarked, signaling the waiter with a single uplifted finger, and getting an immediate response. "A martini, Gloria?" she asked. Then she glanced at Myra and Joni. "Anything for you two, or is Gloria going to be drinking alone again?"

"I'll have iced tea," Gloria Dunne said, her voice as tight as the twist in her hair.

When the waiter finished taking their orders, Myra turned back to Gloria Dunne. "What did you mean, 'half the stories'?" she asked.

Gloria Dunne's perfectly shaped left eyebrow rose a fraction of an inch. "You mean Joni didn't tell you?" Her gaze shifted to Joni Fletcher. "I thought there were full disclosure laws in Massachusetts," she said, a little too sweetly.

"There are," Joni replied. "But they only apply to actual circumstances, not rumors."

Myra's eyes clouded. "Rumors? What are you talking about?"

"Nothing!" Joni declared before either Gloria Dunne or Jane Baker could speak. "Just stories kids tell—you know, the same kind we used to tell. The man with the hook? The girl in the prom dress on the lonely road? That kind of stuff."

"Not exactly," Gloria Dunne said. Ignoring Joni Fletcher's glare, she turned to Myra. "I'm assuming she told you about the murders," she said. Myra nodded. "Did she also tell you about everything else?"

"Everything else?" Myra echoed. "I'm not sure what you mean."

"I mean," Gloria Dunne said, "the fact that no one has ever lived in that house for more than a few months at a time."

"Why?" Myra asked.

"The ghost," Gloria Dunne pronounced. When Jane Baker uttered an annoyed groan, Gloria's expression hardened. "Groan if you want, Jane, but I remember when you wouldn't walk past that house even if you were on the other side of the street!"

"When I was eight," Jane Baker shot back.

"When we were both fifteen," Gloria corrected her. "And it wasn't just us either." She shifted her attention back to Myra. "I'm sure you don't believe in ghosts, and I'm not saying I do either. But that house—" She took a deep breath, then let it out in a deep sigh. "All I can tell you is that no one ever seems to be able to live in it very long. And there are all kinds of stories of people seeing and hearing things out there."

"What kind of things?" Myra pressed.

Gloria shrugged. "All the usual things—noises at night, people smelling smoke, seeing things. I think half the people who ever lived there wound up killing themselves—"

"Gloria!" Joni Fletcher cut in, and now she sounded genuinely angry. "You don't have any idea if any of that is true or not!"

"Everyone in town knows perfectly well—" Gloria began, but Joni didn't let her finish.

"Everyone in town knows perfectly well that one man cracked up, and believe me, I told Myra and Marty all about it when I showed them the house. The rest is just rumor, and frankly, I'm surprised you're spreading them." As Gloria's eyes darkened with anger, Jane Baker quickly stepped in.

"Every town has its haunted house," she said, smiling at Myra. "And all the kids are terrified, and all the adults—except, apparently, this one"—she tilted her head toward Gloria Dunne—"know they're just stories. This is not the seventeenth century, and no one believes in ghosts and hobgoblins and witches and devils and all the rest of the stuff that scares kids half to death. So why don't we just leave it at the fact that you and your family have bought what has always been the 'haunted house' in Roundtree, and assume that now that we have a nice, normal family living in it, the silly stories will finally dry up and blow away."

"Hear, hear," Joni Fletcher said, raising her water glass.

Gloria Dunne started to say something else, but once again Jane Baker preempted her. "Why don't we talk about something else entirely? For instance, what about the Family Day that's coming up this weekend?"

"Family Day?" Myra asked.

"Here at the club," Jane Baker explained. "It's wonderful fun—this month there's a father-son golf tournament and a mother-daughter tennis tournament, then a barbecue and a dance. Or there's a barbecue if it's not too cold, and so far it never has been—Indian summer always seems to last just long enough to cover Family Day."

Myra shook her head. "I'm afraid my husband doesn't play golf, and neither my daughter nor I play tennis."

"It doesn't matter," Jane Baker declared. "I don't play tennis either, so you and I and your daughter will hang around the pool while the boys and men play golf."

"But I really don't think—" Myra began.

Once again Jane Baker took charge. "It doesn't matter what you think," she said. "You're coming, and that's final. Everybody at the club has been dying to meet you and your husband, and I'm sure all the kids will love your daughter. So that's that."

The waiter arrived with their food, and Myra nodded mutely, knowing there was no way out.

Chapter 20

DON'T LISTEN, ANGEL TOLD HERSELF. *IT'S ONLY A sound and it doesn't matter.* She was standing at her locker, trying to concentrate on the combination, but every time she worked the dial, the sound would come again. She knew who was doing it—Jared Woods, whose locker was only about twenty feet down the hall from hers. Seeing him standing in the hall when she first came up the stairs, she almost turned back, but she'd left the heaviest of her books in her locker that morning, and now she needed it. Steeling herself, she'd mounted the last stair and started down the hall, staying as close to the opposite wall as possible. As she passed behind him, she thought maybe he hadn't seen her. But then, just as she started turning the dial on her locker, it began.

The same ugly-sounding kissing noise he and Chad Jackson had been making in the cafeteria.

She tried to just shut it out, but lost track of the combination, and when she tried to lift the handle of the locker, nothing happened. She started over again, but the sound seemed even louder, and she lost track of the number of times she turned the dial between the second number and the third.

Then, as she was starting over for the fourth time, she

felt someone behind her. She froze, her fingers still on the dial, and stole a glance down the hall. Jared Woods was still there, still making the disgusting sounds with his lips, but now he was staring at her, thrusting his hips toward her as if—

The kind of movement Jared was making shoved against her from behind, slamming her up against her locker. Before she could react, she heard Chad Jackson's mocking voice, "This what you want? Huh?" and the awful memory of yesterday and last night rose up in Angel's mind.

Once again she heard her father's accusing voice: *Whore!*

Once again she felt the touch of the unseen hand pressing against her breast in the darkness of the night. Now she recalled her mother saying: *Filth! You will not speak it . . . you will go to church and confess your sins to Father Mike!*

Confess . . . confess her sins . . . confess her guilt. Maybe it was true; maybe all of it was her fault. Maybe—

No! It wasn't her fault! She hadn't done anything!

Bracing herself against the bank of lockers, Angel shoved hard, but Chad anticipated her move and suddenly stepped away. Losing her balance, Angel tumbled to the floor, her left elbow striking the hardwood, her backpack skidding down the hall. As a sharp stab of pain shot from her elbow down into her hand, she sat up.

There were more kids in the hallway now, and they were staring at her.

Jared Woods was still making the horrible noises.

Then Heather Dunne rolled her eyes, shook her head, and turned away.

A few seconds later the hallway was empty, and even the ugly sounds died away as Jared Woods headed down the same stairs Angel had come up only a couple of minutes before. The sound of laughter exploded up the stairwell, and tears of humiliation streamed down Angel's cheeks as she struggled to her feet, finally managed to open her locker, and found her history book.

The bell had already rung by the time she got to her classroom, and a ripple of not quite muted laughter ran through the room as she slunk into her seat.

The afternoon dragged on, and as Angel moved from one classroom to another, she did her best to ignore what was going on around her. But what Chad Jackson and Jared Woods had begun in the cafeteria seemed to have spread through the school like a virus, and each break between classes was worse than the one before. Wherever she went, the kissing sounds followed her, and even though no one else shoved up against her the way Chad Jackson had, more and more of the boys began thrusting their hips toward her as she approached and bursting into laughter as she passed.

Laughter, and more of the increasingly obscene-sounding noises.

Maybe it was her fault—maybe she was doing something. But what?

The day wore on and grew steadily worse, until by the end of the last period, which it seemed to Angel would never come, all she wanted was for the ground to open beneath her feet and swallow her up. Knowing that wasn't going to happen, she simply sat in her chair when the final bell rang, letting all her classmates drain out of the classroom ahead of her. At least half the boys made the sucky-kissy sound as they passed her, and three of them thrust their crotches into her face, but only after making sure Mrs. Holt wasn't looking. *Don't cry,* she told herself. *Just act like nothing's the matter.* The seconds turned into minutes as the sounds of laughter and chatter and slamming lockers rose then slowly began to die away. Only when the corridor had fallen completely silent did Angel finally reach under her desk, pull out her backpack, and begin stowing her books away.

"Angel? Is something the matter?"

She froze, then shook her head.

"You're sure?" Mrs. Holt pressed. "It seemed like some of the boys were acting—well, a little strange."

"I—I didn't notice anything," Angel stammered, and heard the quaver in her own voice as she stood by her desk, ready to leave.

"I don't know," the teacher went on. "It certainly seemed as though—"

"They were just teasing me," Angel broke in, searching for a way to escape before she had to tell the teacher about what had happened to her since lunchtime. "Because I'm new." Finally she turned and hurried to the door, risking a glance at the teacher. Mrs. Holt's brow was furrowed, and Angel could see the pity in her eyes. "Can I go now?" she asked.

Mrs. Holt seemed on the verge of saying something else, but then nodded, and Angel darted out before the teacher had a chance to change her mind.

She headed toward the stairs leading to her locker on the second floor, but then changed her mind—if any of the boys were still waiting to torment her, they'd be upstairs where her locker was. Veering away from the stairs, she headed instead for the front door, pushed her way through the inner set, then paused in the vestibule to peer out into the afternoon sunlight. Seeing no one except Seth Baker, who was on the other side of the street, looking like he might be waiting for her, she pushed the outer door open and stepped out onto the landing at the top of the steps.

She was about to wave to Seth when she heard the awful kissing sound.

Whirling, she saw her cousin standing a few feet away, just far enough to the side so he'd been invisible from inside the doors. As she glared at him, Zack Fletcher thrust his crotch forward, pursed his lips, and made the disgusting sound one more time.

"I'm gonna—" Angel began, then stopped herself, but could see by the malicious sparkle in Zack's eyes that it was too late.

"You gonna *tell?*" he taunted. "What are you—still a baby?"

"Why don't you just leave me alone?" Angel asked, and once more heard the quiver in her own voice.

Zack heard it too. "Ooh, is the baby going to cry now?"

Her eyes welling with tears, Angel turned away from Zack, hurried down the stairs and started toward Seth. But as she crossed the lawn, a car pulled up in front of Seth, he got in, and the car drove away. Wanting to run now, but having no place to run, Angel dropped her head down so no one would see the tears in her eyes. She crossed the street and headed for the corner, but instead of turning toward home, she kept going straight for another block until she came to the corner where the Catholic and Congregational churches stood across the street from each other. The sun had moved far enough across the sky so that the shadow of the larger church no longer fell over the smaller one, but even without the shadow, the little Church of the Holy Mother looked oddly defensive, as if it were afraid that at any moment its far larger and grander neighbor across the street might simply devour it.

Angel made her way into the church, dipped her fingers in the font and crossed herself. No lights were on in the church, and only a few candles were lit for the Holy Mother and the saints, but just enough light made its way through the darkly stained glass of the windows that Angel was able to find the confessional.

It was empty.

Nor was there a sign telling her what time the priest would be available to hear her confession. But if there was no priest, how was she supposed to confess her sins?

Maybe she should just leave—after all, she'd tried, hadn't she? She turned toward the door, but before she'd taken even a single step she heard a voice.

"May I help you, my child?"

Turning back toward the altar, Angel saw the figure of Father Mike emerging from the shadows.

"I—I need to make my confession," Angel stammered.

Father Mike nodded toward the confessional, and a few moments later she was sitting in one side of it, with the priest hidden in the other.

"How long has it been since your last confession?" she heard the priest ask.

"A—A month," Angel said, though she wasn't really sure.

The familiar ritual began, and though she still wasn't certain exactly what she was supposed to confess, she did her best. But fifteen minutes later, when it was over and she had left the church and started home, she felt no better.

Indeed, she felt even worse.

Seth had felt one faint ray of hope as he saw Angel come out the front door of the school. After the last bell rang, he'd gotten out to the sidewalk as quickly as he could, knowing better than to keep his father waiting for even a minute or two. There'd been no sign of the Lexus, but Seth also knew better than to risk leaving without waiting for at least fifteen minutes, and fourteen of them had already passed when the front door of the school opened and Angel Sullivan appeared. He raised his hand to wave at her, but she turned—apparently to say something to her cousin—before she noticed him. Then his father's car rolled around the corner and pulled up next to him.

"Get in," his father commanded. "We're already late."

Seth's hand dropped back to his side and he pulled the door open and got in. His father was pulling away from the curb even before he'd shut the door, and Seth could tell by the throbbing vein in his father's forehead that whatever happened when they got to the country club wasn't going to be pleasant.

"I don't understand how come you're not on the team at school," Blake Baker said a couple of minutes later, barely glancing at Seth as he spoke. "Do you have any idea how much dues I pay the club every year? If you'd just take advantage of the opportunities I provide . . ." His voice died away as he shook his head, both his tone and the gesture letting Seth know how incomprehensible—and annoying—he found his son's behavior.

Seth said nothing, certain that any response would turn his father's irritation into a full-blown rage, and neither of them spoke again until they were inside the clubhouse. As his father checked in at the desk, Seth gazed out the picture window, and once more felt a faint ray of hope—nobody was on the practice range, so at least he wouldn't have to go through the humiliation of having people watch while he tried to master swinging his driver. His heart sank again as he heard his father talking to the guy behind the counter.

"Taking my boy out for a practice round," Blake Baker was saying. "We're gonna kick some serious ass on Saturday."

Five minutes later Seth stood at the first tee box, gazing down the narrow fairway toward the green, which looked like it had to be at least five hundred yards away even though he knew it was only a little more than three hundred. "Easiest hole on the course," his father had told him two years ago, the first time Seth tried to play golf. "Half the guys can drive the green, and even the kids always get on in two." Seth hadn't gotten on the green at all that day—it had taken him five swings with the driver just to hit the ball, and finally his father had told him to pick it up. "Can't hold up play all day," he'd said, giving Seth an encouraging pat on the shoulder and grinning apologetically at the four men waiting a few yards away, watching every clumsy swing he'd made. He'd put the driver back in the bag, picked it up, and tried to sling it over his shoulder the way his father did, and almost lost his balance. His father had steadied him, but as soon as they were alone, Blake Baker's grin had faded. "What the hell's wrong with you?" he'd demanded. "Anybody can carry a golf bag!"

"Go ahead," Blake Baker said now. "Keep it to the left and let it roll into the middle of the fairway."

Seth carefully teed up the ball exactly as his father had shown him, putting the tee between his forefinger and middle finger, then pushing down on it with the ball itself.

As soon as he took his hand away, the ball fell off the tee. He tried it twice more, feeling his father's eyes boring into him.

"Jesus," Blake finally muttered. Edging Seth aside, he set the ball up, leaving it standing steadily atop the tee. "Now, just take it easy and hit it, okay?" he said, his voice making clear his doubt that Seth was going to be able to strike the ball at all.

Seth stood over the ball, trying to remember everything his father had told him. Holding the club in his left hand, he placed his right hand on the shaft so his little finger overlapped his left forefinger. He laid the club head behind the ball, then adjusted his grip so the face of the club was as square to the ball as he could make it.

He bent his knees slightly, and slowly pulled the club back. The head hovered in the air, then Seth brought it around, swinging directly at the ball.

He came close enough that the ball fell off the tee.

"Jesus."

Seth put the ball back on the tee as quickly as possible and tried another swing.

And a third.

On the fourth try he finally managed to hit the ball, but it came off the toe of the club and shied away to the right, into the woods. "I'll find it," Seth said.

"Forget it," Blake Baker snapped. "It's just a junk ball anyway. Tee up another one."

The second ball—to Seth's utter amazement—shot off the tee on his first swing, flying at least fifty yards down the fairway.

"I did it!" Seth cried. "I hit it!"

"You call that hitting it?" Blake replied. "I could kick the ball that far. Let me show you how it's done." Teeing up his own ball, Blake stepped back, took a couple of practice swings, then stepped behind the ball and gazed straight down the fairway for a moment, moved into his stance, and drew the club back.

There was a sharp crack as the club face made contact, and Seth watched the ball soar high into the air, streaking straight down the fairway, finally coming to rest less than a hundred yards from the green.

"See?" Blake asked. "Nothing to it."

Putting their drivers back in the bags, they walked down the fairway to the spot where Seth's ball lay.

"Better use a three iron," his father told him.

Certain it wouldn't make any difference which club he used, Seth pulled the three iron out of the bag, did his best to set up the shot the same way his father did, even taking two practice swings, and standing behind the ball for a few seconds. But when he finally made his swing, the ball only bounced a few feet to the right.

Seth didn't even need to look at his father to feel his disgust—it rolled over him like a breaking wave. Moving quickly to the ball, he swung again, and then a third time, and with each swing he felt his anxiety rising.

Finally, on the fourth swing, the club connected with the ball, but once again the ball only shot off into the woods to the right.

"I'll get another one," Seth said, moving toward his bag.

"You'll find that one," his father told him. "Once it's off the tee, you play it. You've got five minutes to find it or it's a penalty stroke."

Seth looked pleadingly at his father. "I thought we were just practicing," he blurted, and instantly wished he could reclaim his words.

"How are you going to get any better if you don't know how badly you're doing? I'm giving you enough of a break by not starting to count until you're at least decently off the tee."

Putting his iron back in the bag, Seth started toward the woods.

"What are you going to hit it with?" Blake asked, his voice stopping Seth in his tracks.

Seth went back and picked up his golf bag, slinging it over his shoulder, then trudged once again toward the woods. To his surprise, his father came with him.

"Maybe it'll speed things up if I look too," Blake told him. When they finally found the ball, it was lying half hidden under some brush. "Better declare it unplayable," Blake said. "You're just going to get another penalty stroke if you break any of the branches off the bush."

Ten minutes later they finally arrived at the point where Blake's ball lay. He took a pitching wedge out of his bag, swung it a couple of times, then set up the shot. The ball came to rest three feet from the cup.

After three more strokes, Seth's ball finally rolled onto the green.

It took him five strokes with the putter before the ball fell into the hole.

As Seth picked up the flag, his father picked up his own ball from where it had come to rest after the second shot, a little more than a yard from the hole.

"Don't you have to putt it in?" Seth asked.

Blake Baker glared at his son. "From that distance? It's a gimme, isn't?"

Seth said nothing.

"All right," Blake said, his voice taking on a hard edge. "I guess if you won't give it to me, I'll have to putt it out."

Blake set the ball back on the green, and Seth was sure it was closer to the hole than it had originally been. He circled around, studying the putt from every angle. At last he stepped up, took three careful practice swings, and then struck the ball.

It rolled past the hole.

"So it's a four," he said, reaching down and picking up the ball.

When Seth finally got a glance at the scorecard two holes later, he saw that his father had given him fourteen strokes on the first hole.

He'd given himself three.

Chapter 21

THE NEXT DAY WAS EVEN WORSE THAN THE DAY before. Angel had barely slept, lying awake through the long night, terrified that at any moment she would hear the door to her room open and the floorboards begin to creak as her father slunk through the darkness toward her bed. It was worse when she slept, for with sleep came dreams, and in the dreams her father was always there, gazing at her with burning eyes, reaching out toward her, his fingers straining to touch her flesh.

When she turned away from her father, her mother was there, but her back was to Angel, and no matter how Angel begged, her mother wouldn't even look at her.

When she turned away from her mother, she found herself facing Father Mike, who looked at her coldly, then spoke: "Go forth and sin no more."

It was always his words that awakened her, leaving her alone in the darkness, too frightened to sleep and too tired to stay awake.

By the time she got to school, she wasn't sure she could make it through the day at all.

Seth Baker had gotten no more sleep than Angel, the stinging welts from the lash of his father's belt making it impossible for him to lie on his back, and even the weight of his sheet and blanket hurt enough to keep him awake until almost dawn. His father was already gone when he went downstairs, and when his mother asked him if he was going to practice playing golf again that afternoon, he shook his head.

"Do I really have to play in the tournament on Saturday?" he asked as he poured some cereal into a bowl.

"Well, of course you do," Jane Baker told him. "Why would you even ask such a question?"

Because I'm no good at golf and Dad will just give me another beating when we get home. He knew better than to speak the thought out loud, though, and only shrugged in response to his mother's question. And the worst part wouldn't even be the beating. It would be the humiliation of having Zack Fletcher and Chad Jackson and Jared Woods and all the other jocks watch him as he flailed away at the ball. But he knew there was no point in trying to argue with his mother, since she wouldn't argue with his dad any more than he would.

He ate his cereal in silence and left the house in silence, and somehow got through the day.

By the time he had to strip for gym, the welts on his buttocks had faded enough so no one noticed them.

Five minutes after the last bell, he met Angel Sullivan.

"You okay?" he asked as she fell in beside him.

"I guess," she sighed. "What about you?"

Seth shrugged. "I'm used to it." Today's lunch had been an almost exact repeat of the one the day before, with Zack and Heather and their friends making the sucky-kissy noises, and the boys grinding their hips at both Angel and Seth.

Except they hadn't called him Seth, and every time they'd used its rhyme, Angel had seen him cringe. "How come they call you that?" she asked as they began walking out Black Creek Road toward the house that stood at the Crossing.

"I don't know," Seth said. "The same reason they called you all those names in Eastbury, I guess."

"At least they called me girls' names." For a second Seth looked as if she'd slapped him, but then he laughed.

" 'Beth' isn't a girl's name?" he asked.

"That's not what I meant," Angel said. "I meant—"

"Oh, who cares, anyway?" Seth cut in as she began floundering for the right words. "It's just names. Let's talk about something else."

But instead of talking, both of them lapsed into silence, and neither spoke until they were across the street from Angel's house, where, as if by common consent, they both stopped, staring at the house.

It looked exactly as it had this morning, and yesterday, and the day before, and yet, as they gazed at it, neither Angel nor Seth could stop thinking about the strange images that Seth's camera had caught in the window of Angel's room, or the odd drawing that had appeared on the mirror in Angel's room.

Nor could Seth forget what had happened when Angel's father had found them in her bedroom. "Maybe I shouldn't come in," he said, his voice sounding hollow.

Angel looked at him uncertainly. "I thought you wanted to see if there was something under the stairs," she said.

Seth bit his lower lip, then: "If your dad comes home—"

"He won't," Angel said. "And even if he does, we just won't be in my room."

Still Seth hesitated. "I don't know. . . ."

"You were the one that said 'it can't hurt to look,' " she reminded him. But as her eyes shifted from Seth to the house, her voice reflected her own sudden nervousness. "Besides, if my mom's not home either . . ." Now it was her voice that trailed off, and she knew Seth had heard the fear in it. "I mean it's not like I'm scared to be by myself or anything—"

Seth cut her off. "Quit worrying. Let's both go in and see if we can find anything."

They went around to the back of the house, and Angel found the key her mother had hidden under the same pot that had been on the back porch in Eastbury. "If we're supposed to be looking for something under the stairs, shouldn't there be a loose board or something?" Angel asked as she opened a Coke and split it between two glasses.

"I guess," Seth replied. But ten minutes later, after tugging at every stair in the case leading to the second floor, he shook his head. "Even the ones that squeak don't come loose." He looked at Angel. "What about from underneath? Maybe there's some kind of hidden cupboard or something."

They went around to the door of the closet that was built under the stairs, but again found nothing. The walls and the steeply slanted ceiling under the stairs were plastered and painted white, and in the glare of the naked bulb that illuminated the space, they could see that there weren't even any cracks in the plaster, let alone places where it might come open to reveal a hidden space.

"So now what?" Seth asked. But before Angel could reply, they heard a muffled sound, and Seth's eyes widened. "If that's your dad—"

Angel shook her head and held up her hand to silence him.

The sound came again, still muffled, but this time Angel was sure she recognized it. "It's Houdini—he's come back!" Leaving the closet under the stairs, Angel hurried into the kitchen, certain she would find the cat waiting for her.

The kitchen was empty.

"Where is he?" Seth asked as he too entered the kitchen.

Angel shrugged. "I don't know—maybe I was wrong."

But then they heard the sound again, and this time there was no mistaking it. Both Angel and Seth turned to look at the closed door that led to the basement, and when Angel pulled it open, there was the cat. But instead of coming out into the kitchen, he turned and bounded down the steep flight of steps.

Angel and Seth stood at the top of the stairs that plunged down into the basement. For several long seconds they both gazed into the gloom, and as her eyes reached into the darkness, Angel began to feel something—a strange chill seemed to be emanating from the cellar.

Seth took her hand. "Do you feel that?" he asked.

Angel nodded. "It feels like a draft."

"But heat rises," Seth said. "And even when it's the hottest day of the summer, you don't feel any cooler till you go down into the basement. Just opening the door at the top of the stairs doesn't do any good at all."

"M-Maybe there's a window open," Angel said, not realizing that her voice had dropped to little more than a whisper. "That's probably how Houdini got in."

"Or maybe it's something else," Seth replied, his own voice dropping as low as Angel's. "I read once where it gets real cold when . . ." His words died on his lips as the chill suddenly evaporated. When he looked at Angel, he could tell that she felt the sudden change too. "It's gone," he breathed.

Angel once again peered down into the darkness

below. "Houdini?" she called. "Come on, Houdini! Come out of there!"

The cat appeared at the bottom of the stairs, its eyes glowing in the light spilling down from the kitchen, but it did not come up. Instead it meowed again.

"Come on!" Angel said. "You'll get filthy down there."

The cat meowed once more, then disappeared.

"Houdini!" Angel said. She groped for the cellar light switch, found it and turned it on. A bare bulb in the center of the cellar ceiling went on, but its dim glow revealed no sign of the cat.

Then it meowed again, louder.

"What's going on with him?" Seth asked. "It's like he wants us to come down—" He fell silent as he gazed at the cellar stairs. "What if we were looking under the wrong stairs?"

Angel stared at Seth. "He's a cat, Seth! What—"

As quickly as it had vanished, the cat reappeared at the bottom of the steps, meowed loudly, then bounded up most of the stairs. But before it reached the top, it veered off to the right, bounding off the step and dropping to the floor below.

And meowed one more time.

"Let's go down and see," Seth said.

Angel said nothing, but when Seth took the first step down the steep flight of stairs, she hung back. "Maybe we shouldn't go down there," she said as Seth looked back at her.

"Or maybe we *should*," Seth countered, putting just enough emphasis on the word so Angel knew exactly what he meant.

She felt the challenge hanging in the air, and gazed down into the shadows below. As she peered into the gloom, the memories of the last few nights flicked through her mind.

The girl in the closet, surrounded by flames.

The smell of smoke still lingering in the morning.

The presence in her room the night before last, when someone had loomed over her in the darkness, reaching out to her, wanting to touch her.

The sound of the piggy bank crashing to the floor.

And then, the scrawled image on the mirror that she had scrubbed away until there was no trace of it left at all.

A smudge like blood.

The blood of the girl who'd died in the room in which she now slept?

No! It wasn't blood—it was only lipstick, and it had washed away. Everything she'd seen had only been dreams, and there weren't any such things as ghosts.

"All right," she said, trying not to let any of her fears creep into her voice. "Let's go down and see."

Without waiting for Angel to reply, Seth headed down the stairs, and a second or two later Angel followed.

"There's another light at the bottom," she whispered when they were halfway down. "You have to pull a string."

As they came to the last step, Seth reached up, grabbed the string, and pulled. A dim light came on, washing most of the darkness away, but leaving the far recesses of the cellar lost in shadows. They found Houdini under the stairs, which were made of thick oak slabs about the size of the mantel upstairs, mounted on even bigger oak beams, laid in a steep slant with notches cut in them to support the steps. The upper surfaces of the steps were worn smooth—and somewhat concave—from the generations of feet that had tramped up and down them. But on the underside there were still the marks of the hand tools that had hewn and shaped them so long ago.

Houdini was standing on his hind legs, his forepaws

propped against the fourth step, his head stretched high, but his nose still falling short of the fifth step.

As Angel and Seth crouched down to gaze at him, he looked at them, meowed, then stretched upward once again.

"What's he doing?" Angel asked. "What's he want?"

Angel and Seth moved around behind the stairs, then looked up at them from below. Except for a few places where light showed through the tiny gaps between the treads, they saw only darkness.

"Have you got a flashlight?" Seth asked.

"In the kitchen drawer," Angel replied. She hurried up to the kitchen, and opened the top drawer at the end of the counter, where only two days ago she herself had put the contents from the catchall drawer in Eastbury. The flashlight was at the front, exactly where she'd put it.

Back in the cellar, she found Seth crouched down next to the cat, which was still standing on its hind legs, stretching toward the stair that was just out of reach while mewing insistently. As Angel crouched beside Seth and shined the light up at the underside of the stairs, Seth rapped sharply on the three steps nearest the cat.

Twice, they heard nothing but the faint thump of solid wood.

Then he rapped on the fifth step from the bottom.

As his knuckles came in contact with the wood, the sound was much louder, with a resonance to it that made Angel's heart begin to pound.

It sounded hollow!

Seth looked at her, then knocked on the tread once more.

The same sound.

And the cat, apparently now satisfied, moved out from under the stairs, sat down, and began grooming itself.

Seth knocked on the tread above and the tread below, and each time they heard only the same solid sound they'd heard on the rest of the stairs.

Seth went back to the fifth one and began rapping along its entire length.

At each end, it sounded as solid as the adjoining treads. But for six or eight inches in both directions off the center, it had that hollow sound that told them that this tread, at least, was not solid all the way through.

Angel held the flashlight closer while Seth examined the step more carefully. At first he saw nothing, but then, as he looked closer, something didn't look quite right at the point where the tread sat upon the supporting beams. Taking the flashlight from Angel, he held it even closer to the joint, then shifted it first to the one above, then the one below. Though the fits were almost perfect, he was sure he could make out a tiny horizontal gap between the treads and the beams, where the treads were sitting on the notches cut out of the beams to act as risers. But in the fifth step it looked as if the joint went up, as if somehow the tread *were* suspended between the main beams instead of being supported by the notches.

Moving out from under the steps, he examined the end of the fifth tread. From the outside it appeared to be seated atop the notches in the two slanting beams, exactly like all the rest. Frowning, he tapped on the surface of the riser.

It sounded like solid wood.

"What is it?" Angel asked. "Is it hollow or not?"

"It's weird," Seth told her. "It doesn't sound the same from underneath, and it doesn't look the same either."

"Let me see."

With both of them crouching under the stairs now, Seth showed Angel the strange joints. Reaching up, Angel gently rapped on the underside of the tread and heard the same hollow sound Seth had. She frowned, trying to figure out why the joints would look different from below than from the end, and a moment later the answer came to her. "Hold the flashlight," she told Seth. He took it from her, and she pressed the palms of both her hands up onto the bottom of the fifth tread, then pulled them toward her. For a second she thought nothing was going to happen, but then—just as she was about to give up—she felt a slight movement. Pressing even harder, she pulled again, and for a moment it seemed as if the entire tread was moving toward her.

"Wow," Seth breathed. "Look at that!"

Angel kept easing the wood forward, until Seth, who was crouched down low so he could peer up at the bottom of the tread, said, "Hold it—I see something!"

"What?" Angel asked.

"It's like the whole back and bottom of the tread is fake," he said, poking his fingers up into some kind of cavity that had appeared in the bottom of the tread. A second later, his voice trembling, he whispered, "There's something in it. See if you can pull it a little farther."

Angel reached back so her fingertips curled around the edge of the false bottom, and she pulled. The panel slid stiffly for a moment, then suddenly came loose, sliding entirely free of the tread.

Something dropped from the cavity that had been concealed above the sliding panel, falling into Seth's hands.

Neither of them said a word, but simply stared at the object. It was a book, bound in leather that was embossed with faded gold lettering. The letters were so ornate that even if the gilt had not all but vanished, neither of them could have made out what they said. Though the leather of the cover looked almost new, there was still something about it that told them it was far older than it appeared.

And its color was exactly the same as the color of the lipstick Angel had found on the floor that morning, and on her fingers, and on the sheets.

Red.

Bloodred.

Chapter 22

"ET'S TAKE IT UPSTAIRS, SO WE CAN AT LEAST SEE IT," Seth said. "And so I can stand up straight too," he added, awkwardly scuttling out from under the stairs and standing up to stretch the muscles that had begun to ache as he crouched beneath the steep staircase.

Houdini rose to his feet too, stretched, then darted up the stairs to the kitchen.

Angel paused only long enough to replace the sliding panel that hid the compartment carved out of the bottom of the fifth stair. Fitting the two dovetailed tongues on the panel into the matching grooves on the stair step, she pushed it forward until it was exactly as they'd found it a few minutes ago. Shining the light on it one more time to make certain that nothing betrayed its secret, she turned off the two basement lights and followed Seth up to the kitchen, where he was standing at the table, staring down at the book.

Houdini was on the kitchen table, sniffing at it, and as Angel came near, he looked up at her, placed his right forepaw on the volume, and mewed softly.

In the full light of day, the cover looked even redder, but they could also clearly see how old it was. The gilt was all but gone on the ornate symbols, and though the leather itself was uncracked, parts of its polished surface were worn to the texture of suede. Seth was about to open it when Houdini whirled to face the front of the house, his back arched and the hairs on his body standing on end.

As a hiss of warning erupted from the cat's throat, Seth yanked his hand away from the book.

"What's wrong with him?" he asked, staring at the cat. "He's acting like he's going to bite me!"

"It's not you," Angel said. "It's my dad! I hear his car!"

Seth's eyes widened. "Maybe we better put the book back!"

"And have him find us in the basement? He'd want to know what we were doing!" Her eyes flicked around the kitchen. "Where can we hide it?"

Seth picked up the book, shoved it in his backpack, and headed toward the back door. "Come on!"

Waiting only long enough to return the flashlight and grab her own backpack so her father wouldn't know she'd been home, Angel darted out the back door just as she heard the roar of the old Chevelle's engine cut off. She caught up with Seth as the car door slammed, and when her father would have gotten to the front door, they were running down a narrow path that wound into the forest. By the time her father might have glanced out the back window, they were deep enough into the woods that he wouldn't be able to see them at all.

And Houdini was with them every step of the way.

"Where are we going?" Angel asked when Seth finally slowed down.

"I don't know," he said. "Have you ever come back here since you moved in?" Angel shook her head. "This path leads to the old crossing, where the ferry used to be."

Suddenly, Houdini let out a howl, then veered off the narrow path, heading into the trees.

"Houdini!" Angel called. "Come back!"

The cat paused, looked back, meowed, then continued moving deeper into the woods.

"Where's he going?" Angel asked.

Seth shrugged. "How should I know? But I'm not going with him—there isn't even a path there."

Turning away, he started once more along the path that led to Black Creek Crossing. Angel, after another anxious glance at the cat, followed.

Less than half a minute later Houdini appeared on the path a few yards ahead of them. Once again his back was arched and he was hissing and spitting.

Seth stopped so fast that Angel almost bumped into him. "Jeez, what's wrong with him?" He took a step toward the cat, but jerked back when the cat's paw shot out, swiping at his leg.

Angel stooped down and extended her hand, but once again the cat took a swipe with his paw.

"Maybe he's rabid," Seth suggested.

Angel rolled her eyes. "He was fine a minute ago."

"Then let's just go around him." Seth stepped off the path, starting around Houdini.

The cat moved, blocking his way, and hissed again.

Seth moved the other way.

The cat countered, hissing angrily.

"All right, all right," Seth said, holding up his hands and backing off. He turned to Angel. "So now what do we do? Your dad's back at your house, and your cat won't let us down the path."

Then Houdini was at Seth's feet, rubbing up against his legs as if nothing had happened. Seth stared down at the cat, mystified. "What's going on?" he asked Angel. "Is he crazy?"

"How should I know? He's not my cat!"

But now Houdini was rubbing up against her legs as well, and a moment later he bounded back down the path the way they'd come, but stopping a few yards away to turn, mewing plaintively.

When neither Angel nor Seth moved, he darted toward them, meowed, then turned back.

"If he was a dog, I'd think he wants us to follow him," Seth said. "But cats don't do that, do they?"

Now it was Angel who shrugged. "Maybe we should try it." She glanced around at the dense forest of maples and oaks and pines. "What if we get lost?"

"I've been poking around here all my life," Seth told her. "I've never gotten lost yet. Come on—let's at least try it."

Houdini stayed on the path until they came back to the point where he'd left it a few minutes ago, and once again he veered off, pausing a few yards into the woods and looking back as if to see whether Angel and Seth were following.

"Are you sure we won't get lost?" Angel fretted.

"We can't—the road's a few hundred yards to the left, and the creek's off to the right. No matter where that stupid cat goes, we'll be able to find one of them or the other."

They followed the cat as it moved through the woods, down a path neither of them could see. But the cat nevertheless seemed to know where it was going. After a few minutes they came to the creek, which was no more than twenty feet wide, and shallow enough that many of the rocks lining the bottom cleared the surface and were close enough together to act as stepping-stones across. The stream ran through a channel at least ten times wider than it, and Seth thought it was almost ten feet deep.

"Does it ever flood?" Angel asked as she gazed at the meandering stream.

"Not anymore," Seth told her. "In the spring it might get to be four feet deep, but that's all. Most of the water goes into a bunch of reservoirs, and they only let enough out to keep the fish alive."

"Where was the ferry?"

"Back up that way," he said, pointing upstream. "It was like a barge, and there was a rope strung across the river, and the barge guy would haul the barge back and forth."

A few minutes later the cat turned away from the stream again, and the forest seemed to get thicker.

"Do you know where we are?" Angel asked.

"Pretty much," Seth replied. "If we lose Houdini, I can find my way back to the stream. Then it's easy."

"But where are we going?"

"How should I know? I guess we'll just have to follow and find out."

Stepping over a fallen limb, he hurried after the cat. Angel followed him, and moments later they came upon what looked like a path, though it was so overgrown as to be barely visible. As they moved along it, the path narrowed and the trees crowded in, and Angel had to crouch low to get under several branches. The terrain began to get rougher, with granite outcroppings thrusting up, and twice the path disappeared completely.

"Are you sure we're not lost?" she asked as they came into a small open space in front of a bluff of deeply fissured granite.

"I sort of know where we are, but there's nothing out here," Seth told her.

Angel scanned the area but didn't see anything except a small clearing, and beyond that the granite face of the bluff. Still, she followed Seth as the cat moved across the clearing and picked its way over the mound of granite that had fallen from the face of the bluff over the centuries. Now there was no sign of a path at all, and Angel had no idea where they were anymore, even in relation to where they'd come from or even the stream. Then Seth stopped, and a second later Angel caught up with him.

At first she saw nothing, but then, below them and tucked so deeply into one of the fissures in the bluff that it was almost invisible, she spotted something that looked like a wooden wall. "What is it?" she asked.

"I don't know," Seth said. "Nobody ever comes out here but me, and I've never seen this before—I mean, I've been in the clearing, but I always thought the rock was just heaped up against the face of the bluff."

They picked their way down the bank of rubble, to find Houdini scratching at a door that was barely taller than Seth and held closed by a simple wooden latch.

Both of them stared at the door, which seemed so out of place in the cleft of the granite that they could hardly believe it was real.

Finally, Seth reached out and tested the latch.

The door swung slowly open, and the moment the gap was wide enough, Houdini dashed through, vanishing into the darkness. Neither Seth nor Angel made a move to enter until the door had swung far enough that they could see what lay within.

It seemed to be a tiny cabin constructed entirely of great oaken logs, and their unevenness and the adze marks on them made them look to Angel like the hand-hewn timbers that supported the floor of her own house. The cabin was only a single room, but it wasn't rectangular, or even square. Rather, it was oddly wedge-shaped, to conform to the shape of the fissure within whose confines it had been built; none of its four walls were the same length, and every angle where two walls met was different. At the rear there was a crude fireplace built of uneven chunks of granite that must have been gathered from the slag heap at the base of the bluff. The entire surface of the firebox was covered with a layer of soot, and a heavy wrought-iron pothook was mounted in one wall. To one side of the fireplace there was a stack of split wood and a small pile of kindling.

From the pothook hung a kettle that looked every bit as old as the cabin itself.

Glancing nervously at each other, so dumbstruck by what the cat had led them to that neither of them could say a word, first Seth, then Angel, stepped through the small doorway and into the peculiarly proportioned room. A slab of oak nearly four inches thick had been mounted along one wall to serve as a counter, and three worn wooden ladles hung from pegs in the wall. At the far end of the counter an immense block of granite, nearly two feet on a side, had been hollowed out to form a sink.

A sink that was full of water, the surface of which was shimmering even in the dim light that came in through the open door.

Angel stared at it, her heart racing. "Somebody must live here," she breathed.

Seth's eyes were also fastened on the sink, which was full nearly to the rim. But nowhere was there any sign of a faucet, or even a pump handle.

As they stood silently gazing at it, there was a soft *plink*, and the water's surface rippled.

A moment later they heard the plinking sound again, and as the third drop of water fell, Seth finally spotted its source: high up on the wall above the sink, a small piece of wood protruded, and water dripped from the end of it.

"But where's the water coming from?" Angel asked as they moved closer to the sink. Now they could see a notch cut in the rim of the sink, perhaps an inch deep, that let overflow water run out through a small wooden trough that also pierced the wall.

"It probably just seeps out of the face of the bluff," Seth said. "There's a spot up closer to the stream where it does that, even when it hasn't been raining in weeks."

They gazed at the water, which was crystal clear, then Seth took one of the wooden ladles off its hook, dipped it in the water, sniffed it, and tasted it.

"It's good!" He offered the ladle to Angel, but she shook her head.

"Just because it tastes good doesn't mean it's safe. My mother says you should always boil water if you don't know where it came from."

"So does mine," Seth said. "But I've been drinking water out of the stream all my life, and I haven't gotten sick yet." As if to prove his point, he took another deep gulp from the ladle, poured the rest back in the sink, then turned to look at the rest of the room.

There was something that appeared to be a small frame for a mattress in the corner behind the door, though there was no trace of rope webbing to support a mattress, even had there been one in the room. The ceiling was supported by beams low enough so Angel could touch them without stretching, and they had been hewn from the same kind of logs as the walls.

"This is too cool," Seth breathed.

"Who do you think built it?" Angel asked. "It's like nobody's even been here in hundreds of years."

"But there aren't any water stains," Seth said as he

gazed at the low ceiling. "If it's as old as it looks, how come the roof doesn't leak?" Now his eyes roamed over all the other surfaces in the tiny cabin, all of which—the floor, counter, bed frame, even the rim of the sink, except for the notch that served as an overflow drain—were covered with a thick layer of dust that was undisturbed, except for the footprints on the floor where first Houdini and then Angel and Seth had trod. Even the firewood and kindling were almost lost under coats of dust. "It's got to be as old as your house!"

"But if it's that old, how come nobody even knows it's here?" Angel asked.

His eyes fixed on the cat, Seth didn't seem to hear her question. But when he finally spoke, Angel realized that he had. "You think maybe Houdini led us here on purpose?" he asked, his voice carrying a hollow tone that told Angel he'd already answered his own question.

"I—I don't know," she stammered. "I mean, I guess maybe sometimes dogs—"

"He led us to the book," Seth said. He turned away from the cat and looked into Angel's eyes. "He didn't just get us to go down into the cellar—he was sniffing at the exact stair it was hidden in."

Once more Angel felt the apprehension that had come over her when she and Seth stood at the head of the cellar stairs. "M-Maybe he smelled it," she suggested.

Seth's eyes went back to the cat. "You don't know where he came from, do you?"

"N-No," Angel stammered uneasily.

"He just showed up in the closet in your room, with the door closed."

Angel nodded, and tried to quell the uneasiness rising in her stomach.

"And he follows you around, and he showed us where the book was hidden, and then he led us out here."

"Maybe this is where he lives," Angel said, certain she knew what Seth was going to say next, but not wanting to hear it. "Maybe we were just following him home."

"Or maybe we weren't," Seth said. "And we didn't just follow him, remember? He made us go where he wanted us to go. Maybe dogs do that sometimes, but did you ever hear of cats doing it? I saw on TV once where a woman claimed her cat yowled to wake her up when the house was on fire, but if you ask me, the cat was just scared and wanted out before it got burned up."

"But if Houdini really was showing us where the book was, and really did lead us here . . ." Her voice trailed off, and she knew she didn't want to go any further in the direction in which the thought was taking her.

"What about the marks on the mirror?" Seth asked. "The ones that made us look for something under the stairs in the first place?"

"He's a cat, Seth," Angel said, her voice taking on an edge. "Cats don't write on mirrors with lipstick!"

"Then who did it?"

"I don't know! Maybe I did it! Maybe I was sleep-walking or something! But it wasn't Houdini! He's just a cat!"

"What if he's not?" Seth shot back. "What if he's—" He hesitated, then the words came out: "What if he's something else?"

The words hung between them as the silence stretched. They both turned to look at Houdini, who was still sitting on the hearth. But he was no longer grooming himself. Instead, he was staring at them, as if waiting for something.

"I-If he's not just a cat," Angel finally breathed, her voice barely audible, "what is he?"

Now it was Seth who couldn't quite bring himself to voice the thought taking shape in his mind. "I don't know," he said. "But let's try something." He took off his backpack, opened it, and removed the ancient leather-bound book.

As both Angel and Seth watched, Houdini's tail began twitching, then his body tensed as he rose to his feet and stretched his neck toward the book.

"I think we better see if we can figure out what this is," Seth said, setting the book on the counter.

"How old do you think it is?" Angel whispered.

The book lay on the dusty counter, and even though barely enough sunlight filtered through the open door to make it possible to read, the tome had lost none of its strange glow. Indeed, the illusion of it somehow being lit from within was even stronger here than when they brought it out of the shadows of the basement. Nor did it look quite as ancient. The leather seemed slightly less worn, and though the three ornately embossed letters— or symbols—on the cover were still unreadable, the gold seemed slightly brighter than Angel remembered it.

Seth reached out as if to open it, but hesitated, his fingers hovering above the cover. "It's got to be hundreds of years old," he replied, his voice as low as Angel's, even though they were alone in the tiny cabin. "It looks like it might fall apart if I even try to open it."

"But we can't even see the title if we don't open it," Angel said, her voice trembling with anticipation.

Still Seth hesitated. If he tried to open the book and the cover fell off or the pages fell out, the book could be ruined. Yet even as he thought about the damage it might do, his curiosity overrode his caution, and his fingers touched the book.

And instantaneously jerked away.

"What's wrong?" Angel asked.

Seth's gaze remained fixed on the book. "It—It felt hot," he stammered.

Gingerly, Angel reached out, but instead of touching the book, she let her hand hover over it. Though she knew it was impossible—knew it had to be some kind of illusion—the strange glow from within the volume appeared to brighten.

Very slowly, ready to jerk her hand away in an instant, Angel lowered her palm until it was resting on the book.

It felt warm, but certainly not hot.

She lifted the right edge of the cover, gently opening it.

The cover held, and inside it was a page that was blank except for an inscription done in a handwriting that looked so old-fashioned that Seth was certain it had been written when the book was new. It was near the top of the page, slightly off center:

For Forbearance

"Wow," Seth breathed. "Look at that handwriting! It looks really, really old!"

"But what does it mean?" Angel asked, her voice trembling with excitement. " 'For Forbearance'?"

"Maybe it was a present," Seth suggested. "Like if someone was having some kind of trouble, but got through it, you know?"

Gingerly, Angel turned the flyleaf and they found themselves staring at the title page, whose words were in the same ornate lettering as that which was embossed in gold on the cover. Here, though, in stark black against the white of the page, they were far more legible:

Ye Primer of
Ancient Recipes & Remedies

Carefully, Angel reclosed the volume, and now, after they'd seen the title page, the gold embossing on the cover became clear:

𝔓𝔞𝔯

"Do you suppose it's some kind of cookbook?" Seth asked. "Or maybe like folk medicine? You know—herbs and stuff like that?"

Angel reopened the book and began turning the pages.

All of them were beautifully illuminated, the first letter of each word so intricately drawn that they were almost lost in decorative imagery. Indeed, most of the initial letters were only identifiable after they'd deciphered the rest of the words the letters began.

Each page had a heading, but none of them seemed to make sense; beneath the word "Spring" there were four lines of verse that seemed to mean nothing:

𝔇rop of blood
𝔗hrice haired with hog
𝔖ymmerd add
𝔊reen 'neath log

The initial D of the quatrain was entwined in a beautifully colored mass of flowering vines that, though rooted in that first capitalized letter, wandered all over the page, framing the entire verse in flowers and foliage. All but concealed in the vines was some kind of serpent, its mouth wide open, its fangs curving with such menace that Angel shuddered as she gazed at it.

For several long seconds, Angel and Seth studied the verse, and then Angel resumed turning the pages.

On each page there was another verse, each as incomprehensible as the first.

"Do you understand any of it?" she finally asked Seth as she turned the last page and closed the book.

"Yeah," Seth sighed. "A few words."

"It's like it doesn't mean anything," she said. "It's almost like the stuff in *Alice in Wonderland*." As the words came into her mind, Angel began to recite them, letting them roll around on her tongue, enjoying the sound of them now as much as she had when she first read them, back when she was only eight. " 'Twas brillig, and the slithy toves/Did gyre and gimble in the wabe'—"

" 'All mimsy were the borogoves,' " Seth finished. " 'And the mome raths outgrabe.' "

Angel looked at him in surprise. "You memorized it too?"

"When I was a little kid," Seth replied. "The first time I read it. I still don't know what most of the words mean, but they just sound good." His eyes drifted to the book. "But most of these are real words. Or anyway, they sound like real words."

Both of them gazed at the strange book that lay on the table between them.

"What should we do with it?" Angel asked. "It's got to be really valuable, doesn't it?"

"I guess," Seth replied, his eyes still fixed on the book. "Maybe I can find out about it on the Internet."

"But what do we do with it right now?" Angel asked. "You think maybe I should take it home?"

Seth shook his head. "I think we should keep it right here. At least until we can find out what it is."

"Here?" Angel echoed. "What if somebody comes and finds it?"

"Look at this place," Seth said. "Nobody's been in it for practically forever. I bet nobody but us even knows it's here—I mean, I'm practically the only one who ever comes out here anyway, and I didn't even know about it."

"But if we just leave it here and somebody does come—"

"Look!" Seth uttered the word so sharply it startled Angel into silence, and she turned to look where he was pointing.

Houdini was no longer on the hearth. Now he'd moved around to the right side of the fireplace and was pawing at one of the stone blocks just above the floor. The cat moved aside as soon as Seth and Angel went over to get a closer look. Seth crouched down, felt around the rock the cat had been pawing, and a moment later found just enough of a groove for him to grip it. He pulled, and the rock slid out, revealing another cavity, a little bigger than the one in which they'd found the book an hour earlier.

"Still think he's just a cat?" Seth asked as he went to the counter and picked up the old leather-bound book.

Angel tried to tell herself that it was just a coincidence, that the cat couldn't possibly have been showing them anything. But even as she tried to convince herself, Houdini rose to his feet, went over to the book, and sniffed at it.

Then he looked up and his glowing golden eyes seemed to bore straight into her.

And Angel knew that not any of it—finding the book, the cabin, and the niche in the fireplace—was a coincidence. "It's for us," she said, her voice so soft that Seth could barely hear her. She turned to face him, and Seth saw her eyes glowing almost as brightly as those of the cat. "Don't you see?" she said, her voice edged with the excitement growing inside her. "It's for us. That's why he led us here! He wanted us to have the book, and he brought us here! But what are we supposed to do with it?"

"First we have to find out what it really is," Seth said. "So here's what we're going to do. We'll hide the book here, at least until we can find a better place for it. And tonight I'll look on the Internet. Or maybe tomorrow night we'll meet at the library and see if we can find out what it is. Okay?"

Angel hesitated. What if someone did find the cabin and the book? What if they came back tomorrow or the next day and it was gone?

But before she could say anything, Seth slid the book deep into the recess inside the fireplace, and replaced the rock that hid the niche. The stone block slid perfectly into position, leaving no sign that anything could be concealed behind it.

Angel stared at it for a long time, trying to see any hint that the rock that now hid the book was not set firmly into the chimney.

There was none.

The book would be safe.

A few minutes later they left the cabin. When they'd climbed once more over the mound of rubble in front of it, Angel turned to look back. Just as Seth had said, no trace of the cabin was visible at all. From where she stood, all that could be seen was the face of the bluff.

Houdini too had vanished.

"How are we going to find our way back?" Angel asked, knowing there was no way she'd remember all the twists and turns they'd taken while following the cat through the woods. "Are we lost?"

Seth shook his head. "All we have to do is head west, and we should come to Black Creek Road. We should be a little farther out than your house, but not very far."

He started through the forest, and Angel followed him, still not certain they were going in the right direction. But no more than three minutes later they came to what looked like a path. The floor of the forest appeared worn, and here and there she thought she saw marks on the trunks of trees. By the time they came out on Black Creek Road—almost exactly where Seth had told her they'd be—she was almost sure that if she had to, she could find her way back to the tiny cabin by herself.

Almost sure, but not quite.

She was not alone.

Angel could feel it. She'd felt the first twinge of the peculiar sense that there was someone nearby when they turned away from the cabin and began picking their way through the forest, following the path that for a while only Seth could see. At first she thought it must be the cat, but Houdini had performed another of his vanishing acts and was nowhere to be seen.

Besides, the feeling wasn't quite like the one she'd begun to recognize whenever Houdini followed her to school, walked home with her, or curled up in her room when her father wasn't around.

This was a different feeling, as if an unseen being were hovering just beyond the fringes of her senses. It wasn't an unpleasant feeling—not like the creepy feeling when someone was watching her, when the hair on the back of her neck stood up, and she could almost hear people whispering about her. No, this new feeling was almost like having an unseen companion who was there to watch over her.

She must have glanced back over her shoulder three or four times, almost certain there was someone there, following them through the forest, but she'd seen nothing, though she was pretty sure Seth felt the same thing she did.

He kept stopping to look around, but when she asked him what he was looking for, all he said was that he thought he'd heard something.

She had heard nothing.

It was just a feeling, which she was certain would pass as soon as they were out of the forest.

It hadn't. In fact, it had grown stronger, and as she turned off Black Creek Road and started across the patch of unkempt lawn around the little house, it became so strong that she was almost certain Seth was behind her. But when she turned to look, he was on his way home, just disappearing around the bend in the road.

Her father was at the kitchen table, an open bottle of beer in front of him. When he looked at her, Angel could see by the ruddiness of his complexion that it wasn't his first beer.

"Where you been?" he demanded, his bleary eyes narrowing to suspicious slits.

Angel thought quickly. "I—I stopped at church on the way home," she blurted, telling herself it wasn't quite a lie; she actually *had* gone to church yesterday, and she hadn't actually said that she'd gone *today*.

"You sure you weren't with that boy?" her father pressed.

"He's not even Catholic," Angel replied, again not quite telling a lie by avoiding the question.

"I don't like him," her father said. "I don't want him hanging around here anymore. You understand?"

Angel nodded, knowing better than to tell her father that after what had happened the day before yesterday, Seth was almost too frightened even to come into the house that afternoon. "I've got some homework to do," she said, turning away to hurry upstairs before her father could say anything else.

In her room, Angel dropped her backpack on her bed and went to the window. The sun was starting to drop toward the horizon, and the shadows of the huge trees across the street were creeping across the lawn toward the house. She looked to the right and, just above the trees, could see the top of the bluff whose ramparts concealed the tiny cabin in which they'd hidden the book.

The book.

The book whose cover was the same bloodred shade as the lipstick whose markings had been on her mirror.

The book that almost seemed warm the first time she touched it. Had it actually been hot, or had she only imagined it? But Seth's fingers had jerked away too, when he'd touched the book.

Suddenly, the feeling of no longer being alone was so strong that Angel turned away from the window, and for just a moment she thought she caught a glimpse of something—someone?—at the very edge of her vision. But before she was even sure she'd actually seen it, it was gone.

For the next hour, until her mother called her for dinner, she tried to concentrate on her homework, but over and over again she found herself getting up to go to the window, gazing out into the gathering darkness toward the bluff. And each time she went to the window, she had the feeling there was someone else—someone right behind her—looking over her shoulder.

As night fell, she imagined the cabin with a fire blazing in its hearth, the warm glow of a kerosene lantern suffusing it with a soft light, its door closed and its window barred.

The world shut out of a place that no one knew was even there.

No one but she.

She and Seth.

And someone else . . .

Chapter 23

"IT'S WITCHCRAFT."

Angel stared across the table at Seth, certain at first that he must be kidding. But there was nothing in either his expression or his tone of voice that said he was anything but dead serious. In fact, his face looked pale and there was a look in his eyes that she hadn't seen before. It wasn't fear, exactly, at least not the kind she'd seen in his eyes when her father had found them in her room the other day. Today the look in his eyes told her he wasn't so much afraid of what he'd found out already as what he might find out next.

Unless she was wrong. If he was kidding her and she fell for it, she'd feel like a complete idiot. They were in the cafeteria, and Seth had found a table way off in the corner, where no one else ever sat. When she'd seen him sitting there, with empty tables all around him, she'd assumed he'd found out something about the book on the Internet last night and wanted to make sure nobody else could hear what they would talk about. She'd filled her tray, doing her best to resist the macaroni and cheese but failing so miserably that she took a double portion, telling herself she'd share it with Seth, then assuaging her conscience by taking a glass of water instead of a

Coke, even a diet one. It was as she was setting her tray on the table that he'd spoken the two words:

"It's witchcraft."

"You mean like witch doctors?" she asked as she dropped her backpack on the chair next to her and sat down across from him.

"No, I mean like witchcraft," Seth told her, eyeing the macaroni and cheese covetously. "You going to eat all that yourself?"

"Maybe," Angel said, but seeing the look of disappointment in his eyes, she relented. "I got enough for both of us. Here." She handed her plate across to Seth, who transferred a little less than a quarter of it to his plate. "You have to take half—if you don't, then I'll eat it all and be even fatter than I am now."

"You're not fat," Seth told her. "You just look healthy."

"Yeah, right," Angel said, rolling her eyes. "And you're going out for football!"

Seth shrugged. "Okay, so you're a pig! Happy now?" Angel stared at him. "Well, if that's what you want me to say, I'll say it! So, do you want to know what I found out on the Internet or not?"

Angel ignored the question. "You don't really think I look like a pig, do you?" she asked.

Now it was Seth who rolled his eyes. "I already told you what *I* think, but you didn't like it. So I told you what *you* think, even though it's wrong. Make up your mind, okay? Either I'll tell you the truth or I'll tell you what you want to hear."

"The truth, I guess," Angel said. "But I do weigh too much."

"Okay—maybe twenty pounds. Who cares?"

"Would you dance with me? I mean, if we were at a dance or something?"

Seth reddened. "I've never danced with anybody."

"That's not what I asked. I asked if you'd dance with me!" Angel pressed. "And remember, you have to tell me the truth."

"Why wouldn't I dance with you? But you'll have to teach me how. And we're not going to any dances anyway, so what does it matter? Now, do you want to know what I found out about the book?"

"You mean you actually found it on the Internet?"

Seth shook his head. "I Googled 'Recipees and Remedies,' and I didn't find that book, but I found out a bunch of other stuff. I mean, like there's hundreds and hundreds of sites that are all about witchcraft."

"Just because there's a bunch of sites doesn't make it true. There are sites on the Net about everything."

"I didn't say it was true," Seth said. "All I said is that there are lots of sites, and that's what I think the book's about."

"The way you said it sounded like you believe it," Angel said.

An uncertain look came into Seth's eyes. "I don't know—I mean, it seems like if so many people believe it, maybe . . ." His voice trailed off and he shrugged. "I don't know. Maybe it's like voodoo. I read once that voodoo actually works—you know, where they stick pins in a doll, and the person the doll is supposed to be feels the pain?"

"That's just superstition," Angel said. "It doesn't really work."

"It does if the person the doll's supposed to be believes in voodoo and knows someone's doing voodoo on him."

Angel frowned. "Really?"

Seth nodded. "Somebody did a big study about it, and if the person who's being hoodooed believes in voodoo, they'll actually get sick. Sometimes they even die!"

" 'Hoodooed'? What's that mean?"

"It's like a voodoo curse," Seth said.

"I don't believe in curses," Angel said.

"It doesn't matter if you believe in them or not. If someone gets cursed who believes in them, then the curse can work."

"I still don't see what it has to do with the book."

"Maybe nothing at all," Seth said. "But if it's a book of potions—"

"But it's not!" Angel interrupted. "It's a book of recipes and remedies. Yesterday, you thought it might be some kind of cookbook, remember?"

"Maybe it is," Seth agreed. "But when I ran recipes and remedies on the Internet, all I got were a bunch of new-age stuff and a few about witchcraft. I found one that has all kinds of spells and things, and according to that one, there really are magic remedies and potions, and things you can eat that make things happen."

"The only thing that happens when I eat is I get fat," Angel insisted. "And everybody knows none of that stuff works."

"I didn't say it did, did I?" Seth said, starting to sound exasperated. "All I said was that that's what I think the book is."

"Well, how are we going to find out if you're right?"

"Meet me at the library tonight—there's a whole section on the history of Roundtree, and I bet we can find out all kinds of stuff. Even if we can't find out exactly what the book is, I bet we can find out more about your house." His voice rose. "I mean, what if it turns out all the stories about your house are true?"

Angel felt a sudden rush of adrenaline. Could it really be possible that—

No! There was no such thing as witchcraft, no matter

what Seth had found out on the Web. "I don't know—" she began.

"What's the matter?" Seth broke in. "You scared?"

"No! I just don't think—"

But Seth wasn't listening to her. "You are too," he shot back. His voice took on a mocking singsong tone, but he kept it low enough so no one but Angel could hear. "Angel is a scaredy cat, Angel is a scaredy cat—"

"Stop that!"

"Why?" Seth asked, putting on an expression of exaggerated innocence. "It's true, isn't it?"

"No! I'm not scared—I just don't believe in that kind of stuff!"

"Then meet me at the library tonight!"

Angel glared at him. "Maybe I will, and maybe I won't," she finally said, but even as she spoke, she was pretty sure that she'd show up. After all, even though she didn't believe in witchcraft, she still wanted to know what the leather-bound book was about.

"What's going on over there?" Heather Dunne asked, nodding toward the table on the far side of the room where Seth was grinning maliciously at Angel, whose back was toward Heather and her friends, but whose shoulders were hunched over and her head bent down as if she were angry about something. "Looks like Beth and your cousin are having a fight!"

"They better not," Zack Fletcher said. "If they get mad at each other, they won't have any friends at all."

"What I want to know is how come they're sitting way over there?" Chad Jackson asked. "How come they're not sitting at Beth's table?"

"Maybe they want to be *alone*," Jared Woods said,

putting enough emphasis on the last word so everyone at the table began snickering.

"Why would two girls want to be alone?" Chad Jackson asked.

"Maybe Angel likes girls," Heather Dunne said.

Chad Jackson elbowed Zack Fletcher, who was sitting next to him. "Is that it, Zack? Does your cousin like girls?"

Zack's upper lip curled into a sneer. "Even if she did, so what? Even another girl wouldn't go out with her!"

"So what are they up to?" Chad pressed. "I mean, they sit together at lunch, and they go off together after school every day."

"So do you and Jared," Sarah Harmon said. Sarah, whose hair was as dark as Heather Dunne's was blond, usually sat quietly through the lunch hour, content to listen to her friends talk but rarely saying anything herself. Now everybody was looking at her, and she suddenly wished she hadn't spoken at all. But it was too late. "What do you and Jared do every day after school?" she finally asked.

"What do you mean, 'What do we do?' " Chad said. "We hang out!"

"Maybe that's what they do," Sarah Harmon said. "Maybe they aren't up to anything at all!"

"Then how come they're not sitting where they usually do?" Jared demanded.

Now Sarah found herself getting angry. "Maybe because of the way you and Chad act every time they sit anywhere near you."

Heather Dunne stared at her best friend. "Sarah! What's going on with you?"

For a second Sarah wondered if she shouldn't just pick up her tray and go sit somewhere else. But even as the thought formed in her head, she knew she wouldn't do it. She and Heather had been best friends ever since their first day in kindergarten, when they found out their birthdays were only two days apart. She'd known Chad and Jared and Zack just as long, and the half-dozen other kids in their crowd as well. They'd all gone to school together, and hung out at the country club in the summer together, and gone to movies together. They'd done everything together, and Sarah didn't have to think for even a few seconds to know exactly what would happen if she picked up her lunch tray and went to sit somewhere else.

The conversation would switch immediately from Angel Sullivan and Seth Baker to Sarah Harmon.

And that afternoon, when she went to the drugstore, there wouldn't be a seat for her at the table where she and Heather always sat with three or four other kids.

And tomorrow, someone else—probably Shauna Brett, who was sitting across from Sarah and seemed to be hanging on every word she said, just waiting for her to make a mistake—would be sitting next to Heather in the cafeteria.

Besides, who would she sit with? She was far too shy to just go over to another table where there was an empty chair, sit down, and start talking to whoever was there, like Heather Dunne always could. In fact, that was how she and Heather had become friends in the first place—Heather had just sat down next to her in kindergarten and started talking to her, and before her shyness could get in the way, they were already friends. It had been that way ever since—she was Heather's best friend, and all she had to do was follow along and do whatever Heather wanted to do. Heather's crowd was her crowd.

Heather's friends were her friends.

And now Heather was looking at her as if she'd gone

crazy, and Heather's question was still hanging in the air: *What's going on with you?*

And everyone was staring at her, waiting for her to answer.

"Nothing," she said. "I'm fine."

Then she lapsed back into the safety of silence as Zack, Chad, Jared, and the rest of her crowd talked about Angel and Seth.

Chapter 24

MARTY SULLIVAN'S FORK STOPPED MIDWAY BETWEEN his plate and his mouth, his eyes fixed on his daughter. The good mood brought on by the three shots of good Irish whiskey he'd chased down with three equally good pints of Irish beer before coming home that evening had faded rapidly in the face of Myra's pursed lips and disapproving look. Did she think sitting around in a bar listening to Ed Fletcher brag about his country club had been all that great? Besides, he was only about an hour late, and what business was it of hers anyway? But it was Angel that his eyes—now as dark as his mood—were focused on right now. All through supper, which Marty had eaten just to please Myra, even though it wasn't much good, Angel kept looking at the clock.

Like she had a date or something.

Fat chance that was going to happen. The way she was putting away the crappy dinner Myra had made, even that putz that he'd caught in her room with her the other day wouldn't be sniffing around anymore. As she ate the last scrap of ham on her plate, glanced at the clock, and finished up the remains of her second helping of Myra's scalloped potatoes with cheese, "just like her mother used to make"—as if her mother was any better in the kitchen than Myra herself—he put down his fork, leaned back, and crossed his arms over his chest. "What do you think you're up to?" he demanded.

Startled, Angel dropped her fork, which clattered onto her empty plate.

"Jesus!" Marty snorted. "How'd you get to be so clumsy?"

"Marty!" Myra exclaimed, and for an instant Angel thought her mother was going to come to her defense. "Don't take the name of the Lord in vain!"

Angel's faint flicker of hope faded as quickly as it had flared. She stood up to start clearing the table, hoping to distract her father.

"You didn't answer my question," Marty said, his eyes narrowing.

"I—I'm just clearing the table," Angel said, trying the tactic of avoiding the truth by saying something that wasn't quite a lie, which had worked yesterday when she'd gotten back from finding the hidden cabin with Seth.

"You been lookin' at the clock all through dinner," Marty challenged. "And eatin' even faster than usual. You got plans I don't know about?"

Angel bit her lip and willed herself not to flush. Her father's brow was knit into a deep scowl, and the look in his eyes told her she wasn't going to be able to escape the kitchen—let alone the house—without giving him an answer. "I'm going to the library," she finally said. "I've got some homework." Again, the truth that wasn't quite the answer.

"What kinda homework?"

"History," Angel replied. "It's a project about Round-tree."

"You meetin' that boy there?" Marty demanded, and

this time there was nothing Angel could do to keep herself from reddening.

"What boy?" Myra asked.

"That kid I found in her room the other day. What's his name?"

"Seth," Angel breathed. "Seth Baker."

"Oh, I met his mother at lunch," Myra said. "Jane Baker."

Marty swung around to focus on his wife. "Lunch? What lunch?"

"At the country club," Myra explained. "Joni invited me to meet some of her friends."

"They invite you to the big blowout they're havin' this weekend?" Marty asked.

"You mean the Family Day barbecue?" Myra said. "I don't think you could call it a 'big blowout,' really. It's just more like a—"

"I know what it is," Marty interrupted. "I heard your high-and-mighty brother-in-law talkin' about it." He saw Myra's lips purse in that disapproving way again, but so what? "They invite you?" Marty pressed.

"As a matter of fact, they did," Myra said, immediately regretting her words as she saw her husband pull his lips into a mocking imitation of her own expression.

"As a matter of fact, they did," Marty parroted in an intonation close enough to Myra's to make her wince. "And what did you tell them?"

"I didn't really say anything," Myra said, choosing her words carefully, and silently praying that Marty wouldn't lose his temper. "I'm not sure it's our kind of thing—"

"Not our kind of thing," Marty parroted. Then he dropped both his wife's expression and her tone. "How the hell would you know?"

"Don't swear, Marty," Myra said, and once again

wished she could snatch back her words. Too late—
Marty's face was already reddening with anger.

"Don't you tell me how to talk. And don't tell me
what's my kind of thing and what's not either. You know
what, Myra? We're goin' to that party!" He saw Myra's
eyes widen and a look of something like panic come
over his daughter's face. "What's the matter? Neither of
you think we belong there?"

"I—I don't have anything to wear," Myra began.

"You can wear any damned thing you want," Marty
roared. "It's a fuckin' barbecue, isn't it? What's so fuckin'
fancy about a fuckin' barbecue?"

"Marty—" Myra began, but Marty was on his feet
now. "Go to the library, Angel," she said quickly.

"But Mom—" Angel began, but her mother didn't let
her finish.

"Just go. It'll be all right."

Her father was trembling with anger now, and Angel
hurried out of the kitchen, pausing only long enough to
pull a jacket off the hook by the front door before slipping out of the house.

"We're goin' to that party," she heard her father bel-
low as she pulled the door closed behind her. "You call
your goddamn sister right now and tell her we're goin'!"

As Angel hurried away from the house, she told herself that the yelp of pain that came right after her father's last words couldn't possibly have come from her
mother. Her father yelled a lot, but he never hit her
mother.

The same feeling that she was not alone, which she'd felt
last night on the way home from the hidden cabin, came
over Angel again as she started toward the library. But
now, in the darkness of the autumn evening, the feeling

was more frightening than it had been yesterday afternoon when she was with Seth, or in the house, where the lights were on and her parents were downstairs. Now she was by herself, night had fallen, and there was no one else around.

Twice, she looked back over her shoulder as she hurried along Black Creek Road, but saw nothing. *Because there's nothing to see,* she told herself. But the feeling didn't go away, and only when the library was little more than a block away and the glow of the old-fashioned streetlights around the square began to bolster her courage did she slow her pace to a walk. As she passed the drugstore, she saw her cousin sprawled in a booth with Chad Jackson and Jared Woods. Though she was sure he saw her, he pretended he didn't. By the time she reached the foot of the broad sweep of granite steps that led to the fieldstone building's great oaken doors, her heart had finally stopped pounding and her breath was no longer threatening to catch in her throat.

She mounted the steps, pushed open the door, and stepped through the vestibule, then into the library itself. Straight ahead was the front desk, and off to both sides were immense library tables. Unlike the new library in Eastbury, which was lit by bright fluorescent fixtures suspended from the high ceiling with ugly steel cables, here the old milk-white globes still hung from brass rods. The only concessions to technology were the scanner the librarian used to check books in and out, and the three tables on the right that had been divided into carrels equipped with computer monitors. Scanning the tables to the left for Seth, Angel recognized only Heather Dunne and a dark-haired girl whose name she didn't know. She was about to turn away before Heather saw her when she spotted Seth emerging from one of the aisles that led into the long rows of bookcases that filled the back of the building. Seeing her, Seth waved, and Angel started toward the table where he'd already piled a dozen books, threading her way circuitously around the table where Heather and her friends were giggling among themselves, ignoring the glares of the librarian as completely as they were snubbing Angel.

Pulling off her jacket and hanging it on the back of the chair next to Seth's, Angel gazed at the books he'd found on the shelf. One was a slim volume bound in green cloth, the title embossed in flaking gilt that had all but vanished over the years: A BRIEF HISTORY OF ROUNDTREE. Beneath the title there was a stylized image of a tree that was, indeed, perfectly round, supported by an absolutely straight trunk. Two more books had titles that told Angel they weren't going to make her want to use her flashlight under the covers to read them: THE WYNTONS OF ROUNDTREE: A GENEALOGY, and THE PREACHING PARSONS: FOUR GENERATIONS OF PURITAN MINISTERS.

Then she saw the fourth book, and the same kind of chill passed over Angel as when she and Seth stood at the head of the cellar stairs. It was bound in dark red cloth that looked as if it was the same shade as the leather of the book they'd found hidden in the stair. Though it was smaller than the rest of the books on the table, it appeared as close in size to the hidden volume as it was in color. Was it possible that Seth had found another copy of the book, right here in the library?

As she lowered herself into the chair, she reached out and pulled the book over so it was in front of her. Gingerly, as if it might somehow have the capacity to hurt her, she opened it.

The flyleaf was gone, and she found herself looking at the title page, which was printed in the same ornate type she'd seen in the book hidden in the stair:

𝕻𝕴𝖙𝖈𝖍𝖊𝖗𝖞 𝖎𝖓 𝕽𝖔𝖚𝖓𝖉𝖙𝖗𝖊𝖊

Beneath the title the author's name was inscribed in the same ornate typeface:

𝖙𝖍𝖊 𝕽𝖊𝖛𝖊𝖗𝖊𝖓𝖉 𝕻𝖊𝖗𝖈𝖎𝖛𝖆𝖑 𝖀𝖑𝖞𝖓𝖙𝖔𝖓 𝕻𝖆𝖗𝖘𝖔𝖓𝖘

Angel gazed at the words for a long time; somehow, when Seth spoke about witchcraft in the cafeteria, it had been easy for her to dismiss the whole idea. But now, with the old book lying open before her as she sat at a table in the library in the very town about which the book had been written . . .

Her heart quickened again, and her breath caught in her throat, just as it had as she'd walked through the lonely darkness to the library.

But now she was in a brightly lit room and there were people all around her.

She was safe.

Then why did she feel so strange?

She tore her eyes away from the title page and looked at Seth. "I—I don't believe in this kind of stuff," she said, but even as she uttered the words, she heard the doubt in her own voice, and memories began churning through her mind.

The girl in the closet, engulfed in flames.

The smell of smoke still there the next morning.

The strange reflections in her mirror, of another girl's face peering over her own shoulder.

But none of it was real—none of it *could* have been real! Either she'd dreamed it, or was sleepwalking, or there was some other explanation!

The markings scrawled on the mirror that had led them to the book hidden in the stair.

That *had* been real—as had the stains she washed out of her sheets herself.

And finding the book was real, and finding the cabin was real. The cat had led them directly to both the book and the cabin.

The black cat.

The kind of cat that every witch had in every fairy tale she'd ever read.

They all had black cats, just like Houdini.

Was it possible that . . . ?

Then, through her confusion, she heard Seth's voice.

". . . it wasn't an inscription," he was saying. "It was a name."

Angel blinked, trying to make sense of his words. "What?"

" 'Forbearance,' " Seth said. Glancing around, he lowered his voice. "I think that's who the book belonged to. Look." He opened one of the books stacked in front of him—the history of the Wynton family—and turned several pages. "Here," he said, holding his finger under a line in the middle of the page and turning the book so Angel could read it, though the type was so small she could barely make it out:

3. Forbearance—b. 1678 d. 1693.

"She was the daughter of Josiah and Margaret Wynton," she heard Seth saying. "And I found out all kinds of weird stuff about her and her mother."

A ripple of excitement flowed over Angel. "What kind of stuff?"

"They were accused of being witches," Seth told her. "It's all in that book." He nodded to the red volume that lay in front of Angel. "The guy that wrote that? He was her cousin."

"But what did they *do?*" Angel pressed.

"This book says they put hexes on people. Someone swore Margaret made him fall off a horse, and someone else said the girl made lightning burn their house down."

Angel's eyes widened. "You mean like she made it strike the house?"

Seth nodded. "Wouldn't that be cool? Can you imagine the look on Chad Jackson's face if the next time he started in on me, I could just hit him with a bolt of lightning?" He grinned at Angel and stabbed at the air using a forefinger as a bolt of lightning. "*Zap!* Wouldn't that be neat?"

"What did they do to them?" Angel asked. "I mean, was it like what they did in Salem?"

Seth nodded. "Oh, yeah! And when they went after Margaret and Forbearance Wynton, guess where they were living?" The look on his face was enough to tell Angel the answer. "The house at Black Creek Crossing," he said. "Your house."

"You mean it's all true?" Angel asked, her voice louder than she'd intended it. "All the stories everyone tells really happened?" She saw Heather Dunne turn and look at her, then smirk as she turned to whisper to the dark-haired girl.

"It's all here," Seth said. "Look!"

For the next hour and a half, Angel and Seth went through the books, reading and rereading every passage that made any reference to either Forbearance Wynton, her mother, or the house at Black Creek Crossing. Finally, at ten minutes of nine, they gathered up the books and put them on the table for the assistant librarian to return to the stacks.

"Do you think anything really happened?" Angel asked as they walked down the front steps. "I mean, everyone always says the witch hunts were crazy—that those people hadn't done anything at all!"

"That didn't keep them from getting burned at the stake, or drowned, or all the other things they did to them," Seth replied. "And it sure explains why nobody ever stays in your house for very long."

Angel stopped at the bottom of the steps leading to the sidewalk. "You mean you believe the witches were real?"

Seth hesitated, then shrugged. "I don't know. It's just interesting, that's all."

"But do you believe it?" Angel repeated, her voice rising.

Seth looked at her, his head cocked. "Do you?" he countered.

"I asked you first."

"I don't know," Seth said. "I guess—" His eyes shifted away from her and his voice dropped. "I guess I just think it might be kind of neat if it *was* real, you know?"

Angel hesitated, then nodded. "That's what I was thinking too."

There was a hoot of laughter from the top of the stairs, and then they heard Heather Dunne's mocking voice. "You already *look* like a witch," she said, her eyes fixed on Angel. "So now are you going to actually be one?"

Heather and Sarah Harmon were peering down at them. "Why don't you just leave us alone?" Angel demanded. With Heather's words still burning in her ears, she turned away and ran across the street.

A moment later Seth followed.

Neither of them saw Heather and Sarah leave the library, hurry down the sidewalk, and go into the drugstore.

Chapter 25

EATHER'S WORDS WERE STILL RINGING IN HER HEAD as Angel began the walk back home. Seth had come with her as far as the corner of Black Creek Road, but when he asked if she wanted him to walk her all the way out to the Crossing, she shook her head, afraid of what might happen if her father saw her with him.

But as she left the streetlights behind and the darkness of the night began to close around her, Angel once more had the feeling that she was being watched, and wished she'd let Seth come with her. It was too late to change her mind—when she looked back, he'd vanished into the darkness.

She tried to ignore it, to pretend that she felt nothing, but as a cloud passed over the half moon hanging low in the sky, and the blackness seemed to wrap around her like a shroud, she felt her pulse quicken along with her stride.

Then, from somewhere off to the right, she heard a sound.

Angel froze, listening.

Silence.

She resumed walking, but hadn't taken more than three steps when she heard the sound again. It was closer this time, and more distinct, a rustling sound from some-where toward the creek.

"Houdini?" she called out softly. "Is that you?"

The rustling stopped.

"Come on, Houdini," Angel called again. "Here, kitty, kitty. Come on!"

More silence.

Angel stood still, listening, but the night had gone deathly silent.

In the terrible stillness her heart pounded so hard it seemed it would drown out anything else.

But there isn't anything else, she told herself. *It wasn't anything but a mouse or something, poking around in the leaves.* But when she began walking again, she crossed the road to the other side.

Now another sound came out of the darkness—a low, faint hooting. *An owl,* she told herself. But still, she stopped to listen.

The sound came again, closer now.

But there had been no fluttering of wings.

The hooting changed, becoming a moaning sound, and Angel shivered, pulling her jacket tighter around her throat. Then, hearing the sound again, she felt an awful crawly feeling on the back of her neck.

Something was behind her.

Something dangerous.

Crack!

A twig snapped, so close that Angel jumped, and she whirled around to peer into the darkness behind her.

There was a flicker of movement, gone in an instant, swallowed by the darkness so quickly that Angel wasn't sure she'd seen it at all. She backed away, turned, and began to run.

A scream burst out of the night, so loud it stopped Angel in her tracks, but it died abruptly, cut off at almost the instant it began. Now she stood trembling in the darkness. All around her the night had fallen eerily silent after the scream, the silence almost as terrifying as the scream had been.

If it had really been a scream.

It was the owl, Angel told herself. *It was a screech owl.*

Yet even as she reassured herself and headed toward home again, the sounds returned.

Leaves rustling.

Twigs cracking.

She heard a low whistle off to one side, and crossed the road once more, but a moment later there was a moan from the forest—as if someone were in pain. Her heart raced as tendrils of panic slithered out of the darkness, creeping toward her. Then she heard a whimpering sound, and a moment later realized it had come from her own lips.

Another moan, this time from somewhere behind her, and she whirled once more, only to see another shadow vanish into the black depths of the forest.

She turned again, and caught a glimpse of motion out of the corner of her eye. Her breath catching in her throat, she felt the tendrils of panic tightening around her, and now she tried to look in every direction at once, frantically searching for the shapes whose shadows seemed always on the periphery of her vision.

There was nothing but darkness. The lights of the village had disappeared behind her, and the lights of the house at the Crossing weren't yet visible. She looked up into the sky, but it too was darkening as the layer of cloud over the moon grew denser.

Home, Angel thought. *I've got to get home before I can't see anything at all.*

She started running, but the toe of her left foot caught

on something and she plunged forward. She threw out her hands to protect her face, and a moment later felt a terrible stinging as the asphalt of the road tore the skin from her palms.

This time there was no mistaking the cry of pain as coming from anywhere but her own throat, but she managed to choke it into silence almost as quickly as the scream she'd heard moments before had died. She scrambled back to her feet, brushing the dirt from her jacket and jeans. Her eyes blurring with tears, she stumbled on through the darkness. Now there were sounds all around her—leaves rustling and twigs breaking as if some beast hidden in the darkness and the trees were keeping pace with her, preparing to launch itself at her. She veered across the road still another time, but there was no longer any escaping the terrifying cacophony.

Running again, her heart pounding, her lungs heaving, she tried to escape the terrors that surrounded her in the darkness. Now the night took on the quality of a nightmare. Her feet felt sluggish, as if bogged down in thick mud, and the road itself threatened to mire her. A moan escaped her lips, nearly echoing the moans that had come from the forest earlier.

Then, as she came to the bend in the road, she saw it.

The house at the Crossing, light pouring from its windows, washing away the darkness. Angel hurled herself toward the light, veering across the road and onto the small expanse of lawn that wrapped around the house.

The sounds began to die away.

And then, once more, silence.

A silence that was suddenly broken by laughter.

Loud, raucous laughter, rolling out of the forest and across the road and the lawn. Angel felt it crashing against her as she stood on the front porch.

Zack. Now she understood what had happened.

Heather and her friend must have told Zack what had happened. Now he was laughing.

Laughing exactly as they had laughed earlier.

Struggling against the tears that now threatened to overwhelm her, she turned her back on the mocking laughter, slipped through the front door, and headed for the stairs, wanting nothing more than the refuge of her room, where she might blot out the laughter still ringing in her ears.

But as she passed the living room, her mother said, "Angel? Are you all right?"

She hesitated, wanting to tell her mother what had happened, what Zack Fletcher had done. But remembering what had happened when she'd told her mother about her father coming into her room that night, she changed her mind. Besides, if her mother believed her, she would tell her aunt Joni, and her aunt would talk to Zack, and . . .

And everything would be even worse than it was right now.

"I'm okay," she said. "I'm just going upstairs to finish my homework."

"All right," her mother said. "I'll come in and say good night in a little while."

Upstairs, Angel washed the blood and grime off her scraped palms, winced as she dabbed the cuts with iodine, then went to her room. Instead of turning on the light, however, she went to the window and peered out into the darkness. The moon was obliterated now, and it was like looking into the blackness of eternity itself. For a moment she wondered what it would be like to simply disappear into that blackness, to float forever in silence and nothingness.

At last she drew the curtains and turned away from the window, but still didn't turn on the light. Instead she took off her clothes in darkness, and in darkness she slipped into her bed.

When her mother came in to kiss her good night an hour later, Angel pretended to be asleep, and carefully kept her injuries hidden beneath her blankets.

Zack Fletcher was still two blocks from home when he heard a faint rustling sound, just like the sound he himself had made half an hour ago when he, Chad, and Jared caught up with Angel Sullivan as she walked home, making noises in the woods and scaring her so badly she'd started running. So he ignored it as he continued to walk along Haverford Street.

The sounds continued, a distinct rustling in the leaves off to the left, and finally, when he'd passed two more houses, Zack stopped.

So did the sound of rustling leaves.

He resumed walking again.

The sounds began again too.

Zack stopped again. "Okay, Chad!" he called out. "You can come out now—I know it's you."

Nothing.

He began walking again, and the sounds started up again, keeping pace with him.

"Come on, Chad!" he shouted. "You're not scaring me!" But even as he spoke the words, his voice betrayed the lie.

He walked faster, and heard the sound again.

Something, or someone, was moving along next to him, keeping pace with him.

But why couldn't he see them? There were lights on in the houses along Haverford Street, and porch lights were on, and streetlights. Yet he couldn't make out whoever was following him.

Then, as he crossed Prospect Street, he caught a flash of movement.

A cat! Nothing but a stupid cat, like the one that was always hanging around with Angel. His fright vanishing, Zack stepped up onto the curb and started down the last block.

Now the cat was moving alongside him, making no effort at all to stay out of sight.

But strangely, though he could see the cat clearly, moving over the leaves that had fallen from the huge canopy of branches that spread over the lawns along Haverford Street, it was no longer making any sound at all.

The rustling had stopped.

It was as if the cat were somehow floating over the leaves, not even disturbing them.

He stopped.

So did the cat, turning to face him.

Zack took a step toward it. "Shoo!"

The cat only crouched, its tail twitching.

"Stupid cat," Zack said. "Get out of here!" He charged toward it, raising his arms and waving them.

But instead of springing off into the darkness, the cat launched itself straight at him, and a second later Zack screamed as he felt the claws sink deep into the flesh of his face. As his howl of agony rose, the cat dropped away, and as Zack clutched at his face, it darted off, to disappear silently into the shadows.

His face burning with pain and his eyes stinging with tears, Zack ran the rest of the way home, charging up onto the front porch of his house. Opening the door, he lurched inside, then slammed it shut behind him, leaning against it for a moment as he caught his breath.

"Zack?" he heard his mother say from the living room. "Honey, everything OK?"

Feeling tears streaming down his cheeks, Zack moved toward the living room. "It was a cat," he said, his voice quavering. "Angel's cat! It tried to kill me!"

Joni Fletcher gazed at her son, whose face was twisted into a mask of fear and pain. "What?" she asked, rising to her feet. "What cat? What do mean, it attacked you?"

"My face," Zack wailed. "It practically ripped my cheeks off!"

His mother was looking at him with bewilderment. "Honey, what are you talking about? There's nothing wrong with your face."

Zack put his hand to his cheek.

The stinging was gone.

He looked at his fingers.

No blood.

Turning, he looked in the mirror that hung on the wall over the table by the front door.

His face looked perfectly normal—not even a scratch, let alone the deep slashes that should have been there, given how agonizing the pain had been when the animal's claws had sunk into his skin.

He gently touched his cheek with his forefinger.

Nothing—no pain at all.

But a few minutes ago—

He turned back to the living room, where his father had joined his mother, both of them on their feet, looking at him uncertainly. "I'm not lying," Zack said, his voice uneven. "It happened right down at the end of the block."

"What happened?" Ed Fletcher asked.

As best he could, Zack recounted everything from the moment he'd first heard the sound of rustling leaves as he was walking home to when the cat launched itself at his face.

"You're sure it actually attacked you?" Ed Fletcher asked when his son was finished.

"I'm telling you, Dad!" Zack exclaimed, his voice rising in response to the doubt in his father's voice. "It tried to kill me!"

"Well, it certainly didn't succeed, did it? Seems like it did a better job of scaring you than it did of hurting you."

Zack's eyes narrowed and he turned truculent. "You don't believe me."

Ed Fletcher spread his hands as if to ward off his son's angry words. "I'm not saying nothing happened—I'm just saying it doesn't seem to be as bad as you think it was."

"And even if a cat did attack you, why would you think it was Angel's?" his mother asked. "They don't even have a cat. Marty's allergic."

"As allergic as he is to work?" Ed Fletcher interjected, engendering a dark look from his wife.

"It's Angel's," Zack said. "It follows her everywhere. It's all black and—"

"You're claiming you recognized a black cat at night?" Ed Fletcher broke in.

"I did!" Zack was nearly shouting now.

"All right, all right!" Ed said, once more raising his hands as if to fend off his son's anger. "I'm just not sure I would have even seen it, that's all."

"You'd have seen this one," Zack said. "It's huge, and its eyes were glowing, and—"

"All right, that's enough," Ed Fletcher said, his tone imparting his doubt as much as his words. "Even if we agree that this cat attacked you—which, frankly, I doubt—I don't see why you think it belongs to Angel. They don't even live around here, and—"

"It followed me!" Zack blurted, before considering the implication of his words. But it was too late.

"Followed you from where?" Ed Fletcher asked. "Is there something you're not telling us, Zack?"

"No, I—" Zack began, but his father didn't let him finish.

"Why don't you tell us exactly where you were tonight, and what you were doing?"

"I was just hangin' out with Chad and Jared and Heather! And Angel was there, and her stupid cat, and—"

"Why do you keep saying it was Angel's cat?" Joni broke in.

"Because it's always with her! I'm tellin' you—"

"I'm going to call Myra," Joni said.

She picked up the phone, dialed, and when she hung up a few minutes later, her eyes had taken on the same look as her husband's.

"Zack, the Sullivans don't have a cat," she said to her son. "So whatever happened tonight had nothing to do with your cousin. Now, what really happened?"

Seething, but knowing there was no use arguing with both his parents, Zack turned away. "Nothing," he said. "Nothing happened, all right?"

He headed up the stairs, and when his mother called after him, he didn't answer. A moment later he was in his room, slamming the door shut behind him.

As he got ready to go to bed, Chad Jackson was still laughing about the sight of Angel Sullivan running terrified through the night. For him, the best part was when she'd tripped and fallen on her face. He could still remember how much it had hurt two years ago when his bike skidded out of control, across the asphalt in the street right outside. He'd had scabs for weeks, and when his mother insisted on putting iodine on the scrapes—

He winced even now, just thinking about it.

Leaving his clothes piled in a heap on the floor, he climbed into bed and was just reaching for the light switch when his eyes fell on his backpack, full of text-books, and he remembered the math homework he hadn't done.

Well, no point in doing it now—he'd either do it in the morning or make Seth Baker let him copy his. Too bad Seth hadn't been with Angel when they followed her, moving through the woods, where she couldn't see them, making noises. The only thing that would have been bet-ter was if Seth had been there too, getting so scared he'd wet his pants.

That would have made it perfect—if they'd been able to figure out a way to give Seth as good a scare as they'd given Angel.

Angel—what a stupid name.

A stupid name for a fat, ugly, stupid girl.

So stupid she even liked Seth Baker!

And stupid enough to fall for the sounds they'd been making too.

Grinning, Chad softly repeated the hooting sound he'd made in the woods that night. It didn't actually sound like an owl—at least not any he'd ever heard— but it had been good enough to send Angel running for home. He was about to repeat it, and improve on it, when he heard something.

Something from outside the room.

He listened, and heard nothing.

He decided he must have been wrong.

Relaxing, Chad reached for the lamp on the bedside table.

The sound came again, but this time he recognized it. It was the same sound he'd just made.

He lay still, not even breathing, his hand hovering near the lamp.

The sound came again.

What was it? An owl?

But it didn't sound like an owl—it sounded like *him* trying to sound like an owl!

What—

And then he knew! It had to be Jared—or maybe Zack—playing a trick on him.

Or maybe signaling him to come out! He and Jared had snuck out at least half a dozen times last summer and never come close to getting caught. Chad slid out of bed and pulled on his clothes. Going to the door of his room, he listened, then opened it a crack and listened again.

The hall outside was dark and silent, but he could hear his father snoring even through the door to his parents' bedroom.

Closing his door, Chad went to the window, unlatched it, and raised the lower casement. It creaked a little, and the counterweights in the frame rattled, but he knew that even if his mother was awake, she'd have her earplugs in to cut down the racket of his dad's snoring.

"Jared?" he called softly.

There was no reply, except for the same strange hooting sound that had brought him to the window. A cold draft of air flowed in the open window, a draft unlike anything Chad had felt before. The cold seemed to reach inside him, and for a terrible instant he had the feeling he was dying.

Holding perfectly still, he strained his eyes and ears, searching for the source of the sound that had caused him to suddenly freeze.

But he saw nothing, and a moment later realized he heard nothing either—not even the last of the crickets and frogs that were so loud during the summer that they kept him awake, and which he'd still heard outside when he'd gone to bed tonight.

Now the night was utterly silent.

Why? What had silenced the frogs and crickets?

He listened with concentration, and then, from no more than a few feet away, was startled by a loud screeching.

Chad jumped, banging his head against the frame of the open window.

What was it?

An owl? A cat?

He turned in the direction from which the sound had come, and at first saw nothing. But then he saw something glimmering in the blackness, barely visible.

Chad's pulse quickened as he strained to see better.

The glimmer turned to a glow, and then the glow came into focus.

Eyes.

Two darkly glowing eyes, the pupils huge, were peering at him from a branch of the tree that was just far enough away to be out of his reach.

An owl. That's what it had to be—a screech owl! He'd imitated it better than he thought!

Chad waved his arms toward it, certain it would leap from the branch and fly away. But instead of seeing an owl burst out of the tree's canopy in startled flight, something as black as the night outside came through the window. For a terrible instant Chad felt as if the darkness itself was reaching for him, but a fraction of a second later he knew he was wrong.

A cat!

A black cat, with a single white blaze in the middle of its chest.

Angel's cat!

Claws that felt like acid-tipped scalpel blades suddenly slashed deep into the bare flesh of his shoulders, and teeth sank into his neck.

A scream of pain and shock choking in his throat, Chad lurched backward, tumbling to the bedroom floor. He tried to get his hands on it to tear it away from his throat before it killed him, but before he could, the cat was gone.

Gone so quickly and so completely that for several seconds Chad wondered if anything had actually happened at all. But then the pain of the cat's claws sinking into the flesh of his shoulders began to burn, and he pressed his hands against his neck, terrified that the animal might have torn open his throat. Stumbling from his bedroom down the hall to the bathroom, he turned on the cold water and began washing his neck and shoulders even before turning the light on.

The coolness of the water soothed the burning of his wounds, and after using a washcloth to wipe most of the water away, he turned on the light and looked at his reflection in the mirror.

Nothing.

Not a cut anywhere—not even a scratch!

Then, as he stared at his image in the mirror, he saw it.

The cat's face, its lips pulled back to show its teeth, looming behind him, just over his right shoulder.

Spinning around, Chad raised his arms to fend off the cat's attack once more.

And again he saw nothing.

For almost a full minute he stood trembling in the bathroom, his heart racing, too terrified even to turn off the light and go back to his room.

He searched the bathroom then, even looking in the shower and behind the old-fashioned claw-foot bathtub, for any sign of the cat, but the cat had vanished even faster than it had vanished from the tree outside.

If it had been in the bathroom at all.

As his heart finally slowed back to normal, Chad told himself he couldn't have seen anything in the mirror, that it had to have been his imagination playing tricks on him.

But what about before, when he was peering out the open window and the cat had attacked him and he'd felt the pain of its claws sinking into his flesh?

Could he have imagined that too?

How?

How had it happened?

Maybe nothing had happened.

Maybe he had imagined it all.

But when he went back to his bedroom, Chad left the light on in the bathroom, and when he went to sleep, he left the light on in his room too.

The black cat slipped through the night like a wraith, moving silently in the darkness, no sound at all betraying its presence. Rather, it was the silence itself that signaled every living thing within its reach that something was wrong.

That danger was nearby.

And sensing the danger—the presence of the wraith-like creature—every living thing took on a stillness that lay over the night like a cloak so dense that even the light breeze of the autumn night died away.

But even the cloak of silence wasn't enough to slow the cat as it moved toward its prey, for there was nothing in the night the cat could not hear.

Nothing it could not see.

Nothing it could not sense.

After it had passed, the silence slowly lifted.

Crickets concealed beneath the bark of trees once more rubbed their wing covers together.

Tree frogs in the gardens began to puff out their throats once more.

Birds in their nests and on their perches twittered softly in their sleep.

Even the leaves dying on the trees began to rustle as the breeze in the air came back to life.

Moments later farther down the street, the black wraith slithered silently up a tree, then moved out onto a limb.

Dropped onto a steeply sloping roof.

Crept around to a gable.

Peered through the window.

Saw Jared Woods asleep in his bed.

A moment later, though Jared had left no window open, and locked his bedroom door, the cat named Houdini was inside the room.

In his dream, Jared Woods was once again in the forest near Black Creek Crossing, barely able to contain his laughter as he heard Chad Jackson hooting softly in an almost perfect imitation of an owl.

Perfect enough to send Angel Sullivan veering back across the road to the other side, where Zack Fletcher was waiting to crack twigs again.

As he watched Angel hurry her step and veer first one way and then another to escape the ominous sounds coming out of the darkness, Jared felt the same thrill that always came over him when he saw the frightened look in Seth Baker's eyes whenever he and Chad were about to subject him to some new humiliation.

Terrifying Angel was even better, because she had no

idea what was happening or who was hidden in the darkness.

Now, as she veered away from the fear of Zack's cracking sticks and started back toward him, he readied himself, his lungs filled with air, his mouth opening.

Just when he was certain she would come no closer, Jared unleashed the scream.

Which lasted only a split second before something slammed into him.

As the scream abruptly died, Jared jerked awake, still feeling the sickening sensation of something having struck him in the stomach, knocking the breath out of him.

For a moment a wave of panic washed over him as he realized he couldn't breathe, then his diaphragm began to function again and his lungs filled with air.

And then he felt a searing pain in his stomach, as if someone had just plunged a knife into him and was twisting it in his guts. Howling as a second stab slashed at his belly, he tried to reach for the lamp on the table beside his bed, but as a third stab struck him, his whole body went into a spasm and he tumbled from the bed, dragging the bedclothes with him.

Screaming, he thrashed at the sheet and blanket that were tangled around him, but even as he tried to free himself, he knew there was something else in the jumbled mass too.

Something that was twisting and writhing as frantically as he, but not because it wanted to escape.

It was thrashing and twisting and writhing because it wanted to kill him, and as another scream built in his throat, he felt it tear at his belly yet again.

Panic erupted inside Jared as he felt teeth and claws sinking deeper into his flesh.

He was going to die!

He was going to die right now on the floor of his own room.

Now, he could feel his limbs starting to go numb, and a strange kind of darkness—far blacker than the night—was starting to gather around him.

A nightmare!

That was it—he was having a terrible nightmare, and in a moment he would wake up.

But the nightmare went on and on, and the darkness was closing in on him, and he knew that if it finally gathered him in its folds, he would never see again.

Never breathe again.

He rolled over, still flailing to free himself from the tangle of bedding.

Then he heard a voice.

"Jared? Jared—what's going on in there?"

His father!

The jaws at his throat were suddenly gone, and Jared sucked in a huge gulp of air. He rolled over once more and tried to stand up.

"Jared?" his father called out again.

It was as if his father's voice had freed him from the bedding, and he pulled himself to the bed table, reached up, and switched on the lamp.

The room filled with light, and a cat—the black cat he'd seen before, weaving around Angel Sullivan's feet and rubbing against her legs—sprang to its feet. As Jared managed to stand and started toward the door, the cat's back arched, and it hissed menacingly and tensed as if it were about to leap at him again.

"I'm coming," Jared called back to his father, but the pain in his torn belly was so bad he could barely get the words out. His eyes never leaving the cat, Jared backed toward the door, reaching behind him and groping for the key. His fingers closed on it, but it wouldn't turn.

He struggled with it for a moment, terrified that if he turned his back, the cat would strike, but when the key still wouldn't turn, he knew he had no choice. Spinning around, he twisted at the key frantically, and this time it clicked open. A second later he flung the door open.

"It's a cat!" he cried. "It tried to kill me!"

Jared's face was pasty white, and Steve Woods could see the terror in his son's eyes. But as he scanned the room, he saw no sign of a cat, though the covers were pulled half off the bed, and the rag rug Steve's grand-mother had made for him when he was about Jared's age was rumpled up the way it used to get when Steve and his friends used it for a wrestling mat. Steve scanned the room once more, then looked again at his son. "A cat? What are you talking about?"

"Over there—" Jared began as he turned to point at the spot where the cat had been crouched. But the cat had vanished.

He looked around the room, searching for the cat.

Nothing.

"There was a cat!" he insisted. "It attacked me! Look! Look at my stomach—it almost killed me!"

Steve Woods cocked his head, and a small smile played around the corners of his mouth. "Sounds to me like you had one hell of a nightmare," he said. He began straightening out the rug with his foot. "I'm not sure I ever had one so bad I was fighting on the floor, but—"

"It wasn't a nightmare!" Jared cried. "It was a cat!"

His father's smile faded. "Jared, take a look around. Do you see a cat?"

Again Jared scanned the room, searching for some-place the cat might be hiding. But the closet door was closed, as was the one to the hall.

The window was closed tight as well.

Crouching down, he looked under the bed, and under

his desk, and behind the chair, and anyplace else the cat might be hiding.

It had vanished so completely it might as well never have been there at all.

Then, as he rose to his feet again, he caught a glimpse of himself in the mirror on his closet door.

There wasn't a mark on his stomach, or anywhere else.

It was as if none of it had happened.

But it had.

He knew it had.

And he knew whose cat it was that had attacked him . . .

Chapter 26

THE TERROR ANGEL HAD FELT AS SHE WALKED HOME from the library the night before gave way to anger in the morning sunlight, with the shadows of the forest washed away and Houdini frolicking around her feet, dashing away every now and then to chase a squirrel or a rabbit, but always coming back before more than a minute or two had passed.

How could she have been so stupid last night?

How could she not have figured out that the sounds she'd heard weren't made by some kind of dangerous animal stalking her? In the full light of day, even the memory of the strange hooting she'd heard didn't sound like an owl, or any other kind of animal. Rather, it sounded like someone trying to sound like an owl, and not even doing a good imitation of one.

Stupid! She'd been stupid, and Zack and his friends would tell everyone else about it all day. She could already picture everyone looking at her in the cafeteria at lunchtime, and hear them giggling and laughing just loud enough to make sure she heard them.

She considered skipping school that day. But ten minutes later, standing across the street from the school and seeing Zack, Chad, and Jared hanging around on the front steps just like they always did, she changed her mind.

Better to just ignore them.

She bent down to say good-bye to Houdini. Instead of nuzzling her hand the way he usually did, he was gazing across the street, his eyes fixed on the three boys on the front steps, his tail twitching.

He knows! Angel thought. *He knows what they did!*

"It's okay, Houdini," she said softly, stroking the cat's fur. "They're just stupid boys!" Giving him one last pat, she straightened up, hitched her backpack higher on her shoulders, and started across the street.

Houdini darted in front of her, hissed in the direction of her cousin and his friends, and pressed against her legs as if to keep her from going any farther.

Angel looked at the cat quizzically. "Houdini, I have to go to school! Just go on back to wherever you go every day, and I'll see you after school!" Stepping around the cat, she continued across the street.

Houdini darted in front of her again. This time, though, he didn't try to stop her; instead he stalked ahead of her, his head low, his teeth bared.

As she came to the bottom of the steps, he moved halfway up the flight and crouched down. Now the fur on his neck was standing up and his tail was twitching dangerously.

His hiss turned into a low growl.

Angel watched in surprise as Zack and his two friends seemed to shrink away from the cat.

"What do you think you're doing?" Zack Fletcher demanded of her. "You can't bring your stupid cat to school." But there was a tremor in his voice that belied the truculence of his words, and both Chad Jackson and Jared Woods appeared just as nervous as Zack sounded.

"He's not my cat, and I didn't bring him to school. He just came."

"Well, make him go away," Chad Jackson said.

As if understanding Chad's words perfectly, Houdini took a step toward him, bared his teeth, and hissed angrily.

Chad shrank back against the wall.

"It's okay," Angel said, stooping down to soothe the cat. "They're just not as brave as they were last night." She looked up at Jared, who hadn't said a word so far. "What's the matter? Cat got your tongue?"

Jared's face flushed, but his eyes never left Houdini, and now he was edging toward the front door of the school. "I—I gotta go find someone," he mumbled, then slipped through the door before either of his friends could try to stop him.

Zack Fletcher licked his lips nervously and tried once more to sound braver than he was feeling. "You better get him away from here, or I'm gonna tell Mr. Lambert."

Coincidentally, even as he spoke, the door opened and the principal stepped out. "Tell me what, Zack?" Phil Lambert asked. Seeing Houdini, he smiled and crouched down, extending his hand. "Well, who are you?" he asked. "Aren't you a pretty kitty?"

Houdini, relaxing, moved toward the principal, sniffed at his extended hand, then slid under it to get a scratch on the back of his neck.

"You better watch out," Chad Jackson blurted. "He bites."

Phil Lambert took both of Houdini's cheeks in his hands and gently shook his head. "Ooh, is the mean kitty going to bite me?" he asked. When he released him, Houdini rolled over onto his back and batted playfully at the principal's hands, his claws sheathed. After playing with the cat another moment, Phil Lambert straightened up and gave Chad an amused look. "I certainly see what you mean. Never saw a cat as vicious as this one."

Chad's face turned scarlet, and Angel saw his eyes darting around to see how many people were witnessing the principal making fun of him. Then, like Jared before him, he disappeared into the school. Zack followed before the door had even swung closed again.

When they were gone, Mr. Lambert turned back to Angel. "Were they giving you a problem?" he asked.

Angel shook her head.

Phil Lambert tilted his head, as if he knew there was something Angel wasn't telling him. "If they were, you can tell me, you know. It won't go any further, but if anyone's harassing you, I need to know about it."

"I'm okay," Angel said, but couldn't quite bring herself to look the principal in the eye as she uttered the not-quite-truth that wasn't quite a lie.

"Okay," Mr. Lambert sighed. "But if you want to talk to me, you know where my office is, don't you?" As Angel nodded, the principal's gaze shifted to Houdini. "He's yours?"

Angel shook her head, again deciding to tell not quite all of the truth. "I guess he's a stray. I think he lives out by our house somewhere, and he just sort of started following me around."

"Does he have a collar?"

Again Angel shook her head.

Lambert frowned. "Maybe we should call the pound—"

But Angel didn't let him finish. "Don't do that," she cried. "He didn't do anything—he's a really nice cat!"

"Chad and his friends don't seem to think so," the principal observed. "Why would they be afraid of him?"

Because he knows what they did, Angel thought. But

she said nothing aloud and only shrugged in response to the principal's question.

"All right," Mr. Lambert sighed. "Tell you what—I'll pretend I never saw the cat today. But Chad's right about one thing—you can't bring it to school, and if it keeps following you here, I'll have to call the pound. Okay?"

Angel nodded, and when the principal had gone back into the building, she crouched down to stroke Houdini's fur. "You have to go somewhere else," she said softly. "If you stay here—"

But Houdini, again responding as if he understood what she was saying, took off before she'd finished, bounding down the steps and dashing out into the street. Only when he was on the other side did he stop, turn around, sit down under the huge oak tree that stood opposite the school, and wrap his tail around his feet.

Angel looked at him for a few seconds, waved once, then turned away to begin the day at school.

"I hate that cat," Chad Jackson said as he stood with his back to his locker, talking to Zack and Jared while he waited for Seth Baker to show up. "Did you see? It was all set to come at me! Jeez! It coulda killed me!"

"It *did* try to kill me," Zack Fletcher said. "It must have followed me back from the Crossing last night."

Chad's pulse quickened and he forgot all about Seth Baker. "What do you mean, it tried to kill you?"

"I mean, it jumped me. I was almost home, and suddenly it just came at me!"

"Where?" Chad asked.

Zack's eyes narrowed. "What do you mean, where?"

"Like, where'd it go at you?"

"My face," Zack blurted out, remembering only after

he'd spoken the words that there wasn't a mark on him anywhere. "I just barely fought him off before he got me." He looked quizzically at Chad, who had a strange look in his eyes, as if he was frightened. "What's going on?" he asked.

"It—It came after me too," Chad stammered. "At least, I think it did." His eyes flicked from Zack to Jared, both of whom were now staring at him. "I mean—well, I *think* it came after me."

Zack's eyes narrowed. "What do you mean, you think it came after you? Did it or didn't it?"

"I—I think it did," Chad stammered. "It felt like it slashed at my face. I mean, I thought it was gonna rip my eyes out. But when I looked in the mirror . . ." His voice trailed off.

"There wasn't anything, right?" Zack said, his voice hollow.

Chad shook his head. "It was like it hadn't happened at all. Except I know it did."

"That's what happened to me too," Jared Woods said, his voice trembling. Both Chad and Zack turned to look at him. "I thought it was a dream." Slowly, still uncertain whether it had happened, he told his friends what he thought the cat had done to him last night. "But it couldn't have been in my room," he finished. "I mean, it was all locked up, and when my dad came in to see what was wrong—" He cut himself short an instant too late.

"Your dad?" Zack echoed. "You screamed so loud your dad came in?"

"I was asleep!" Jared said. "I mean—"

"So what's the big deal?" Chad asked, glaring at Zack. "So what if he screamed? The only reason my folks didn't hear me was the freakin' cat had me by the throat."

"That's not what I meant," Zack said. "I mean, could

the cat have gotten out of your room when your dad came in?"

Jared shook his head. "The lights were on, and I was right by the door, and so was my dad. It was like it was there one second, and then it was just gone."

The three boys looked at each other for a long moment.

"What are we gonna do?" Jared asked.

"It's simple," Zack said. "She says it's not her cat, so she won't care if something happens to it, right? So let's find out if it's her cat or not."

"You got it?" Zack asked as Jared began working the combination to his locker, which was just two down from Zack's own. When Jared nodded, Zack signaled to Chad Jackson, who slammed the door of his own locker and sauntered over to lounge against the wall across from Zack and Jared. The lunch bell had rung five minutes ago, and on any other day the three of them would have already been inside the cafeteria, first in line. But today they'd taken their time, hanging around in front of their lockers, waiting for the corridor to empty.

"This is gonna be fun," Chad said, his lips twisting into a malicious grin.

"If it works." The uncertainty in Jared Woods's voice only made Chad's grin turn even uglier.

"Why shouldn't it work?"

"How do you even know we can find the stupid cat?" Jared countered.

"We know where Angel is," Zack told him. "So we know where the cat's going to be, right? It's been there all morning. I checked after every class."

"But she says it's not even her cat," Jared reminded Chad and Zack.

Now both of his friends were eyeing him, and Jared knew what they were thinking. "I'm not chickening out," he said. "But what if we get caught?"

Zack rolled his eyes. "If it looks like we're going to get caught, we won't do anything. What do you think I am, stupid?" He glanced up and down the hallway, which was now deserted. Dumping the contents of his backpack into his locker and shutting the door fast enough so nothing fell out, he flattened the backpack and stuck it inside his jacket, pulling the zipper halfway up so he didn't have to hold the pack in place. "Come on."

Leading his friends down the stairs and out the front door of the school, he threaded his way through the knot of nerds who habitually sat on the front steps playing chess while eating their lunches out of the kind of lunch boxes that Zack and his friends had quit carrying in fourth grade. Ignoring them, Zack headed across the lawn to the sidewalk, and then wondered if he might not be wrong.

The black cat was nowhere to be seen.

"I thought you said it was here all morning," Jared Woods said, trying to keep the relief from his voice.

"It was," Zack said, starting across the street toward the spot under the big oak tree on the corner where he'd always seen the cat sitting in the morning.

But now it was gone.

"I don't get it," he said, frowning as he scanned the area around the tree and looked up and down the street. "It's been here the whole morning." As he uttered the words, the hairs on the back of his neck stood on end, and feeling a terrible presentiment of danger, he spun around.

Nothing.

He turned around again, and saw Jared and Chad gazing up into the tree.

Jared was slowly backing away, and though Chad wasn't moving, his face had gone pale.

Zack peered up into the tree too, and found himself looking into the golden-yellow eyes of the coal-black cat, whose lips drew back, baring its teeth.

Zack's heart pounded heavily as he remembered the cat hurtling out of the darkness last night and sinking its claws deep into the flesh of his face. Now, the cat emitted a low hiss, and again Zack felt the agonizing pain that had ripped through him a little more than twelve hours earlier. It was all he could do to keep from backing away the same as Jared had, but somehow he managed to hold his ground.

The cat's tail twitched and it crouched lower, stretching toward him.

"Watch out," Jared said, his voice barely above a whisper. "If he jumps at you—"

"He won't jump at me," Zack said. "He's just as chicken as you are." His eyes still locked on the cat, he pulled the backpack out of his jacket. "That's right, isn't it?" he asked, staring up at the cat. "You're real brave in the dark, but when it's light—"

Reacting to the words as if it understood them, the cat suddenly launched itself at Zack, springing from the branch with its forepaws outstretched, its claws bared, a furious yowl erupting from its throat.

Zack stepped aside at the last second and lashed at the cat with the backpack, catching it in the side and flipping it over.

The cat fell to the ground on its back but rolled over so fast Zack barely even saw it, and an instant later was on its feet again, crouched low, hissing and snarling as it faced him.

"What's the matter, cat?" Zack taunted. "Don't like it?"

He struck out at the cat with the backpack, and the animal lashed at the pack with its forefoot.

Zack jerked the backpack away a moment before the cat's claws could sink into the nylon.

Now Chad joined in, peeling off the nylon jacket he was wearing over his flannel shirt and rolling it up the way he and his friends rolled towels in the locker room to flick at each other after they'd showered. As the cat kept its eyes fastened on Zack, Chad moved around and slashed at its flanks with one of the jacket's sleeves.

Screeching, the cat leaped into the air, whirled around, and came down on all fours, hissing and spitting at Chad with even more fury than it had directed at Zack.

A second later one of the shoulder straps of Zack's backpack came down on its back, and once more it whirled.

"Come on, Jared," Zack said. "Take a lick or two." Jared Woods had moved back another pace, and shook his head silently as his friends kept baiting the cat.

"What's the matter, Woods?" Chad teased. "Afraid he might get into your room again tonight?" As Zack kept baiting the cat with his backpack, Chad snapped his rolled up jacket at Jared, who jerked back as the snap on the jacket's sleeve stung his wrist. "You a pussy too?" Chad taunted.

With the challenge hanging over him, Jared unfastened his belt buckle and pulled it out of the loops in his pants.

As if sensing the new danger, the cat whirled to face Jared, every muscle in its body tensing as it prepared to strike. His nerve fading in the face of the animal's fury, Jared took a step backward.

The cat moved closer to him, the tip of its tail twitching as dangerously as the rattle on the tail of a snake. Behind the cat, Jared could see Zack opening the backpack and edging closer.

Seeing what Zack was doing and understanding what he had in mind, Chad whispered to Jared, "Take another step back. Wave the belt at him."

Taking the backward step was easy—every instinct inside Jared was screaming at him to turn and run before the cat launched itself at him and once again sank its claws into his belly. The cat, sensing Jared's fear, edged closer, its yellow eyes glinting, its tail twitching faster.

Jared froze, too terrified now even to move.

The cat crept closer, a venomous sound coming from its mouth that sounded to Jared even more dangerous than the hiss of a snake about to strike.

The belt fell from his hands.

The cat moved closer yet, its eyes fixed on Jared as if it could see the terror in his soul, and Jared felt a cold sweat break out on his skin. He tried to step back again, but his legs suddenly felt weak.

Then, just as the cat was about to strike, Jared saw a sudden movement behind it.

The cat, sensing the movement, leaped into the air to turn on the threat behind it.

Too late!

Zack dropped the open backpack over the cat while it was still in the air, and dove to the ground, his full weight falling on the backpack as he fumbled for the zippers that would close its flap.

Beneath him he could feel the cat squirming and thrashing, slashing at the heavy nylon with its claws.

He found the zipper and pulled it closed. With the cat still thrashing, and now yowling with rage, Zack scrambled to his feet, grabbed the backpack by the shoulder straps, and swung it hard against the trunk of the oak tree from which the cat had leaped only moments before.

The cat howled.

Zack smashed the backpack against the tree once more, and the cat fell silent. The boy glanced up and down the street. No one across the street, by the steps of the school, seemed to be paying attention, perhaps because the battle with the cat had been shielded from view by the large tree. And except for a woman who was just coming around the corner a block away, the street itself was deserted.

"Come on," Zack said. "Follow me."

With Chad and Jared behind him, he hurried across the street, but instead of heading for the front door of the school where the nerds had finally finished their chess games, he veered off to the side, headed down to the end of the building, and went around the corner. By the time Chad and Jared caught up, he was halfway up the steps that led to the door that opened into the staircase connecting the main floor not only to the second floor, but to the basement as well. Then all three of the boys were in the maze of pipes and ducts that filled the basement of the school, and Zack led the way to a dark corner near the furnace.

"What are we going to do?" Chad asked. "Burn it?"

Zack shook his head. "I've got a better idea. But first we're going to make sure it's dead."

Gripping the shoulder straps of his backpack, he raised it, swung it high over his head, and smashed it down onto the basement's concrete floor.

A grunting sound came from inside the bag, and there was a faint movement. Zack handed the pack to Chad Jackson. "Your turn."

Chad hesitated only a second before hefting the bag as if to test its weight, tightening his grip on the shoulder straps, then swinging it high a couple of times before smashing it to the floor.

From inside the bag there were two more muffled grunts.

Chad tossed the bag to Jared Woods, who let it drop to the floor at his feet. "Now you."

Jared gazed uncertainly down at the bag.

"We said we'd all do it," Zack Fletcher said.

"Y-You didn't say what—"

"Do it," Zack cut in, his voice as hard as his balled right fist. "You want to keep on being our friend, you do it."

Jared scanned the far reaches of the dimly lit basement, half hoping someone might come out and give him an excuse not to pick up the backpack, but he neither saw nor heard anyone.

They were alone.

With no one to save him, Jared bent down and picked up the backpack. He could feel some weak movement inside the bag, but nothing like the violent thrashing of a few moments ago.

He hefted it in unconscious imitation of Chad Jackson.

"Go on, pussy—do it," Zack commanded.

Wincing at the nickname—and knowing Zack would hang it on him forever, just as he'd done to Seth Baker when he'd renamed him "Beth" when they were still just little kids—Jared steeled himself, tried to put down the nausea rising in his stomach, and swung the backpack against the wall.

He told himself he didn't hear the yip of pain from inside the pack.

Told himself he hadn't swung the pack hard enough to really hurt the cat. Not like Zack and Chad had anyway.

Told himself the cat was probably already dead.

Besides, the cat had attacked him last night, hadn't it?

But even as he tried to convince himself, the nausea rose in his stomach again. He dropped the bag at Zack's feet. "I did it, okay?"

His lips curling into a faint sneer, Zack picked up his backpack. "And now you're gonna puke, aren't you?"

Jared shook his head, though he wasn't at all sure Zack was wrong.

"Okay, let's go," Zack said, slinging the pack onto his shoulders as if it still contained nothing more than his schoolbooks.

Staying half a step ahead of Chad and Jared, he led them back to the stairs, then up to the second floor corridor where their lockers were.

Theirs—and Angel Sullivan's.

While Zack kept a careful eye on the empty corridor, Chad began working the combination to Angel's locker.

Chapter 27

THE SUDDEN CHANGE IN THE ATMOSPHERE OF THE cafeteria told Angel that her cousin had finally come in. Yet it wasn't anything she could really put her finger on, it wasn't that the temperature changed, or a cold draft swept through, or even that the hum of conversation changed. No, it was something subtler.

A creepy feeling that made her skin tingle.

A sense of apprehension, as if some unseen threat was lurking close by.

"Here they come," Seth said sourly, glancing toward the food line where Zack, Chad Jackson, and Jared Woods were grabbing whatever food was left as Mrs. Carelli began clearing out the steam table. "Just as I was starting to think we might actually make it through lunch hour without even seeing them."

Angel didn't have to turn around to feel them looking at her, and seeing the puzzled expression on Seth's face, her odd feeling of foreboding grew stronger. "They're doing something, aren't they?"

Seth's brow furrowed. "They keep looking over here—at least Chad Jackson does. And he's got this weird look on his face, like he's trying not to laugh. And every time he starts to lose it, Zack's punching at him."

"What about Jared?"

"He looks like he just puked his brains out. I mean, his face is all pasty and he looks sick."

Her curiosity overcoming her apprehension, Angel turned to get a look at the three boys, all of whom quickly turned away from her.

Her feeling of apprehension deepened. "How come they looked away when I turned around?" she asked.

Seth shrugged. "How should I know? Maybe they're embarrassed that you caught them talking about you."

Angel and Seth stared at each other for a couple of seconds, and then the absurdity of what Seth had said got the better of both of them and they began giggling. "And maybe Chad's going to invite me on a date, and maybe Heather Dunne's going to ask you to the Sadie Hawkins Dance."

"And maybe pigs really can fly!" Seth added. "Okay, so what's going on?"

Angel shrugged. "I don't know. But the weird thing is, I felt something when they first came in. I mean, I didn't even see them, or hear them, or anything, but just before you looked up, I felt something."

"Felt something like what?"

"I don't know," Angel said again. "It's just a weird feeling—like something bad's going to happen."

"That's not weird," Seth said. "That's just reality. It sucks, but what are we supposed to do about it?"

Angel shrugged, and as Zack and his friends threaded their way toward their regular table, they went back to their lunch. "You want to go over to the old churchyard after school and see if we can find a grave for Forbearance Wynton?"

Angel cocked her head. "Why would there be one? If they burned her as a witch, they wouldn't bury her in the churchyard, would they?"

Seth rolled his eyes. "So if we find her grave, we know

they didn't think she was a witch, right? At least we'll know more than we do so far."

"Okay," Angel said. "Unless . . ."

"Unless what?"

Angel glanced at Zack and his friends, who seemed to have forgotten about her. Yet she still had that strange feeling that something was wrong, that something was going to happen. She let out the breath she didn't even know she'd been holding in a long sigh. "Nothing, I guess. I'll meet you after school."

The bell ending lunch hour rang a few minutes later, and as she picked up her backpack, Angel glanced one last time at her cousin.

This time, their eyes met.

And she saw a dark, cruel glint, as if he knew something.

But what?

As his eyes remained fixed on her, and the strange feeling of apprehension gripped her once again, Angel turned away and hurried out of the cafeteria.

The day wore on, and by the time the last bell rang, Angel was beginning to wonder if she'd just been imagining things in the cafeteria. But when she came to the second floor landing and started toward her locker, she knew that she hadn't.

Zack and his friends were clumped around Zack's locker, and though he tried not to be as obvious as he'd been in the cafeteria, Chad Jackson kept glancing at her as she started down the hall toward her own locker.

And she was certain Zack was trying not to laugh.

As she drew closer to her locker, the strange feeling of apprehension grew stronger.

Her locker!

Had they done something to it?

She remembered last year, when someone sprayed paint through the vents of her locker back in Eastbury.

Her step slowed.

Maybe she shouldn't even open it, she thought. The only thing inside was the heavy history book she didn't want to lug around all afternoon, and since Mr. Mc-Dowell hadn't given them homework tonight, she didn't need to take it home.

She glanced back at Zack, Chad, and Jared.

Jared was gone.

But Zack and Chad had been watching her. And they'd done something—she could tell by their postures and expressions, with Chad trying too hard to look innocent.

Making up her mind, she turned away from her locker, hurried back down the stairs, and left the school by the front door. Seth was waiting for her. "I think they did something to my locker," she said as they started down the steps and across the lawn. They walked toward the cemetery behind the Congregational church, and Angel told him how they had stood around, eyeing her as if hiding a secret, when she'd gone to her locker.

"What are you going to do?" Seth asked. "You have to open it sometime."

"I know," Angel said. "I just didn't want to open it with them standing right there. I just didn't—" Her words caught as a lump rose in her throat.

"How about we go back after we look in the cemetery?" Seth said. "They'll be gone by then, and whatever they did, we'll clean it up. Okay?"

Angel nodded, still struggling to control the sob in her throat. Why couldn't they just leave her alone? What had she ever done to them?

And what had they done to her locker?

Ten minutes later they were standing at the gate to the

old cemetery that was all but hidden behind the Congregational church. An enormous tree loomed in the exact center of it. Nearly bare of leaves now, its branches were silhouetted against the sky, its trunk was absolutely straight, and its canopy was almost perfectly round.

Angel stared at it for several long seconds. "How do they keep it looking like that?" she finally asked.

Seth grinned at her. "They don't—it just grows that way. It's supposed to be the tree the town was named for."

"But trees don't grow that way."

"That one does," Seth said. "Come on—the oldest part of the cemetery's over there."

He started toward a far corner of the graveyard, beyond which was a small stone chapel with an abandoned look that made Angel feel almost sorry for it. "What's that?"

"It's supposed to be the first church built when the town was founded. They're always talking about making it into a museum but they never do."

As they drew closer to the old chapel, the shiny granite headstones near the gate gave way to more weathered stones, and when they came to the area directly behind the ancient stone church—which couldn't have seated more than a hundred people, even if they were packed inside—the headstones were so weathered that whatever inscriptions had been chiseled into them were barely legible.

"Let's start here," Seth said, stooping down to try to make out the name on a stone that was leaning at a precarious angle and was missing one corner.

Even the once jagged break had long ago been worn smooth by the centuries of harsh New England weather that had all but eroded it away.

Seth squinted at the inscription. " 'Jabez Conant,' " he read. "Wow! He died in 1672!"

Angel crouched down in front of the next headstone. " 'Abigail Conant,' " she read. " 'Wife of Jabez.' "

"When did she die?"

Angel reached out and brushed some moss away. "It looks like 1661. Or maybe 1667."

They moved on down the row, reading all the inscriptions they could, then started up the next one. Most of the stones were too worn to be completely legible, though, and even most of those they could read were so faint they weren't sure they were reading them right.

Halfway up the third row, they found an area neatly bordered by a rectangle of granite blocks that were about four inches wide and three feet long. In several of them, holes had been bored that showed signs of rust. "I bet there used to be a fence mounted in the stones," Seth said. "But it's so old the whole thing rusted away." Within the rectangular plot bordered by the granite footings, which was about twenty feet long and almost as wide, there were at least two dozen headstones, one of which was much bigger than the others.

Even from the path in front of the plot, both Seth and Angel could read the name engraved on the largest stone: THE REVEREND PERCIVAL WYNTON PARSONS.

"The guy who wrote the book," Seth breathed. "The one about the witches."

Spread around the large headstone were many smaller ones; they found grave markers for the minister's wife, his son, two of his grandsons, and his father, along with the stones marking the graves of the men's wives, and at least a dozen infant children, some of whom had been buried without names.

Three of the women who had married into the Parsons family and were buried in its plot—by far the largest in the cemetery—had been named Wynton.

"I bet there's a Wynton plot too," Seth said when they'd deciphered the inscriptions of as many of the stones as they could.

Five minutes later they found it.

It was near the northern edge of the graveyard, and, like the Parsons plot, was surrounded by granite blocks with the same holes bored in them that might too have once supported a wrought-iron fence.

They searched the headstones, brushing away the moss that covered most of the inscriptions, and were almost ready to give up when they noticed one more stone.

It was set apart from the rest of the grave markers, and as Seth and Angel gazed at it, they both got the eerie feeling that they'd found what they were looking for.

They moved closer, crouched down, and tried to read the inscription. Though the granite was deeply pitted, and whatever decorative carving may once have adorned it had long since eroded away, the name was just readable: JOSIAH WYNTON.

Beneath the name was the date the man had been born and the date he died.

He'd been just a little past forty when he died in 1694.

Beneath the dates were two more lines. Angel and Seth looked at them for a long time, neither of them saying a word.

The first line read: "Husband of Margaret."

The second line read: "Father of Forbearance."

But the space around Josiah Wynton's grave—the space where his wife and daughter would have been buried—was empty.

Indeed, after Josiah, no other person had ever been buried in the plot.

They found the rest of the Wyntons, what few there were, in another plot, on the opposite side of the graveyard.

As they left the graveyard and started back toward the school, neither Angel nor Seth said anything at all.

The steps in front of the school were deserted by the time they got back from the graveyard, and when they went through the front door, the downstairs corridor was empty. They started up the stairs to the second floor, but when they got to the landing where the stairs turned, Angel stopped.

"Maybe we should just go home," she said, the memory of Zack's smirk still fresh in her mind.

Seth shook his head. "You'll just have to open it Monday morning. And you better believe that Zack and Chad and Jared will all be there, waiting to see what happens when you do."

Angel took a deep breath, knowing he was right. Whatever Zack was up to, it was better to face it now, with no one there except Seth. She started up the rest of the stairs.

The second floor corridor was as empty as the first, and as they walked the twenty yards to Angel's locker, their footsteps echoed off its walls with a hollowness that matched the feeling in Angel's belly. When they were finally standing in front of the locker, she stared at the lock for nearly a full minute.

How did they get in?

How did they know the combination?

Maybe they didn't!

Maybe it was nothing—maybe they were just trying to freak her out.

Clinging to that faint hope, she began working the

combination, and a moment later lifted the handle of the locker.

She swung it open.

And saw Houdini lying on top of the thick history text that lay on the floor of her locker.

Except that he wasn't actually lying on it at all.

Rather, his broken body was sprawled across it. He was on his back, his legs splayed out at strange angles, and his eyes, wide open, were staring at her.

Except they weren't staring—their light had faded away, leaving only the cold empty look of death.

Blood was caked around his ears and the corners of his mouth.

Angel stared at Houdini's broken corpse, barely able to believe what she was seeing.

How could they have done it?

What had Houdini ever done to them?

A sob rose in her throat, and Angel tried to choke it back but failed. As a second sob gripped her, followed by a wracking moan, Seth moved around her so he could see inside the locker too.

"Oh, Jeez," he whispered.

Angel turned away from the locker and buried her head on his shoulder. Seth, his eyes fastened on the dead eyes of the cat almost as if he was mesmerized by them, put his arms around her and patted her gently as her sobs began to build. He felt Angel stiffen in his arms a moment before she pulled away from him. Her face was streaked with tears, but she reached into her backpack, found a handkerchief, and wiped them away.

"Let's bury him," she said, her eyes fixed on Seth's.

Seth frowned. He'd buried a hamster when he was six, but now he was fifteen.

As if reading his mind, Angel said, "I'm not talking about holding some kind of dumb funeral for him. I just want to take him somewhere and bury him—somewhere nobody will ever find him. Then I'm going to act like nothing happened at all."

"But tomorrow morning—"

"Zack will be waiting for me to open my locker, just like he was this afternoon," Angel said. "Only there won't be anything in it."

Suddenly Seth understood. "And if you don't let on we found him today—"

Angel glanced into the locker again, and another sob rose in her throat. "Let's just do it, okay?" she asked, her voice trembling as she struggled not to start crying again. "If we talk about it . . ." Her voice trailed off.

Seth could read her emotions from the tremor in her voice and the pain in her eyes. "I'll put him in my backpack," he said.

As Angel struggled to control her roiling emotions, Seth transferred the contents of his backpack to Angel's, and then, placing himself between Angel and the locker, gently lifted Houdini's broken body out and slipped it into the pack.

"Come on," he said softly. "I know exactly the place where no one will ever find him, and I know where we can get a shovel."

They'd paused only once more before leaving the village, when Angel insisted on picking some flowers from one of the gardens in the old cemetery. "It just seems like he should have them," she'd explained. "I mean—" She'd faltered, then shrugged helplessly. "It just seems right, that's all."

The yellow aster and three red chrysanthemums were still clutched in her hand, and Angel thought they might wilt before they got back to the little cabin where she knew Seth was taking them. Indeed, it seemed to her that the path they had set out on almost half an hour ago had completely disappeared, and now nothing around her looked familiar. Seth hadn't slowed down even when the trail disappeared, and even though she'd been able to keep up so far, she was starting to feel out of breath.

"Are you sure we're going the right way?" she finally asked.

To her relief, Seth stopped and turned around. "It's only about five more minutes," he said.

"But nothing looks anything like it did the day before yesterday when we followed—" Her voice choked when she tried to say Houdini's name, and despite her silent vow that she wasn't going to cry, her eyes blurred with tears. She wiped them away with the sleeve of her sweatshirt and sniffled to clear her nose.

"It's okay," Seth said, his brown eyes reflecting the pain she was feeling almost as if he were feeling it himself. "Nobody's around except me. If you want to cry—"

"I don't want to cry," Angel interrupted, a little too quickly. "I just asked if you were sure you know where we are."

"I'm sure," Seth insisted. "I've been coming out here forever, and I've never gotten lost yet." He pointed off toward what Angel was pretty sure was the east. "The bluff's over that way—in a couple more minutes you'll be able to see it." He turned away and started walking again, either following a trail Angel couldn't see or knowing his way so well he didn't need any path at all. Taking a deep breath, she followed, silently counting the passing seconds just to see if he was telling her the truth.

She'd counted the 110th second when suddenly, through the trees ahead, the face of the bluff appeared. Seth turned back to her, grinning. "See? Here we are." He pointed off to the right. "The cabin's down that way."

A few minutes later they climbed over the berm of rubble that hid the cabin from anyone who might happen to run across the small clearing between it and the forest, and Angel gazed down at the strange structure that was so well hidden in the face of the bluff that it was still almost invisible.

"I still can't believe no one knows it's here but us," she said.

"We wouldn't know if Houdini hadn't showed it to us." Seth clambered down the steep face of the berm, leaned the rusty shovel they'd taken from his mother's potting shed against the door of the cabin, and swung his backpack off his shoulders, setting it gently on the ground.

They took turns digging a grave for the cat, making it deep enough so no wild animal would be tempted to dig the creature's corpse up and eat it, and when they were finally satisfied, Seth gently laid Houdini on the grave's bottom. Then Angel knelt down and carefully laid the three red chrysanthemums on the cat's body, their stems together so they formed a bouquet. She added a thin layer of earth over the chrysanthemums, then laid the yellow aster so its bloom was resting on Houdini's head. "So you'll always have a patch of sunlight," she whispered. Picking up the shovel, she quickly began filling the hole in, tamping down the dirt as best she could. When she was finished, there was still a mound of leftover earth, and she used the shovel to spread it around, mixing it with the fallen leaves and shattered rock that covered the rest of the thin strip of earth between the base of the berm and the wall of the cabin. By the time she was finished, the spot where Houdini was buried looked no different than anyplace else.

Seth hefted a large slab of loose granite from the berm and set it above the grave. "Nobody but us would ever even notice it," he said. "But at least we'll know where he is."

Angel's eyes met his. "And we don't say anything to anybody."

Seth nodded.

Angel's eyes shifted to the cabin. "You want to try something?"

Her tone made Seth's pulse quicken. "What?"

Angel licked nervously at her lower lip. "I was thinking—what if we tried out one of the recipes, and something really happened?"

Seth looked at her uncertainly. "Like what?" he asked, his voice reflecting the uneasiness he was feeling.

Angel shrugged. "I don't know." She hesitated, then: "But wouldn't it be neat if we could actually do something to Zack and his friends?"

The beginnings of a grin played around the corners of Seth's mouth. "You mean like a hex, or a curse, or something?"

"What are you laughing about?" Angel challenged. "Last night you were the one who was talking about how many people believe in stuff like that."

Seth's grin faded as he gazed at Angel. "All right," he said after several seconds had gone by and the challenge in her eyes didn't fade. "Let's try it."

They went into the tiny chamber, leaving the door open. Seth lifted the rough wooden bar that held the single shutter covering the window closed, and swung it open. As light and air flooded through the opening, they looked around.

Nothing had changed, yet somehow the little room felt different to Angel.

It felt oddly empty, as if something were missing.

Yet as she gazed around, everything appeared to be exactly as it had been when they first found the cabin.

The kettle still hung from the pothook in the fireplace. A thick layer of dust still covered everything.

And yet . . .

Then she knew. It was Houdini that was missing. Once again she had to struggle against the tears that threatened to overwhelm her, and when she spoke, her voice caught on the terrible lump that had risen in her throat.

"I hope it is real," she said, crouching down to pull the loose stone from the fireplace and reaching deep into the recess behind it. Taking the book from its hiding place, she stood up and moved to the counter that ran along the longest wall. "I hope—" she began as she set the book down, but her words died on her lips as the book fell open and she saw the single word at the top of the page:

 rief

Beneath the single word were two brief verses:

ix lover's blood
Drawn by knife
Symmer long
To bring back life.

' bit of earth
From loved's grave
The blur of grief
Will help to save.

Angel and Seth read the two verses over and over again. Finally, Seth asked, "How come it opened to this one?"

"Houdini," Angel breathed, her voice breaking as the memory of the cat's body lying broken and twisted at the bottom of the grave rose up in her mind. "I just— I can't—" At last the tears she'd been struggling to control since they'd opened her locker overflowed, and a wracking sob seized her. "Why did they do it?" she cried. "Why—" Another sob choked off her words, but the little she'd said was enough for Seth to understand exactly how much pain she was feeling.

"Let's try it," he said. "Let's see if we can figure out what we're supposed to do."

Angel struggled against yet another sob, forced it down, and again wiped her tears away with her sleeve. Her eyes focused on the first line. " 'Lover's blood . . .' " she whispered, then looked at Seth. "What does it mean?"

"I think it has to mean your blood," he replied, his voice barely louder than hers. "I mean, you loved Houdini, right?" Angel nodded, and Seth went outside, picked up his backpack, and brought it in. He fished around in the front pocket of the pack and produced a small Swiss Army knife. "Think you can do it?"

"H-How much do you think it means?" Angel stammered, staring at the knife but making no move to take it from Seth.

"It doesn't say."

"It has to," Angel said. "Recipes always tell you how much you need." Wiping the last vestiges of her tears away, she turned back to the book, but this time opened it at the front. The first page bore nothing but the title.

The second page listed all the recipes the book contained.

On the third page there was a poem that bore no title:

> Symmer all; in kettle boil
> Fresh spring water, never oil
> Each and ev'ry other thing
> In weest trace will majyk bring.

She read the verse twice more, then gave the book to Seth. "It looks like all we need is a drop."

Seth read the verse through, then turned the pages until the book was once more open to the recipe. "Put some water in the kettle while I build a fire."

While Seth began stacking kindling and wood on the hearth, Angel took the large iron kettle off the pothook and dipped it into the deep stone basin that was still full of crystal clear water, the steady dripping from the roof seemingly unchanged since the last time they were here. It took only about a quarter of the contents of the basin to make the kettle half full.

"What if someone sees the smoke?" Angel asked as Seth struck a match and held it to the kindling. The bone-dry wood ignited in an instant, flames leaping from one piece to another until the whole pile was ablaze. It took only a few seconds. As if to answer Angel's question, there was a flash of brilliant white light and a clap of thunder so loud the floor trembled beneath their feet.

A second later a pounding rain began to fall.

"Nobody will see anything through this," Seth said, staring out at the downpour that had materialized so suddenly.

"How are we even going to get home?" Angel asked.

"Maybe it'll quit as fast as it started." Seth hung the kettle back on the pothook and was about to swing it over the fire when Angel stopped him.

"I have to put the blood in." Picking up Seth's pocketknife, she moved close to the kettle, opened one of the blades, and held it against the forefinger of her right hand. Biting her lower lip so hard it hurt, she steeled her nerves, then jabbed the point of the knife into her finger. Handing the knife to Seth, she held her wounded forefinger over the kettle and squeezed it hard.

Two or three drops of blood fell into the water and instantly vanished.

"Do you think it's enough?" she asked, watching as the water seemed to swallow up her blood without a trace.

Seth shrugged. "How should I know?" His gaze shifted to the open door and the downpour outside. "Think you have to get the dirt from Houdini's grave, or can I?"

Angel's brows knit. "I probably better." She moved to the door and peered out. The sky—crystal clear when they'd arrived only a little while ago—was leaden now, and the clouds seemed to be getting darker even as she watched. Certain that the rain was only going to get worse, she darted out the door, snatched up a pinch of muck from the spot marked by the stone Seth had laid over Houdini's grave, and ducked back inside.

Surprisingly, though it was pouring outside, she'd barely gotten wet.

She went back to the kettle and dipped her fingers in. The fire was blazing under it, and the water had already turned warm. Rinsing her fingers clean of the dirt from Houdini's grave, she wiped them dry on her sweatpants and looked at Seth, who was once more studying the book. "Now what do we do?"

"Let it boil, I guess. But what about this other thing? What's 'blur of grief'?"

Angel figured it out immediately. "My tears," she breathed. "Every time I think about Houdini, I get all—" Her voice broke once again, and almost as if in response to her words, her eyes blurred with tears. She moved quickly back to the kettle, swung it out of the fireplace, leaned over it, and thought once more of what her cousin had done to her pet.

Half a dozen tears dripped into the kettle.

Angel swung it back over the fire.

"That's all it says," Seth said softly. "Now we wait."

Chapter 28

HE FLASH OF LIGHTNING, AND THE CRASH OF THUN-der that seemed to come at the same instant, made Marty Sullivan flinch so badly he dropped the pneumatic hammer he'd been using, which smashed down onto Ritchie Henderson's toe.

Henderson jerked his injured foot out from under the heavy tool, bellowing with pain. "Jesus! What the hell—" But the rest of his words were lost as the sky seemed to open and a torrent of rain began pouring out of the roiling clouds overhead.

Holding his arms up in a futile effort to fend off the sudden downpour, Marty loped toward the site office, a slapped-together shed that was more of a lean-to than anything else. With most of its floor space already taken up by the wide counter covered with architectural plans for the project, there was barely enough space for Jack Varney himself, let alone all the men who worked for him. *First come, first served,* Marty thought as he ducked under the structure's steeply sloping roof.

"Where the hell'd this come from?" Varney asked, gazing up at the sky as Marty tried to shake off some of the water that had already soaked through his shirt and jeans. "Am I nuts, or was it clear as a bell five minutes ago?"

Before Marty could respond, Ritchie Henderson hobbled into the crowded shelter. "What the hell goes with you, Sullivan?" he snarled, glowering at Marty with unconcealed fury. "First you drop the hammer on my foot, then you don't even stick around to see if I'm okay."

"You got here, didn't you?" Marty shot back. "So I guess you're not hurt too bad."

Jack Varney gazed out into the downpour. "The pneumatic hammer?" he asked.

Ritchie Henderson nodded. "Lightning made him jump so bad it fell right out of his hand."

"I coulda been killed!" Marty howled. "What'd you expect me to do?"

"I expect you to take care of the tools you use," Varney interjected before Henderson could say anything. "Where is it now?"

"How the hell should I know?" Marty growled.

"You were using it—you're responsible for it," Varney replied, deciding to ignore the contempt in Sullivan's voice. "What did you think—Ritchie would bring it in for you?"

"It's fuckin' pouring out there—" Marty began.

"Then you better get that hammer now," Varney snapped, his eyes narrowing angrily. "It starts rusting out there, I'll take it out of your paycheck."

"You can't do that," Marty complained.

"The hell I can't," the foreman growled. "If you don't like it, talk to Ed Fletcher." His eyes bored into Marty, who stood his ground for only a few seconds before breaking.

"Maybe I'll just do that," Marty groused, but the truculence in his voice was tinged with enough of a whine that Varney knew he wouldn't.

With the rain still pouring down, Marty left the shelter of the lean-to and slogged out toward the spot where he and Henderson had been working when the storm suddenly broke. The rain was coming down so hard that puddles had formed all over the site. They were fast merging together, turning the whole area into a muddy pond. Twice, he nearly sprawled out into the mud, but finally he found the pneumatic hammer, disconnected it from the air hose, and was about to start back toward the lean-to when another bolt of lightning struck, instantly followed by a thunderclap even louder than the first. This time, though, Marty was prepared for it, and ducking his head low into the rain, he began running back to the shed.

He was still a dozen yards away when he lost his footing and sprawled face forward into the mud. Swearing under his breath, he pulled himself to his feet and lurched the last few yards to the lean-to, where Jack Varney and Ritchie Henderson weren't even trying to conceal their laughter.

"Here's your damn hammer," Marty rasped, his fury building. "And guess what? I'm through for the day!"

"We all are," Varney replied, taking the pneumatic hammer. He wiped it off with a rag and laid it on the counter where the plans were spread out. "No way we can get anything more done today, even if this quits. See you Monday."

Too soaked and muddy even to stop for a drink somewhere, Marty got into his old Chevelle, started the engine, and cursed when the windshield wipers refused to work. Jamming the car into gear, he slammed his foot on the accelerator and watched with grim satisfaction as the rear wheels spewed enough mud that neither Henderson nor Varney could avoid it. *Serves 'em right,* he thought as he sped away into the storm.

The only stop he did make on the way home was to

buy a couple of six-packs, and by the time he got home he'd already consumed one of them.

"Angel?" he called out as he lurched through the front door. "You here?" When there was no answer, he went through the house to the kitchen, peeled off his muddy clothes and left them in a pile in the corner, then cracked open another beer. Wearing nothing but his underpants, he flopped down onto his favorite chair and stared moodily out at the raging storm. Where the hell was Angel? She should have been home by now. But even as the question came into his mind, Marty Sullivan knew the answer.

She was with that kid again.

And if he caught them, this time there'd be hell to pay.

Myra Sullivan had instinctively crossed herself and uttered a silent prayer to the Blessed Mother when the first bolt of lightning had struck, and repeated the prayer as the thunderclap rattled the windows of the church.

"Merciful heavens," she breathed as Father Mike came through the door that led to the tiny sacristy a few minutes later. "It felt like the lightning was so close it might have hit the steeple!"

Father Mike smiled wryly. "I like to think that if God is going to strike us with lightning, He'll at least have the good sense to strike down the heretics across the street." When Myra Sullivan showed no sign of understanding that he was making a joke, his smile faded. "Actually, it probably hit the tree in their cemetery," he said. "There used to be a legend that every time that tree was struck by lightning, it meant someone in town was practicing witchcraft."

Myra's eyes widened. "Surely no one believes such a thing!"

"I don't, and I suspect no one else does either. In fact, you'd better hope no one does."

"Me?" Myra asked. "What are you talking about?"

"You remember the storm that hit on Saturday morning?" he asked. "The day your family arrived?"

"We were just starting to unload the truck," Myra said, shuddering at the memory. "It could have ruined everything we own."

"Well, at least one bolt of lightning hit the tree in the cemetery across the street. And with you moving into the old place out at the Crossing . . ." He let his words trail off, shrugging.

"What are you talking about?" Myra asked.

"I'm sure it's nothing," the priest said. "Just all the old stories." The look of incomprehension in Myra's eyes made him cock his head slightly. "Didn't your sister tell you about the stories?"

Myra frowned. "She told me about the last people that lived there," she said.

Father Mike's brows lifted a fraction of an inch. "There are legends that the two women who were accused of being witches here in Roundtree were burned under that tree, and from what I'm told, at least three people swore they saw the tree being struck by lightning at the same time that the women were casting spells."

Myra's expression darkened. "I don't believe in witchcraft."

"Nor do I," the priest agreed. "And I doubt there's a single person in town who does. But four hundred years ago they believed it enough to burn two women."

"Surely it's only a story," Myra breathed.

"If it is, it's pretty well documented—at least the burning part." When Myra still looked doubtful, he led her toward the front door of the church, opening it just wide enough so they could peer at the storm raging outside. "It's that tree over there," he said, pointing to the barely visible form of an enormous tree that stood in the far reaches of the cemetery behind the Congregational church. "See the little stone building near the tree? That's the original church. In fact, the women who were burned as witches were apparently relatives of the minister. His brother's wife and daughter, I believe, or maybe his uncle's. At any rate, the story is that they dragged them in from—"

He stopped abruptly, and Myra could tell by the look on his face that there was something he'd been about to say that he changed his mind about. "From where, Father?" she asked.

Father Mike Mulroney hesitated a moment, then decided there was no point in not finishing the story. It was, after all, just a story; whatever crimes the two women may have committed four centuries earlier, they certainly had nothing to do with witchcraft, no matter what people at the time might have thought. "Actually, they lived in your house," he said. Seeing the shock in Myra's eyes, he suddenly wished he hadn't said anything at all.

Then, as Myra turned to gaze at the tree once more, a brilliant flash of light crossed the sky, and a jagged bolt of lightning, crackling and making the air smell of ozone, lashed down from the thunderheads above, struck the topmost branches of the great tree in the cemetery, and vanished in a thunderclap that shook the building.

"Saints preserve us," Myra breathed.

Father Mike nodded absently, but his eyes stayed on the tree.

Just like last week, the lightning had struck the middle of the tree, and he assumed it must have passed all the way down through its trunk to reach the ground.

Last week, after the storm had passed, he had walked across the street to have a look at the tree.

And he'd seen nothing. The tree showed no signs of damage at all.

No burns on its bark.

No broken limbs.

Nothing.

Later this afternoon, he decided, when this storm had also blown on through, he would go across the street again, just to make sure. But even from here he could see that once again the tree had been struck by lightning and nothing had happened to it.

Nothing at all.

Chapter 29

ANGEL AND SETH HAD NO IDEA HOW LONG THEY SAT cross-legged on the floor staring at the fire that burned steadily under the kettle hanging from the pot-hook. After the first two bolts of lightning faded away and their accompanying thunderclaps rolled into silence, the steady beat of rain outside and the flickering flames on the hearth had taken on an oddly hypnotic quality, so that when the rain suddenly stopped and the fire flickered abruptly out, neither of them was quite certain what had happened. For a moment they didn't move.

Was it possible that the fire had gone out at the exact moment the rain stopped?

Finally, Seth unfolded his legs, realized how sore they were as he stood up, and looked at his watch. His eyes widened and he glanced at Angel. "How long do you think we've been sitting here?"

Angel cocked her head, frowning. "I don't know—ten or fifteen minutes, I guess."

"Try an hour and a half," he said.

Now Angel scrambled to her feet, and the stiffness in her legs was enough to tell her that Seth was right. "What time is it?" she breathed.

"Five-thirty," Seth replied. He went to the fireplace

and knelt down. The fire under the kettle was completely out—not even the red glow of smoldering embers showed beneath the gray ash that was the only sign the fire had been there at all.

When he held his hand out, he felt no warmth. "It's like it's been out for days," he said, his voice faintly hollow.

He reached out and touched the kettle.

It, at least, was still warm, but not so hot that his reflexes jerked his hand away. Gingerly, he reached for the rod from which the pot hung.

It wasn't even warm. He pulled on the rod, swinging the kettle out of the fireplace.

Now Angel was next to him, and for a long moment they gazed into the kettle. All that was left of its contents was an inch of fluid at the bottom of the huge soup pot. "But it was almost half full," Angel said. "How could that much of it have boiled away?"

Both of them swung around to look at the stone sink from which Angel had filled the kettle, but there was no longer any way of telling how much water she'd taken from it, for the basin was filled to the brim and a steady stream of water was flowing in through the wooden trough mounted high in the wall. The overflow was running out through the second trough below. As they watched, the inflow quickly slowed to a trickle, and then the trickle turned into the same rhythmic drip as when they first discovered the cabin.

Except they hadn't discovered the cabin—Houdini had led them to it.

"I don't get it," Seth said. "If that much water boiled away, how come the fireplace isn't even hot anymore, and the kettle's cool enough so you can touch it?"

Instead of answering Seth's question, Angel asked one of her own. "What are we supposed to do with it?" she asked, her eyes fixed on the small pool of liquid that covered the bottom of the kettle.

"I guess you're supposed to drink it," Seth said. When Angel paled, he added, "Well, what else would you do?"

"Would you drink it?" Angel challenged.

The words hung in the air as Seth too gazed into the depths of the kettle. When he finally answered her, his words sounded far braver than the tone of his voice. "Sure! I mean, why not? Practically all that's in it is water, and I already drank the water from the sink."

"And there's blood, and dirt from outside," Angel reminded him.

Seth chewed his lower lip for a moment, then shrugged. "I'd still drink it."

Angel looked at him. "I dare you," she said.

Once again her words hung in the air, and she could see Seth trying to make up his mind. He shrugged again, but this time with such an elaborate show of bravado that Angel knew he was a lot more frightened than he was willing to admit. "Okay," he said. "I will if you will." He went to the counter next to the huge stone sink and took one of the ladles from a hook. Reaching deep into the kettle, he dipped it into the liquid at the bottom, scooping up as much as the ladle would hold.

When he lifted it out again, it was still only half full.

He and Angel stared at it for several long seconds, but even in the ladle it looked no more dangerous than a ladle of water.

There was no hint of color.

No strange odor.

Holding the ladle between them, Seth looked into Angel's eyes. "If I try it, you'll try it?" he asked, and this time Angel had the feeling that if she so much as nodded, he'd drink from the ladle.

And then she would have to do it too.

The seconds ticked by until a full minute had passed. And then, almost against her own volition, Angel nodded and a single whispered word escaped her lips:

"Yes."

Seth's hand trembled as he lifted the ladle to his lips. He took a deep breath, tipped the ladle, and sucked half its contents into his mouth.

And tasted absolutely nothing.

It was as if he'd filled his mouth with the purest rainwater.

He swallowed the broth, then offered the ladle to Angel.

"Wh-What did it taste like?" she whispered, making no move to take the wooden dipper from him.

A sly grin came over Seth's face. "Why should I tell you?" he said. "You promised to try it if I did, didn't you?"

For a fraction of a second Angel was tempted to renege on her promise, but she put the impulse aside almost the moment it came over her. Reaching out, she took the ladle from him, took a deep breath in unconscious imitation of him, then held the dipper to her lips, tipped it back, and drained it into her mouth.

Water!

It was nothing but water!

It felt faintly warm in her mouth, but that was all.

She swallowed, and the water went down her throat.

Now the warmness she'd felt spread through her, but there was nothing unpleasant about the sensation.

"It's warm," she breathed.

Seth looked at her blankly. "What do you mean, it's warm? It's just water."

Angel nodded. "I know. But it feels warm—I can feel it spreading out into my arms and legs! Don't you feel it?"

Seth slowly shook his head, his eyes never leaving Angel. Was she getting sick? But if she was, she didn't look sick. In fact, she looked better than she had since they'd opened her locker and found Houdini. Then it dawned on him: Grief! That's what the recipe was called! That's what it was for! "How do you feel?" he asked, his voice now edged with excitement.

"Fine!" Angel said. "I told you—"

Seth didn't let her finish. "I mean, how do you feel about Houdini?"

Angel looked at Seth in utter incomprehension for a few seconds. How did she feel about Houdini? She felt terrible about—

And then, in the midst of the thought, she realized it wasn't true.

She didn't feel terrible about him at all.

The hard knot of grief that had almost choked her only an hour or so ago was completely gone! She missed him, but thinking about him didn't hurt anymore, and when she visualized him in her mind, the only image she got was of him bounding out of her closet the day they'd moved into the house at Black Creek Crossing. When she tried to conjure up a memory of his body the way it had been when she found it in her locker this afternoon, she couldn't. She could remember finding him, but couldn't visualize what he had looked like. It was as if her memory had been wiped clean of that terrible image.

"I'm all right," she breathed. "I miss him, but it's okay. It—" She hesitated, searching for the right word. "It doesn't hurt anymore," she finally said.

"Wow," Seth whispered. "It worked. It really worked!"

Angel gazed at him. "But it was only water," she whispered.

"Water, and your blood, and earth from his grave, and your tears," Seth reminded her. "That's why nothing happened to me at all—it wasn't about me! It was about you, and it worked!"

As his words sank in, Angel's eyes went to the book that was still open on the counter. Was it possible?

Could it be possible?

"Let's go home," she whispered as she gazed at the worn volume. "Let's just put it back in the chimney and go home, okay?"

A few minutes later they stepped out into the fading daylight of the late afternoon. The last vestiges of the storm were gone, and the sky above was dark blue. As they started to climb the berm, Angel paused and looked at the rock beneath which lay the remains of the only pet she'd ever had.

"I wish you were still alive," she whispered. "If you were, I wouldn't ever let a bad thing happen to you again." She turned away and began clambering up the heap of rubble that hid the facade of the cabin from the clearing in the forest.

Had she stayed, she might have seen the ground beneath the stone marking Houdini's grave sink lower into the ground. . . .

Marty Sullivan pulled the first bottle out of the second six-pack, twisted the cap off, and tossed it in the general direction of the wastebasket. It missed the plastic container by a foot, bounced off the wall, fell to the floor, and wound up lying upside down in front of the sink. Marty stared at it dolefully for a moment, then left it where it was and headed back to the living room and the comfort of his favorite chair. Half an hour ago the storm that closed down the worksite had vanished as suddenly as it had appeared. If he hadn't known it was impossible, he'd have sworn the rain had been pouring down out of coal-black clouds one second, and the sky was clear the next.

More likely he'd just dozed off for a few minutes.

Now, as he glanced blearily out the front window trying to figure out how a storm that bad could have vanished that fast, a movement caught his eye, but it wasn't until he moved closer to the window and pulled the sheer curtain aside that he saw what it was.

Angel.

Angel, and that little putz he'd caught her with the other day.

The putz he'd told her to stay away from.

And they weren't coming from the direction of the village either.

What the hell was going on?

He started toward the front door, his anger growing with every step. But just before he pulled it open, he had a better idea. Better to just wait until they came in. Settling himself into his chair, he raised the beer bottle to his lips and drained half of it in a single long gulp.

A minute or two later he heard the front door open, and then Angel came in. "Where the hell've you been?" he growled, his eyes fixed malevolently on her.

Hearing her father's voice, Angel knew he'd been drinking, and when she saw the half-dozen empty beer bottles that were scattered around the chair he was sprawled in—and the full bottle in his hand—she knew she'd better be careful about what she said.

But before she could speak at all, her father's bloodshot eyes fixed on her and he said, "You were with that kid."

Her eyes flicked toward the window. Her father's back was to it, but if he'd been getting another beer when she and Seth had come out of the woods . . .

Better not try to deny it.

"W-We were out hiking," she stammered.

Her father's eyes narrowed to slits. "Ever since school let out?"

Angel nodded, and instantly wished she hadn't. But it was already too late—her skin began to crawl as she felt her father's eyes moving over her. "Don't lie to me," he said, shifting his weight in the chair. "If you'd been out in that downpour, you'd be soaked."

"I—I am wet," she said. "I better go up and change." Before he could say anything else, she hurried out of the room and up the stairs.

Liar, Marty thought. *That's what she is—a lying little slut.* He drained the rest of his beer, lurched to his feet, and headed back to the kitchen. The next beer cap wound up only a couple of feet from the last one, only this time in front of the refrigerator instead of the sink. Pouring half the newest bottle down his throat as quickly as he'd drained the last one, Marty headed for the stairs.

Wet, huh? She hadn't looked wet to him, and if she'd really been where she said she was, she'd be a lot more than just wet. She'd have come in dripping, with her hair plastered down, and that ugly sweatshirt she was always wearing would've been clinging to her body.

So she hadn't been out hiking.

She'd been out doing something else.

And he knew damned well what it was.

He started up the stairs, but his foot caught on the first step. Swearing loudly as he lost his balance and lurched forward, he threw out his hands to catch himself. The half-full bottle of beer struck the wall, clattered onto the stairs, rolled down a couple of steps, then came to rest on its side, the last of its contents draining onto the step below. Cursing again, Marty picked up the bottle, drained the last few drops from it, and tossed it down to the floor below. He started to take another step, swaying as the beer he'd been pouring down his throat for the last two hours tightened its grip on his brain. This time, though, his hand closed on the banister and he caught himself before he sprawled out on the stairs. Muttering darkly, he continued on up the stairs, but when he came to the point where his head was level with the upstairs landing, he suddenly stopped.

A cat!

A black cat with a small white mark in the center of its chest was sitting on the landing above him, looking down at him.

Marty hated cats. He'd always hated them, even when he was little. He could still remember the time when he was only three or four—before he'd even gone to kindergarten—when his father had brought home a kitten. When Marty had first seen the shoe box punched full of holes his father was holding, he'd been sure it was the puppy he'd been begging for. But when his father set the box on the floor and let him open it, all he found was a kitten.

A stupid kitten!

His first impulse was to pick it up and throw it against the wall, and as he'd reached for it, the animal seemed to sense what he was about to do and lashed out at him with its tiny paw. The miniature claws, already needle sharp, slashed deep into the skin of his hand, and he screamed in pain.

The kitten had been given away that very afternoon, but ever since, Marty Sullivan had hated cats.

And been terrified of them.

And now there was one in his house, sitting on the upper landing, staring down at him. He froze, his eyes fixed on the cat, and a dim memory rose out of his alcohol-clouded subconscious. A memory of a dream.

A dream in which a cat had leaped out of the darkness, scratching his face.

He couldn't remember much else about the dream, just that he'd been in the dark and a voice had been whispering to him, telling him what to do, and then he'd heard a cat hissing at him. Hissing at him, and then leaping out of the darkness, slashing at him!

Marty's hand rose to his face, and his fingers touched the scabs over the not quite healed cuts he'd thought he must have accidentally inflicted on himself while he'd been shaving the other morning. But maybe he hadn't cut himself.

Maybe it hadn't been a dream.

Maybe the cat had gotten into the house the other night and come after him.

He gazed up at it malevolently, and as if sensing his hatred—and his fear—the cat rose to its feet and its back arched.

It bared its teeth and a low hissing sound came from its throat.

The same hissing Marty had heard in his dream.

The cat's eyes began to glow with a light that seemed to come from within, and its gaze held Marty in an almost hypnotic thrall.

As he stood frozen on the staircase, the cat edged closer to the lip of the landing and its muscles tensed.

Marty's heart began to pound and he felt a cold sweat break out over his body.

It was going to kill him.

The cat, which couldn't weigh more than ten or fifteen pounds, was going to kill him!

And he couldn't move!

It was as if every muscle in his body had gone rigid, and no matter how hard he tried, he couldn't force himself to turn around, or even back away.

He tried to swallow, but his throat was too constricted, and now he realized he wasn't even breathing.

And the cat was gathering itself for the attack, its claws already extended, its jaw yawning wide, exposing all its teeth.

Then, just as it was about to launch itself at his throat, there was the slam of a door and a voice.

"Marty? Angel?"

The sound of Myra's voice jerked Marty out of the strange trance the cat had induced, and he spun around, almost lost his balance again, and grabbed at the rail. A second later Myra appeared at the foot of the stairs. Her eyes were hard and she held an empty beer bottle in her hand.

"How many?" she demanded, raising the bottle toward him so there was no mistaking her meaning.

"A—A couple," Marty stammered.

"A couple six-packs," Myra replied. "And if you think I'm cleaning up your mess, you're wrong." Then, seeing the ashen color of her husband's complexion, her tone softened. "Are you all right?"

"A cat," Marty said. "There's a cat up here."

Myra frowned. "What are you talking about?"

"A damned cat!" Marty said, his courage returning now that Myra's voice had softened. "It was gonna come at me!"

Myra's lips pursed. "Oh, really, Marty—"

"You don't believe me?" Marty asked, his voice taking on a hint of a whine. "It's up here right now!"

Myra started up the stairs. "Why would there be a cat up there?"

"How should I know?" Marty countered truculently. "Maybe you left a window open, or Angel—"

"I don't leave windows open, and neither does Angel," Myra cut in. Passing Marty, she came to the upper landing and looked around. "And if there's a cat here, I don't see it!"

Marty climbed the rest of the stairs, searching for the cat.

There was no sign of it.

The door to the bedroom he and Myra shared was closed, as was Angel's, and the one leading to the back bedroom.

Only the bathroom door stood open, and Marty, emboldened by his wife's presence, went to it. There was no more sign of the cat in the bathroom than there was anywhere else. "I'm telling you, it was here," he said, his voice rising. "Just a second ago, when you came in!"

Then the door to Angel's room opened and she came out, wrapped in her bathrobe. "What's going on?" she asked.

"Your father seems to think there's a cat in the house," Myra said, her tone reflecting her doubt about what Marty claimed to have seen.

"It was black!" Marty growled. "With a white mark on its chest. And it was going to attack me. If your mom hadn't come in—" He fell silent as Angel's face turned ghostly white. "What's going on?" he asked. "Did *you* bring a cat in here?"

"No!" Angel cried. "I just—"

Her father pushed past her into her room. The window was closed and so was the closet. Marty pulled open the closet door, searched every corner and shelf, then looked under Angel's bed and behind the chest.

"It was here," he said, his voice dropping to a sullen growl. "I saw it."

"After as many beers as you drank, I'm surprised you didn't see a herd of pink elephants in the living room," Myra snapped. "Now, if I were you, I'd get some clothes on and get downstairs and clean up your mess."

Knowing better than to argue, Marty did exactly as Myra had ordered.

When her parents were gone, Angel went back into her room and closed the door, her father's words echoing in her head. . . . *black* . . . *with a white mark on its chest* . . .

But it wasn't possible!

It *couldn't* be. . . .

Chapter 30

Do you believe that?" Heather Dunne said, nudg-ing Sarah Harmon and whispering softly enough so only she could hear her. "What's *she* doing here?"

They were in their favorite store—Meryl's, Of Course—and Heather had tried on at least a dozen sweaters but wasn't even close to finding one she wanted to buy. Now, with a blue cashmere cardigan over her arm that Sarah Harmon was sure was going to be the eventual winner of this round of what she always thought of as "Heather's Shopping Derby," Heather tipped her head toward a rack in the far corner. When Sarah followed her gaze, she knew right away who Heather was talking about: Angel Sullivan was going through the rack with a tall, thin woman whom Sarah was certain had to be her mother, given what her own mother had told her after she'd had lunch the other day with Zack's mother and aunt. "Myra Sullivan's nothing like Joni Fletcher at all," her mother had said. "She's scrawny and mousy and has no sense of humor, and I think she's some kind of religious fanatic." Then her mother had brightened, adding, "Well, at least if Joni and Ed put them up for the club, we can blackball them!"

"Shouldn't she be going to that fat girl's shop at the outlet mall?" Heather asked, pulling Sarah out of her reverie. "How's she think she's going to fit into anything here?"

As they watched, the woman with Angel pulled a pink dress off the rack, one with a full skirt and lots of frills around the bodice. Heather had been laughing about it only half an hour ago. Angel took the pink dress and headed for the dressing room.

"Do you believe she's looking at *party* dresses?" Heather whispered. "Who'd invite *her* to—" Then the light dawned and she stared at Sarah. "I bet she's going to the country club tonight," she breathed.

Sarah rolled her eyes. "You've got to be kidding!"

"Where else would she wear that dress?" Heather asked.

"Nobody else would wear it at all!" Sarah said.

But Heather was no longer listening. Instead, her eyes were following Angel as she disappeared through the curtains that hung at the door to the dressing room area, and Sarah Harmon could tell just by the look on Heather's face that an idea was forming in her head. A moment later Heather turned back to Sarah, and her voice dropped to a whisper. "Here's what we're going to do . . ." she said.

Sarah listened as Heather laid out her plan, and less than a minute after Angel had walked through the curtains, they did too.

Only one of the three dressing rooms was occupied. Holding a finger to her lips, Heather led Sarah into the one next to Angel's.

Angel gazed despondently at the dress.

Everything about it was wrong. Even with it still on the hanger, she could tell it wasn't going to fit, and even if it did fit, it would only make her look fatter.

"The bodice is modest, and the skirt will give you some shape," her mother had told her when she'd found the dress a few minutes ago. *Like anyone was even going to be looking at the breasts that were just barely beginning to show, and the full skirt—*

She didn't even want to think about how it would look.

And she certainly didn't want to be here. What she wanted to do was talk to Seth. She'd hardly slept last night. Instead, she'd lain awake in bed, recalling her father's words.

. . . a cat . . . black . . . with a white mark on its chest . . .

Of course, it wasn't possible—her father was drunk, after all, and probably hadn't seen a cat at all.

And yet . . .

She remembered the strange feeling that had come over her after she drank the watery broth left at the bottom of the kettle after it had boiled for almost two hours.

The awful knot of grief that had gripped her the moment she'd found Houdini's body in her locker was completely gone. So completely gone, in fact, that she'd had to keep reminding herself that he wasn't going to come bounding out of nowhere to rub up against her legs and beg to have his ears scratched.

And she'd kept thinking about the strange verse that had been the recipe they'd followed when they made up the broth:

Mix lover's blood drawn by knife/Symmer long to bring back life.

A bit of earth from loved's grave/The blur of grief will help to save.

One fragment of it had echoed all through the long hours of the night:

. . . symmer long to bring back life . . .

When morning had finally come and she went downstairs, she'd wanted to call Seth, to tell him what her father had said, and see what he thought.

And maybe even go back out to the cabin and . . .

But the minute she'd picked up the phone, her father demanded to know who she was calling. And when she turned to her mother for support, her mother shook her head. "Nice girls don't call up boys," she'd pronounced. "Nice girls wait for boys to call them. And besides," she added, "we're going to go shopping this morning. We're getting you a brand-new dress for the dance tonight."

So here she was, in a dressing room with the worst dress she'd ever seen, and her mother waiting for her to come out and model it. Knowing there was no point in trying to postpone the inevitable, Angel began taking off her jeans and sweatshirt.

She was just hanging the sweatshirt on a hook when she heard a familiar voice from the dressing room next door.

"So what are you wearing tonight?" Heather Dunne asked.

"I hate costume parties," someone replied. It was a voice Angel didn't recognize.

"Oh, come on," Heather said. "It'll be fun. Besides, if you don't wear a costume, you'll be the only one, and then how will you feel?"

"I'd feel like Angel Sullivan," the other girl said. Then: "Are you sure no one told her it's a costume dance?"

Angel felt her face begin to burn.

"Who would?" Heather said, snickering. "I mean, who even speaks to her?"

"Beth Baker," the other girl answered.

"Oh, like he's even going to go to the dance!" Heather said, giggling. "What would he go as? A fairy princess?"

"What are you going as?" the other girl said after the laughter died away.

"The Queen of Hearts," Heather declared. Then: "And you could be the White Rabbit." There was a short pause, then Heather said: "I know! Why don't you go as Alice?"

"I love it!" the other girl said. "But where am I going to get a costume?"

"It'll be easy," Heather said. "I've already got most of it from last year, and we can just pin it to fit you instead of me! At least you won't look as stupid as Angel Sullivan when she shows up without any costume at all!"

There was a flurry from the next stall as the girls left, and Angel barely breathed as she prayed none of them had noticed her in the store. Five minutes later, just as she was wondering if it was safe to leave the dressing room, she heard her mother's voice.

"Angel? What's wrong? If the dress doesn't fit, I'm sure they have it in a larger size."

With the dress in her hand, Angel came out of the dressing room. "It doesn't matter if it fits or not," she said. "It's a costume party."

Myra looked blank. "It's what?"

"A costume party," Angel repeated. "I heard Heather Dunne and some other girl talking about it. She's going as the Queen of Hearts, and the girl she was with is going as Alice."

Myra frowned uncertainly. "Then I suppose we'll have to find you a costume."

Angel shook her head. "I already have one," she said. "And it'll be perfect!"

*   *   *

Myra knew even before she and Angel walked into the house that Marty had been drinking. It wasn't just that the leaves she'd asked him to rake while they were in town were still scattered over the lawn and the rake she had left on the front step, where he couldn't miss it, hadn't been moved. Those things only reinforced the dark sense of apprehension that came over her as she moved toward the front door. She had lived with Marty long enough so that she knew yesterday's bender was still going on, and today she was certain that Angel also knew what was waiting for them inside the house. For a moment she was tempted to turn around and just walk away. She and Angel could get lunch at the drugstore and then maybe go visit Joni.

Except she couldn't afford lunch at the drugstore, or anywhere else, and Joni—along with Ed and Zack—was already at the country club. The country club that only this morning Marty had declared he'd never set foot in.

"You were the one who wanted to go," Myra had said when he'd announced his decision while she was fixing breakfast.

Marty only shrugged. "So I changed my mind."

"It's Family Day," Myra began. "Joni said—"

" 'Joni said, Joni said,' " Marty mocked. "What do I care what your snotty sister said? I'm not going, okay? So just don't bother me with it."

Myra had hoped that by the time they got back from shopping he'd have quit drinking and changed his mind yet again, but even as she opened the front door, she knew he had done neither. Just as she expected, Marty was sprawled in his chair, a beer in his hand and three empty bottles on the floor next to him. He peered balefully at her through eyes that were already bleary, even though it was barely lunchtime. "Figured you'd be at that fancy-ass country club by now," he said, his words slurring.

Myra's expression tightened. "You don't have to talk like—"

"I'll talk any way I want to! This is my house, and—"

"Angel, why don't you see if you can find something for lunch?" Myra cut in. Only after her daughter had left the room did she turn to her husband again. "I don't want to have a fight," she said, her voice quiet but her eyes hard. "But—"

Marty rose out of his chair and towered over her. "You don't want to have a fight?" he asked, his voice as low as Myra's but carrying a dangerous edge. The fingers of his right hand gripped the beer bottle so tightly that his knuckles turned white, and he raised it up so it was hovering in the air above Myra's head. "Well, guess what, sweetheart?" he spat. "This is my house, and you're my wife, and I'll do any damned thing I please, and you'll do any damned thing I say. And I say that if I don't want to—"

Suddenly his words choked off and his eyes widened.

The hand holding the bottle began to shake, and Myra saw his face turn pale.

Was he having a heart attack? Or a stroke?

"Marty?" she said, reaching out.

"Get it away!" Marty said, taking a step backward.

Get it away? What was he talking about? For a moment Myra thought she must have misunderstood Marty's slurred words, and then she realized that he wasn't even looking at her. His eyes, now utterly terrified, were looking past her, as if there were something behind her.

Then she heard it.

A hissing sound, so soft it was barely audible, but carrying a note of menace that made Myra's blood run cold.

Marty took another step backward, and the beer bottle dropped from his hand, clattering to the floor. "No," he whispered, his voice suddenly sounding stone sober. "Get it away from me—get it away!"

The hissing sound came again, a low angry sibilance that sent another chill through Myra.

A snake?

Myra had never even seen anything but a garter snake, and even though she'd heard that every now and then someone came across a timber rattler, she didn't know anyone who had actually seen one.

The hissing came again, and now Marty had backed all the way to the wall. His face was still ashen and there was a sheen of sweat on his forehead. Her heart pounding, Myra turned to see exactly what had so terrified her husband.

A cat!

A black cat with a white blaze on its chest. It was crouched low on the floor, its twitching tail stretched straight out behind it, and it was creeping slowly forward as if stalking prey that might sense the impending danger at any second and flee to safety.

The cat's golden eyes seemed to glow with a fire from within, and they were fixed on Marty.

Myra gazed at the cat for a moment, then quickly moved toward it, stamping her foot and waving her hands. "Shoo! Scat!"

The cat seemed not even to be aware of her, let alone frightened or startled.

"Shoo!" Myra said again, and once more moved toward the cat.

This time the cat moved. But instead of darting out of the room, it shot past Myra in a dark blur, and a second later she heard Marty utter a choking scream. Spinning around, she took a step toward him, then stopped in her tracks.

Instead of a cat, she saw a figure clad in an old-fashioned black dress and a bonnet. The figure's back was toward her, and its arm was raised as a moment ago Marty Sullivan's own arm had been raised.

But instead of a beer bottle, the black-clad figure held a knife with a stiletto-sharp blade that glinted even in the shadowed light of the living room.

The blade was stained red, and over the figure's shoulder Myra could see a bloody slash across Marty's cheek.

The figure turned, and for an instant Myra got a glimpse of a young girl—perhaps a little younger than Angel—with a cameo brooch pinned to the breast of her black dress.

As Myra gazed at the vision—for surely that was what it had to be—the face changed. Its flesh began to dissolve, skin and muscle falling away to leave nothing but a skull.

A skull with sharply pointed teeth jutting from its jaws, and golden embers glowing deep in the empty eye sockets.

An instant later, so quickly that Myra wasn't sure she'd seen it at all, the horrible apparition vanished.

Marty was on the floor now, his back against the wall, his knees drawn up. He held his hands to his face and was whimpering. "No . . . please . . . get it away from me. . . ."

Stunned by what she'd seen, Myra remained rooted for a moment, her mind reeling as she tried to make sense of the apparition. But there was no sense to be made of it—the images that churned in her mind wouldn't fit together.

A cat—

A girl—

A skeleton—

And now nothing! No trace anywhere in the room of the cat, or the girl, or the knife the girl had held. But a moment later, when Marty dropped his hands away from his face and looked up at her, she saw the deep slash in his cheek—a slash that began just beneath his eye and ran all the way down to his jaw—and she knew that no matter how impossible it had been, she had indeed seen something.

But what?

Then, from behind her, she heard a strangled voice and whirled around to see Angel standing in the door to the kitchen, her face as ashen as Marty's, her eyes wide. It took no more than that single glance to understand that whatever it was she'd seen, her daughter had seen it too.

Mother and daughter gazed at each other, and the silence between them seemed to stretch to eternity. It was Angel who finally broke the silence, her eyes shifting from her mother to her father. "Is—Is Dad okay?"

Before Myra could say anything, Marty lurched to his feet. "That cat," he rasped. "It tried to kill me." His eyes fixed furiously on Myra. "And you saw it too, so don't tell me it didn't happen!"

"I—I saw something," Myra breathed, her mind still reeling.

"It tried to kill me!" Marty repeated, wiping away the blood that was streaming from his wound.

And it kept you from killing me, Myra thought, remembering the look in Marty's eyes and the fury in his voice as he'd stood above her only a few moments ago, the beer bottle raised high, poised to come crashing down into her face. "I don't know," she finally said. "I don't know what I saw."

I know what you saw, Angel thought as her mother began tending to her father's wound. *You saw Houdini. And you saw Forbearance.*

And they are the same . . .

Chapter 31

WELL, AT LEAST I DON'T HAVE TO WORRY ABOUT beating my biggest client," Blake Baker sourly observed as he and Seth gazed at the list that had them matched up against Ed and Zack Fletcher. His eyes shifted from the list to Seth. "Just try not to look like too much of a damn fool out there, okay?"

The words stung almost as much as the lash of his father's belt, but Seth stared straight ahead, trying to pretend he hadn't heard them. Besides, it could have been worse, at least for him—he could have gotten matched up against Chad Jackson or Jared Woods, who made fun of him even more than Zack Fletcher did. They and their fathers had managed to get paired together, which Seth figured had a lot to do with the fact that Chad's father was the chairman of the tournament committee, and Jared's father was Chad's father's best friend. Not that it was supposed to matter who was paired with whom, since the father-son "tournament" wasn't supposed to be a real tournament at all.

It was just supposed to be fun.

It wasn't supposed to matter who won, and it wasn't supposed to matter how good anyone was. Besides, it wasn't even like a real tournament where everyone had to play their own ball. It was just a best-ball foursome of match play, where Seth and his father would take turns playing the same spot while Zack and Ed Fletcher took turns hitting from theirs, and in the end whoever won the most holes won the match. The total number of strokes wouldn't even matter, and twenty minutes later no one would care who won. They'd all go have a barbecue, and everyone would have a good time, and that would be the end of it.

Except that wouldn't be the end of it for him, because no matter how hard he tried, he wouldn't be able to play well enough for his father, and even though his father didn't want to win—at least not against his biggest client—he didn't want to be embarrassed by his son either.

What his father wanted, Seth knew, was to lose, but only by a hole or maybe two at the most.

But not by the whole eighteen. If they lost every single hole, which Seth was pretty sure they would, he wasn't the only one who would be teased about it. It would be his father too. And then, when they got home—

Seth felt the lash of his father's belt rise out of his memory, and half an hour later when he shanked his first swing on the first tee and sent the ball flying off to the right, where it had rolled into the shrubbery around the tee box, he'd felt the lash yet again.

And heard Zack Fletcher snickering.

Then, to make it worse, Zack had stepped up to the tee, set up a ball, and driven it almost 250 yards straight down the fairway.

Seth felt like crying as he thought about what was to come, and as the afternoon wore on, it only got worse. The more Zack snickered at him, the worse he played. And the worse he played, the angrier his father grew. Hole after hole, the torture went on. It seemed that every ball he hit went either nowhere or in the wrong direction, and every time his father hit a good shot, Seth managed to spoil it with his own following shot. Zack and his father won hole after hole, usually by two or three strokes.

And Seth could feel his father's rage building.

When they came to the eighth tee, Seth gazed dolefully at the green.

"Gee, too bad it isn't Seth's turn to drive," Zack Fletcher said. "Didn't he hit one almost that far, back on Five?" Then, as if just remembering, he slapped his forehead. "Oh, yeah! I forgot—it went in the water, didn't it!"

Seth's face burned with embarrassment.

And his father's burned with fury.

Ed Fletcher teed up, took a couple of practice swings with his seven iron, and stepped up to the ball. He drew the club back, paused for a moment at the top of the backswing, then swept the iron downward.

Seth watched as the ball arced through the air and dropped onto the green about twenty feet from the pin. Turning, he bowed to his son with mock grandeur. "Just get it close, and we have another par."

Then Blake Baker stepped onto the tee box, set up his ball, and after taking almost a dozen practice swings, finally took his shot.

The ball rose off the tee and rose toward the sky, heading directly toward the pin.

"Looks good," Ed Fletcher said.

The ball struck the ground about ten feet in front of the green and bounced straight forward.

"Member's bounce," Ed said. "Looking even better!"

The ball rolled straight toward the hole, and suddenly both the Fletchers and the Bakers were standing still and silent, watching.

When the ball finally stopped rolling, it was only a foot from the cup.

"Another foot," Blake Baker groaned as the four of them started from the tee box toward the green. "One lousy foot and I would have had an ace."

"And if Seth weren't putting, you'd have a sure birdie," Zack said.

Seth felt a knot form in his stomach as his father laughed at the joke but said nothing. When they got to the green, he marked the ball his father had driven, then watched as Zack carefully circled around the green, studying the twenty-some-foot putt from every angle. There was a rise between the ball and the cup, and once the putt crested the rise, it would start to speed up. If Zack didn't hit the ball hard enough, it wouldn't make it over the rise, but if he hit it too hard and missed the hole, it might very well end up going ten feet past it. Finally Zack crouched down, cupped his hands over the bill of his cap, and peered at the line from the ball to the hole one more time. At last he stood up, squared the putter behind the ball, and swung.

The ball started up the slope of the rise, moving more and more slowly, until at last it came to the top, where it almost stopped.

But it didn't stop.

Instead it made one more slow revolution, then began rolling down the gentle slope, curving slowly to the right.

It picked up speed, and the curve straightened out, sending the ball directly toward the hole. It was still gaining speed, and even Seth could see that if it missed the hole, it wouldn't go just ten feet beyond the cup, it would go at least fifteen, or maybe even more.

But it didn't miss the cup.

Instead, it rolled directly into the center of the hole, struck the opposite side, then dropped out of sight.

Now it was Zack who turned to his father with an exaggerated bow. "Looks like our hole," he said. "Unless Seth can figure out how to make his putt."

The knot in his stomach tightening, Seth carefully replaced the ball on the spot he'd marked, then stepped back to look at the putt.

One foot, straight at the hole.

No slopes, at least not that he could see.

The knot in his stomach throbbed.

He felt his father's eyes fixed on him and knew exactly what would happen if he missed the putt.

His arms trembling, he swung the putter back a few inches and gently tapped the ball.

It started slightly left, and for one horrified moment Seth was certain it had happened. He'd missed a twelve-inch putt—a putt that anyone but Zack Fletcher would have given him. Then, just as the ball was about to roll past the cup, it veered slightly right, hovered on the edge for a moment, and fell in.

"Not your hole," Blake Baker said. "We split."

Zack rolled his eyes scornfully. "Ooh, I'm so scared! Now we're going to lose."

"I've gotta go to the bathroom," Seth mumbled fifteen minutes later, after he and his father had lost the ninth hole by two strokes. Without waiting for his father, he rushed to the men's locker room, ran directly to the toilets, slipped into one of the stalls, and threw up. For almost ten minutes he crouched by the toilet, puking his brains out until there wasn't anything left to vomit up. But no matter how much he threw up, the terrible knot in his stomach never loosened. The retching finally eased up and he was sitting on the toilet catching his breath when he heard the door open.

Then he heard his father's voice: "You can't hide in here all day, Seth. You're holding up the whole game."

The terrible knot in his stomach tightening even more, Seth nevertheless flushed the toilet and left the stall. Knowing that telling his father his stomach hurt too much to play would only make things worse than they already were, Seth trudged back to the course.

Ed Fletcher had already driven his ball down the right, where it drifted into the trees. As Seth watched, his father sent his ball into the bunker that lay two hundred yards out on the left side of the fairway, then glowered at Seth as if somehow the shot had been his fault.

Seth could already feel the sting of the extra lash he'd get from his father's belt later tonight.

Now Zack was teeing up, and a moment later he began his backswing, his club coming smoothly up, his athletic body twisting until the club was extended horizontally behind his neck. The driver's enormous head hovered for a moment, and then, just as Zack began his swing, there was a sudden blur of motion as something darted out of the boxwood hedge behind the tee box, shot past Zack's ball, and disappeared into a tangle of ivy. Startled by the sudden movement, Zack pulled the shot. The ball soared in a huge hook, disappeared into the stand of ancient maples that bordered the fairway, and a second later they all heard it clatter off at least two trees.

Zack hurled his club at the ivy into which the animal had vanished. "No fair!" he howled. "I should get the shot over!"

"This is a tournament," Blake Baker replied. "There aren't any mulligans."

"Come on," Ed Fletcher said. "It's not like it was his fault—anybody would have jumped when that happened. I jumped, and I wasn't even at the tee!"

Blake Baker shrugged impassively. "Doesn't make any difference. The rules are the rules."

Ed Fletcher's eyes narrowed angrily. "For Christ's sake, Blake—he's a kid!"

"Do you see me giving Seth mulligans?" Baker asked. "Or even asking for them?"

"If you did, we'd be here all day," Ed Fletcher shot back. "He hasn't hit a decent shot yet."

Seth barely heard what Ed Fletcher had said. His eyes were still fixed on the spot where the animal had vanished into the ivy.

It had looked to him exactly like the black cat he and Angel Sullivan had buried yesterday.

But that was impossible. Houdini was dead! He'd been dead when he took him out of Angel's locker.

"So what's it going to be?" he heard his father saying. "Is he going to play it as it lays, or be three off the tee?"

"Who cares?" Zack said, his voice trembling with anger. "It's best ball anyway, and we'll just use Dad's— he's farther out than you, and you're stuck in the bunker."

Blake Baker's eyes narrowed angrily, but he said nothing, rather than risk offending Ed Fletcher. Instead, he gave his own son a tight-lipped nod that told Seth it was time for him to get on with it.

Pulling his driver out of his bag, Seth set up the ball, but by now all he wanted was to get the whole tournament behind him. So this time he didn't even bother to aim, or take a practice swing, or any of the other things his father had pounded into him the other day when they were out practicing. Instead he just straightened up from the tee, stepped back, pulled the club up, and swung it, barely even bothering to watch where the ball was.

Except for the sharp *thwack* when the face of the club struck the ball, Seth would have sworn he'd missed completely, for he didn't feel the contact at all. But the ball shot off the tee, arced high into the afternoon sky, seemed almost to hover in the air for a few seconds, then began its descent.

It landed in the exact center of the fairway.

More than two hundred yards out.

There was a long moment of silence, then Ed Fletcher uttered a low whistle, followed by a quizzical expression. "Where the heck did that come from?"

Blake Baker only rolled his eyes. "You know what they say—even the stupidest pig finds a truffle now and then."

But Seth barely heard him, for his entire attention was focused on the black cat, who had now emerged from the hedge and was sitting on the edge of the tee box, its tail wrapped around its legs exactly the way Houdini's always had.

Its eyes fixed on Seth for a moment, then it vanished back into the hedge.

Five minutes later, after first Ed Fletcher and then Zack had blown the shot out of the woods—winding up with their third shot coming out of the light rough and no farther ahead than before—Seth stood over his own ball, not quite certain what to do. It was the first of his balls that he and his father had used all day, and until now he'd simply used whatever iron his father had used, knowing it wasn't going to make any difference anyway. But he'd just caught a glimpse of the black cat again. It was sitting in the shade of the closest tree, and he would have missed him except for the white blaze on his chest.

The blaze that looked to Seth to be identical to Houdini's.

And the cat was staring at him again.

Almost like it was trying to tell him something . . .

"Looks like a five iron," Seth heard Ed Fletcher say. "Or maybe a six."

With no better idea of his own, Seth pulled the five iron out of his bag, stepped up to the ball, and once again swung without thinking.

And again the ball soared into the air.

This time it dropped onto the green.

"Well, well, well," Ed Fletcher said quietly. "Looks like we got a sandbagger."

Seth stared at Zack's father. "I—I don't know how I did that," he stammered.

Ed Fletcher's brow lifted. "Looked to me like you did it perfectly." His gaze shifted to Blake Baker. "Want to just take that one and get on with it?"

Blake shrugged. "I guess I can live with it—should be good for a par anyway."

With their next shots the Fletchers still weren't on the green, but with their fourth they managed to leave the ball only three feet from the pin.

As Seth set up his putt, he once more saw the cat watching him, this time from the top of the bunker at the back of the green, and when the putt was finished, the ball lay only six inches from the cup.

Ed Fletcher conceded the hole.

"Not sandbagging, huh?" Ed Fletcher said as they approached the eleventh tee.

"I never hit a ball like that before," Seth said. "I mean, never!"

Ed Fletcher shrugged. "You know what you did different?"

Seth shook his head.

"You relaxed. That's the key to golf—just relax. Trouble is, most of us just can't do it."

"And flukes can happen to anyone," Blake Baker said. "Even Seth."

Something that looked like anger flashed through Ed

Fletcher's eyes so quickly that Seth wasn't certain he'd seen it, and then it was gone.

But as Seth was setting up for his tee shot, Ed Fletcher said, "I've got twenty bucks that says it wasn't a fluke."

Blake Baker eyed his client uneasily. "You want to bet on *Seth?*" he asked with disbelief. When Ed Fletcher nodded, Blake shrugged. "Fine—easiest twenty I'll ever take from you."

As his father agreed to bet against him, Seth felt his eyes start to sting with tears, but rather than either wipe them away or risk anyone seeing them, he simply pulled his driver back and took a swing at the ball.

Once again it soared into the air and flew down the fairway, landing to the right, where it would be easy to send the next shot around the dogleg toward the green. As the ball rolled to a stop, Seth saw the black cat disappear into a thicket behind the tee box.

Seth's next shot hit the green five feet from the cup.

With the black cat watching from the shadow of one of the granite outcroppings that dotted the course, Seth sank the putt.

"What the hell's going on?" his father asked him as they walked toward the next tee.

"I don't know," Seth said. "All I'm doing is just hitting the ball!"

" 'Just hitting the ball'?" his father echoed. "Nobody 'just hits the ball' like that!"

Seth stared at his father in bewilderment. "But I'm doing good, aren't I?"

Blake eyed him darkly. "You know what a sandbagger is?"

Seth swallowed. "I—I guess it's someone who suddenly does better than anyone thinks he can do."

Blake Baker's voice hardened. "It's someone who pretends he can't do something to sucker someone else in."

"But I'm not any good at golf," Seth said. "You saw me just the other day, when we were practicing!"

"Or I saw you faking," Blake replied.

By the fifteenth hole, when not one of Seth's shots had gone wild and he and his father had won every hole since the ninth, the word had begun to spread that something strange was going on. As they walked down the eighteenth fairway, with each team having won eight and a half holes, and having split one, the green was ringed with all the teams that had already finished, and most of the people who'd been spending the afternoon at the pool as well.

Zack Fletcher looked furious, and even Ed Fletcher's tone had changed. While he'd actually seemed amused at how well Seth had been doing on the first few holes of the back nine, his good humor drained slowly away as the difference in the two teams' scores had narrowed.

Now that he seemed to be on the very verge of defeat, he'd stopped talking altogether.

And finally they came to the green, where Zack and Seth would be the first to putt for their teams.

Zack was twenty feet from the hole, Seth about fifteen.

Heather Dunne and Sarah Harmon were standing with Chad Jackson and Jared Woods, and all of them were rooting for Zack.

Zack studied the putt from every angle, carefully took two practice swings until he was sure of the line, then stepped up to the ball and putted.

The ball rolled straight toward the hole.

"You're the man, Zack!" Chad Jackson yelled as it drew closer to the cup.

Zack raised his fist into the air, ready to pump it the instant the ball dropped into the cup.

And then it veered off, drifted half an inch past the hole, and came to a stop.

The beginnings of the cheer that started to rise from the crowd around the green died abruptly away, leaving Zack staring unbelievingly at his ball.

And Seth, his eyes drawn by a slight movement from the other side of the green, glanced over to see the black cat seat itself on the edge of one of the sand traps that ringed the putting surface.

The black cat with the white blaze on its chest.

Seth's eyes met those of the cat as Zack, swearing, marked the spot where his ball had stopped.

As the murmur of sympathy for Zack's failed putt died away, Ed Fletcher placed his ball at the spot from which Zack had putted, spent even more time analyzing the putt than his son had, and finally struck the ball.

And missed.

Seth walked over to his ball, glanced once more at the cat, which was still sitting by the sand trap, and swung his putter.

The ball dropped into the hole.

As the crowd realized what had happened, Seth looked one more time at the sand trap.

The cat was gone.

The Fletchers, Zack and his father, had lost.

And Seth could see the fury not only in his father's eyes, but in everyone else's as well.

But he hadn't cheated.

He wasn't a sandbagger.

He'd simply won.

And everyone—including his father—hated him.

Chapter 32

MYRA SULLIVAN GASPED AS THE FIGURE APPEARED in the kitchen doorway, and the memory of the terrifying specter she'd glimpsed in the living room only a few hours earlier instantly leaped back to the forefront of her mind. Her hand flew to her breast as if to still her suddenly racing heart, then moved on, unconsciously making the sign of the cross as she mouthed an inaudible prayer so deeply rooted in her subconscious that she was barely aware of its utterance at all.

The figure stood still in the doorway. Clad completely in black, a cape falling from its shoulders nearly to the floor, the ghost-white face seemed almost to float like a disembodied object above the body.

The mouth was a scarlet slash, the eyes—enormous in the ghostly face—were circled with black. The lips parted to expose fangs so distended that Myra lurched back a step. Then, just as a scream began to form in her throat, she heard the sound of laughter.

Angel's laughter!

"Got you!" her daughter crowed, her bloodred lips broadening into a grin. She stepped farther into the kitchen and whirled around so the cape billowed out, and pulled away the black scarf she'd wrapped around her head so her hair fell back to her shoulders. "What do you think?"

"Dear God," Myra breathed, her right hand still on her breast. "For heaven's sake, Angel, what are you trying to do to me?"

"It's my costume!" Angel cried. "What do you think?"

Myra took a deep breath as her pulse began to slow. "I think it's a little early, don't you? Halloween's still a few weeks away. And where on earth did you get that cape?"

"Last year, remember? When you said Zack was going to invite me to his—" She fell abruptly silent as the pain of the invitation that had never come rose inside her. She'd looked forward to it for almost a month, and bought the vampire kit the day the drugstore in Eastbury had stocked its shelves with Halloween decorations.

Even on the afternoon of Halloween, she'd been sure the phone would ring and her cousin would invite her to his party.

It hadn't happened.

She'd put the costume away and tried to pretend it didn't matter, and never even asked Zack about it. Now, suddenly, as the pain of what had happened almost a year ago came flooding back, she knew what had happened this year. Nobody had told her the country club was having a costume party tonight, and if she hadn't overheard Heather Dunne and her friend talking in the dressing room this morning, she would have been the only one to show up without a costume.

And she would have felt even worse this year than she did last, when she hadn't been invited to the party at all.

But what about Seth? Why hadn't he told her? But she knew the answer even as the question rose in her mind— no one had told him either. And it was way too late to call him—he was stuck in the golf tournament with his father.

Half an hour later Myra pulled the old Chevelle into the parking lot at the country club, which was mostly filled with Mercedes-Benzes, BMWs, and Lexuses. Myra finally spotted a handful of cars that looked more like the Chevelle than the fancy models parked closest to the front door, and only realized when she was locking the car that she'd parked in the employees' area. As she gazed at the contrast between her car and those of the members, Myra wondered once more if coming had been a mistake—it still wasn't too late to get back in the car and go home.

Home, where Marty would be going back to his beer, despite the promises he'd made just before they left. Besides, Joni and her friends had been so insistent that she come, and it would be a great opportunity for Angel to come out of her shell and start making more friends than just that one boy Marty had told her about.

It would be fine.

Less than five minutes later, she and Angel passed through the front doors of the country club and were scrutinized by a hostess who seemed reluctant to tell them that the barbecue was on the patio around the pool. And then they stepped through the French doors out onto the terrace overlooking the pool, she knew she was wrong. It wasn't going to be fine at all.

There were at least forty youngsters gathered around the pool, ranging in age from ten to sixteen or seventeen.

The boys were wearing khaki pants, polo shirts, and loafers, mostly without socks.

The girls who weren't wearing clothes almost identical to the boys were wearing skirts with white or plaid blouses, and had sweaters draped around their shoulders that Myra could see were cashmere even from this distance.

Not one of them was wearing any kind of costume at all.

As Myra and Angel stood gazing down at them, the youngsters began looking up at the terrace and fell into silence.

Someone snickered.

Then someone else snickered.

Then the snickering turned into a ripple of laughter.

Then a single voice rose above the laughter: "Ooooh, I'm sooo scared! Is it a vampire or a witch?" A pause, then: "Oh, no—I'm wrong! It's an *Angel!*"

As the laughter erupted into a roar, Angel turned and fled back into the shelter of the clubhouse, Heather Dunne's mocking voice echoing in her mind. By the time she'd found the ladies' room, tears were streaming down her face.

Now she knew what had happened. Heather had seen her in the store, then followed her into the dressing room area and—

How could she have been so stupid?

A sob welled up in her throat, but she choked it back as she heard the door open. If it was Heather or one of her friends, she wasn't about to let them see her crying.

But to her surprise, she heard Seth's voice. "Angel?" he called softly. "Are you in here?"

"You can't come in," she said, her voice catching on the sob that still threatened to overwhelm her. "It's the ladies' room."

But a moment later she sensed Seth standing behind her, and when she looked up and into the mirror and saw the worried expression on his face, she turned around, wiping her eyes with a fold of the cape. "I'm not going to die," she told him. "It's just . . . just . . ." Her

tears welled up again and her chin quivered. "How
could they do that?" she asked. "How come they want
to be so mean? What am I doing wrong?"

Seth took an uncertain step toward her and clumsily
put his arm around her. "You're not doing anything
wrong," he said. "They just need someone to pick on.
And I guess it's us."

Us. Not *you.* He'd said *us.*

But he wasn't wearing a costume. What had they done
to him?

Sniffling back her tears, she pulled away from him,
and Seth could read the question in her eyes.

"Zack's really pissed at me," he said. Then, unable
to hold back a grin, he told her what had happened on
the eighteenth hole. "And you're not gonna believe
this," he finished, "but the cat that spooked him on the
tee showed up again at the green. It was—"

"It was Houdini, wasn't it?" Angel breathed.

Seth nodded. "I know it isn't possible, but—"

"I saw him too," Angel broke in. "He was at my
house." Quickly, she told him what had happened when
she and her mother got back from the store, and what
she'd seen.

Or at least what she thought she'd seen.

"I thought I must have imagined it," she said. "But if
you saw him too . . ." She left the thought unfinished,
still not ready to say aloud what she knew they were
both thinking. Instead she asked, "What are we going
to do?"

"First, we're going to go out there and show them you
don't care what kind of tricks they pull on you. Have
you got your makeup?"

Angel nodded. "I brought it all, 'cause I figured it
might start wearing off in the middle of the party."

"Great," Seth said. "Okay, first let's get rid of the

cape. Turn it around and put it on backward so you don't mess up your clothes while you wash some of that white guck off."

"How do you mess all this up?" Angel fretted. "Besides, I'm not going back out there—everyone else is wearing really expensive clothes, and I don't have anything but what I have on!"

"Quit worrying," he told her, eyeing her black sweater, skirt, and leggings. "By the time we're done, you're gonna look great!"

As they began to work on her makeup, the door opened and they heard Angel's mother. "Angel?" she said. "Are you all right?"

"I'm fine, Mom!" Angel called out.

Seth jumped into one of the stalls before Myra appeared. "Perhaps we should just go home," her mother began, but Angel shook her head.

"I'm okay," she said. "I—I guess I just misunderstood. I'm just taking off this stupid vampire makeup, then I'll be out."

"If you'd rather just go home . . ."

Angel shook her head. "I'm all right."

Myra still hesitated, then, mentally assessing the contents of the refrigerator—and Marty's likely alcohol consumption—she shrugged. The barbecue outside was already lit, and she'd seen the cut of steaks they were serving. "All right," she said. "But if you change your mind—"

"Go find Aunt Joni," Angel told her. "I'll be out in a few minutes."

Fifteen minutes later, Seth led Angel out of the ladies' room, back through the clubhouse, and out onto the terrace. The black cape was gone—rolled up and stuffed into the black shoulder bag she'd brought to hold the makeup. Most of the white was gone from her face, and the vampire fangs had joined the cape in the shoulder bag. They'd used the makeup kit to put shadow on her lids, and Seth had carefully applied mascara to her eyelashes, which now looked twice as long and full as before. He'd plaited her hair into a single long braid that hung down her back, and the black clothes now made her look thinner. With her hair pulled back from her face and her features accentuated with the makeup Seth had applied, she barely looked like herself anymore.

And nobody laughed.

Nobody except Heather Dunne.

"Well," Heather said as she and Seth passed. "I guess we know which it is—she's obviously not a vampire, but she sure looks like a witch!"

Though Angel tried to keep moving, Seth stopped her and turned to face Heather. "Maybe you're right," he said. "Maybe she is a witch. But if she is, I'd think you'd want to be a little more careful what you say." Leaving Heather glaring furiously at him, he turned around and walked away, with Angel hurrying after him.

"Are you crazy?" Angel said when she was sure Heather couldn't hear her. "What did you want to say that for?"

Seth shrugged. "Maybe I'm just sick of putting up with them all the time," he replied. "Besides," he added, dropping his voice, "maybe you really are a witch. I mean, how else did Houdini come back to life?"

Angel gasped. "What are you talking about? I didn't—"

"But you did," Seth said. "And we both know how you did it."

For the rest of the afternoon and into the evening, Angel thought about what Seth had said, and it almost blotted out the whispers passing through the rest of the crowd.

Almost blotted them out, but not quite . . .

It was as if an inaudible signal went off at precisely ten o'clock. Even though no one actually heard it, the members of the Roundtree Country Club reacted exactly as factory workers half a century earlier had reacted to the whistle signaling the end of the workday. Abandoning the remains of the barbecue around the pool and the dance in the "ballroom"—the main dining room with its tables moved to the walls, and a makeshift dance floor installed over the carpet—the members began their exodus, herding their younger children ahead of them and reminding the older ones that they should be home by midnight.

By ten-fifteen the club was all but abandoned to the staff, and Joni Fletcher found herself waiting with only Jane and Seth Baker on the front porch, facing a parking lot that was empty except for the Fletchers' Mercedes-Benz, the Bakers' Lexus, and a collection of battered and rusting old cars that belonged to the staff. "I don't believe they're still at it," Joni said, glancing impatiently at her watch. "If I'd known those two were still going to be playing this late, I'd have caught a ride with Myra."

"Go get them, will you, Seth?" Jane Baker asked.

The knot of anxiety that had only just begun to release him from its grip tightened again, and for an instant Seth wondered what would happen if he tried to beg off. But what would be the use? His father was already mad at him, and what would happen when they got home wouldn't get any worse just because he'd brought a message from his mother. Turning away from the porch, he went back into the clubhouse and down the stairs to the poolroom in the basement.

Though the club had banished smoking a year ago, the low-ceilinged, walnut-paneled room that housed the club's single billiard table still reeked of the thousands of cigars that had smoldered in the room over the decades, and Seth almost gagged when he stepped through the door to see his father lining up a bank shot. Knowing better than to utter even a single word before his father completed the shot, Seth waited until the cue had clicked, the ball his father had been aiming at had failed to drop into the far corner pocket, and the cue ball had come to rest in an almost unplayable position against the rail, next to the nearest corner pocket. "Mom says she's ready," he said when Blake finally glanced over at him.

"Nice timing," Blake Baker said, his eyes fixed balefully on his son. "In case you're interested, what I'm trying to do here is win back the money you managed to lose for me this afternoon."

"Come on, Blake," Ed Fletcher said. "It wasn't Seth's fault—all he did was make a couple of good shots. Seems to me it was you and Zack who lost the money."

Out of the corner of his eye, Seth saw Zack Fletcher's jaw clench and his fingers tighten on the pool cue he was holding. "But Mom said—" he began.

His father didn't let him finish. "Tell your mother that if she's in such a hurry, she can catch a ride with Joni. I'll drop Zack and Ed off after we're done here."

"And at the rate it's going, that might take all night," Ed Fletcher said. Leaning over his cue, he lined up his shot carefully, then sent the cue ball the length of the table, banking it off the far end so it came back, glanced the six ball into the side pocket, then sent the four ball into the corner pocket that lay only a couple of inches from where the shot had begun. Seth backed out the door, then turned and started back up the stairs. He'd just gotten to the landing when he heard Zack's voice.

"I want to talk to you, Beth."

Seth froze. Part of him wanted to run, to dash through the lobby and out the front door before Zack could get to the top of the stairs. But then he realized even Zack wouldn't dare start something right in front of his mother. And by tomorrow Zack would have told everybody he knew that he had run away.

Run away and hid behind his mother's skirts.

He thought of Angel Sullivan, staying through the party and facing Heather Dunne, Sarah Harmon, Chad Jackson, Jared Woods, and all the other kids who hadn't spoken to her but kept talking about her just loud enough to make sure she heard every word they said.

If she could face them, he could face Zack Fletcher.

So instead of running, he waited at the top of the stairs until Zack caught up with him.

And suddenly, having made the decision not to run away, he was no longer afraid. "So what do you want to talk about, Zack?"

Zack hesitated—he'd been sure that Seth would run away from him. And tomorrow he would have had one more story to tell everyone about what a chicken "Beth" Baker was. But he hadn't run. Instead, Seth was just standing there, looking at him as if he wasn't scared at all.

"What did you do?" Zack finally asked.

Seth stared at him as if he didn't understand the question. Indeed, he didn't.

"This afternoon," Zack said, his voice rising. "How'd you make all those shots?"

Seth's mind raced as he tried to think of something—anything—that Zack might accept. But recalling the black cat that had stayed with him all the way through the back nine, watching every shot so closely, as if it was controlling them, he realized what to say.

The truth.

The simple truth.

"It was easy," he said softly. "I did it the same way I messed up your last putt. I used witchcraft on you!"

Zack gaped at him, then pulled back his fist and smashed it into Seth's face. Seth jerked aside at the last second, just enough to avoid the full force of the blow, but Zack's fist still caught him on the jaw and sent him sprawling to the floor. Instead of bursting into tears, however, or trying to scuttle away, Seth only looked up at Zack.

"I don't think you should have done that," he said, his voice cold. He picked himself up, and his eyes locked on Zack's. "And my name isn't 'Beth,' " he added. "It's 'Seth.' "

Then he turned around and walked away.

Chapter 33

MYRA SULLIVAN LAY AWAKE THROUGH MOST OF THE night, waiting for Marty to come upstairs and praying that he wouldn't. When they'd come in at a little after nine, he was sprawled in his chair with the lights off, the droning television providing a dim glow, enough for her to see that the collection of empty beer bottles around his chair had almost doubled while she and Angel were at the country club, and a pint bottle of bourbon had been added to it. She wasn't sure whether she was angry or relieved that he'd spent the hours she was gone drinking himself into a stupor. Part of her didn't want to cope with him, or even talk about what had happened that afternoon when she'd seen something she couldn't possibly have seen. But another part of her hoped he'd be sober enough when they got home that she could at least tell him he'd been right about the party at the country club—she and Angel shouldn't have gone at all. She'd known it the minute she saw all those kids dressed in their preppy clothes, in contrast to Angel who looked foolish in her vampire costume.

Why had those girls Angel overheard in the dressing room done it? She knew that Angel had never done a thing to them.

Had it been up to Myra, they would have left right

then, but before she could even say anything, Angel had dashed away, and when she found her daughter hiding in the ladies' room, Angel had insisted she was all right. So Myra had gone back to the party, found Joni, and tried to make the best of it.

But the "best of it" turned out to be the forced smiles a few of Joni's friends managed to come up with, while the rest of it was pretending she didn't notice the disapproving stares most of the club members were giving her and the backs that were turned wherever she went. What kept her from finding Angel and leaving within the first hour was the knowledge that the only place they could have come was home, and she suspected that being home that evening would be even worse, not only for her, but for Angel too. So she'd stuck it out, and so had Angel, who at least had Jane Baker's boy—Seth, that was his name—to keep her company. Not that she was certain that was a good thing—knowing what boys wanted from all girls.

Though the subject of sex had always made her uncomfortable, she'd tried to talk to Angel about it on the way home.

"Seth's not like that," Angel had insisted, shaking her head. "He's not a boyfriend—he's just a friend!"

"All boys want the same thing," her mother had said darkly, and Angel had rolled her eyes. "Maybe you should talk to Father Mike," Myra had suggested.

"Why?" Angel shot back. "It's not like I have anything to confess!"

"Don't take that tone, young lady," Myra snapped, and that had been the end of the conversation.

They'd driven the rest of the way home in silence, and remained silent as Angel disappeared into her room without so much as a "Good night."

Myra went to bed, but hadn't slept for more than a few minutes, and every time she did, the strange spectral figure she'd seen in the living room that afternoon appeared in her dreams, the knife dripping blood held aloft, the empty eyes of the fleshless skull staring at her.

But of course it hadn't happened—it had just been a cat, and the rest of it was simply her imagination.

Except that Myra had never had much of an imagination. Even as a child, she was never frightened by the fairy tales her father read her, because she always knew they were only stories and nothing in them was real.

And she'd never dreamed either—at least nothing she could ever remember.

Still, by the time dawn broke, she convinced herself that she couldn't have seen the black-clad figure, and by the time she got downstairs to fix breakfast, she'd managed to dismiss the dreams as well.

Then she saw Marty.

He was sitting at the kitchen table, still wearing the same clothes he'd had on yesterday. His eyes were bloodshot, his complexion was pasty, and his jowls were covered with stubble.

And the wound—the terrible slash that had run from just beneath his right eye all the way down to his jaw—was gone. But that was impossible! It had to be there—she'd seen it! She'd helped him clean it up, washed the blood away, put iodine on it—

As if sensing her presence, Marty raised his head. "What are you staring at?" he growled.

"The—The cut," Myra stammered. "Where the cat—"

Marty's eyes darkened with anger. "Goddamned animal . . ." he began, raising his right hand to touch his cheek. As his fingers touched his flesh, his lips and his eyes widened. Frowning, he rose to his feet, swayed unsteadily as his hangover threatened to overwhelm him, then lurched toward the mirror that hung in the hall. A few seconds later he was back, leaning heavily against the door frame, his complexion ashen. "I saw it," he whispered. "You saw it. . . ." His voice grew louder. "It happened, goddammit! We both saw it!"

All Myra could do was nod mutely.

Nod, cross herself, and whisper a nearly inaudible prayer.

Two hours later, as Father Mulroney began chanting the benediction, Myra uttered another silent prayer, this time begging forgiveness for having been unable to concentrate on the mass. Angel was fidgeting next to her, and as Father Mulroney's voice died away and the rest of the congregation stood and began to exit, Myra laid a hand on her daughter's arm to keep her in her place. Then, while the little church quickly emptied, Myra continued to pray.

Only when the last sounds of shuffling feet and murmuring voices were gone did she stand, move into the aisle, genuflect before the cross one last time, and lead Angel out into the morning sunlight. Just as she'd hoped, Father Mulroney was still on the steps of the church, bidding farewell to the last parishioner. He turned to Myra with his hand extended and a warm smile lighting his face, but seeing the expression in her eyes, his smile faded.

"Myra?" he said uncertainly. "Is anything wrong?"

Myra shook her head so slightly the gesture was almost invisible. But she'd already made up her mind that she had to tell the priest what had happened yesterday, and she wasn't about to turn back now. "Can I talk to you for a few moments?" she said softly. Her eyes flicked toward Angel so briefly that the priest almost missed it, but then he too nodded.

"Of course. Why don't we go into the vestry?" Without waiting for a reply, he led Myra back into the church, down the aisle, then around the altar to the cramped room that served as office, vestry, sacristy, and storeroom. "What is it?" he asked, doing his best to ignore the look of disapproval from Myra as he shed his clerical robes in favor of the comfort of his favorite corduroy jacket.

Slowly, knowing how strange and impossible the story sounded, Myra did her best to tell him exactly what had happened yesterday afternoon, sparing none of the details, not even how much Marty had been drinking. The priest listened in silence until she was finished, then frowned thoughtfully.

"You're absolutely sure there was a cut on your husband's cheek?"

"Blood was running down his face," Myra replied. "If you don't believe me, ask Angel—she saw it too. I'm not lying, Father!"

"I'm not doubting that you think you saw exactly what you've told me," Father Mulroney assured her. "But if the cut healed overnight—"

"Not just healed," Myra interrupted. "It's as if it had never happened at all. It's like—" She fell silent as she realized the word she'd been about to utter, but the priest picked up where she left off.

"Like a miracle?"

Myra shook her head. "It was more like a—" She'd been about to say "vision," but stopped herself. She still hadn't told Father Mulroney about the glimpses of the

Holy Mother she'd had, and she didn't want the priest to just pass her off as someone who sometimes "saw things." She finally said, "I don't know what it was like. I just don't know."

"Then perhaps you should just try to forget it," the priest told her. "Some things we can understand, and some things we can't. You were upset yesterday, and so was your daughter. Our emotions can play tricks on us, and make us think all kinds of terrible things." He began leading Myra out of the vestry and back up the aisle toward the door. When they were outside the church once again, in the bright morning sunlight, he placed a gentle hand on Myra's shoulder. "Try not to worry," he said. "I'm sure everything will be all right—the saints will look after us."

His eyes shifted to the crowd that had poured out of the Congregational church across the street, two or three of whom had been part of his own flock until recently. Even Angel Sullivan was over there, talking to Jane and Blake Baker's son.

"Of course it would be nice," he sighed, "if the saints could not just look after us, but send a few more people our way, but I suppose we must be content with what we have." He winked at Myra. "But if I were you, I'd keep my eye on Angel before Seth Baker corrupts her completely." As a shocked look came into Myra's eye, he quickly backtracked. "It was a joke, Myra," he assured her. "Even if he doesn't go to my church, Seth is still one of the nicest boys in town. So stop worrying so much—everything will work out."

But as Myra walked down the steps and started across the street to reclaim her daughter, Father Mulroney found his eyes wandering to the great tree in the cemetery across the street, which only the day before yesterday had twice been struck by lightning in a storm that came out of nowhere, then vanished as quickly as it had come.

And yesterday, in the house at Black Creek Crossing, a little girl all dressed in black had appeared for an instant.

A little girl, wielding a bloody knife.

Crossing himself, Father Michael Mulroney retreated back into his tiny church and began to pray.

The sun was just reaching its zenith as Angel and Seth climbed to the top of the shattered granite berm and looked down at the area of flat ground that fronted the single visible wall of the cabin. Neither of them was certain what to expect, but what they hadn't expected was to find that nothing had changed.

The flat stone marking the spot where they'd buried Houdini was exactly where they'd left it, but seemed to have sunk lower into the ground. Yet nowhere did the ground look as if it had been disturbed.

For almost a full minute the two of them stood side by side, gazing down at the invisible grave below. Finally, Seth broke the silence.

"M-Maybe it wasn't Houdini," he said so softly that Angel wasn't certain that he knew he'd spoken out loud. "Maybe it was another cat—one that just looked like Houdini."

Angel shook her head. "It *was* Houdini. My dad saw him, and my mom saw him, and I think my mom saw . . ." She cut her words short, still not quite ready to tell him about the strange vision—if that's what it was—that she'd had when the cat attacked her father yesterday.

Indeed, the more she'd thought about it, and tried to make sense of it, the harder it was to believe that she'd seen it at all. She'd barely been able to sleep at all last night, and whenever she had, her dreams had mingled with her memories, and the darkness was filled with strange images of her father reaching for her, and the cat leaping at him and tearing at his face, and the girl— the girl clad all in black with the white brooch on her chest—plunging a glittering silver knife deep into her father's chest over and over again. But no matter how many times the knife struck deep into his chest—no matter how much blood gushed from his wounds—he kept looming over her, reaching for her, wanting to touch her, to press his body against her own, to—

How many times had she awakened, her skin clammy with the sweat of pure terror, her whole body trembling in fear of the touch that had never quite come? And every time she'd awakened, the memory of the cat had risen in her mind, and then the cat had been transformed once more into the girl, except that in the blackness of the night all she saw of the cat was its glowing golden eyes and the white blaze on its chest, and all she ever saw of the girl was the pale skin of her face and the white of the ivory brooch on her breast. By the time dawn had finally broken, she was no longer sure what was real and what to believe, and as she now gazed down on the spot where they'd buried the cat two days ago, her confusion only grew worse.

"You think your mother saw what?" she heard Seth ask.

Instead of answering him, she scrambled down the face of the berm and pushed the large rock away from the top of the grave. Using her bare hands, she began digging, and when Seth brought the shovel from the cabin a moment later, she shook her head. "If we use the shovel, we won't know," she said.

Seth cocked his head. "Know what?"

"The flowers," Angel said. "If we use the shovel, we won't know if they're still the way we put them."

Laying the shovel aside, Seth dropped to his knees next to Angel and set to work, scooping the soft earth from the grave and laying it aside, taking more care with each handful he removed. They had dug nearly a foot of earth from the hole when Angel stopped and looked at Seth. "I feel one of the stems." Now they took even more care, slowly removing the earth bit by bit, until finally the first of the four flowers they'd buried with Houdini's body lay exposed.

It was a bright yellow aster, and as she gazed at it, Angel could remember laying it carefully on Houdini's head to provide him with sunlight even in the darkness of his grave. The flower still lay at precisely the angle at which she'd placed it, and its petals hadn't even begun to fade. But his head was not beneath it.

She and Seth glanced at each other, then she picked up the flower, shook the dirt from its petals, and laid it carefully to one side.

"He *must* still be here," Seth whispered, speaking the words that Angel was thinking. "Even if he wasn't dead when we buried him, there's no way he could have gotten out without moving the flowers, and if somebody dug him up—"

"Nobody dug him up," Angel said. "If they had, wouldn't something have gotten moved from the way it was?"

"Maybe it did," Seth said, "Maybe we just didn't remember it exactly right."

Angel shook her head. "Who even knew we'd buried

him? You were the one who said no one even knows this place is here."

But even though they knew what they were about to find, they kept digging anyway, taking out the rest of the flowers and removing handful after handful of the earth that hadn't yet solidified since they'd dug into it the first time, certain that with each handful of earth they removed, they would reach Houdini's corpse. And then, suddenly, it was over. All the loose dirt was out of the grave, and all that was left was an empty hole—a hole exactly as large and as deep as they both remembered having dug it to hold Houdini's broken corpse.

But the corpse was gone.

They stared into the empty grave for almost a full minute before Seth finally spoke. "I was right," he whispered. "You really did bring him back to life."

Though she heard the words, Angel tried to shut them out, tried to reject them, because to accept them was also to accept the rest of what Seth had said last night: *Maybe you really are a witch.* Her eyes still fixed on the empty grave, she shook her head. "I couldn't have," she whispered. "It isn't—"

There was a soft mewing then, and they both turned to see Houdini sitting in the open doorway of the tiny cabin. As they stared at him, he turned and disappeared inside.

Neither of them speaking, Angel and Seth stood up and followed the cat into the tiny room hidden in the cleft. The cat was sniffing anxiously at the niche in which the book was hidden, and when they retrieved it from its hiding place and put it on the table, it seemed to fall naturally open to the same strange verse they'd read the first day they'd discovered the book:

Spring

Drop of blood
Thrice haired with hog
Symmerd add
Green 'neath log.

Wishing thence
Upon a stone
Tasts it whence
Thou wisht it thrown.

They read it through three times, then Angel turned to Seth. "Do you know what it means? I mean, what it's supposed to do?"

Seth shrugged helplessly and his eyes shifted to Houdini, who was now sitting on the counter near the huge water catchment basin, his tail twitching nervously as he watched them. "But I think we ought to try it, and see what happens." As soon as he uttered the words, Houdini appeared to relax, stretching out on the counter, curling up, and going to sleep.

Angel looked doubtfully at the page. " 'Thrice haired with hog,' " she read. "Where are we supposed to get hairs from a hog?"

"There's a farm about half a mile farther out the road," Seth replied.

An hour later they were back in the tiny cabin, carrying half a dozen long hairs they'd found in the mud of the pigsty on the farm down the road, and a variety of mosses from under fallen logs in the woods. As they entered the cabin chamber, Houdini woke up, bounded off the counter, and came over to stretch up and sniff at Angel's hand.

While Seth built a fire, Angel took the kettle from the pothook, filled it half full with water, replaced it on the hook and swung it over the quickly growing fire.

As the water began to heat, there was a sudden flash of lightning, followed a few seconds later by a clap of thunder.

As first Seth, then Angel, cut their fingers and squeezed a few drops of blood into the kettle, a gentle rain began to fall.

As they added the rest of the ingredients they'd collected, the shower built into a downpour.

With Houdini curled up beside them, Angel and Seth watched the flames.

Chapter 34

STARTLED BY THE FLASH OF LIGHTNING, FATHER Michael Mulroney's whispered prayers died on his lips, and as the thunderclap that instantly followed on the heels of the lightning bolt rattled the windows of the church, he got to his feet and hurried up the aisle to the door. The first drops of rain were just beginning to fall, but the storm that had suddenly blackened the sky had not yet unleashed enough water to drown the wisp of smoke rising from the enormous tree that stood in the old graveyard across the street. As he stood in the shelter of the tiny church foyer and the rain began coming down harder, Father Mike felt a chill pass over him— a chill far colder than the slight drop in the temperature could account for.

A second bolt of lightning struck, slashing out of the sky, reaching down to the tree like giant fingers intent on gripping the mighty oak, ripping it from the ground, and tossing it aside as if it were no more than a weed. In an instant the lightning had vanished and the deafening roar of its accompanying thunder once again shook the structure of Father Mike's church to its foundations. As the thunderclap rolled away and the skies seemed to open—as they must have at the beginning of the Flood, the priest reflected—he backed deeper into the church, closing the doors as if to shut out not only the storm, but the fear that was congealing deep within his soul.

Abandoning his prayers, he retreated to the small room behind the altar and sat down at his desk. Unlocking the bottom drawer on the left hand side, he took out a worn book that had been left in the desk by his predecessor, or perhaps even by someone who had served Roundtree's small Catholic congregation several centuries ago. When he'd first come upon the book nearly twenty years ago, he'd thought it little more than a curiosity, for what possible relevance could seventeenth century speculations on witchcraft have to his parish? He'd glanced through it, more amused than anything else by the obvious terror the author felt for everything he discussed in his short essay on how the town had tried to rid itself of two women—or, rather, a woman and her teenage daughter—who had been accused of "Vile Majyk"—as it had been called in the book— nearly a century before the Revolutionary War. His first impulse had been to give the book to the local library, where it properly belonged, but for some reason—a reason he'd never quite understood—he put it back in the drawer, where it had remained locked away for almost two decades.

Then, almost two years ago, he was awakened in the middle of the night by a sudden storm that whipped up out of nowhere. The first crash of thunder woke him, and the second flash of lightning was so bright that he went to the window to make certain it hadn't struck the church next door. A moment later the third bolt struck, lashing down out of the sky into the great round tree in the middle of the cemetery. For almost half an hour he stood at the window watching as bolt after bolt of lightning struck the tree and deafening thunder crashed against his ears, shaking the tiny parsonage. In less than an hour the storm died away as suddenly as it began, and he went back to bed. But as he rose at dawn the next morning and looked out the window, instead of seeing the shattered and scarred remains of a tree, as he'd expected, the immense old oak stood as it always had, its canopy forming an almost perfect sphere, none of its branches showing any signs of the violence to which it had been subjected only a few hours earlier.

Then, late that afternoon, he'd heard the first rumors of violence that had taken place in the house at Black Creek Crossing the night before.

And something clicked in his mind.

He'd gone to his desk, unlocked the bottom drawer, taken out the book and thumbed through it until he found the passage that had suddenly risen out of the depths of his memory:

> . . . it being known that Storms struck out of empty Skyes when they practiced the Evil Majyk and three Witnesses swearing that they saw ye Round Tree struck by lightning but never Burned, they were thus Bound to that Tree, there to be Burned themselves . . .

Father Mulroney read the passage three times before turning the page to read the rest of the story of what had happened when Margaret and Forbearance Wynton had been burned:

> . . . and when ye Flames did finally Die and ye Smoke blewe away on the great Winde that rose up, naught was left of ye Witches nor the Rope that Bound them, yet ye Great Tree still stood.

The priest locked the book up once again and went to his prayers, certain that the Holy Mother would guide him. He'd followed the trial of Nate Rogers, and once or twice wondered if perhaps he should talk to the man's lawyer, perhaps show him the book he'd found locked in his desk. But in the end he kept silent, saying nothing about the strange passages he'd read in the old book, knowing that whatever had been written in it couldn't possibly have any bearing whatsoever on the case of Nate Rogers, who had never been able to give any explanation at all for what he'd done.

"There was a voice," was all he'd ever said. "It told me to do what I wanted to do."

Besides, Father Mulroney had reasoned, if he said anything, people would only have thought he was as crazy as Nate Rogers had been found to be.

Then, on the day that Marty and Myra Sullivan and their daughter moved into the old house at Black Creek Crossing, thunderheads had churned up in a clear blue sky, and an electrical storm as violent as the one on the night when Nate Rogers murdered his wife and daughter had lashed out at the village for almost three hours before vanishing as suddenly as it had arrived.

The sky had once more been crystalline blue, and within minutes of the cessation of the rain, thunder, and lightning, no trace of the clouds remained.

Another had struck only two days ago.

And now a third had struck.

For the third time, Father Mulroney opened the old book and tried to make sense of the strange and impossible things described within its covers.

As the fire under the cast-iron kettle died away, so also did the storm that had been raging outside. Once again neither Angel nor Seth was certain how long they had sat staring into the flames. But when they looked outside, the sun was just above the trees; soon dusk would begin to fall, and the darkness would gather quickly.

Seth swung the kettle out of the fireplace, and together they peered into its depths. Just as before, most of the water had boiled away, and what was left seemed utterly devoid of either color or aroma. And when they breathed in the steam still rising from the surface of the broth, neither one of them felt anything unusual.

"How much of it do you think we should drink?" Angel asked.

Seth shrugged. "All of it, I guess."

Angel peered uncertainly into the kettle, which was far fuller today than it had been when the fire burned out the day before yesterday. "But what's it going to do?"

"How should I know?" Seth asked. Fetching the ladle and lifting it to his lips, he blew on it, then tipped his head back and poured the contents into his mouth.

Far from burning his tongue, which he'd feared, the liquid seemed cool in his mouth, and he felt the same cool sensation as it moved through his esophagus and down into his stomach.

"You won't believe it," he said as he dipped the ladle into the kettle once again, this time offering it to Angel. "It's not even hot."

Though Angel could see the steam rising from the ladle, she still held it to her lips and took a careful sip. Seth was right—it was cool! Tipping the ladle further, she drained it quickly, and felt the coolness spread through her. Houdini had now approached and sat by her feet. Dipping the ladle once more into the kettle, Angel held it close to the floor, right under the cat's nose. Not even bothering to sniff it first, Houdini lapped thirstily, sucking up the liquid until the ladle was empty.

Ten minutes later, with the kettle empty, the ladle put back on its peg above the counter, and the book returned to the niche behind the loose stone in the wall of the fireplace, they closed the cabin and climbed the stone berm.

When they got to the top, Angel turned around and looked down at the stone they used to mark the spot where they'd buried Houdini. "Let's try something," she said to Seth as she recalled the strange words of the recipe's second verse. Focusing on the stone, she tried to visualize it rising into the air until it was level with the cabin's roof.

For several long seconds nothing happened. Then, as she and Seth watched, the stone slowly rose from the ground, seemed to float in the air for a moment, and dropped back to the earth.

Chapter 35

NEITHER ONE OF THEM SPOKE AS THEY FOLLOWED Houdini back along the trail to Black Creek Road, but as they emerged from the woods and stepped onto the solid asphalt of the roadway, Seth finally voiced the question that had been in his mind ever since they'd turned away from the cabin and started home: "You think it really happened?"

Angel shrugged. "We both saw it, didn't we?"

"But how?" Seth pressed. "I mean—"

"I don't know!" Angel broke in. "But I know what we both saw, so it must have happened."

"But—"

"All I did was what the book said to do."

Sensing that Angel had no more idea than he did about the rock rising into the air, Seth lapsed back into silence until they came to the last bend in Black Creek Road before Angel's house would become visible—which meant they would be just as visible from the house. "What if your dad sees me?" he asked, stopping before the house came into view.

"Then I guess he'll be mad at me," Angel sighed. "But if Mom's there, it'll be all right."

"What if she's not there?"

Angel shrugged as if it wouldn't make much difference, but she knew that if her mother wasn't there, and her father had started drinking—*She'll be there,* she told herself. *And Dad won't be drinking.*

But a few minutes later, when they saw the house, she knew she was wrong about at least one thing—the car wasn't in sight, which told her that at least one of her parents had gone somewhere. And if it was her father who was home, and if he'd been drinking . . .

She felt Houdini pressing up against her leg, and bent down to scratch him behind the ears. "You'll take care of me, won't you?" she asked, trying to make her words lighter than her mood.

"M-Maybe we should go get a Coke at the drugstore, or something," Seth suggested. But as Angel glanced around at the gathering darkness, she shook her head.

"I better go in." Yet she made no move to start across the lawn toward the house. Seth waited for her to speak again, and at last she did. "A-Are you scared?" Angel asked, her stammer betraying her feelings.

Seth nodded. "I—Well, I didn't really think any of it would—I mean—" His eyes dropped to Houdini, who was looking up at them as if he understood every word they were saying. "I guess I still thought maybe he wasn't really dead, and must have dug his way out of the hole even though we couldn't see how. But when . . ." His voice faded away, but he didn't have to finish for Angel to know what he was talking about.

"Maybe we shouldn't go back there," she said. "Maybe we should just pretend like we never found the book or the cabin at all."

"But we didn't find it," Seth said. "Houdini led us to it, and—"

"*Angel!*" The single word rang out like a shot, and Seth and Angel whirled around to see her father standing on the front porch of the old house, a bottle of beer clutched in his upraised fist. "You get in here, you hear me?"

Angel glanced at Seth, her face paling. "I've got to go," she said. "I'll see you tomorrow."

Seth held up a hand as if to stop her, but her father was already off the porch and starting across the lawn toward them.

"Didn't I tell you to stay away from my daughter?" Marty snarled.

"We weren't doing anything wrong," Angel began, stepping in front of Seth, as if to block her father.

"You get in the house," Marty said, shoving her aside. "I'll get to you when I'm done with him!" But Seth was already gone, running down Black Creek Road toward town. "Coward!" Marty bellowed. Draining the last of the beer in a single long swallow, he flung the bottle after Seth, then turned back to the house as it shattered on the pavement thirty feet short of where he'd been aiming.

Retreating back into the house, he slammed the door behind him. There was no sign of Angel in the living room, so Marty continued on into the kitchen, pulled another beer out of the refrigerator, knocked the cap off on the edge of the counter, then sucked half of it down his throat before mounting the stairs. When he got to the top, he paused for a moment, glowering at the closed door to his daughter's room.

His daughter, who didn't seem to give a damn about what he told her.

Well, now was as good a time as any to teach her a lesson.

He started toward her door, lost his balance, but caught himself before he fell. Twisting the doorknob, he flung the door open without knocking.

Angel was on the bed, huddled up against the head-board, her knees drawn up to her chest.

In her arms she held a cat.

The same black cat with the white blaze on its chest that had attacked him yesterday.

"Get that thing outta here," he said, his voice rasping, his fingers clenching the beer bottle.

The cat bared its teeth, hissing at him.

Draining the beer, Marty flipped the bottle around so he was holding it by the neck, then smashed it against the floor. As razor-sharp shards of brown glass shot across the floor, he straightened up again. Now he held the broken neck of the bottle in his right hand. Three jagged points, one much longer than the other two, were pointing at the cat.

The cat, and Angel too.

"Wanta try it again, cat?" Marty whispered, moving closer to the bed, jabbing at the cat with the broken bottle.

Angel's eyes widened as she stared at the broken beer bottle and the fury in her father's eyes. "Daddy, don't," she pleaded. "I—I'll put him outside."

"I don't want him outside," Marty replied, moving closer. "I want him dead! Should've killed him last time . . ."

Angel felt every muscle in Houdini's body grow tense as he prepared to launch himself at her father. For a moment she felt paralyzed, but then her mind focused, and again she remembered the rock that had suddenly lifted off the ground and flown through the air.

And in her mind, she visualized not a stone, but her father, and not the top of the bluff, but the bottom of the stairs.

As if grasped by some immense unseen force, Marty Sullivan was suddenly propelled backward out of the room, his head crashing against the top of the doorway as he passed through. A moment later Angel heard him tumbling down the stairs.

Stunned by what had just happened—barely able to believe it—Angel remained motionless on the bed until Houdini squirmed free of her grasp and bounded through the open door. Then Angel got up and quickly followed.

Looking down, she saw her father lying at the foot of the stairs, sprawled out on his back, his eyes closed. The neck of the beer bottle lay next to his right hand, and he was bleeding from a deep cut in his cheek where the broken glass must have slashed him as he tumbled down the stairs.

Houdini sniffed at the wound, then licked at the blood that was running down Marty's cheek.

Was he dead?

Angel started down the stairs, but then her father stirred, tried to sit up, and dropped back down again. "I'm gonna kill you," he mumbled, trying to push the cat away. "I'm gonna . . ." His voice faded away and he passed out again, and Angel suddenly knew what she had to do.

Hurrying downstairs, she skirted around her father, found the dustpan and broom in the closet under the stairs, and hurried back up to her room. A moment later she was back downstairs, where she dumped the broken glass from the dustpan onto the kitchen floor and put the dustpan and broom back where she'd found them. Then, picking up Houdini, she went back up to her room, closed the door, and sat down to wait, silently praying that her mother would come home before her father woke up again.

*   *   *

After he left Angel's—or, to be completely honest with himself about it, after he'd run in the face of her father's fury—Seth didn't slow down until he was certain he was around the bend and out of sight. When he finally paused to catch his breath, he started feeling guilty, and wondered if he shouldn't go back and make sure Angel was all right. The sun had finally set, though, and as he realized how late it was getting—and how late he'd be for dinner—the thought of his own father's rage made him continue toward town.

Night had almost completely fallen by the time he came to the village, but that hadn't bothered him—he'd learned years ago that the darkness of night was his best protection from Chad Jackson and his friends; if they couldn't see him, they couldn't start after him. He walked past the cemetery, as he'd done hundreds of times, and as always, was not the least bit scared. Of course, this was the first time he'd walked past it since he and Angel came upon the story of Forbearance Wynton and her mother in the library, and then found the graves of their family—but not their own—the next day.

Still, he hadn't done more than glance into the grave-yard, and there was nothing there that frightened him. No shadowy figures lurking among the gravestones, no rustling sounds, no oddly cold drafts, nor anything else that might have suggested the presence of anything out of the ordinary.

He peered into the drugstore as he passed it, but it had closed half an hour ago, and the only lights still on were way at the back, where the pharmacy and the office were. If Chad and Jared had even been there earlier, they were long gone.

In fact, everyone seemed to be gone.

The streets were empty, and no cars passed him as he

walked past the square, turned the corner onto Court Street, and started up toward Elm.

As he was passing the small park next to the courthouse, the first sense that something wasn't quite right came over him, but as some instinct deep inside him sounded the first warning, he tried to dismiss it.

Still, he quickened his pace.

The feeling persisted, but as he continued up Court Street, he told himself it didn't mean anything. And besides, it would be weirder if he didn't feel anything strange after what had happened out at the cabin. Even now, he wasn't sure how much of it had actually been real. Certainly, he had a clear memory of going out and gathering the stuff he and Angel needed to follow the recipe in the book, but he still couldn't quite believe there wasn't some more reasonable explanation for how Houdini had come back to life and gotten out of the grave where they'd buried him than some kind of magic.

But Houdini had been dead—he was sure of it.

And he was just as sure that no one else had been out there messing with the grave either.

A chill passed over him—the same kind of chill that occurred in horror stories when there was a ghost in the room. But he wasn't in a room, and wasn't even anywhere near the graveyard anymore.

He walked even faster, then forced himself to slow down, sure that if he began running he'd get even more scared than he was right now.

But there's nothing to be scared of, he told himself. *There's nothing in the park—or anywhere else.* Yet even as he silently reassured himself, the eerie feeling only grew stronger that something—or someone—was there, just outside the limits of his vision.

Hiding in the darkness.

He gave in to the impulse to move faster past the park,

yet his presentiment of danger only grew stronger. At the next corner, he paused in the bright pool of light flooding from the fixture hanging in the middle of the intersection. But instead of feeling safer, the bright light left him feeling exposed. Whatever the danger was, it was creeping through the darkness, surrounding him, using the shelter of night to trap him in a noose that would slowly tighten until—

A strangled sound welling up from his throat, Seth darted off the curbing, dashed across the street, and hurried along the sidewalk until he was out of the pool of light and the shadows of the trees swallowed him up.

Then, just as the terrible feeling of danger lurking close by began to ease, a figure stepped out from behind a tree to stand in the middle of the sidewalk ten yards ahead, blocking his way.

Seth stopped dead in his tracks, his heart pounding as the sense of danger came flooding back. But this time it was no presentiment. This time he could see the danger, and even before he heard the voice, he knew who it was.

"Hi, Beth," Zack Fletcher said softly. "Thought you might be coming this way."

Seth stood perfectly still, wondering what to do. He was still three blocks from home, and there was no way he could outrun Zack, even if Zack were by himself.

Which, Seth was certain, he wasn't.

Chad Jackson and Jared Woods would be hidden somewhere in the darkness nearby, guarding Zack's flanks.

And making certain he had no way to escape.

"Tell me how you did it," Zack said with a cold quietness in his voice that frightened Seth far more than any furious yell would have.

"D-Did what?" Seth countered, knowing what Zack was talking about and stalling for time. He glanced around, searching for some sign of Chad and Jared, but saw no flicker of movement in the darkness and heard no crackling of the unraked leaves that lay thick on the lawn beside him.

"Don't mess with me, Baker," Zack snarled, moving closer, his right hand squeezed into a fist. "You couldn't beat me at anything on the best day of your life. So you cheated."

"Like you and your friends cheat off my homework whenever you can?" Seth heard himself say, the words having risen unbidden into his throat and emerging from his mouth before he realized he was going to speak. And yet, even as he saw Zack's whole body tense with anger, the fear that had filled him a second ago began to drain away. He glanced around again, and once more neither heard nor saw any sign of Chad Jackson or Jared Woods.

And then he heard himself speak again, and once more had no memory of formulating the thought before he uttered it: "By yourself, aren't you, Zack? Big mistake."

Zack, who was slowly but steadily closing the distance between them, stopped, and for just an instant appeared taken aback.

And now, Seth knew what he was going to say before he spoke: "Why don't you just go away?"

Zack Fletcher's eyes widened. "You gone nuts, Beth?" he asked, but the dangerous, quiet tone in his voice was gone, and Seth thought he heard a quaver, at least of uncertainty if not quite of fear.

"Don't ever call me that again," Seth said. "I don't think I like it."

At that, Zack seemed to regain his self-confidence. "Yeah? Why should I care what you like?" He moved closer again, his fist cocked, and Seth could almost feel the pain of the blow that was about to strike him. "You're nothing but a—"

But before Zack could finish, he rose off his feet, his head smashing against the lowest branch of the oak tree in whose shadow both boys stood. And then he dropped back to the sidewalk, sprawled out flat on his back, his head crashing against the concrete sidewalk.

As Zack moaned and whimpered, cradling his head in his hands, Seth edged around him. "I warned you," he said quietly. "All you had to do was walk away."

Chapter 36

MYRA SULLIVAN WAS LATE, WHICH SHE KNEW MEANT that Marty would be angry, which meant he'd be drinking. As she pulled the bag of groceries out of the trunk of the Chevelle she braced herself for the tirade she would almost certainly face the moment she opened the front door. It was her fault, of course—she should have gone to the store earlier, which she would have done if the thunderstorm hadn't swirled in out of nowhere. In fact, she'd been about to leave the house when the first bolt of lightning lashed out of the sky and a moment later the house shook under the crash of the thunderbolt that came on the heels of the lightning.

And then the skies had opened.

She'd peered out the window for a few minutes, waiting for the rain to let up, but finally took off her coat and went back to unpacking the last of the boxes that were still in the unoccupied bedroom upstairs, while Marty settled in to watch a football game. The lightning was ruining the reception and he could barely see anything on the flickering screen, but instead of shutting off the set and helping her with the boxes, he kept opening more beers and grumbling that she should have had the cable turned on last week. Knowing better than to argue with him, she kept working until the storm finally passed, then went out to get what she needed to feed them that evening.

Apparently, everybody else had the same idea, so it took her twice as long to get out of the store as she'd planned, and now Marty would be angry. Well, it couldn't be helped. He was her cross to bear, and whatever pain she had to endure in this life would be rewarded in the next.

As she lifted the groceries out of the back of the car and headed for the house, she saw a light glowing in Angel's window, which was a relief. At least she could stop worrying about where Angel might be.

Preparing for whatever anger Marty might have been nursing while she was gone—and knowing it would be amplified by her lateness—Myra wondered for a brief second what it might be like to have a husband who actually came out to carry the groceries in for her. Banishing the thought almost as quickly as it occurred to her, and offering up a quick prayer for forgiveness to the Holy Mother, she pushed the front door open.

And instantly sensed that something had changed.

Though the TV was still on, Marty wasn't watching it.

Frowning, she picked up the remote from the arm of his chair and shut off the TV.

The silence that fell over the house did nothing to banish her uneasiness; indeed, the quiet only amplified it. She started toward the kitchen, her strange sense of apprehension growing with every step. And then she saw him.

Her husband was sprawled out on his back, the shards of a shattered beer bottle spread out around him, his eyes closed. "Marty?" she gasped. "Marty, what—" Her eyes still fixed on him, she set the groceries on the counter. "Angel?" she called as she sank to her knees next to her supine husband. Then her voice rose to almost a scream: "Angel!"

A moment later Angel appeared at the top of the stairs. Myra gazed up at her, then turned back to her husband. "Call an ambulance," she said. "Your father's—"

She stopped as Marty moaned softly. His right arm moved, and then he opened his eyes. He focused on Angel, who was halfway down the stairs, and sat bolt upright, his eyes widening. "Get away," he said, his voice little more than a garbled croak. "Get away from me!" Angel froze on the stairs, and Marty, his face pale, clutched at Myra's arm. "She did it!" he said. "She threw me down the stairs!"

Myra stared at Marty, the shock of finding him unconscious on the floor giving way now to utter confusion. "Threw you?" she echoed. "Marty, what are you—"

"She did!" Marty cried as Angel came down the rest of the stairs. He shrank back from his daughter. "She—"

But Myra had heard enough. Whatever sympathy she'd had for him a moment earlier drained away. "You're drunk, Marty," she said, rising to her feet.

"I'm not!" Marty protested. "She—"

"Don't!" Myra said. "I can see what happened, Marty. You sat here drinking all day, and when you finally tried to go upstairs, you tripped and fell down." As Marty tried to object, Myra shook her head. "A falling down drunk, that's what you are. And I won't have it! To blame your daughter! Shame, Martin! Shame on you!"

"But, Myra—" Marty whined, reaching out as if to grab the hem of his wife's skirt.

"No!" Myra snapped. "I won't have it! Now get up and get this mess cleaned up, and then go sleep it off."

Marty wilted in the face of his wife's sudden fury. But as he hauled himself to his feet, his anger began to build once again. "I'm tellin' you, it wasn't me!" he said. "It was—"

Before he could finish, Myra turned, raised her hand, and slapped him so hard across the face that he reeled away.

Clutching at his stinging cheek, he lurched toward the back door. "The hell with you," he muttered. "The hell with you both." Jerking the door open so fast it slammed against the wall, Marty Sullivan stumbled away into the darkness outside.

"Zack should have been home half an hour ago," Joni Fletcher said, frowning as she glanced at the clock above the kitchen sink. "I told him six o'clock and absolutely no later."

"Hey, he's a teenager," Ed replied. "So he's a few minutes late—what's the big deal?"

"The 'big deal,' as you call it, is that I've got a roast almost ready to serve. And not just any roast—it's the kind of prime rib that you and your son love the most. It was done exactly fifteen minutes ago, and it can rest for exactly fifteen more minutes before it's going to start getting less than prime. And in half an hour, it'll start getting cold, and after that—"

"Okay, okay!" Ed Fletcher held up his hands in exaggerated surrender. "So if he's late, he's late. I vote we eat it when it's perfect, and if he's not here, that's more for me."

"And I vote," Joni retorted, "that you hop in the car and go see if you can find him. He knew what I was serving, and he swore he wouldn't be late. He's probably over at the Jacksons', so how long can it take?"

Ed rolled his eyes. "Come on, Joni—do you have any idea what it's like for a sixteen-year-old to have his daddy come looking for him? I remember—" But before he could begin expounding on every dire consequence that could pertain to the humiliation Joni was suggesting, the phone rang.

"Where?" Joni his wife asked after listening briefly, the receiver pressed to her ear. "All right—we'll be right there . . . not more than two minutes." As she hung up, and looked at him, Ed guessed what the call was about.

"Zack?" he asked.

Joni nodded, but was already heading toward the door that led from the kitchen to the garage. "I'll tell you on the way."

In less than a minute, Ed was backing down the driveway.

"That was Sheila Jacobson," his wife explained. "She lives on Court Street? That's where we're going. Anyway, she heard something in front of her house a few minutes ago, and when she went to look, she found Zack on the sidewalk. He's—oh God, Ed, he was almost unconscious, and she's already called an ambulance, and—" Her voice caught. She struggled against the lump rising in her throat, forced it back under control, then went on. "Just hurry."

When he pulled into the Jacobsons' driveway on Court Street, Joni leaped out of the car. At nearly the same time, an ambulance, lights flashing and siren screaming, raced around the corner and pulled up to the curb. Now, in the light of the ambulance's headlights, Joni could see the still form of her son lying on the sidewalk, with a man bent over him. A moment later, as Ed joined her, they rushed over to kneel next to Zack, where medics had edged the man aside and were examining the boy.

"Please, God," Joni whispered, unaware that she was speaking out loud. "Don't let him be dead! Let him be—"

"I think he's okay," one of the medics said. "Get a stretcher and—" Before he could finish, Zack groaned, lifted an arm, then tried to sit up. "Easy," the medic said. "Just take it easy."

Zack let the medic ease him back down onto the sidewalk, but gingerly touched the top of his head with his fingers, winced, and pulled them away.

The fingers were red with blood.

Joni gasped. "My God, Zack—what happened to you?"

Zack said nothing for a moment, then his eyes narrowed angrily. "Seth Baker," he said. "The prick jumped me! He—He hit me with a rock or something!"

The medic was already examining Zack's head, while his partner held a powerful flashlight on the wound. "Something in his hair, here," he muttered softly, and carefully picked a fragment of something that looked like wood out of Zack's blood-matted hair. "Looks like bark." He grinned. "Sure you just didn't try to tackle a tree, big fella?" he asked.

"He threw me!" Zack said. "He threw me right up into—" He fell abruptly silent, as if realizing just how strange he must sound.

The medic with the light frowned, and then shined the light up into the tree directly above Zack. Standing, he moved around, playing the light over the lowest branch. "For Christ's sake," he said, holding the light still. "Would you look at that?" He jumped up, barely managed to touch the branch, then looked at his fingers.

More blood.

Now Zack was sitting up, and it was apparent that his injuries weren't terribly serious.

"You say Seth Baker did this?" Ed Fletcher said, eyeing his son skeptically.

"He jumped me!" Zack repeated. "He grabbed me

from behind and—" He seemed to lose track of what he was saying for a moment, then shook his head as if trying to clear it of an idea that made no sense. "It was weird," he finished.

"And he was by himself?" Ed asked. "Nobody was with him?"

Zack started to shake his head, then changed his mind. "I—I don't know."

"Well, did you see anyone?" Ed Fletcher pressed.

"It was dark!" Zack complained. "I could barely even see him!"

Ed seemed about to say something else, but Joni spoke first. "Can we please take care of Zack first, then figure out exactly what happened?" She turned to the medics. "Do you have to take him to the emergency room?"

"We'd better," one of them replied. "That's a pretty nasty cut, and it'll probably take a few stitches to close it up. And it won't hurt to make sure there's no concussion."

"All right," Joni said. "We'll follow you."

A few minutes later Ed backed the Mercedes out of the Jacobsons' driveway and fell in behind the ambulance.

"Okay," Joni said. "Do you really believe Seth Baker attacked Zack?"

Ed glanced over at his wife. "What do you mean? He said—"

"I heard what he said," Joni cut in. "But it just seems so unlikely—I mean, *Seth Baker*? He's never even tried to fight back during all the years the other kids have picked on him. And I'm including Zack in that," she went on before Ed could interrupt. "Why would that suddenly change tonight?"

"Maybe it didn't suddenly change," Ed suggested. "I mean, look what he did at the club yesterday, sandbagging us by pretending he couldn't play golf for nine holes, then never missing a shot on the back nine! I mean, at the beginning I thought it was a fluke, but nobody goes through nine holes the way he did without knowing exactly what he was doing."

Joni was silent for a moment, then: "And I saw the look on Zack's face when Seth beat him yesterday, Ed. He looked like he wanted to beat Seth up on the spot. And you weren't very happy about losing to Blake Baker either. So with Zack being mad at Seth rather than the other way around, why would Seth have jumped Zack? And what was Zack doing there in the first place? Court Street is on the way to the Bakers' house, not ours."

Ed's grip on the wheel tightened. "So what are you saying? That Zack's lying?"

Faced with the starkness of her husband's question, Joni found herself unable to answer it directly. "I— I don't know," she finally temporized.

"No, you don't," Ed said in a tone that Joni recognized. It was the one he always used when he was about to stop discussing something. "And I don't either. But I know something's going on with Seth Baker, and tomorrow I'm going to have a talk with Blake and find out just what it is."

Neither of them spoke again until they were parked in the lot next to the small hospital. "So what do we do?" Joni finally asked. "What do we say to Zack?"

Ed took a deep breath, then slowly let it out. "Nothing," he finally said. "Tomorrow I'll talk to Blake and see what he's got to say. For tonight, we take Zack home." He looked pointedly at Joni. "And you at least act like you believe what our son told us, all right?"

Joni hesitated, then reluctantly nodded. Yet as they entered the hospital, she had the feeling that nothing was going to be as simple as Ed seemed to think. Something had happened to Zack, and while she knew that her son's explanation didn't make much sense—especially since he'd changed it after the medic found blood on the branch high up in the tree—she also knew there had to be something Zack wasn't telling them.

Marty Sullivan stared dolefully into the bottom of his empty glass, shifted his gaze to the greasy mirror behind the bar, and shoved the glass out for a refill.

"Haven't you had about enough?" the barman asked, eyeing him with a look of such boredom that Marty didn't bother to respond to the question. "Your funeral," the bartender sighed as he filled Marty's glass with the watered-down whiskey he kept in the well for people like Marty, who had already consumed enough alcohol that they'd barely notice that their drinks no longer carried the punch of the first half dozen, and weren't in good enough condition to fight even if they caught on and tried to object. "Just try to make sure you don't kill anybody but yourself on your way home."

Marty uttered a disinterested grunt, drained the drink, and threw a wad of bills on the bar. The bartender eyed the crumpled paper, decided there was more than enough to cover the tab and a good tip for himself, swept it off the counter, and moved down to the other end, where he began pouring a round for a group near the pool table that were even drunker than Marty.

As he pushed his way through the door and out into the cool of the night, Marty considered the possibilities.

He could go to another bar, have a couple more drinks, and maybe pick up a pool game.

He could go home, where Myra would be all over him for getting drunk, and Angel—

Angel!

He shuddered as the vision that had hung before him through the long hours he'd sat drinking in the bar rose once again, this time hovering in the quiet darkness of the village's empty streets.

Angel, holding that damned cat and staring at him with a look he'd never seen before. For a second she'd appeared frightened and her face had gone all pale, but then, just before she came at him, something in her face had changed.

It was her eyes. They'd suddenly taken on the same golden glow—like there was a fire burning inside them— that he'd seen in the cat's eyes as it lunged at his face.

Then, so quickly he hadn't seen it at all, she'd come at him, shoving him so hard he flew off his feet, tumbled backward down the stairs, and—

Nothing.

Except that there was one other image that kept popping up in his mind too. It was after Angel had pushed him down the stairs. He'd been lying on the floor, just barely conscious, when he'd felt something.

Something sniffing at him.

The cat! The damned cat!

He'd struggled to open his eyes, raised a hand to fend off the animal, but when he finally managed to lift an eyelid, what he'd seen wasn't a cat at all.

It was a girl—a girl about the same age as Angel. But she didn't look like Angel. Her face was ghostly white, and her eyes were the palest blue he'd ever seen. She was wearing an old-fashioned black bonnet, and a black dress, and there was some kind of brooch on her chest that looked like it was carved out of ivory or something.

Then, in an instant, her face changed. The flesh began to fall away, leaving nothing but a skull with that terrible golden light shining from the empty eye sockets. And as she leaned forward, her lips dropped off to expose her teeth.

Long, curved, feline teeth, each of them tipped with blood.

As she moved her face closer to his, her mouth opened, but instead of a tongue, a serpent emerged. Its jaws were spread wide, and its fangs, already oozing venom, came directly at him.

The worst terror he'd ever felt had risen up in him, and then—

Nothing.

He'd passed out, and remembered nothing else until he awakened to find Myra looming over him, and wished he could escape into unconsciousness again.

And now he was standing alone on a street corner, whiskey burning in his belly, a sour taste rising in his throat, and so dizzy he had to hold on to the lamppost to keep from falling down.

And all the images—all the impossible memories— were still there.

As his stomach finally rebelled against the alcohol he'd poured into it, Marty sank to his knees, leaned over, and threw up into the gutter. Over and over again his stomach contracted, until finally there was nothing left to spew out of his throat. At last he leaned back, resting against the lamppost, a cold sweat breaking out over his body. His breathing came in shallow gasps and the sour taste of vomit filled his mouth, while its acid burned in his throat.

A car drove by, and through his bleary eyes Marty saw the driver glance at him, then look quickly away.

Finally, half pulling himself up on the lamppost, he got back to his feet and began walking, cutting diagonally across the intersection, then weaving along the sidewalk on the other side of the street, neither thinking about nor caring about where he was going.

After a few blocks—he didn't know how many, exactly—he found himself in front of a church.

A little church, with its name neatly chiseled into a granite plaque attached to the wall next to the front door.

CHURCH OF THE HOLY MOTHER.

Marty gazed at the sign for a long time, trying to remember the last time he'd been in church.

He couldn't.

He gazed at the church door, and suddenly felt a need to go inside.

Except this late on Sunday night, it would be locked up tight.

But when he gave the door a perfunctory pull, it opened.

Marty stepped though the open door into the tiny foyer. Though no lights were on, candles were burning everywhere, and the small sanctuary was filled with a soft golden light that seemed to swirl around him as the candle flames danced in the draft of the open door.

Automatically, he dipped his fingers in the font, crossed himself, and mouthed a quick prayer.

As he was starting down the aisle, a figure rose in front of the altar and turned toward him.

"How may I help you?" the priest asked.

For almost a full minute Marty Sullivan simply stared at him. Then, almost unaware of what he was doing, he sank to his knees. "Something happened," he whispered. "Something terrible."

Father Michael Mulroney walked slowly up the aisle and laid a gentle hand on his shoulder. "You're Marty Sullivan, aren't you?" he asked.

Marty looked up at the priest, his eyes wide. "H-How do you know who I am?"

The priest smiled. But there was something in his smile, and in his eyes as well—a sadness that seemed to come from somewhere deep within him—that sent a chill through Marty. "I've been expecting you," he said.

Chapter 37

WITCHCRAFT? WHAT THE HELL WAS A PRIEST DOING, talking about witchcraft? And about his daughter too!

Only an hour had passed since Marty Sullivan had wandered into the Church of the Holy Mother, but as he now made his way uncertainly through the darkness of the night, it wasn't only the alcohol he'd consumed that impaired his gait, but also the strange story Father Mulroney had told him as they sat in the tiny room behind the church altar.

At first he had figured the priest was just pulling his leg, talking about all the weird stuff that had happened in Roundtree. But after a while he'd started to get scared. Well, not really scared—he didn't believe in witches any more than anybody else did—but still, the way the priest told it, a lot more weird stuff had happened in Roundtree than anybody had ever told him about, and it seemed like most of it had started right there in the house he'd bought.

Except it wasn't really the house *he'd* bought. It was the house Myra had *made* him buy. Myra, and her snotty sister, Joni. If even half of what Father Mulroney had told him was true, he should sue Joni. And not just Joni either—he'd sue Ed Fletcher too. And the guy who set up the loan on the house, and everyone else as well. By the time he got done, they'd all wish they had never messed with Marty Sullivan!

The righteousness of his fury drove out the last of the fleeting uneasiness Marty had felt as he listened to the priest's story, and as he came to the Roundtree Tavern, he was already starting to think about what he'd do with the money he was going to get. Deciding he deserved a drink to celebrate the good fortune about to come his way, he pushed through the door and slid onto a stool at the end of the nearly empty bar.

"Just about to close up," the bartender said, eyeing Marty dolefully.

Marty pulled out his wallet and lay a twenty dollar bill on the bar. "That be enough to keep you open for a Johnnie Walker Black? Straight up." The bartender shrugged, poured the drink, and scooped up the twenty as he set the glass in front of him. Marty took another twenty out of his wallet and dropped it on the bar. "Pour yourself one too."

After a hesitation so short Marty didn't even notice it, the man behind the bar poured a second shot of whiskey into a glass, lifted it, and gestured toward Marty. "To whatever we're celebrating."

"The witches of Roundtree," Marty declared, raising his own glass. "They're going to be taking care of me the rest of my life!"

The bartender's glass hovered a few inches from his lips. "What the hell are you talking about?" he asked, suddenly suspicious.

Marty let out a bark of laughter and drained his glass in a single gulp. "My house! Father Mulroney over at Holy Mother just told me about the people who used to live there. He told me about the witches, and the trials, and everything else. So I'm gonna sue the bitch who sold the place to me, and the son of a bitch she's married to, too."

The bartender set his drink back on the bar, untouched. "You talking about the old place out at the Crossing?" When Marty nodded, the bartender shook his head. "You think you're gonna get anything out of all those old stories about that house, you better think again. You want to win a lawsuit, you got to prove there's somethin' wrong. And a bunch of old stories kids tell about witches aren't going to get you nothing."

"Yeah?" Marty shot back, the ebullience he'd been feeling only a moment ago starting to dissolve into anger. "What about the guy who killed his whole family in there?"

"He was a nutcase. And you knew about it when you moved in, didn't you?"

"How do you know what I knew and what I didn't?" Marty challenged.

The bartender rolled his eyes, picked up Marty's glass, and drained his own still full one into the sink. "Everybody knows everything around here," he said, putting the two twenties back on the bar in front of Marty. "Tell you what—why don't we just call it one on the house?"

Marty glowered as the heat of the alcohol spread through him. "You throwin' me outta here?"

"I'm just trying to close my place up for the night," the bartender replied. He glanced toward the opposite end of the bar, where the only other customer in the place was draining a beer. "You about done, Sergeant?" he called out, then glanced back at Marty. "All the cops in town hang out here," he drawled. "Probably why I never have any trouble."

Marty's dark gaze shifted from the bartender to the man at the far end of the bar, who was now staring at him. "Fine," he said, shoving the bills into his pocket and rising unsteadily to his feet.

"You need a lift, I can—" the bartender began, but Marty cut him off.

"I'm okay," he said. Before either the bartender or the cop could argue with him, Marty shoved through the door and out onto the sidewalk. Sucking his lungs full of the cold night air, he started down the street.

A minute later the cop and the bartender stepped out onto the sidewalk and watched as Marty weaved his way toward Black Creek Road. "What do you think?" the sergeant asked. "How drunk is he?"

The bartender shrugged. "Not enough to get in any trouble. He'll just stagger home and pass out." Then he laughed. "'Course, that's not saying he won't be having any hallucinations on the way." As they went back inside and he drew each of them a beer from the tap, the bartender began telling the cop what Marty Sullivan had said.

"Oh, Lord," the cop sighed. "Here we go again. I figured Father Mike would be the last one to start talking about all that crap, but what the hell do I know?" He shook his head. "Witches," he sighed. "Jesus, don't people have anything better to do?"

The heat of the last shot of Johnnie Walker was beginning to fade as Marty came to the edge of the village. He pulled the zipper of his jacket all the way up to his neck as the wind began to blow out of the northeast. Overhead, clouds scudded across the sky, and as he left the warm glow of the streetlights behind, the darkness closed around him like a shroud and fragments of the things Father Mulroney had told him began to rise unbidden from his memory.

. . . storms come out of nowhere . . .

Storms like the one that had struck this afternoon.

. . . it only seems to happen when there's an adolescent girl in the house . . .

A girl Angel's age.

. . . people see things . . . a cat . . . a girl dressed in black whose eyes glow like a cat's . . .

The same things Marty had seen.

Marty's pulse quickened, and so did his step.

The moon came out, and for an instant the darkness was washed away in a silvery glow.

And ahead of him he saw a figure.

A dark figure, little more than a shadow in the faint light of the moon. But Marty recognized it, and his breath caught in his throat as he froze in his tracks.

It was the girl—the same girl he'd seen in the living room when the cat attacked him.

The figure in the darkness moved closer, and Marty instinctively raised his arms as if to fend her off.

A cloud drifted over the moon.

The silvery light faded.

The figure vanished, but Marty remained rooted where he was, his heart pounding, his breath coming in short, labored gasps. A terrible chill fell over him—an iciness far colder than the night that reached deep inside him and gripped his soul. The cold made him shiver, and his teeth began to chatter, but still he couldn't make himself move.

His eyes searched the darkness for any sign of the black-clad figure that had been there only moments ago, but now all but the faintest glimmer of light seemed to have been blotted out, and even the shapes of the trees had vanished into the blackness surrounding him.

Not real, Marty told himself. *Too much to drink . . . stupid stories . . .*

Slowly, his heart began to slow, his gasping breath to even out. But still he stayed where he was, for even though he could see nothing and his whole body was numbed with cold, he could still feel the presence of something lurking in the darkness.

Then, out of the corner of his eye, Marty caught a faint flicker of golden light. He jerked his head around as his heart once more began to race, but whatever he'd seen was gone, vanishing into the darkness as quickly as it had come.

Then he saw it again, this time out of the corner of the other eye. But now the golden light didn't vanish when he turned toward it, and as he saw the two glowing eyes staring at him, the iciness in his blood ran even colder.

The eyes drew nearer, staying close to the ground.

They vanished, only to reappear a few seconds later, three or four feet to the left and a few feet closer.

"Scat!" Marty said, but even to his own ears the word sounded oddly hollow. "Go on! Get away!"

Instead of vanishing, the eyes moved nearer still. Now the invisible creature's eyes fixed on his own, and Marty had the horrible sensation that if he couldn't look away, couldn't tear his eyes from the golden orbs floating in the darkness, the creature would reach into him and tear away his very soul.

The eyes stopped moving, but their hypnotic gaze still held Marty pinned to the spot where he stood. Seconds passed—seconds that felt like minutes—but still Marty couldn't move.

He felt the creature tensing, could almost see it readying itself to leap at him, almost feel its claws and fangs sinking into his flesh.

As his fear coalesced into panic, a broken howl of anguish rose in his throat, and finally he managed to lash out with his foot at the staring eyes.

The eyes vanished, and then Marty was running, bolting through the blackness, driven as much by his own panic as the terror of what might be pursuing him. But he lost his footing, pitched forward, and fell face-first into the drainage ditch that ran next to the road. Swearing, he pulled himself up to his knees, wiping the muck from the ditch away from his eyes with his sleeve. A sob of pain mixed with fear and frustration rose in his throat, and he crawled back onto the road, bracing himself for the attack he knew was sure to come. He was just starting to haul himself back to his feet when the moon came out again and the wind died away. Marty blinked in the brightness of the silvery light, and searched for the creature that had stalked him only a moment ago.

Nothing.

He was alone on the road.

He peered in every direction, then began edging cautiously along the road. But with every step he took, he imagined that something was behind him, and the skin on the back of his neck began to crawl until he spun around, braced to defend himself against whatever might be behind him.

But there was only the night.

He felt another sob rise in his throat, and moved out into the center of the road, terrified that whatever was stalking him was hidden in the trees.

He was stumbling now, nearly tripping over his own feet, and another sob threatened to strangle him. Then, in the distance, he saw a light glowing. His first instinct was to turn and run, to try to race back into whatever safety the darkness might offer. Then he realized that this time the light was not the terrible glowing of the creature's eyes, but the porch light of his own house.

Sucking in a breath deep enough to break through the

terror that had built inside him, he ran again, but this time he wasn't running away from something, but toward the safety of his house.

Halfway across his own front yard he stopped once more.

Stopped, and gazed at the house.

And once more he recalled Father Mulroney's words.

But now, with the sky clear and the moon bright, and nothing peering at him out of the darkness, he was able to turn away the fear those same words had brought only a few minutes ago.

"Crap," he whispered as he continued toward the front door. "Nothin' but a pile of crap."

Marty wasn't sure exactly when the voice had begun whispering to him. The house had been silent when he slipped in through the back door, and for a moment he'd had the eerie feeling that the house was empty, that somehow Myra and Angel had vanished while he was gone. But that was impossible—where would they go? He turned on the light, and headed for the refrigerator, figuring one more beer couldn't hurt him.

But where earlier there had been most of a six-pack on the bottom shelf, there now was nothing. Frowning, Marty searched the refrigerator more carefully.

No beer.

Suspicion growing in his mind, he went to the sink, pulled open the cabinet below it, and peered into the wastebasket. Sure enough, there were five empty beer bottles, and they weren't just tossed in as he would have done. Instead, they were laid out side by side, exactly the way Myra would have done it after pouring the contents down the drain.

Bitch!

His first impulse was to go back out and find another six-pack—or maybe even a whole case—then sit and drink the whole thing just to show her. In the end, though, he just dug around in the cupboards until he found her cooking sherry and finished that off instead.

Then, his stomach feeling sour, he went upstairs, peeled off his clothes, and slid into bed beside Myra.

If she was awake—and he was pretty sure she was—she didn't say anything, and when he edged closer to her, snuggling up against her, she let out a muffled groan and turned away.

The hell with her—who needed her anyway?

He rolled over and closed his eyes, but as Myra's breathing finally fell into the gentle rhythm of sleep, he still lay awake.

Then the voice came out of the darkness, so soft at first he barely heard it. "*It's time . . .*" the voice whispered. "*. . . you know it's time . . .*

"*. . . now. . . .*" the voice pressed. "*It's time . . . you know it's time. . . .*"

Marty rolled over again.

"*You want to do it,*" the voice whispered. "*You have to do it . . . you know you do . . .*"

Marty's eyes opened.

"*. . . now. . . .*" the voice whispered. "*Do it now. . . .*"

He got up from the bed and left the bedroom, pulling the door shut so quietly there was barely the faintest click to disturb Myra's sleep. . . .

Chapter 38

ANGEL LAY IN THE DARKNESS, LISTENING.

She wasn't sure how long she'd been in bed, or whether she'd slept or not. But she must have slept, because the memory of the dreams she'd had was as fresh in her mind as if they'd actually happened, and happened only a few moments ago. They weren't at all like the dreams that made no sense and faded away the moment she awoke, leaving her with nothing more than a vague memory of having dreamed, but no memory at all of what the dream was actually about. No, the dreams she'd had this night were different.

She'd been on the road, and it was night, and even though the moon was blotted out by a thick layer of clouds, she could see a figure in the darkness ahead of her. She knew it was her father, even though his shape was no more than a faint silhouette and his features were utterly lost in shadows. But tonight she felt none of the fear of him that had been growing in her every day since they'd moved into their little house. The figure drew closer, and still she felt no sense of danger. Then, as the wind began to grow, the clouds broke and the light of the moon flooded through. Her father stopped, and she instinctively moved toward him. But then, as the moon fell full on him, she hesitated.

Instead of the clothes her father had been wearing when he stumbled out of the house a few hours ago, the figure ahead of her was clad almost entirely in black, with a close-fitting coat with a broad collar, and lapels buttoned up almost to the throat.

The face wasn't her father's either. It was longer, and narrower, and had a sort of pinched look to it.

He was staring at her now, and she could see the fear in his eyes. But why was he frightened? It was she who had been frightened of him this afternoon, and yesterday, and the day before that. Why—

Once again the clouds scudded over the moon, and the figure vanished into the blackness.

But suddenly she could see it again, only now she was looking up at it, as if she were lying on the ground.

And even though the moonlight was gone, she could see almost as well as she could during the day. Except everything was black and white, with no color at all.

Her father was staring at her again, backing away, and then he started running. As she watched, he ran off the road, tripped, and plunged face first into the ditch between the road and the forest.

"Dad!" she started to call out.

It was the sound of her own voice that awakened her from the dream, but the odd thing was, when she awoke, her heart wasn't pounding and she felt none of the terror that had seized her when the other dreams held her in their grip. And instead of feeling a sense of relief to find herself in her own bed in her own room, she felt vaguely surprised, as if she shouldn't be there at all. Only a second or two ago she was certain she'd been out in the road.

She'd gotten up and gone to the window, and seen her father coming across the lawn just as if he too had stepped out of her dream and into reality. Except now he was wearing the right clothes again, and when the moonlight spilled onto his face for a moment, she recognized him clearly.

As he headed around the corner of the house to the back door, she hurried back to bed, slipped in, and silently offered up a prayer to whatever saint might be listening that tonight her father wouldn't come into her room. She pulled the covers up close around her neck and listened.

She heard him rummage around in the kitchen.

Heard him come upstairs.

She held her breath, her heart pounding, and waited.

He went into the room where her mother was sleeping.

Angel breathed again.

But still she didn't sleep, for every other night in which her father had crept into her room, he'd gone to bed first.

Gone to bed, and waited until her mother was asleep.

Angel waited.

Outside, the wind began to rise again, and then the moonlight faded away as the clouds once again began racing across the sky.

Angel tried to shut out the sound of the wind sighing in the trees beyond her window, tried to focus her ears only on whatever sounds might be coming from within the house.

Seconds crept by, and turned into minutes, and every minute felt like an eternity.

He was asleep . . . he must be asleep.

And if he was asleep, it was safe for her to sleep.

She felt her muscles relax.

And then she heard it!

A faint creaking sound, so soft she almost missed it.

Had it come from inside the house? Maybe not. Maybe

it came from outside. Maybe one of the huge old maples had a cracked branch and—

It came again, and this time there was no mistaking it. The creaking had come from inside the house.

Angel froze, willing her heart to remain calm so its throbbing wouldn't drown out any sound that might betray whatever danger was creeping through the house.

Again she waited, straining her ears, unconsciously holding her breath.

Nothing.

Maybe she'd been wrong—maybe she hadn't really heard anything at all! Maybe whatever it was had come from outside. Slowly letting out the breath she hadn't known she was holding, she once more let herself relax.

And the sound came again.

This time she was certain it was right outside her door, and she had to fight to keep the scream that was building in her throat from erupting.

But maybe she should scream! Maybe she should scream as loud as she could, so her mother would wake up and—

Then she remembered what had happened when she tried to tell her mother about what her father was doing. And tonight, her father would just say he'd been worried about her and was listening to make sure she was all right.

And her mother would believe him.

Biting her lips, she held back her cry.

And heard the soft click of the door opening.

The squeal of its hinges as someone pushed it open.

The wind cleared the clouds away from the moon, and a silvery glow flooded through the window.

And Angel saw the same figure standing in her doorway that she'd seen standing in the road in her dream.

But she was awake now, and it wasn't a dream, and

even though the figure was wearing the strange black coat with the wide collar and lapels and didn't even look like her father, she knew that it *was* her father.

She could feel him looking at her, feel his eyes peeling away the blanket and the sheet, stripping off her pajamas.

She clutched at the covers, holding them as tight around her neck as she could, but still felt as if she was lying naked on the bed, with her father gazing at her.

The figure moved, stepping into the room.

No, Angel cried silently. *Oh, please, no!*

The figure moved closer, and once again her heart was racing, and she shrank back into the pillows and prayed she could just disappear and—

Long fingers with cracked and torn nails closed on the bedding, and Angel felt it being pulled away.

Now the hand was reaching for her pajamas.

Just as the fingers were about to close on the thin material that covered her breast, she focused her mind the way she had that afternoon and visualized her father hurtling through the door.

But instead of flying backward as he had that afternoon, this time her father only hesitated.

His hand trembled in the air a few inches in front of her.

In the dim silvery light spilling through the window, she could see him struggling.

Then his hand came closer.

Angel shrank back and concentrated harder, closing her mind to everything but the image she visualized of her father being pushed away, pushed out of the room, pushed to the top of the stairs, and then—

Slowly, almost imperceptibly, the hand reaching for her breast began to move away.

She could see it trembling again, see her father once

again struggling against the unseen force. But this time she held her concentration, focused her mind so utterly on the one single image that she no longer even saw her father, or the room around her, or even the light of the moon.

She felt herself tiring, felt every muscle in her body begin to ache as if she'd been running for hours.

The image in her mind wavered.

She struggled to regain it, but it was too late.

Exhausted, she let go of the image. It was as if all the tension in her body were released at once, and as a muted cry escaped her lungs, her head collapsed into her pillow and all her muscles suddenly turned to jelly.

But when she opened her eyes, the dark figure of her father was gone.

She was once again alone in her room.

The door was closed.

The wind outside had died away.

The light of the moon was once more suffusing the room with a bright silvery glow.

And the house was silent.

Angel waited, listening for any sound at all that might betray her father's return. Finally, after several long minutes, she slipped out of her bed and went to the door.

Opening it a crack, she peeked out into the hallway.

At the far end, her father was sprawled in a heap, as if he'd passed out just as he reached the top of the stairs.

Almost certain he wouldn't awaken for the rest of the night, she silently closed her door and returned to her bed.

And this time she slept. But she didn't sleep until close to dawn.

Chapter 39

MYRA SULLIVAN NEARLY DROPPED THE FRYING PAN full of scrambled eggs as she turned away from the stove and caught sight of Angel for the first time that morning. For a moment she was too stunned to say anything as she gazed at the black-clad figure that stood framed in the doorway. Angel's face was made up exactly as it had been on Saturday for the party at the country club, her skin a ghostly white, her eyes enlarged with shadow and liner, her lips the deep glistening red of blood. Myra could only gape, and then her mouth opened as if she were about to speak, but no words came out. Tearing her eyes away from Angel, she turned to Marty.

And saw that his face was almost as pale as Angel's. His gaze was fixed on Angel, and his features were twisted into a look of such utter terror that for a second Myra thought he must be having a heart attack.

"Marty?" she finally managed to say. "Marty!"

It wasn't until she spoke his name for a third time that Marty reacted to his wife's words, and then it was only to rise unsteadily from the table, backing away so quickly that the chair behind him tipped over with a crash. "Get her away," he said, his voice shaking. "Get her away from me!"

Now it was her husband Myra was gaping at. Had he gotten so drunk last night, and been left so hung over this morning, that he didn't even recognize his own daughter? "For heaven's sake, Marty, calm down—you look like you've seen a ghost! It's only Angel."

The shock of Angel's appearance receding as quickly as it had washed over her, she pursed her lips and turned back to her daughter. "What on earth are you thinking of?" she asked. "You practically frightened your father half to death. Now go upstairs, change your clothes, and take off that ridiculous makeup. Of all the—"

"It's not ridiculous, and I'm not taking it off," Angel said, sitting down at the table and pouring some orange juice from the carton Myra had taken out of the refrigerator a few minutes ago. "May I have some eggs?"

Startled into silence by her response, Myra automatically scooped a spoonful of eggs onto Angel's plate, then scooped another onto Marty's plate, not even noticing that half of her husband's serving dropped directly onto the table. Not that it mattered, for Marty was as oblivious of the eggs as Myra, his eyes still fixed on Angel.

"You do what your mother tells you," he said, but there was a note in his voice that betrayed his fear.

"I can wear what I want," Angel said, looking directly at her father.

Marty's gaze wavered, then broke. "If you get kicked out of school, don't come crying to me," he mumbled. Picking up his lunch box, he moved toward the back door.

"Marty!" Myra protested. "You haven't even eaten your breakfast!"

"I'll get a doughnut on the way to work," he said. And with one more quick glance at Angel, he was gone.

Frowning, Myra turned back to her daughter. "What

on earth are you trying to do?" she demanded. "You scared your father half to death! Your own father!"

For a moment Angel said nothing. Then looking directly into her mother's eyes, she asked, "Why do you think that is? Why do you think Daddy would be scared of me?"

Instead of answering her daughter's questions, Myra turned away from her, just as a few days earlier she'd turned away from Angel's fears about her husband.

It's not true, she told herself. *It can't be true. Marty wouldn't do that.*

A heavy silence hung between mother and daughter, a silence that wasn't broken even when Angel left to begin the long walk to school.

Seth Baker gazed at himself in the mirror and rubbed a hand experimentally over his chin, but just as on every other day, there was no trace of a beard—just the same soft, smooth skin that had been there every other day of his life.

But this day he felt different, if for no other reason than what had happened last night when Zack Fletcher was about to beat him up and instead wound up lying semiconscious on the sidewalk. When Seth got home, he'd been terrified his father had already discovered what had happened. But his father was watching a football game on TV and barely noticed him as he scurried up the stairs to his room. Still, he'd been certain that sooner or later the phone would ring and his father would be told what he'd done. But the phone hadn't rung. In fact, his father hadn't paid any attention to him at all last night. And that was a good thing, because even after what he'd been able to do to Zack, Seth wasn't sure he'd have the nerve to try the trick on his own father.

But when he awoke this morning, he felt better than he could ever remember feeling. He was no longer afraid of Zack Fletcher and Chad Jackson and Jared Woods. The feeling of well-being that had come over him persisted as he went into the bathroom, used the toilet, brushed his teeth, washed his face, and finally checked to see if there was yet any sign of a beard.

It hadn't bothered him that there still wasn't even a single whisker. He hadn't really expected to find one. Besides, a beard—no matter how thick—didn't have anything to do with what he'd done last night.

It was so easy. He'd just pictured Zack rising into the air, and it happened, just like it had happened with the rock out by the cabin where he and Angel had made the potion.

Now, turning away from his image in the mirror, he looked for something to experiment on, and focused on the bar of soap sitting on the edge of the sink.

In his mind, he pictured it rising into the air and floating over to the bathtub.

And nothing happened.

The soap remained where it was.

Stuck! That must be it—the soap was stuck to the sink!

Seth picked the bar of soap up, turned it over so its wet side was up, and set it on a dry spot on the sink.

Once again he imagined it rising into the air, and once again it remained where he'd put it, not moving even a fraction of an inch.

He stared at the bar of soap, focusing as hard as he could, and a cold knot of fear formed in the pit of his stomach as he realized what it meant if the bar didn't rise.

The soap stayed exactly where he'd put it.

He took a deep breath and tried once more, but already knew what had happened: during the night, the effect of the strange broth he and Angel brewed in the kettle had worn off, just the way every medicine wore off if you didn't keep taking it.

The knot of fear tightened in his belly, and he felt almost sick, thinking about what would happen that day.

Seth took the long way to school that morning, certain that if he followed his normal route, not only Zack Fletcher, but Chad Jackson and Jared Woods would be waiting for him somewhere. And he didn't think that this morning they'd stop with just taking his backpack, or pantsing him, or figuring out some other way to humiliate him.

Today they would be out for blood.

"Where the hell is the little prick?" Zack Fletcher asked, his voice shaking with fury. He and Chad Jackson were around the corner from Seth Baker's house, well enough concealed by a thick laurel hedge that there was no way Seth would be able to see them. And Jared Woods was stationed across the street, ready to cut Seth off if he happened to spot them and made a run for it.

"He'll show up," Chad said, staring at the lump on Zack's head, which was now covered with a bandage. "Jeez, man—what did he do to you?"

"Jumped me," Zack said. "He was hiding over on Court Street—you know, where the Jacobsons live?"

"What do you mean, hiding?" Chad asked.

Zack glared at him. "Like, hiding, all right?"

"You mean he was waiting for you?"

"Well, you don't think I just let him walk up and hit me with a baseball bat do you?"

Chad's eyes widened as he pictured Seth Baker stepping out from behind a bush wielding a baseball bat and taking a swing at Zack's head, and he winced as he thought about how hard the bat must have hit Zack to raise a lump the size he was sporting. "So, did you call the police?"

"You gotta be kidding! I didn't call anybody—I was flat on my back, out like a light. Mrs. Jacobson found me, and called my folks and an ambulance. I had to go to the hospital and everything."

"So, is your dad gonna sue the Bakers? I mean, you could have died, couldn't you?"

"That little bastard Seth is going to die when I get my hands on him," Zack said, his eyes narrowing to little more than slits. "I swear to God, I should've brought my own bat this morning."

Jared Woods appeared then, dashing across the street.

"Are you nuts?" Zack demanded. "If he sees you, he'll never come this way!"

"He's not coming this way anyway," Jared retorted. "You know what time it is? It's ten of eight," he went on, without giving either Zack or Chad time to answer. "You guys can keep waiting if you want, but if I get one more tardy, I'll get three hours in study hall after school."

"Well, where is he?" Zack asked. "He couldn't have just walked right by us."

Now it was Jared Woods who rolled his eyes. "Jeez, Zack! Seth's geeky, but he's not stupid. You think he didn't figure out you'd be waiting for him this morning? Bet he went over his back fence and through the Shroeders' yard, then cut down a couple of blocks."

"Too chicken to face us," Zack sneered.

"I guess he wasn't too chicken last night," Jared said,

eyeing the lump on Zack's head with a hint of a grin playing around the corners of his mouth.

"I told you," Zack shot back, his voice belligerent. "He jumped me!"

Jared shrugged and started down the block. "Hey, anything you say." As Zack glowered at him, Jared shifted his gaze to Chad. "You coming, or not?"

Chad glanced from Zack to Jared, then back to Zack.

"You calling me a liar?" Zack shouted at Jared, who was already a quarter of the way down the block.

Jared stopped short and turned back to face Zack. The other boy's fists were clenched, and Jared knew that if he didn't say exactly the right thing, Zack would come after him, and if he did, Chad would too. That was how it worked. "I'm not calling you anything," he said, backing down as he saw the anger in Chad's eyes as well as Zack's. "All I'm saying is that if Baker was coming this way, he'd have been here long ago, and if we wait any longer, we're all gonna be in trouble."

Zack took a deep breath and one last look toward the corner where Seth Baker should have appeared at least fifteen minutes ago. "Okay," he said, finally giving in. "But after school—"

"After school," Chad broke in, "I'm gonna do what I should've done a long time ago. I'm gonna get him, and by the time I'm done with him, he's gonna wish he'd never come near you last night."

As Zack's lips twisted into an ugly grin of anticipation, Jared Woods wondered whether Chad was just trying to impress Zack or if he was really going to help Zack Fletcher give Seth Baker the kind of beating he was talking about.

Teasing Seth all those years had been one thing.

Actually hurting him was something else.

* * *

Heather Dunne was waiting nervously by the front door as the three boys raced up the steps just as the first bell was ringing. As Zack reached the top step, Heather's eyes widened. "Zack? What happened?"

"I'll tell you later," he muttered, unwilling to try to convince Heather that there'd been nothing he could do to defend himself from Seth Baker, not until he had enough time to figure out an answer for every question she might ask. "Got to get to class." Chad and Jared had already gone into the building and were racing up the stairs to their lockers, and now Zack hurried after them.

"Zack!" Heather called out. "Wait a minute! You're not going to believe—"

"Later!" Zack yelled back over his shoulder. "Tell me at lunch!"

Not even pausing at the landing halfway up the staircase, he took the second flight two steps at a time. He came through the door to the stairwell running, and almost crashed into Chad and Jared. Instead of frantically working the combinations to their lockers, as they should have been, they were standing frozen in place, staring down the corridor. Barely keeping his balance, Zack was about to push Chad aside when he saw what his two friends were gazing at.

Halfway down the corridor, standing in the very center of the corridor, was a figure clad completely in black. The face was an almost ghostly white, slashed with a bloodred gash of a mouth.

Two enormous eyes—eyes far larger than Zack would have thought possible—seemed to be staring right through him.

As he too stood frozen between his friends, the figure

moved slowly toward him, and just as slowly, Zack recognized the face.

Angel.

His cousin.

Except this morning everything about her had changed.

It wasn't just the makeup she was wearing, and the
black clothes.

There was something else.

Something in the way she moved.

Instead of edging along the wall as she usually did,
looking like she hoped no one would notice her, she
walked down the center of the wide corridor, her eyes
fixed on him.

Fixed on him in a way that made his blood run cold.

As she drew closer, he involuntarily took a step back,
then wished he hadn't. But it was too late.

She'd seen it.

And so had Chad and Jared, who were now edging
away from him.

"Get out of the way, Zack," Angel said. "I want to go
downstairs."

Zack's mouth opened but nothing came out. What
was going on? What did she think she was doing? But
before he could figure out how to react, Angel slowly
raised her right arm and pointed at him.

"I know what Seth did to you last night," she said,
"and I can do it too."

As the terrible memory of being hurled straight up
into the tree rose in his mind, Zack backed away.

Backed away, and let Angel pass.

Pausing at the top of the stairs, she turned and looked
back at him once more.

"It's witchcraft," she said softly. "Or didn't you tell
Chad and Jared what really happened last night?"

His face ashen, Zack watched as Angel disappeared

down the stairs. When she was gone, he turned back to Chad and Jared, to find both of them staring at him.

Staring at him almost as coldly as Angel had stared at him a moment ago.

Angel Sullivan paused outside the door to her first period class. She was late, but not very late—maybe a minute or two. But she didn't care, because the look on Zack Fletcher's face when he'd seen her coming down the hall was still fresh in her mind. He'd looked just as scared of her as her father had when she came downstairs this morning.

Having people look scared of her instead of the other way around was a whole new experience for her, and for the first time in her life, Angel didn't care if people looked at her. In fact, as she'd walked to school that morning with Houdini frolicking along beside her, she actually looked forward to school for the first time.

Looked forward to walking through the group of girls who were always clustered around Heather Dunne on the front steps.

Looked forward to walking into the cafeteria at lunchtime. By then everyone in school would have heard about what she was wearing, and they would all turn and look at her.

Stare at her.

And she no longer cared.

It had happened after she forced her father out of her room last night. She had to use all of the strange power given to her by the broth she and Seth drank that afternoon. But it didn't matter because this afternoon they could make more.

Or experiment with some of the other recipes in the book.

Forbearance Wynton's book.

As she lay in the dark last night she'd thought about Forbearance Wynton. And about Forbearance Wynton's father.

It was him she'd seen in the moonlight that night, reaching toward her—she was sure of it.

She'd shuddered in the darkness, remembering the hands that pulled the bedding away . . .

Had reached toward the buttons on her pajama top . . .

Had been about to put his hands on her. . . .

But the man hadn't only been Forbearance Wynton's father—he'd been her father too. How could that be? She turned it over in her mind, trying to figure it out, and then Houdini had appeared out of the darkness. As on that first day in the house, she had no idea how he'd gotten into the room—the window was closed, and so was the door—but somehow he was there, leaping up onto the bed, sliding under her hand so she could scratch his ears. And as she stroked the cat, she began to understand.

They were all one.

She was Forbearance Wynton, and her father was Forbearance Wynton's father, and everything that happened hundreds of years ago was happening again.

How many other people in the house had been part of it? She was sure about the last family. Rogers was the name. Nate Rogers had killed his wife in her parents' bedroom before he killed his daughter in the room that was now hers. Had the same things happened to Nate Rogers's daughter that had happened to her? Had Nate Rogers crept into his daughter's room at night, touching her and caressing her and—

Angel had cut off the thought before it was fully formed, but in the darkness, with Houdini purring softly beneath her hand, she'd begun to understand last night that what was happening to her now had happened over and over in this house. It didn't matter who lived here— it was something in the house itself.

But Forbearance Wynton's book had saved her, had given her the power to protect herself. Forbearance had been able to protect herself too, though in the end they accused her of being a witch, and they killed her.

In the darkness of the night, Angel had conjured up a vision of what it must have been like. She'd pictured Forbearance Wynton and her mother bound to the great oak tree in the old cemetery, with wood, kindling, and brush piled around them.

She saw a man step out of the crowd to ignite the fire.

Margaret Wynton's husband.

Forbearance Wynton's father.

Her father . . .

Angel had imagined herself tied to the tree then, her father coming toward her, bearing a great flaming torch that he held high as he gazed furiously into her eyes.

"You should have loved me," he whispered. "All you had to do was love me."

He bent forward to kiss her, but she pulled away, and after gazing at her one more time with eyes that were filled with a fury greater than any she'd ever seen before, he touched the torch to the piled brush and the flames began to dance around her, leaping ever higher until—

She'd shut down her mind then, but the memory of what she'd already thought and pictured lingered.

A witch.

Josiah Wynton had called his daughter a witch.

And in the night, stroking Houdini's soft fur, she'd known he was right. Forbearance had used the strange book she and Seth had found to protect herself.

But Angel was certain that Nate Rogers's daughter

had never found it at all. And she had died. Her father had killed her.

But it hadn't happened to Angel.

She and Seth had found the book, and used it, and it had protected them.

So there it was—Forbearance Wynton had been a witch, and so was she.

And so was Seth . . .

But they didn't burn witches anymore. In fact, no one even believed in witches anymore. So she was safe.

She and Seth were both safe.

Finally, she'd fallen asleep, and when she awoke this morning, she knew exactly what she would do.

She would be herself. Not the self she'd always hated, but the one that Seth had shown her when he first put the makeup on her face, accentuating the features she'd always hated. So she dug through her drawers and found a black turtleneck shirt and black jeans, and when she put them on and looked at herself in the mirror, she realized that Seth was right. She wasn't as fat as she'd always thought; in fact, if she lost ten or fifteen pounds, she might actually have the beginning of a real figure!

And when she threw the black cape over her shoulders, she saw that Seth was right again. She didn't look terrible at all.

And she didn't feel terrible either. She felt better than she'd ever remembered feeling on any morning of her whole life, and when she went downstairs and saw the look on her father's face, she felt even better.

This morning she hadn't been afraid of him; this morning, he'd been afraid of her.

And it was true at school too. After Seth had told her what had happened last night, she decided to wait in the upstairs corridor until Zack showed up, just to see the look on his face when he saw her. When Chad and Jared showed up without Zack, she'd been afraid that her cousin might not show up at all, that perhaps he hadn't come to school that day. But the expressions on the faces of both Chad and Jared told her that the effect she was having on them was what she'd been hoping for. And then when Zack finally showed up and looked like he might actually faint at the sight of her, it had been all she could do to keep from laughing out loud.

She'd managed to keep a straight face, and when she walked straight toward him, he hadn't tried to block her. He just got out of her way, as if afraid she might put some kind of hex on him.

Now, in the silence of the hallway, Angel took a deep breath, pulled the door to her classroom open, and stepped inside.

Mrs. Brink was just turning to write something on the chalkboard, but catching sight of Angel, she froze, her mouth hanging open, the chalk hovering in her fingers a few inches from the board.

The entire room went dead silent as her classmates turned to stare at her.

Yesterday, Angel would have wished she could fall through the floor and vanish.

Today, she simply went to her desk, took her textbook and notebook out of her backpack, settled herself into her seat and let them stare.

It felt good.

In fact, it felt very good.

Chapter 40

BLAKE BAKER KNEW SOMETHING WAS WRONG THE moment Ed Fletcher walked unannounced into his office. He assumed it had to be the golf game—the game Ed had not won. "Hey," he said, holding up his hands in an exaggerated gesture of mock defense. "I don't like being sandbagged any more than you do, and I told Seth as much. I don't know when he's been practicing, but the way he was playing those last nine holes, he looked like a scratch golfer!"

Ed Fletcher's countenance only darkened. "So what else has Seth been working on that you don't know about? Martial arts, maybe?"

"Seth?" Baker said. "You gotta be kidding. He's—" He hesitated, then shrugged helplessly. "Look, Seth's my kid, but let's not kid ourselves—he's not what anyone would call the fighting kind." When Fletcher said nothing, Baker went on, now uncertain where the conversation was headed. "Come on, Ed—we both know how the other kids have always treated him, and I've been telling him for years that sooner or later he's got to learn to take care of himself."

"Think there's any chance that he finally did?" Fletcher asked coldly.

"You want to tell me what this is about?"

"Zack got beaten up last night," Ed Fletcher said, keeping his unwavering gaze on Blake Baker.

"By Seth?" Baker asked incredulously, as what his client was implying dawned on him "Come on, Ed, Seth's afraid of his own shadow, for Christ's sake!"

"According to Zack, the shadows were exactly where Seth was waiting for him," Fletcher said sarcastically.

As he related Zack's version of what had happened last night, Blake's incredulity only grew. "What time did all this happen?" he asked, interrupting before Fletcher was finished.

"About six-thirty. That's when Sheila Jacobson called, anyway."

"So why didn't you call me last night?" Baker asked.

Fletcher glared at him. "By the time we got back from the emergency room and got Zack cleaned up, it was late."

Baker's eyes narrowed. "Not that late. Especially given what you claim happened."

Ed Fletcher took a deep breath. "Which is part of the reason I didn't call last night," he said. "The thing is, Zack gave us a couple of different versions of what happened. First he said Seth hit him, then he said Seth threw him into a tree."

Blake Baker's brows arched. "Oh, yeah," he said, his voice heavy with sarcasm. "My hundred and thirty pound kid who spends most of his time at a computer screen is going to throw your hundred and eighty pound football player into a tree. I mean, come on, Ed!"

"I'm just telling you what Zack told us," Fletcher said.

"What about Sheila Jacobson?" Blake asked. "What did she say?"

Fletcher shrugged. "She didn't see it—she just found Zack and called us and the ambulance."

"So all you have is Zack's word."

"Why would he lie?" Fletcher demanded. "I mean, getting beat up by Seth? It makes him look like a wimp!" Before Baker could respond, Fletcher reined in his anger. "I'm sorry—I shouldn't have said that about Seth. He's a good kid—he always has been. But the thing is, I just can't figure out what happened last night. Being thrown into a tree—I know, that's hard to believe. And I know as well as you do how pissed off Zack was after Seth beat us Saturday afternoon. I'd hate to think my own son would beat anyone up because he lost a tournament. But I know that Zack has a temper, and that he hates to lose. So for the sake of argument, let's just say that it wasn't Seth that jumped Zack. Let's say it was the other way around. So how did Seth manage to slam Zack's head against the limb of a tree?"

"You sure that's how he got hurt?"

Fletcher nodded. "The paramedics saw the blood on the limb last night, and I checked again this morning. It's there. And it's at least nine feet off the ground."

"Nine feet!" Blake said, incredulous. "You're saying that Seth—if it *was* Seth, which I'm not admitting—"

"I'm not suing anybody, Blake," Fletcher quickly said, "whatever the situation or circumstance might have been. After all these years, you of all people should know I fight suits. Have I ever actually initiated one?"

Blake Baker shrugged. "There's always a first time."

"Well, this isn't it," Fletcher said. "I'm just trying to figure out what happened last night, okay?"

Baker tipped his head in assent. "Okay, for the sake of argument, let's assume it was Seth. And let's also assume there's no way he could have picked Zack up and slammed his head against a limb of a tree that's nine feet up. At least not by himself."

"Then he had help," Fletcher said. "From who? I don't

mean this as anything against Seth, but let's face it—he's never had a lot of friends."

Now it was Baker's turn to fall silent. He nodded, took a deep breath, and said, "Until a couple of weeks ago, I'm not sure he had any."

"But now he does?" Fletcher asked.

"So Jane tells me," Baker replied. "Your niece. Seems Jane saw them dancing together Saturday night." He met Fletcher's eyes. "So where does that get us?"

Instead of answering the question, Ed Fletcher glanced at the clock on Blake Baker's desk. "It's almost noon," he announced. "I've got a lunch and then a meeting. What do you say we meet around two and go have a talk with my brother-in-law? At least we should find out where his daughter was last night."

"What am I gonna do?" Seth asked as the clamor of the bell announced the end of lunch hour. All through lunch, Angel and Seth had felt the eyes of their classmates on them and heard the whispered murmurs as the tale of what had happened to Zack Fletcher last night swirled through the cafeteria, getting more exaggerated with every telling. Seth sat with his back to the room, but he felt Zack's furious glare as clearly as if they'd been sitting across the table from each other.

And he heard the rumors about what would happen after school. It didn't seem to matter where he went that day—there was always a group of boys whispering among themselves, then glancing at him and nudging each other.

At least half a dozen boys—most of whom had never before bothered to speak to him at all—had brushed roughly past him, offering one promise or another just loud enough for him to hear.

"You're dead meat, Baker."

"Zack and Chad are gonna kill you, you little creep."

"Who do you think you are, jumping Fletcher?"

"Your ass is *so* in a sling."

It wasn't just Zack's friends either—it was everyone. Everyone who'd never said a thing when Zack, Chad, and Jared used to pants him or shove him into a wall or push his head into a toilet. And the worst of it was, it wasn't even true! Zack had jumped *him*.

Now, as the rest of the kids swarmed past Seth and Angel—and one of them "accidentally" shoved him hard enough to send the contents of his lunch tray cascading over Seth—they stayed at the table, trying to figure out the answer to Seth's question: What was he going to do?

Seth had all but given up on finding an answer when Angel brightened. "Meet me at your locker right after school, okay?" she said.

Seth cocked his head. "What are you—" he began.

"Just meet me, okay?" she said, and then she was gone, hurrying out of the cafeteria with her backpack. By the time he cleared the mess from their table and went after her, the last bell rang.

He was already late for class, and he still had to go to his locker. As Seth moved through the silent and deserted hallways—free of the whispered conversations, the barely suppressed snickers, and the angry stares of Zack's friends—the tendrils of fear that had been gripping him more and more tightly as the day wore on began to loosen.

Then just as he reached his locker, someone behind him said, "What you doing, Beth?"

Chad Jackson's voice startled Seth so badly that his backpack slipped from his fingers and fell to the floor.

"Scared, Beth?" Chad asked, his voice low, but carrying a note of menace that made Seth's stomach churn.

Bluff, he told himself, and turned to face Chad, who

was flanked by Zack Fletcher and Jared Woods. "Why should I be scared?" he asked, and prayed that they hadn't heard the tremor in his voice.

"Because now you're all by yourself," Chad said. "And Zack's not." He moved closer, and Seth could see a hint of uncertainty in his eyes, as if unsure what Seth might be able to do to him.

"I was by myself last night too," Seth said.

"Were you?" Chad replied. "Or was your girlfriend with you?"

"She's not my girlfriend," Seth said, and instantly wished he could reclaim the words.

Chad's lips twisted into a sneer. "I bet she's not," he said. "In fact, I bet you wish you were someone's girlfriend, don't you, Beth?" He cast a sidelong glance toward Zack. "How about it? Is that why you were following Zack last night? Do you wish you were his girlfriend, Beth?"

"Don't call me that," Seth said, but now the tremor in his voice was so bad, he knew Chad couldn't miss it. Sure enough, Chad's eyes glittered with malice, and as Zack snickered, he moved closer to Seth.

"Why not?" Chad asked. "What do you think you're going to do about it?"

The urge to turn and run was almost irresistible, but Seth steeled himself against it. "The same thing I did to Zack last night," he said softly.

Not even a flicker of fear crossed Chad's expression, but Seth was sure he'd seen Zack flinch. Chad only moved even closer, so he was towering above him. "You think you can jump me like you jumped Zack?" he demanded.

"I didn't—" Seth began, then realized it didn't matter what he said. The attack he'd been afraid of all day would take place anyway. Grabbing his backpack, Seth tried to duck away, but it was too late. Chad smashed him up against the bank of lockers, slamming his head so hard against the metal that for a second Seth thought he might pass out.

"You listen, you little shit," Chad hissed, clutching Seth's shirt and shoving his face so close that Chad was spitting on him as he spoke. "You jump Zack, you might as well have jumped me! So I'm going to make you wish you were dead, get it? I'm going to hurt you so bad you'll never—"

At the sound of footsteps coming up the stairs, Chad let go of Seth as quickly as he'd grabbed him. By the time the principal appeared at the top of the stairs, Chad was busily working the combination of his own locker, and Zack and Jared appeared to be paying no attention to Seth either. Phil Lambert, though, had been the school principal long enough to read the entire situation in an instant, and he focused on Chad, the only one of the four boys in the corridor who wasn't looking at him. "Something wrong, Jackson?" he asked.

Chad turned around, shrugging. "Just can't get my stupid lock to work."

"Then maybe you should get the custodian," the principal suggested. "And even if Jackson has a problem," he said, addressing the others, "shouldn't the rest of you be in class?"

Zack Fletcher and Jared Woods jumped at the opportunity to escape the principal unpunished, and Seth held back just long enough to let them start downstairs before he hurried down the hall toward his trigonometry class.

Though every eye in the room shifted from the teacher to stare at Seth when he entered, and the teacher himself was glaring, all Seth was aware of were the words Chad had spoken to him.

*I'm going to make you wish you were dead. . . . I'm
going to hurt you so bad . . .*

Marty Sullivan swore in disgust as he stared at the sod-
den tuna fish sandwich, the already blackening banana,
and the thermos of coffee that, even if it weren't cold, he
knew would be as bitter as the bile rising in his throat at
the thought of eating one more of Myra's crappy
lunches. Christ, wasn't it bad enough that he had to eat
out of a tin box every day? The least she could do was
try to come up with something decent for him. But no,
every day, the same damned thing—a soggy sandwich,
some kind of half-rotten fruit, and a thermos of her
lousy coffee. There was a tavern half a mile away, and
since Jack Varney had already made him work through
what should have been his lunch hour, maybe he should
just dump Myra's whole mess of a lunch in the trash
barrel and go treat himself to some fish-and-chips and a
couple of beers.

And take the rest of the day off.

He was still considering that possibility when Varney
called his name. *Well, the hell with him,* he thought.
He'd already given Varney two extra hours in the morning, and he knew the rules—unless it was an emergency,
he had a right to an hour to himself.

Then Varney yelled at him again, and this time Marty
looked up, more out of irritation than any interest in
what the job foreman might want. When he saw Ed
Fletcher wearing one of his fancy-ass suits and leaning
against his Mercedes, his irritation grew into anger. If
his snotnose brother-in-law was here to fire him, he
wouldn't give him a chance. He'd quit, and the hell with
all of them. The hell with the Fletchers, and if Myra gave
him any crap, then maybe he'd just say the hell with her

too. Moving to Roundtree was the dumbest thing he'd ever let her talk him into, and if she still wanted to stay, then maybe he'd just let her. She and her weird kid both. After the way Angel had been acting—and the way she'd looked this morning, like some vampire witch from Hell—he figured he could do just fine without them. Maybe he'd just take off to California, or even Hawaii; God knew he wasn't looking forward to another winter in New England.

"For Christ's sake, Marty," Ed Fletcher yelled. "You gone deaf in your old age?" Marty heaved himself to his feet, glowering, and started toward his brother-in-law. "Hey, take it easy," Fletcher protested when he saw that Marty's right hand was already balled into a fist. "I just want to talk to you."

"It's lunch hour," Marty growled. He shot a furious look at Varney. "It shoulda been lunch hour two hours ago!"

Ed Fletcher's eyes rolled impatiently. "God forbid I should transgress on one of your precious union rules."

"I'm just sayin'—"

"I know what you're saying," Fletcher cut in. "So why don't you for once in your life find out what's going on before you get mad?" Before Marty could answer, Fletcher tilted his head toward the man leaning against his car. "You know Blake Baker?"

Marty's eyes narrowed to suspicious slits. "Should I?"

Blake Baker extended a hand toward Marty. "My boy knows your girl. Seth?"

Marty ignored the other man's hand and spat into the dirt. "I don't want that little punk hanging around my daughter. And I told him that too," he said, suddenly certain that he knew what was going on. This Baker prick was trying to get him fired. "Caught him with her once, but all I did was tell him to stay away. I didn't hit

him or nothin' like that." He spat again, and snorted de-
risively. "'Course, I'd'a had to catch up with him to hit
him, and the way he was running, that wasn't gonna
happen. Guess I put an end to him messin' with Angel."

"Not according to Zack," Ed Fletcher said.

Marty cocked his head. "What do you mean?"

Ed shrugged. "Seems Seth and Zack got into it last
night."

"Shit," Marty said, "Zack'd bust that little punk's
face so fast it'd make your head spin."

Ed Fletcher's expression tightened. "Well, that's not
exactly how it turned out. He wound up at the hospital
getting four stitches."

Marty stared at his brother-in-law in disbelief. "You
gotta be kiddin' me!"

"I wish I were. The thing is, neither Blake nor I can
figure out exactly what happened. But Zack says Seth
has been acting weird since he started hanging out with
Angel."

"I already told you," Marty said, "they're not hanging out!"

Ed sighed heavily. "That's not the way I hear it. Zack
says they eat lunch together every day, and they were at
the library together the other night, and now they've
started taking off after school together."

Marty wheeled on Blake Baker. "If your kid's messin'
with my girl—"

Ed Fletcher cut him short. "Will you just keep your
shirt on long enough to listen? No one's saying Seth's
'messing' with Angel, as you put it. But he sure messed
with Zack last night." Before Marty could start talking
again, Ed told him as much as he knew about what had
happened last night—or at least as much as Zack had
told him. "The thing is, he keeps changing his story, but
even when he changes it, it doesn't make any sense. And

it doesn't make any sense that they found blood on a tree branch that's nine feet off the ground. It's almost like someone threw him up against the branch."

Suddenly, Marty recalled what had happened yesterday afternoon, when Angel shoved him down the stairs, knocking him unconscious.

Except that he had no memory of being shoved down the stairs. Sure, he'd been drinking a little, and he remembered the storm that struck in the afternoon, and going up to Angel's room. . . . In fact, now that he thought about it, he remembered that Angel heard him open the door, and she turned, but hadn't actually come at him.

And the cat hadn't come at him either.

But something had come at him—some kind of force he couldn't see. It was like he was just picked up and thrown backward, and a second later he was tumbling down the stairs.

Like Zack had been thrown?

Then he remembered what Father Mulroney had told him, the legends about what had gone on in Roundtree centuries ago, and the storms that came up sometimes.

Storms like the one yesterday afternoon, when Angel hadn't been home, and when the Baker kid hadn't been home either, according to Ed Fletcher. "I think maybe you better go talk to Father Mulroney," Marty finally said, his voice hollow.

Blake Baker gazed at him in bafflement. "Father Mulroney? What's he got to do with this?"

"He told me some stuff," Marty said. "He told me what's been going on around here, okay? So don't talk to me—go ask him!"

Ed Fletcher drew in a deep breath. "All right, Marty, suppose we do go ask Father Mike? What's he going to tell us?"

Marty opened his mouth to speak a single word: *witchcraft*. But he couldn't bring himself to utter it. Let them hear it from the priest; let them think it was the priest who was crazy. "You ask him," Marty said once more. "Let him tell you."

Chapter 41

"I NEVER HEARD SUCH A PILE OF CRAP IN MY LIFE."

Father Mike Mulroney shrugged almost disinterestedly and offered Blake Baker a faint smile. When Baker and Ed Fletcher had rung the rectory bell half an hour ago, he'd been surprised to see them. Both of them were members of the Congregational church across the street, and as far as Mulroney knew, neither of them had ever set foot in his church. He had a vague memory of Fletcher's wife, Joni, showing up a few times—mostly on Easter—but even that had stopped years ago, and he suspected that her churchgoing habits were dictated far more forcefully by her profession than her convictions, which meant that she too was now a Congregationalist. Thus, when two prominent members of the church across the street appeared at his front door on a Monday afternoon, he'd assumed it must be church business of some sort. After they told him how they'd come to be there, he decided that he was right, at least in an oddly abstract way. After all, the church these two men went to was the same one that burned Margaret and Forbearance Wynton several centuries ago.

Now, in response to Blake Baker's crude summation of his remarks, Mulroney tipped his head in recognition that, despite their crudeness, he wasn't going to utterly discount Baker's words. "I'm just telling you the same thing I told Martin Sullivan last night," he said, "which is nothing more than what I've read over the years about the history of the town."

"It sounds like you expect us to believe in—what?" Ed Fletcher hesitated, searching for a better word than the one that came to mind. But he didn't find one. "Witchcraft?" he finally said. "Come on, Father—this is the twenty-first century. We don't believe in superstition anymore."

Mulroney spread his hands. "The difference between faith such as yours and mine, and what people like us often like to call superstition, is something that seems to elude me more and more with each passing year."

He rose from his chair, moved to the window, and gazed at the huge old oak tree that stood in the grave-yard across the street like a great silent sentinel. "Doesn't anything about that tree ever strike you as strange?" he asked. He turned back to the other two men. "Its canopy is almost perfectly round, which is peculiar in and of itself. Still, it could in part be accounted for by careful pruning, except the tree doesn't show any signs of ever having been pruned at all. Also, according to every record I've been able to find, the tree was already there when the town was founded. The town was named after the tree, gentlemen, and that was more than three hundred and fifty years ago. Even the trees down at Oak Alley in Louisiana aren't anywhere near that old."

"So it's old," Blake Baker said. "And no one's ever pruned it—so what?"

The priest shrugged. "Maybe nothing at all. I just find it curious that not only does the tree show no signs of ever being pruned, it shows no signs of ever having burned or been struck by lightning either."

Ed Fletcher frowned. "Maybe it never has been."

Father Mulroney met Fletcher's gaze. "But it has, Ed. I've seen it myself. The storms that came up out of nowhere yesterday and a couple of days before that? I was watching, and that tree was struck half a dozen times. And there's not a mark on it."

For the first time, a flicker of uncertainty came into Blake Baker's eyes. "Well, there's got to be some kind of explanation. I mean, maybe—" But before he could go on, a gust of wind slammed into the rectory, and outside, a huge thunderhead took shape. "Jesus!" Baker said. "Where did that come from?"

As the sun vanished behind the dark cloud that seemed to have come literally out of nowhere, another blast of wind struck the rectory. The structure shuddered again, followed by a blinding flash of lightning and then a crash of thunder that rattled the windows. Blake Baker flinched under the onslaught, but Ed Fletcher remained where he was, gazing out the window.

"You see?" Father Mulroney said softly as rain began to slash down from the sky.

As if to underscore the priest's question, another bolt of lightning shot out of the sky, lashing into the top of the great oak tree and vanishing in a shower of sparks as another clap of thunder exploded. The uncertainty in Blake Baker's eyes coalesced into fear. "I don't get it," he whispered, almost to himself. "What's going on?"

"According to the oldest legends in Roundtree," Father Mulroney said almost placidly, "someone is practicing witchcraft even as we are talking."

Baker's eyes fixed on the priest. "Who?" he demanded.

Father Mulroney's lips curved into a sardonic smile. "Wasn't it you that just said something about all this being—what was it?" He hesitated, as if trying to remember the exact words, then continued. "Ah! 'A pile of crap,' I believe you said."

Blake Baker ignored both the priest's tone and his words. "If you know what's going on, you'd better tell us," he said, as yet a third bolt of lightning shot out of the sky, and the rectory once more trembled under the crash of thunder.

"According to the legends, it always comes from one place," the priest said as the thunder died away. "The old house at Black Creek Crossing. And it always involves an adolescent girl." Before either of the other men could say anything, there was a sharp rapping at the study door. "Come in," Father Mulroney called, certain he knew who it was.

The door opened, and Myra Sullivan stepped in. "Father, what's hap—" she began, but her words died on her lips as she saw the two men who were with the priest. "Ed?" she said. "What are you doing here?"

Instead of answering her question, Ed asked his own. "Did Angel go to school this morning?"

Myra's eyes flicked from her brother-in-law to the priest. "What—" she began again, and this time was interrupted by Blake Baker.

"Angel?" he repeated. "That's your daughter?"

Myra frowned. "I don't understand," she said.

"Well, I don't understand either," Blake Baker stated, his voice hardening. "According to Father Mulroney, here, your kid's some kind of witch or something, and—"

Myra turned to face Father Mulroney, her face ashen. "You're a priest!" she breathed. "How could you say such a thing? How could you even think such a thing?"

"I didn't say Angel is a witch, Myra. I—"

"You might as well have," Baker fumed, wheeling on the priest. "And given the way my kid is acting, maybe she is!" He turned to Ed Fletcher. "I think it's time you and I got to the bottom of whatever happened last night. I'm going over to the school and finding Seth. If Zack was telling the truth, my boy's in so much trouble, he'll never forget it." His furious eyes fixed on Myra. "And if I find out your girl was involved—"

"My Angel wouldn't—"

But Blake Baker wasn't listening and cut her off. "You coming, Ed?" he asked, and stormed out of the study without waiting for an answer. Ed Fletcher followed a moment later.

A shocked silence hung in the room as Myra Sullivan gazed at Father Mulroney in bewilderment. Finally the priest sighed, gently took her elbow, and guided her toward the front door. "School will be out in another twenty minutes," he said quietly. "I think maybe you should be there. And I'd better go with you."

Seth Baker had been thinking about it ever since lunch, when first Angel had taken off, then Chad, Zack, and Jared cornered him upstairs by his locker. If Mr. Lambert hadn't come along—

But Mr. Lambert *had* come along, so his nose was still unbroken, his eyes unblackened, and his teeth intact. This afternoon, however, after school, things would be different. They wouldn't come after him at school, of course, where one of the teachers might well see them. No, they'd wait until later, when they were all away from school, and corner him somewhere. And then, judging from the fury in Chad's eyes after lunch, they'd give him a beating that would be far worse than anything his father had ever given him.

At least his father only hit him with the belt.

Chad and Zack—and maybe even Jared—would come at him with anything that came to hand.

He knew it wouldn't do any good to just hang around after school either. By now, Zack would have told everyone he knew to keep an eye on him, and even if he out-waited everyone, sooner or later they'd lock up the school and he'd have to leave. And Chad would be wait-ing, with Zack—his head bandaged—right beside him. He would have no chance at all. It was all Seth thought about through fifth period, and during the break before his history class he knew people were watching him, whispering, and he wished he could just disappear.

Like Angel had disappeared. But where had she gone?

Then, when he saw the flash of light through the win-dow at the far end of the corridor, followed so quickly by the crash of thunder that he knew the lightning had struck within a block or two of the school, he knew where Angel had gone. She was in the cabin, and the fire was burning on the hearth, and the old wrought-iron kettle was heating. And Seth knew what he had to do.

Instead of going to his sixth period history class, he hurried back to his locker, packed everything he needed into his backpack, and headed down the stairs at the far end of the corridor. As the bell rang signaling the begin-ning of the last class of the day, he pushed the door open and stepped out into the breaking storm.

Another jagged bolt of lightning ripped out of the roil-ing clouds overhead as he started down the steps, and Seth watched as it slashed to the ground over by the old cemetery. As the thunderclap exploded around him, he dashed across the street, ducking his head against the pouring rain. By the time he reached the corner of Black Creek Road, he was already soaked to the skin, but he didn't care. He was away from the school, and away from Chad, Zack, and all the rest of them.

For now, at least, he was safe.

It had taken him almost fifteen minutes to get out to the head of the trail that would lead him to the cabin, and by then he was shivering with the cold and the slashing downpour nearly blinded him. He had to step off the road twice to avoid oncoming cars; both times, he was about to duck into the woods to avoid someone stopping to ask him what he was doing out in the raging storm, but the cars didn't even slow down. Apparently the drivers were having as much difficulty seeing through the storm as he was.

At the trailhead, he turned off the road and began slogging through the squishy mire the path had already become. Finally, he gave up on the path and edged his way alongside it, weaving through the trees and pushing through the thickets, but never moving so far from the path that he lost sight of it. Soon his shoes were as soggy as his clothes and heavy with mud.

Still, the canopy of the forest gave him a little protection from the rain, and the flashes of lightning came often enough so that even under the blackness of the sky and the even deeper darkness of the forest, he was able to keep track of where he was.

At last he came to the clearing on the far side of which he saw the berm of shattered granite. He searched for any sign of smoke coming from the chimney of the tiny cabin, but the darkness of the day and the fury of the storm made it impossible to see anything.

He climbed to the top of the berm and looked down to the spot where the cabin was hidden.

And saw nothing at all.

It was as if the weathered wall of the cabin had vanished into the rock.

But that was impossible! He'd already been to the cabin three times. And this was the right spot—he was sure of it!

As another flash of lightning slashed across the sky, and the roar of thunder echoed off the sheer granite face of the cliff, Seth began scrambling down the mound of rubble.

His left foot caught between two rocks, and he choked back a yelp of pain as his ankle twisted. A moment later he worked his foot loose, twisted it experimentally a couple of times, then continued on down.

And found that the cabin was still there.

Indeed, he could see a faint glimmer of yellowish light flickering in the crack under the door.

He moved forward, hesitated, then pushed the door open.

For a moment he saw nothing in the dim light inside, but then his eyes adjusted to the gloom.

A fire was burning on the hearth, and above it the ancient kettle was already steaming.

Houdini was sitting near the hearth, his tail wrapped around him. As his eyes met Seth's, the cat rose and moved toward him.

Angel was sitting at the table, the red leather-bound book open before her. As Seth stepped inside, she looked up.

She smiled.

"I knew you'd come," she said.

In the warmth of the cabin, the pain in Seth's ankle melted away, and so did the shivering that had seized his body.

He was safe.

At least for a while . . .

Phil Lambert glowered at the storm raging outside. When he woke that morning to see a cloudless sky with no trace of the sudden squalls that had been cropping up during the last week, he'd decided to get in a couple of hours of fly-fishing on the creek after school. He even put his rod and creel—along with his waders and his favorite fishing hat—in the car so he could get out as soon after the last bell as possible. And all day, the weather had held—a perfect fall day with a brilliant sun hanging in an utterly cloudless sky. And then, barely an hour before the day would be over, the sky suddenly turned black, a flash of lightning startling him so badly that he slopped coffee all over the report he was preparing for the superintendent. And then the whole school trembled under the thunderclap that struck before the lightning even faded fully away. Which meant that instead of spending two quiet hours trying to tease the trout in Black Creek into snapping at one of his hand-tied flies, he would instead spend those same two hours in his office, working on the endless mass of reports that his job seemed to have devolved down to.

Maybe he should have kept teaching, he thought, and never become the principal at all.

Or maybe this storm would blow through faster than the ones that struck last week and then again yesterday, and in another half hour the sky would once again be clear. The odds of that, he thought as he turned away from the window to gaze at the four people ranged in front of his desk, were about the same as being able to finish five hours of reports in only two or three, even without the sudden arrival of a priest and three upset parents, at least one of whom—Seth Baker's father—was even more unpleasant than usual. After listening to Baker for ten minutes, he decided it would be easier to simply bring the three kids involved to his office now, rather than try to convince all of them to wait for the bell to ring in half an hour, especially since he was clinging to a faint ray of hope that by the time school let out for the day, the storm would have passed and he could still go fishing.

There was a tap at the door, and his assistant, Stacy Moore, stuck her head in. "Zack Fletcher is here," she said, "but neither Angel Sullivan nor Seth Baker are in their classrooms." One of Phil Lambert's eyebrows lifted questioningly. "Apparently no one's seen Angel since lunch, but Seth was in his next to last class."

"You mean she's not here at all?" Myra Sullivan asked.

"So it would appear," Phil Lambert observed dryly. "Give us a minute, please, Stacy? I'll buzz you when we're ready to see Zack."

As Stacy Moore backed out and pulled the door closed, Lambert leaned back in his chair, tented his fingers under his chin, and surveyed the three parents. Myra Sullivan looked worried and Ed Fletcher looked perplexed. And Blake Baker appeared to be growing angrier every second. "Here's the situation as I see it," Lambert said. "Obviously we're not going to be talking to either Angel or Seth this afternoon, but I can assure you that tomorrow morning I'll personally be speaking to both of them. When kids start skipping out of school in the middle of the day, I want to know why. Although," he went on, turning to Ed Fletcher, "I suspect I know exactly why Seth is gone. At the end of the lunch hour today, I happened to find Zack and his two closest friends in the hall upstairs. I didn't get there in time to see anything directly, but from what I saw, they were either hazing Seth Baker or getting ready to." He held up a restraining hand as Blake Baker started to say something. "Now, given what happened last night, and what I saw today, my guess is that Seth decided to cut his last class today rather than risk running into Zack and his pals after school."

"Who were the other two?" Blake Baker demanded. "Were they Chad Jackson and Jared Woods?"

"Since I didn't actually see them doing anything, I'm not sure there's any real point in naming them," Lambert said mildly. Another flash of lightning flared across the sky, and once again the building trembled under the thunderclap that instantly followed. "Now, I suppose we could have Zack come in here and try to explain what happened last night one more time, but I'm not sure what that would accomplish. Frankly," he said, standing up and coming around the end of the desk, "it seems to me that the best thing is to do what Seth apparently did—simply go home. By tomorrow I suspect that most of whatever went on between Seth and Zack last night will have blown over, and in any case, I can assure you I'll be keeping a careful eye on both of them."

"But what about Angel?" Myra Sullivan fretted. "If she's been gone since noon . . ." Her voice trailed off.

"We take attendance in the homerooms in the morning, Mrs. Sullivan," Lambert explained. "If someone doesn't show up in a class later in the day, the teachers assume the absence was reported in the morning. The only other way we'd know about it is if one of the other students reported it." He uttered a hollow chuckle. "Needless to say, the incidence of one student reporting that another is cutting classes isn't very high. In fact, most of them cover for each other." He moved toward the door. "So why don't we all call it a day, and see what happens tomorrow, all right?" He offered Blake Baker a reassuring smile. "I wouldn't worry too much about Seth—these things usually blow over pretty fast." He pulled the door to his office open and stepped out into the anteroom, where Zack Fletcher was sitting uneasily on the plastic chair that was the only piece of furniture in the room other than Stacy's own desk and chair.

As not only his father, but his aunt and Seth's father, came out of the principal's office, he rose to his feet.

"Did they tell you?" he asked his father. "I'm right, aren't I? Seth jumped me last night, and Angel was with him, wasn't she?"

Ed Fletcher searched his son's eyes, trying to see something, anything, that would give him a hint as to whether Zack was telling the truth or not, but there was nothing. "Seth and Angel aren't even here," he said. "So everything's on hold till tomorrow. Come on—we're going home."

Zack shook his head. "I have football practice."

Now it was Ed Fletcher who shook his head. "Not today you don't—not with that bandage on your head, and the rain pouring down. I'm taking you home and you're going to take it easy, and then tomorrow we'll see how things stand." His eyes fixed first on Blake Baker, then on Phil Lambert. "We'll see how things stand with everything, right?"

Blake Baker seemed about to say something, then apparently thought better of it.

Phil Lambert smiled. "Not to worry, Ed—in all the years I've been doing this job, I've never yet seen a problem with the kids that couldn't wait until morning. And you'd be surprised how many times the problem that seemed huge one day has completely vanished by the next."

Chapter 42

ANGEL HAD LISTENED IN SILENCE AS SETH TOLD HER what happened after she left that day and why he decided not to wait around until the last bell rang.

"But what are you going to do tomorrow?" she asked when he finished.

"I don't know—I guess I'm hoping that by tomorrow Zack won't be as mad as he was this morning."

Angel rolled her eyes. "Like that's going to happen."

"Maybe I'll just cut school."

"For how long?" Angel shot back. "I mean, what are you going to do, hide in your house for the rest of your life?"

Seth couldn't quite meet her eyes. "Didn't you ever wish you could do that?"

Angel was silent for several long seconds, then shook her head. "Not anymore. Now I wish I never had to go back to my house. I wish I could just stay here."

Seth glanced around the tiny cabin. With the fire burning on the hearth, the tiny chamber was almost too warm, but even with the heat, he could still feel drafts coming in from the cracks in the front wall and the gaps in the shutter over the window, and there was practically a steady breeze coming through the gap under the door. Only the light of the small fire brightened the gloom, and though most of the smoke from the fire was streaming up the chimney, enough of it curled out of the fireplace so that his eyes were burning, and he kept feeling like he had to sneeze. Yet he knew exactly what she meant. "So what are we going to do?" he asked.

Angel reached out and turned the ancient book of recipes so he could read the page to which it was opened. "I think we should make this."

Seth bent down and peered at the page, which was barely legible in the dim light. Only when Angel tilted the book toward the fire could he make out the ornate print:

Reckoning

From pulsing Toad
And weeping Tree
It also yearns
For Blood from Thee.

Not while Fire
Still doest Burn
Add the last
To Thine own Urn.

Thus the payn
Will turn from Thee
And Fall upon
Thine Enemie.

Seth read the strange verses through twice. "Have you figured out what it means?"

Angel shrugged uncertainly. "I'm not sure. I mean, I'm pretty sure the first line means we have to put in some blood from a live toad." She shuddered at the thought, but Seth was too engrossed in studying the verse again to notice.

"I bet the 'weeping tree' part means a weeping willow. There's one at the edge of the clearing, right where the trail comes out. But what are we supposed to use? The leaves? Or maybe the bark?"

"I think it has to be the sap," Angel said. "It says 'It also yearns for blood from thee.' So wouldn't that mean we need the sap from the tree? I mean, isn't sap sort of like blood?"

"It's exactly like blood," Seth said. "So what does this second part mean? Aren't we supposed to drink it straight from the kettle like we did with the other stuff?"

Angel shook her head. "I think we're supposed to wait until the fire goes out, and then add some of our own blood to what we're going to drink. I put my blood in mine, and you put your blood in yours."

Seth read the verses one more time, then looked up from the book. "What do you think it does?"

"I think maybe it sort of turns things around. So whatever someone tries to do to you turns back on them."

Seth repeated the single word printed above them. " 'Reckoning.' " He looked at Angel. "You think maybe it's like a day of reckoning, when everything evens out?"

"What else could it be?" she asked.

"But how would it work?" Seth countered, then picked up the book. "Did you find anything else in here?"

"I made some more of the stuff that makes things rise," Angel replied. "But I couldn't figure out what the rest of them mean. In fact, I could hardly read most of them."

Seth went through the pages of the book one by one. On half the pages the designs were so ornate and the words so strange that he had no more idea of what they said than Angel did, and even when he could figure out what the words were, their meanings were buried so deep in riddles that he couldn't begin to fathom them. Finally he went back to the recipe for "Reckoning." At least it seemed relatively straightforward. "Okay. Let's try it."

He put his coat back on as Angel pulled a plastic poncho out of her backpack, and together they went out into the storm. Houdini, abandoning his place by the hearth, followed them, and by the time they'd picked their way up the slag heap, he was darting across the clearing toward the willow tree, making a zigzag course that made no sense until they caught up with him in the shelter of the huge tree's canopy.

Held firmly in the cat's jaws, but kicking wildly enough to give testament to the fact that it was still very much alive, was a large toad.

As Angel stared at the squirming creature, Seth reached up, grasped a branch of the tree, and tried to snap it. Though the core of the branch broke, the softer bark only split and tore, but the branch still held to the tree. Seth worked it back and forth, but the tough bark refused to give way.

"Where's your knife?" Angel asked.

"In my backpack," Seth replied as he twisted the branch. As the bark twisted tighter, sap began to ooze out of it, and Angel reached out and caught a gob of it on her finger. "Maybe this is enough," she said as a flash of lightning briefly lit the sky, and another thunderclap echoed off the face of the cliff.

"I guess it has to be," Seth sighed, letting go of the branch. "I should have brought my knife."

They ran back to the cabin, ducking their heads against the rain.

Even before she took off the poncho, Angel scraped the sap from her finger into the boiling kettle. Seth retrieved the knife from his backpack, squatted down and took the toad from Houdini, who released it the moment Seth had it in his grasp.

"D-Do you really have to hurt it?" Angel asked as he carefully opened a tiny slit in the skin of one of the toad's large hind legs.

"I barely cut it," Seth replied, holding the toad over the kettle and squeezing the leg until a few drops of blood fell into the roiling liquid. A moment later he released the toad out the front door and watched as it hopped toward the pile of rocks and disappeared. "I don't think he even felt it," he told Angel as he closed the door.

As the fire burned and the cauldron boiled, the storm outside raged on. . . .

As the sun began to set, the fire finally died away. The bubbling in the black kettle settled down to a slow simmer as the storm outside spent the last of its rage; the flashes of lightning weakened, the thunder lost its strength. The light seeping through the cracks in the wall and door brightened. When water stopped pouring into the granite sink, the last rumble of thunder had died away, and the fire beneath the kettle had shrunk to a pile of glowing embers, Seth opened the window.

The air, washed clean by the storm, smelled sweet. As Seth gazed upward, the last remnants of the clouds evaporated into nothing. But for the freshness of the

air and the dripping of the still soggy trees, the storm
seemed to have left no trace at all, for even the wind that
had driven the rain into a slashing torrent had died so
completely that Seth felt no breeze against his cheek. He
pushed the window shutter wide and opened the door as
well. The fresh air left by the storm flushed out the acrid
fumes left by the fire as the last rays of the setting sun
washed away some of the gloom in the tiny cabin chamber.

Seth came back to the table and watched Angel ladle
the contents of the kettle into a small jar. Meanwhile,
Houdini twined himself first through Angel's legs and
then through Seth's, and finally stretched out in the
small patch of sunlight that found its way through the
doorway.

"Now what?" Seth asked as Angel set the jar on the
table.

"One of us adds our own blood to the jar and drinks
it. Then we wash the jar out, and the other one does it."

Saying nothing more, Seth picked up the knife, cut his
finger, and squeezed a few drops of blood into the clear
liquid in the jar. It vanished in an instant, leaving not
even a hint of pink to betray its presence. Waiting only
until the fluid was cool enough so it wouldn't scald his
mouth, he lifted the jar to his lips and swallowed the
contents.

He rinsed the jar at the sink and Angel refilled it. Repeating the same ritual Seth had just performed, but
using her own blood instead of his, she too drained the
contents of the jar.

A moment later she picked up a second jar from the
counter and handed it to Seth. "It's the other one," she
said. "The one that lets you lift things. At least you can
stop Zack from coming after you for a while."

Silently, Seth tipped the second jar up, draining it even faster than he had the first.

A few minutes later, leaving no sign that they'd been there at all, Angel and Seth followed Houdini out the door of the cabin, pulled the door closed, and scrambled to the top of the berm of shattered granite. Climbing down the other side, they crossed the clearing and disappeared into the forest. Even though it was almost completely dark now, they had no trouble following Houdini as he led them back toward Black Creek Road.

"Maybe we should go to the drugstore and get a Coke or something," Seth suggested. They were in front of the Sullivans' house, and both of them could see her father framed in the window, staring out at the darkness of the evening.

Angel shook her head. "I better not. He can't see us, but if I'm any later, he'll just be even madder when I get back."

"I guess," Seth agreed, and Angel could hear the disappointment in his voice. "I guess I'd better be going." Despite his effort to cover it, Angel could hear the fear in Seth's voice, just as she had when he'd asked her to go to the drugstore for a Coke the last time.

"Are you going to be okay?" she asked.

He cocked his head and managed a small grin. "Well, I was okay last night, so I guess I should be able to make it home, shouldn't I?"

"Zack probably won't try anything," she said.

"Maybe," Seth replied, but his expression told her that he was worried about it. "So, I guess I'll see you tomorrow," he finally said. Still, he lingered another few seconds before turning and starting to walk away.

Houdini, who had been sitting patiently while they

talked, stood up, looked up at Angel, then started after Seth. The cat took a few paces, paused, and turned to gaze at Angel, and for a moment seemed uncertain. But then, turning away from her, Houdini hurried after Seth, catching up to him before he was fifty yards down the road.

"Hey," Seth said, bending down to scratch the cat's ears. "What are you doing?" He straightened up and looked back at Angel, but before he could send the cat back, she waved and turned toward her house. "You sure you want to come with me?" Seth asked, squatting down. Houdini promptly rolled over to have his stomach scratched. "Okay," Seth sighed as he complied. "I'm not going to try to tell you what to do."

Twenty minutes later he was only a block from his house, and so far had seen no sign of Chad, Zack, or Jared. Instead of going up Court Street as he usually did—where Zack had caught him yesterday—this time he went around to the other side of the park and walked up Church Street, staying across the street from the park, just in case. Coming to Elm Street, he didn't make the turn toward his house, but went halfway up the next block. Now all he had to do was cut down the alley and come into his house through the back door.

He paused at the mouth of the alley, and as he peered down the long, shadowy row of garages—behind any one of which Zack, Chad, Jared, or anyone else could be hiding—he wondered if it wouldn't be better to go back down to Elm Street and use the front door. Even if Chad and Jared were around, they'd be at the other end of the street anyway.

But if they saw him . . .

Better to use the alley, he decided.

With Houdini darting ahead of him, Seth started

down the narrow graveled lane, leaving the faint yellowish glow of the streetlights behind.

As the darkness gathered around him, he thought he saw a faint movement off to the right, but when he turned to look, there was nothing.

Nothing but a gate that was slightly ajar.

Was that what he'd seen?

Had it moved?

Or had someone come through it? Someone who was now hiding in the shadows of the garage, which were even darker than the night?

Hunching his shoulders against the darkness—and whatever it might conceal—he hurried his step.

He was halfway to his own garage when Houdini suddenly froze.

As the cat's back arched and it stared straight ahead, Seth felt the hair on the back of his neck stand up, and knew then that someone was behind him.

He'd walked into a trap.

Spinning around, he found himself staring at a dark figure silhouetted against the glow of the streetlight at the end of the alley. For a moment both Seth and the dark figure froze, and then the figure raised one if its arms. Now Seth could see the broken beer bottle clutched in the hand at the end of the uplifted arm, and as the figure raised it even higher, so that one of its jagged points was aimed directly at him, it caught the light from behind. As if mesmerized by the glittering object, Seth's mind went blank, and a cold sheen of sweat broke out over his body.

Behind him, he heard a low hiss from Houdini, then a voice.

Jared Woods's voice!

"Jeez! It's that cat!"

The silhouetted figure moved closer, and now the

razor-sharp blade of broken glass was just a few inches from Seth's face. He could almost feel the glass tearing into his flesh, laying his face and neck open, slashing at his arteries—

From behind Seth came a muted scream, just loud enough to break the strange spell the broken glass had cast on Seth. He whirled around to see the barely visible figure of Jared Woods clutching at his face.

Houdini! The cat must have leaped at Jared and—

The thought was cut off by another scream, and once again Seth whirled.

What he saw made him stagger back a pace. The figure holding the broken bottle—who Seth was now sure had to be Chad Jackson—was standing stock-still. The broken bottle was still clutched in his right hand, but even in the dim light coming from the streetlight at the end of the alley, Seth was certain he could see something dripping from it.

Blood.

What had happened?

Had Chad slashed himself? He remembered, then, the last lines of the verse whose instructions he and Angel had followed only an hour earlier: . . . *the payn will turn from thee and fall upon thine enemie.*

As Seth stood frozen and gaping, Chad moved again, and then was hurling himself toward Seth, the broken bottle raised high. Even in the darkness he could see an insane light glowing in Chad's eyes, and he knew what was about to happen.

Chad was going to kill him.

Seth's reflexes instinctively took over, and his mind conjured a single image.

An image of Chad's attack turning back on him, just as the verse had said.

At almost the same moment, Chad lurched backward,

as if an unseen force had pulled him from behind, and then he was writhing on the ground as he tried to escape the weapon that was wielded by his own hand. Out of the corner of his eye Seth saw Jared Woods, staring in stupefaction at the struggling figure thrashing in the alley, then turning to stagger away into the darkness.

A moment later, just as the lethal point of the bottle was about to rip into Chad's neck, Seth let go of the vision he'd conjured in his imagination.

And as the image of Chad slashing at his own neck vanished, Chad dropped the broken bottle. Then he lurched to his feet and stumbled after Jared.

As they disappeared into the darkness at the far end of the alley, Seth turned back to the gate to his own backyard, but paused to look for Houdini.

The cat had disappeared.

With the image of Chad struggling in the darkness to avoid the ravages of his own weapon still etched in his memory, Seth pushed through the gate, slipped into his house, and went up the back stairs to his room. He closed the door, dropped his backpack on his bed, then looked at himself in the mirror.

On the outside, he looked exactly as he had this morning when he went to school.

But on the inside, he knew something had changed.

He could have made Chad Jackson kill himself just now, could have made him use the broken bottle to slash his own throat.

Instead, he'd let Chad go.

But now, in a small dark corner of his mind, all the things Chad had done to him over the years rose up out of his memory, all the humiliations and all the beatings, and he found himself wishing that he hadn't let Chad go.

He wished, instead, that he'd finished what Chad had begun.

In his mind Seth Baker began to visualize what he could have done, and as the images of Chad destroying himself grew clearer, Seth felt a strange power growing inside him.

Maybe, after all, it wasn't too late.

Maybe he could still have a day of reckoning with Chad.

Focusing his mind, he once more turned his enemy upon himself. . . .

Chapter 43

E TRIED TO KILL ME!" CHAD JACKSON HOWLED. "That little shit tried to fuckin' kill me!" He and Jared were in Chad's bedroom.

The broken bottle was gone—dropped somewhere as he'd fled down the alley to the safety of his house. As he stared at the blood covering his right hand, he felt as if he were going to throw up. He hurried to the bathroom and got there just in time to drop to his knees in front of the toilet before a violent contraction seized his stomach and he felt the remains of his lunch rise in his throat and spew out of his mouth.

Gagging and retching, Chad hung onto the toilet, and three more times the nausea overwhelmed him. When his stomach was finally empty, he dropped down onto the bathroom floor, half panting and half sobbing. What had happened? How had Seth—Seth *Baker,* for Christ's sake—done it? He and Jared had spotted him half an hour ago, and it hadn't taken them long to figure out what he was up to. They followed him almost all the way, concealed in the darkness in the park, then cut down Elm Street and through a couple of yards when they saw him heading for the alley.

It should have been easy—Jared was ahead of Seth, and Chad was behind him.

He was caught.

Caught!

Caught all by himself, except for that stupid cat.

Where had it come from? And how could it be alive? They'd killed it, all three of them, and stuffed it in Angel Sullivan's locker. It boggled Chad's mind to the point where he could only dismiss it, stop thinking about it. And anyway, it was nothing but a stupid cat! If Jared had just kicked it or something—

That was it—it was Jared's fault.

The last of his nausea giving way to anger, Chad scrambled to his feet, intending to find Jared, and—

Jared was standing in the bathroom door.

Standing there staring at him.

"What are you looking at?" Chad snarled.

"Jeez, Chad," Jared breathed. "All that blood—I thought we were just going to scare him!"

Now it was Chad who was staring. "I should have killed him!" he screamed. "After what he did to me!" He put his finger to the cheek the broken bottle had slashed only a few minutes ago, and yanked it away as he felt the sting of his own touch. "He coulda killed me!" He turned and gazed into the mirror at the throbbing, burning wound. But he also saw Jared Woods gazing at him, and he saw the doubt in Jared's eyes. What was going on? "You saw him," he said to Jared's image in the mirror. "Jeez, Jared—you saw what he did to me!" As he turned to face Jared directly, he saw his friend pull away. "You saw it!" he said again.

"It—it was dark," Jared stammered.

Chad's voice rose. "He came at me! He grabbed the bottle and—"

"I didn't see that," Jared said, taking a step backward. "I only saw you holding the bottle."

"So what are you saying?" Chad demanded. "You

think I did this to myself?" Again he put his fingers to his throbbing cheek.

Jared shook his head. "It was dark, and . . . Jeez, Chad—*you* had the bottle." Chad moved toward him, but again Jared backed away.

"You *saw* it," Chad said, the fury in his voice dissolving into a whine. "You—"

"It was dark," Jared said. "I couldn't really see—" He licked his lips nervously, then: "I think I better go home." He turned and hurried down the stairs. A moment later Chad heard the front door slam.

What had happened? Why didn't Jared believe him? He turned back to the mirror and gazed once again at his face.

How had it happened? It was Seth's face the broken bottle should have laid open, not his own. How could Seth have gotten hold of him and twisted the broken glass around like that?

And why couldn't he remember it happening?

He could only remember charging at Seth with the shattered bottle, feeling the warmth in his belly as he anticipated the razor-sharp glass sinking into Seth's flesh.

But it hadn't happened. The glass had sunk into his own flesh instead, and torn at his own face.

Had he tripped?

But he didn't remember tripping.

All he remembered was Seth watching him, staring at him—

He caught a flicker in the mirror and whirled around, half expecting to see Jared again standing in the doorway to the bathroom.

But the doorway—and the hall beyond—were empty.

Chad turned back to the mirror, and froze. The image was back, but this time it wasn't just a flicker of motion. This time it was a face, and the face was clear.

It was Seth Baker, and Seth was staring straight at him, his eyes cold and boring deep into his.

As he gazed back, something inside Chad Jackson began to understand the truth, and he knew that the pain he was feeling now wasn't the pain of his own wound.

Now he was feeling the agony of all the wounds he had ever inflicted on Seth Baker.

As the seconds stretched out, Chad's eyes remained fixed on the image of Seth in the mirror, and a terrible urge came over him. Against his own will and with his eyes still fixed on the image of Seth Baker, which seemed to be suspended somewhere deep in the infinity behind the mirror, Chad opened the top drawer of the counter beneath the bathroom sink and picked up the razor that had been his grandfather's and was now his father's and would someday be his.

But he needed the razor now.

He picked it up in his right hand, opening the blade with his left. He didn't test the blade—didn't even see it, really.

All he did was raise it so its point lay against his neck just below his left ear.

He knew what was going to happen next but there was nothing he could do to stop it. It was as if the force of Seth Baker's will had taken control of his body, and it was a force Chad Jackson was utterly powerless to resist.

With one quick motion he pressed the blade of the razor deep into his neck, cutting through skin and muscle and sinew. As blood began to flow from the wound, he jerked the razor across his throat, and watched in shocked awe as his throat gaped open and the flow of blood surged to a pulsing gush as the blade ripped through his larynx and aorta.

As his life drained away, the razor fell from Chad's hand and clattered into the sink, but as he sank to the floor and the darkness of eternity began to close around him, all he heard was the faint sound of laughter.

Seth Baker's laughter.

In the quiet of his own room, Seth clung to the fading image of Chad Jackson for a few more seconds, watching as Chad's life drained away into the pool of blood spreading around him. Only when Chad lay still and the flow of blood had slowed to a trickle did he finally turn away from the mirror over his dresser, in which the vision of Chad's death had been so vivid that Seth was certain it had happened exactly as he'd seen it.

The day of reckoning had come, and the first of his tormentors had fallen.

Chapter 44

ALL AFTERNOON JANE BAKER HAD BEEN TRYING TO make sense of what her husband was saying, but after more than three hours, she still didn't understand. Still, she knew better than to try to argue with Blake when he was angry, and when he'd come home this afternoon, he was angrier than she'd ever seen him and telling her things that just sounded crazy.

Like Seth attacking Zack Fletcher last night. Seth was terrified of Zack, and always had been. But if he'd finally decided to fight back, wasn't it about time?

And witchcraft? Where had that come from? Of course, she'd heard the stories about what had happened in Roundtree centuries ago—who hadn't? But surely Blake didn't believe them! And what was he doing talking to Father Mulroney anyway?

But Blake had been too upset and too angry for her to reason with him, so she'd just listened and tried to understand, and waited for his rage to pass before it focused on her. And for a little while—the last half hour, anyway—she thought it was going to be all right.

But a few minutes ago they heard Seth going up the back stairs, and then Blake's fury came flooding back, and suddenly she wished she could take back the words she'd just spoken: "What are you going to do to him?"

"I'm going to get the truth out of him," Blake rasped, his eyes as hard as his voice. "I'm going to find out where he's been and what he's been doing."

As he turned on his heel and started toward the stairs, Jane stood up and reached toward her husband, as if to stop him. But she said nothing as he mounted the stairs, and let her hand drop to her side, certain that anything she said or did would only make matters worse. *Besides*, she told herself, *he won't hurt Seth.* Sinking back onto the sofa, Jane picked up a magazine and began leafing through it, believing that if she could concentrate on something else, she wouldn't dwell on whatever might be happening in Seth's room.

And it was better not to know, really, since there wasn't anything she could do about it anyway.

Seth heard his father rap once on his door. Then, as always, he opened it without waiting for Seth to respond. But this evening, for the first time in his memory, Seth didn't feel frightened.

"What the hell have you been doing?" Blake Baker demanded, stepping into the room and closing the door behind him.

With a strange feeling of detachment, Seth turned around to face his father. He could see that his father was furious with him, but somehow his father's rage wasn't tying his own stomach into knots, or making his knees tremble, or bringing him to the brink of crying.

In fact, his father's anger wasn't making him feel anything at all.

"You answer me, boy," Blake said, his voice dropping dangerously. "What have you been doing?"

Seth cocked his head, and his brow furrowed as he tried to decide what to tell his father. Not that it would make much difference—his father wouldn't believe the truth, and had already made up his mind what he was going to do. He was already unbuckling his belt.

"You're not going to do that anymore," Seth said quietly.

His father froze, the belt half out of its loops. "What did you say?" he asked, his eyes boring into Seth with the coldness that always made Seth cower.

This time, Seth didn't move.

"I don't want you to hit me anymore," he said.

"Since when do you decide what I do and what I don't do?" Blake grated. "You do what I tell you. And since you didn't answer either of the questions I asked you, you know what happens next." He pulled the belt free from the rest of the loops and wrapped the tag end around his hand a few times so the buckle was dangling from two feet of leather. "Drop your pants, Seth—I'm going to teach you some respect."

Seth shook his head.

A vein in Blake Baker's forehead began to pulse as he slapped the belt buckle against the palm of his free hand. "You don't want to do this, Seth," he said. "You're only making it worse for yourself."

Seth shook his head again.

Blake's right fist tightened on the belt, and his arm rose in the air.

And Seth focused his mind.

Blake Baker's arm began its downward arc, but instead of lashing out at Seth, the buckle whipped around and struck his own face. As the metal tore into the flesh of his cheek, Blake Baker roared in pain, lurched backward, then lashed out at Seth once more.

Again the belt buckle swung all the way around and ripped into Blake, this time catching him in the right eye.

Another howl of agony erupted from his throat, and

he hurled himself at Seth, still trying to lash out with the belt.

As if seized by some invisible power, Blake crashed face first against the wall, grunted, and sank to his knees as blood began to gush from his nose. For a moment it seemed he might slide to the floor, but then he gathered his strength and heaved himself back to his feet just as the door flew open.

Jane Baker, her face ashen and clutching a fireplace poker in one hand, gazed at her bleeding husband. "Seth!" she screamed. "What are you—"

Seth whirled around. "Go away!" he yelled. "Just leave us alone!"

But it was too late. Blake lurched toward Seth once more, the belt raised high again. But at the last moment he veered off toward his wife. Instinctively, Jane Baker raised her arms to fend off her husband's careening body, but it was too late. His full weight crashed against her, and she uttered a muffled grunt as the spur of the poker plunged deep into her own neck. A second later blood began to ooze from the wound. With a look of something akin to surprise in her eyes, she reached out to brace herself against the wall, and the poker fell from her neck, clattering to the floor.

Blake, stunned at the sight of the wound in his wife's throat, let the belt fall to his side and took a step toward her.

The color already fading from her face, Jane Baker slowly sank to the floor, blood now spurting from the deep puncture in her throat. As the reality of what was happening to her slowly sank in, she gazed up at her husband. Her mouth worked, but instead of sound only blood bubbled from her lips.

Paralyzed by what he was seeing, Blake stared down

at Jane, his own face going pale as the geyser of blood from his wife's punctured aorta began to slow and the last of the color drained from her face. As the gush slowed to a trickle, her body slumped to one side, her head lolling back so the wound the poker had opened gaped lewdly.

As the realization of what he'd done sank in, Blake came back to life. Straightening, he tightened his grip on the belt once more, and wheeled around to face Seth. Blood was still streaming from his nose and his wounded eye, but now his rage overwhelmed the agony of his own wounds. "You killed her!" he bellowed. "God damn you, you—" The belt raised high, he charged at Seth.

And at the last instant, as the belt buckle slashed toward him, Seth stepped aside.

His father lumbered past him, staggered through the open door of Seth's room, and lurched against the banister over the stairwell. Losing his balance, he pitched forward. For a second or two he seemed almost to hover in midair, his free hand flailing wildly in search of something to hang onto. Then he tilted forward and, just before he fell, his fingers found the banister. But it was too late. Slippery with his own blood, his fingers lost their grasp and he pitched headfirst to the floor below. His single brief howl of shock and terror was cut off as his head struck the limestone floor of the foyer.

As the silence that fell over the house stretched from seconds into minutes, Seth Baker gazed at his mother. Finally, he went over to kneel beside her. Reaching out, he gently touched her cheek. "You never stopped him," he whispered. "You just let him do it."

Then he stood, left his room, and gazed down at the floor below. His father's body lay facedown on the blood-smeared limestone, and Seth could tell by the angle of his father's head—and the stillness of his body—that he was dead too.

At last he turned away, went down the same stairs he'd come up only a short while ago, left the house by the back door, and walked away into the darkness of the night.

Chapter 45

MYRA SULLIVAN HAD THOUGHT THE DAY WOULD never end. She could barely believe it when Phil Lambert told her that no one had seen Angel since lunchtime. Afterward, she'd gone straight home, certain that Angel would be there. Father Mulroney went with her, and insisted on coming into the house. When they found no sign of Angel, he hadn't wanted to leave her alone.

"Not in this storm," he'd said, and though he tried to pretend that he was only worried that the electricity might go out, she knew right away that there was more to it than that. She'd seen it in his eyes as they flicked around the rooms of her house as if looking for something he knew was there even though he couldn't see it. She heard it in the hollowness of his voice as well, as he made the explanation she hadn't believed. Not that she wanted to stay in the house by herself—not after the terrible stories Father Mulroney had told her, and the strange things she'd seen in that house.

So she went back to the church with Father Mulroney, and spent the afternoon repeating her prayers again and again, and telling herself over and over again that the things Father Mulroney had told her couldn't possibly be true. Yet as the storm raged outside and she stayed on her knees in front of the altar, her fingers moving over the rosary beads in perfect unison with the silent rhythms of the prayers she repeated, she could not banish the memories of the strange things that had happened in her house and the strange vision she'd seen.

The vision of the girl dressed in black, the way Angel had been dressed when she left the house this morning.

It *had* been a vision—she knew that. But not the same kind of vision she sometimes had when, after long hours of praying, she caught glimpses of the Holy Mother in the curling smoke of the votive candles, or in the rippling surface of the holy water as she dipped her fingers in the font. The Holy Mother was real—as real as she herself.

And those visions had comforted her.

The black-clad figure had not comforted her at all. Indeed, even its memory filled her with the kind of chill she could only think of as coming from death itself.

So she'd prayed.

And finally the storm had ended.

And still she prayed, until now her knees were so stiff and sore, she could barely stand up, no trace of daylight was visible through the stained-glass windows, and the candles she'd lit hours earlier had burned to little more than flickering stubs.

Leaving the church at last, Myra made her way home through the darkness. She was late, and she knew Marty would be angry, but even the thought of his fury didn't quicken her step. Indeed, as she left the town behind and started out on Black Creek Road, the closer she came to the house at the Crossing, the slower were the steps she took. When she came around the bend in the road and could finally make out the shape of the house silhouetted against the night sky, she stopped walking entirely.

And gazed through the darkness at the house.

And knew there was a reason why her steps had slowed.

It wasn't just the things Father Mulroney had told her, or the recollection of the things she'd seen, or the uneasiness she'd felt in the emptiness of the house a few hours ago. No, this time it was different.

This time the house wasn't empty.

And something was wrong.

Part of Myra wanted to turn away and go back to town, back to the church, back to Father Mulroney.

But instead she made herself go on.

Marty Sullivan wasn't sure when the voice had started whispering again. He was slouched low in the chair in front of the television, but he'd long since stopped watching its flickering images or listening to its droning sound.

Instead he was listening to the voice that was whispering to him, and he was watching the images in his head.

"*You can have her. . . .*" the voice whispered.

"*You want her. . . .*"

He'd finished the last of the beer an hour before Angel came home, but found half a bottle of bourbon in one of the boxes in the kitchen that Myra had never bothered to unpack.

Myra!

Where the hell was she, anyway? Spending all her time at that stupid church, praying and taking care of the damned priest when she should have been home taking care of him.

Just the thought of the priest made Marty add an extra couple of inches of whiskey to his glass. By the time Angel walked into the house, he'd worked his way through three more shots.

He didn't have to ask Angel where she'd been—he knew! Out with that son of a bitch Blake Baker's kid. And he knew what they'd been doing too. Myra might not believe it, but he knew.

His daughter was a slut.

A slut who had taken a boy she'd barely even met into her bedroom.

"It isn't him she wants," the voice whispered, *"it's you . . . she wants you just the way you want her. . . ."*

That was why she hadn't spoken to him when she came in, why she just glanced at him as she headed for the stairs, acting like she didn't see him at all. But she had seen him—he could tell.

And she wanted him.

Just like the voice said.

He could feel it.

He listened to her going up the stairs, and heard her close the door to her room.

"You know what she's doing. . . ." the voice taunted.

Oh, yeah, he knew. She was taking off her clothes. . . .

The thought made Marty tremble, and he poured more of the whiskey from the bottle into his glass, then drained the glass.

"She wants you to see her," the voice continued. *"She wants you to touch her. . . ."*

As the television droned on, and the image on the set continued to flicker, Marty drank the rest of the whiskey and listened to the voice.

"Go on," it whispered. *"You know what you want to do . . . you know what you have to do. . . ."*

At last, with the voice whispering to him, Marty rose from his chair and went into the kitchen. He opened the drawer next to the sink, and a moment later his fingers closed on the handle of Myra's favorite knife.

The thumb of his other hand traced its edge, testing its sharpness.

"That's right," the voice whispered. *"You know what you want to do . . . what you have to do. . . ."*

The knife in his right hand, Marty started up the stairs.

Angel heard the footsteps on the stairs and knew exactly what they meant.

He was finally coming for her.

The door to her room was shut, but it wasn't locked—he'd taken away the key—and she knew that if he wanted to come in, he would.

Nothing would keep him out.

As soon as she'd entered the house, she knew it was a mistake—she should have gone with Seth.

Or gone to her aunt's.

Or gone anywhere.

But she hadn't done any of those things, and now she was alone without even Houdini to help her, and he was finally coming for her. *But it's going to be all right,* she told herself. *I can make him stop. I know I can.*

She was standing next to the chair by her desk, still dressed in the clothes she'd worn to school. She'd considered putting on one of her old sweatshirts when she got home, but changed her mind when she remembered her father walking in on her the other day, staring at her half-naked body with a look in his eye that told her what he was thinking. So she hadn't risked taking off any of her clothes.

Nor had she been able to absorb any of her English assignment. She'd reread the same page over and over, her eyes scanning the words but not seeing them, so focused was she on listening for the sounds that would betray her father's presence outside her door.

Now, as his footsteps drew closer, she tried to prepare herself. She gripped the chair.

And she waited.

The planking in the floor groaned as if protesting every step he took, and Angel could almost see him walking with exaggerated care, but weaving from all the beer and whiskey he'd been drinking.

He was outside her door now, but before the door opened she sensed something at her feet and looked down to see Houdini gazing up at her. As the bedroom door began to open, the cat jumped into her arms.

The door swung slowly open to reveal the figure of a girl holding a cat as black as the clothes she wore, and once more Marty Sullivan heard the voice whispering in his head.

"Yes . . . oh, yes . . . my little girl . . . my perfect little girl. . . ."

He clutched the knife in his right hand even more tightly and stepped forward, crossing the threshold and entering Angel's room.

"Yes . . ." the voice inside whispered. *"Closer . . . close enough to touch her . . ."*

With the voice whispering hypnotically inside his head, Marty moved closer.

Angel held Houdini tightly as she saw the knife in her father's hand, and as he slowly moved toward her, she felt the cat tense and heard his low growl shift into a warning hiss. But her father kept coming, and as he drew near, with the knife raised high and aimed at her face, she imagined its point sinking into one of her eyes, stabbing deep—

The thought died as she recoiled from the pain, which was so vividly imagined that she could actually feel it, and even see the blood pouring from the wound.

A scream erupted in the room, a scream that perfectly reflected the pain Angel was imagining and the carnage she saw in her mind's eye. Except the scream hadn't erupted from her throat, and the blood wasn't pouring from a wound in her own face, but rather, from her father's! And her father was reeling now, his free hand reflexively pressed against his eye. Blood was streaming from it, oozing through his fingers, running down his face and his neck, spreading over his shirt.

But how had it happened? The knife was still in his other hand, and still pointing at her.

But it was covered with blood!

How? She'd been watching, and she hadn't seen him do anything! She'd just imagined the knife plunging into her own eye and—

And her father's own eye had bled!

What if she'd imagined it sinking into her breast?

Another howl burst from her father's throat, and now blood was spurting from a great gash in his chest. Then the howl died away and he was moving toward her again, and his lips were moving, and she could hear words.

But it wasn't her father's voice. And as the voice poured forth from the bloody figure lurching toward her, the cat in her arms launched itself outward.

"Killing me . . ." the voice whispered. *". . . have to touch her . . . have to have—"*

The cat struck Marty Sullivan's face, its claws extended, its fangs bared. As its teeth tore into the flesh of Marty's face, he let out another scream of agony, and finally turned away, lurching toward the door, groping with his free hand as he staggered out of the room.

Myra Sullivan heard the first scream as she was coming through the front door. She froze, but when she heard the second scream, and knew it was coming from the second floor, she left the front door standing open and hurried toward the foot of the steep staircase. "Angel?" she called out. "Angel!"

Now she could hear movement upstairs, and muffled grunts, and a sound like sobbing.

Angel!

She mounted the stairs, but before she was even halfway up, a figure appeared on the landing above, and as she gazed at it, Myra could barely believe her eyes. Blood was spurting from the figure's chest, and half its face seemed to be torn away. Transfixed by the terrible vision above her, she gazed at it in awe. Then, seeing the knife in the figure's right hand, she realized it wasn't a vision at all. "Marty?" she breathed.

Instead of answering her, the great bloodied form of her husband teetered at the top of the stairs for a moment, then began tipping toward her. Reflexively, Myra raised her arm to fend off the falling form of her husband, but it was too late. The arm holding the knife stretched straight ahead of him as Marty Sullivan plunged headfirst down the stairs.

The long blade of the knife tore through Myra's breast, and she uttered a grunt as her eyes widened in shock. She felt herself falling backward, and a moment later was sprawled on the kitchen floor. Then Marty's body crashed down on top of her, and as the full force of his weight struck her, the blade of the knife twisted in her breast and slashed through her heart.

Just before Myra died, she caught a fleeting glimpse of a figure at the top of the stairs.

It was a girl, clad all in black, holding a cat.

But it was not her daughter.

It couldn't be her daughter.

After all, her daughter was an angel. . . .

Chapter 46

SETH BAKER CAME AROUND THE BEND IN THE ROAD and saw the house that stood at Black Creek Crossing looming against the night sky. Even though there were lights on, the house had a look of terrible foreboding about it, and as he made his way across the lawn, part of him wanted to turn away and go somewhere else.

But there was nowhere else to go.

Not after what had happened in his house.

As he approached the front door, the awful sense of foreboding grew stronger, and he paused at the door, which was standing wide open, and listened.

A silence seemed to emanate from the house, a silence that felt as if it was about to swallow him up. Once again he wanted nothing more than to turn away, to leave whatever was inside the house undiscovered, and again he knew he could not. Steeling himself, he stepped over the threshold into the living room.

The television was still on, but somehow even its droning didn't dispel the strange sense of silence that imbued the house.

Knowing he didn't want to see whatever it was that lay beyond the living room, but knowing there was no alternative, he moved deeper into the house.

He found Angel at the bottom of the stairs, staring at the bodies of her parents, who were lying on the floor— her father on top of her mother—in a pool of their own blood. Myra Sullivan's eyes were open, and as he looked down at her, Seth had the uneasy feeling that she was looking back at him. Turning away, he looked at Angel. "It happened at my house too," he said softly.

Angel gazed at him, and for a second Seth wasn't sure she even saw him. A moment later, though, she spoke, her voice hollow:

"I know what we have to do."

Seth said nothing and when she led him out of the house, he silently followed.

They crossed the lawn to the road, and instead of turning right, toward the trail that would lead them to the cabin hidden in the cliff, Angel turned left.

Once again, Seth followed. . . .

Chapter 47

FATHER MIKE MULRONEY HAD A SENSE THAT SOME-
thing was wrong from the moment he awoke the
next morning. At first he thought he'd slept late, but
both the faintly glowing hands of the clock on his bed-
stand and the darkness of the room told him that was
not so.

It was five o'clock, the time at which he always
awoke.

Nor did he feel in any way ill.

Then what was it? Rising from his narrow cot and following the routine of years, he used the small prie-dieu
in his bedroom to offer his first prayers of the day. Then,
still before the sun had risen, he showered, dressed, and
prepared his breakfast of orange juice, two fried eggs, a
single slice of wheat toast, and a demitasse of the kind of
rich bitter coffee he'd fallen in love with the year he'd
spent in Rome, before being ordained into the priest-
hood by His Holiness himself.

And the feeling that something was wrong stayed with
him.

After cleaning up what little mess his breakfast had
caused in the kitchen, he moved through the rectory,
seeing nothing amiss, but with his feeling of unease
growing stronger. Finally, as the blackness outside began

to give way to the first faint gray of the coming sunrise, he went to his desk to begin organizing the day. Not that there was much to organize: Tuesday was the closest thing to a day off Father Mulroney had, and this Tuesday nothing at all was on his schedule.

So why was he certain that something was amiss?

His eyes fell on the old book recounting the legends of Roundtree's past—if they were legends at all—and he remembered the storm that had struck yesterday, exploding out of nowhere to batter the town for nearly three hours, and vanishing as quickly as it had come.

Three hours during which Angel Sullivan had not been in either of the places people had expected her to be.

Her mother had expected to find her at school, where she should have been all day.

Father Mulroney, though, had not expected her to be in school—indeed, he would have been very surprised to find her there. However, he'd been very surprised when she hadn't been at home either. In fact, one of the reasons he'd insisted on accompanying Myra Sullivan back to her house in the afternoon was his certainty that Angel was there, and he was curious to see what she might be doing. Yet the house had been empty, and finally he brought Myra back to the rectory with him, where she'd worked until after sunset, and refused his offer to take her home.

He let her go—after all, the storm had passed.

Now, picking up the book, he locked it back into its usual desk drawer and returned the key to its place in a small box on the mantel. As he turned away from the mantel he glanced out the window behind his desk. The sun had finally risen above the horizon, and across the street, silhouetted against the morning sun, stood the ancient oak tree.

It was a sight Father Mulroney had witnessed thousands of times before, but one he never tired of. And this morning it was almost perfect. The sun was directly behind the tree, which stood in stark contrast to the pale blue of the cloudless sky, its limbs casting black fingers across the brilliance of the morning, which reached all the way to the rectory.

But this morning it wasn't only the tree that caught the priest's attention, for there were two other shapes etched starkly against the pale canvas of the morning sky.

Two shapes that Father Mulroney recognized immediately.

Two shapes that told him exactly what had felt so wrong this morning.

Picking up the telephone, he dialed a number, spoke rapidly for a few seconds, and then left the rectory, hurrying across the street to the cemetery.

The sound of sirens was already wailing through the town by the time Father Mulroney was close enough to the ancient oak to see the faces of Angel Sullivan and Seth Baker.

Their jaws had gone slack and their eyes were open.

Father Mulroney crossed himself and began to pray, but even as he prayed, he couldn't take his eyes from the terrible visages of the two children who had hanged themselves from the tree in the darkness of the night. . . .

Epilogue

*W*HY CAN'T IT JUST BURN DOWN?

Joni Fletcher wondered how many times she'd asked herself that question during the year that had passed since the night Angel Sullivan and Seth Baker had killed their parents and then hung themselves from the old oak tree in the Congregational cemetery. Nor was she the only person in town who had asked the question; someone had asked it just last night at the town council meeting, suggesting that the town buy the property, donate the building to the Volunteer Fire Department as fuel for a practice fire, then sell off the land after the house was gone. It had fallen to Ed to explain—for at least the hundredth time—that the house couldn't be burned down, or torn down, or even moved. It was an historical building, and thus protected by law. Unless it caught fire by accident, it would stand until it finally rotted away.

In fact, someone had tried to burn it down at least three times over the last year, and strangely, all three times the fires went out of their own accord. The two in the basement had done little more than leave the smell of smoke in the cellar—and throughout the rest of the house, whenever it rained—and the one in Angel's room only succeeded in ruining the paint, which Joni and Ed themselves had paid to have replaced. Each time a fire had been set, the police chief and his deputy had gone out to the old house to take a look, and most of the people in town, including Joni, were sure that the police were more interested in trying to figure out why the fires had burned out than in finding out who had set them. Certainly no one had been charged with the three acts of arson, nor had the chief ever mentioned a suspect.

The bank had slashed the price again, and though Joni had done her best to talk the woman in the passenger seat next to her out of even looking at the house, in the end she'd decided that at least she would be honest about the place. She'd been in the business long enough to know that any other real estate agent—or at least the ones from the surrounding towns, who were also showing the property—would say no more than they were legally obligated to. Now that she was here, though, Joni wasn't sure she could bring herself to go through with the showing.

"Well, it certainly looks solid enough," the woman said.

Joni gazed bleakly at the house. "Oh, it's solid enough, Mrs.—" For the first time in her career, Joni Fletcher completely blanked on her customer's name, and finally had to glance down at the information sheet she'd filled in only two hours ago. "—Flint," she finished. Then: "May I call you . . . ?" She left the question open, like a space in a form waiting to be filled in.

"Margie," the woman said automatically, her eyes still fixed on the house. "If there's nothing wrong with it, why is it so cheap?"

"Because everyone who lives in it dies," Joni replied, her voice flat.

Margie Flint turned to stare at her. "Excuse me?" she

said, thinking she could not possibly have heard the other woman correctly.

"The last people who lived here were my own sister and her husband and daughter. And I sold them the house myself." Then, in as much detail as she could bear to recount, she told Margie Flint what had taken place almost exactly a year ago. "They weren't even in it for two weeks," she finished, her voice sounding as drained as she felt after repeating the story of how Myra, Marty, and Angel had died. "Which is why I don't want to sell the house to you. Not to you, or to anybody else."

"You sound like you think there's some kind of curse on it," Margie said, turning away from Joni to gaze once more at the little house that sat far back from the road, almost as if it were trying to disappear into the surrounding forest.

Now Joni's eyes also shifted back to the old house, which seemed so utterly harmless under the clear blue sky and bright sunlight of the perfect fall day. "I don't know if it's a curse, but—" Her words died abruptly as Margie Flint turned back to her.

"Can I see it?" Margie asked, opening the car door before Joni could respond.

"See it?" Joni echoed blankly. After what she'd just told the woman, she still wanted to see the house? "I— I don't know—" she floundered. "I thought—"

Margie Flint's demeanor instantly changed, the eager light in her eyes fading into an expression of sympathy. "Oh, I'm sorry," she said. "Of course you wouldn't even want to set foot inside it, would you?" She hesitated, glancing back toward the house once more. "But what if—well, would it be all right if I just went in?" At the stricken look on Joni Fletcher's face, she spoke again, her words tumbling out. "It's just that I came all this way, and the price is so low, and I know terrible things happened in it, but—" She fell silent, then shrugged. "I don't know—it's just a feeling I have. Can't I just go in for a minute and take a look? Please?"

Joni's expression hardened. "We've had dozens of people wanting to see it," she began. "Maybe even hundreds. Frankly, I think it's morbid the way—"

Margie Flint's eyes widened in shock as she realized what Joni Fletcher was saying. "Oh, no!" she said. "That's not it at all. It's just—I don't know." She shrugged helplessly. "I don't want to know any more about what happened in the house, and I don't want to know where—" She was about to say "where the bodies were found," but thought better of it. "I just feel like I have to see it," she said. "We've been looking so long, and nothing's been right, and—" Her voice faltered again as she turned back to gaze at the house. "There's just something about it," she said finally.

When she turned back to face Joni, her eyes were practically pleading, and Joni could see that the woman didn't have so much as a trace of the morbid curiosity that the dozens of other people who had asked to see the house over the last year exhibited.

Reaching into her purse, Joni found the key and handed it to Margie Flint. "I'll wait here," she said.

Mrs. Flint got out of Joni's Volvo, closed the door behind her, and started toward the house. As she drew closer she found herself gazing up at one of the windows on the second floor. Pausing, she wondered what had drawn her attention, but could see nothing that distinguished that window from the other two that looked out over the weed-choked lawn to the road. Yet, though she saw nothing different about the window, she still felt as if she were being drawn to the room behind it.

At the front door, she hesitated. Maybe she shouldn't go into the house after all—maybe she should just go back to the car, get in, and have Joni Fletcher show her something else.

Even as she entertained the thought, however, she slid the key into the lock, turned it, and opened the front door.

And stepped inside.

Though the room was devoid of furniture, Margie Flint felt none of the emptiness she'd experienced in the other unoccupied houses she'd looked at over the last few months. In the rest of them, she'd shared the feelings of her family—what her daughter had started calling "the empty house creeps." But this house had none of that, and as she moved through it, Margie could see perfect places for every piece of furniture she and her husband had collected over the years, scrimping to save up the money and restoring the pieces themselves.

And this house—no matter what had happened in it before—was the perfect place not only for their furniture, but for them. She and Alex could do all the restoration work themselves, and by the time they were done, the house would provide the ideal backdrop for everything they had.

Her excitement grew as she mounted the stairs and went through the bathroom and the master bedroom.

Then, at last, she came to the door of the room whose window had caught her attention a few minutes ago. Opening the door, she stepped inside the little bedroom at the front of the house. Like the rest of the house, it was empty of furniture, but it didn't matter.

In her mind's eye she already saw how it would look with all of Gina's things in it. And with some curtains on the windows—

She jumped as something brushed her leg, and she looked down.

A black cat was sitting on the floor, gazing up at her.

"Well, who are you?" Margie asked, bending down to scratch the cat's ears. As the cat began to purr and rolled over to have its belly rubbed, she saw the single white blaze in the center of its chest. "What a pretty kitty—we'll have to think of a wonderful name for you." Margie gave the cat another scratch, then straightened up. "The question is," she said, smiling down at the cat, who was now weaving back and forth around her legs, rubbing first one side, then the other, "how did you get in here? And how will you like having to share the house?"

The cat mewed softly.

Margie went through the house one more time, but knew she'd already made up her mind. Yet as she started back to the car, she paused to look back at the house once again.

Her eyes came to rest on the window of the small bedroom on the second floor. And for an instant—a moment so brief she wasn't sure it had happened at all—she thought she saw two faces looking back at her.

A girl and a boy, in their mid-teens.

The images vanished so quickly that Margie assumed she'd imagined them. Squinting in the bright sunlight, she peered once more up at the window.

The cat was looking back at her.

Nothing else—just the cat.

And it was a cat that seemed to like her, and had mewed happily at the suggestion that it was going to have to share the house. So that was all she'd seen—not two barely visible faces, but just a cat that was not only completely visible, but very real, and wanted her there as much as she wanted to be there. Her fleeting doubt dispelled, Margie Flint pulled out her checkbook as soon as she was back in the car. "How much earnest money will you need?" she asked.

Joni Fletcher stared at her in disbelief. "You're not seriously going to—" she began, but Margie Flint didn't let her finish.

"I am very serious. The house is perfect, and I have no interest whatever in what might have happened here in the past. Just tell me how much the bank wants to hold it until we can get the deal settled."

"I—I'm sure a thousand dollars will be fine," she began. "But—"

But Marge Flint was already writing the check, and finally Joni Fletcher started her car and headed back to the office.

"This is so wonderful," Margie said as they drove back into the heart of the little town a few minutes later. "It's almost like I'm coming home again!"

Joni Fletcher glanced at her as she pulled into a spot in front of her office. "Are you from around here?"

Margie Flint shook her head. "Not me—I grew up in Colorado. But my father said his family used to live around here."

"Really?" Joni asked. "What was their name?"

"Wynton," Margie said. "That was my maiden name. Margaret Wynton."

Joni Fletcher felt an icy chill close around her soul. The house at Black Creek Crossing, she knew, would never burn.

It would, in fact, be there forever. . . .

If you enjoyed John Saul's
Black Creek Crossing,
You won't want to miss
His new terrifying novel of suspense

PERFECT NIGHTMARE

Available August 30th, 2005 in hardcover
From Ballantine Books

*Please turn the page
for an exciting sneak preview . . .*

I prowled through their house for a long time last night before I finally did what I knew I had to do.

I loved the house the first time I saw it—loved it almost as much as I loved the girl who lived there. And last night it was as perfect as it has ever been.

It was the candlelight, I think.

I remember the house being candlelit the first time I saw it—indeed, I think perhaps it was the candlelight itself that drew me to it.

Like a moth drawn to a flame?

It's a cliché, I know, but didn't someone once say that a cliché is only a cliché because it's true?

And the candlelight did mesmerize me, almost as much as the girl's face.

Her face, and her body.

The first time I remember being in the house, the candles were lit. The family was having some kind of a party.

A birthday?

I don't know.

I shall never know.

It doesn't matter that I shall never know, of course, just as it never mattered that I didn't know her age.

All I know is that she was perfect, that I knew I loved her from the moment I saw the candlelight flickering on her face, making her flesh glow as if with an inner light.

A light I have never known.

Could that be why the candles fascinated me? Because of their strange, flickering light that warms as much is it illuminates?

I don't know.

Nor do I care, if I am going to be absolutely honest about it. All I know is that the first time I saw the house it was glowing with candlelight, and her beautiful young face radiated even more heat than the candles, and I was drawn to that heat.

After that first night, I came back to the house as often as I could, slipping into it at night and lighting the candles—just enough for me to make my way around. And the first time I slipped into her room, feeling my way through the darkness of the corridor, moving so silently I could hear my own heart beating—but nothing else—I knew.

I knew she was mine.

She, you see, loved candles as much as I do.

Her room was filled with them. She had them on her dresser and on the table by her chair, and on her desk and on the nightstand by her bed.

Most of them were out, of course, but there was one still burning.

I remember it even now, remember how I stood at her door, which I had opened just far enough to peep inside, and found myself gazing at a flame.

A flame that drew me toward her even from that very first moment.

I slipped into the room, closing the door so silently there wasn't even the softest click to betray my presence. Inside the room—her room—an odd sensation came over me. It was as if I was floating, drifting over the thick rug on the floor as if my feet weren't even touching it.

When I was close by her bed, I looked down and beheld her perfect beauty in the light of that single candle, and knew that we belonged together.

I didn't touch her that night. No, I was content merely to hover above her, gazing down on her youth and innocence.

It was a long time before I finally touched her. I don't know how long.

And she didn't mind.

I know she didn't, for she lay still, and let my fingers trace her soft contours, let my lips brush hers.

So perfect . . . so very perfect.

I thought it would stay that way forever, that we would share our perfect love, but then one night she pushed me away.

Just like the other one had.

And I knew what I had to do.

I even knew it had to be last night.

Last night, after all, was Christmas Eve.

I'd seen the house once before on Christmas Eve, as I lurked hidden in the shadows, watching the candles being lit one by one, each of them pushing the cold and darkness a little farther away, until the entire house was suffused with a flickering golden light.

Even the Christmas tree, standing in front of the great picture window that overlooked the lake, was aflame with candles, each set in its own holder, clipped to the very ends of the branches so no wick had a twig above it.

It was a beautiful sight, that tree, and last night I lit it once more.

They had all gone to bed by then of course, and I was alone downstairs.

I only lit that one room, but I lit every candle in it. The ones in the sconces on the walls, and the ones in the uplifted hands of the pair of brass figures—they look oddly Russian, though I don't know why—that stands on the mahogany table where they always play games. I even lit the six tapers in the three pair of sterling silver candlesticks atop the glass fronted bookcase that fills the wall opposite the picture window.

Then I lit the tree.

For a long time—I don't know how long—I gazed at the tree, knowing it would be the last time I saw it.

Knowing it would be the last time I saw this house.

Then I carefully extinguished every candle I had lit, and went upstairs.

As always, she had a single candle lit by her bed, and I gazed at it for a long time, too.

It, and the perfect face it was illuminating.

Her hair was spread around her face like a halo, glowing in the soft light of the candle's flame, and as I beheld her innocence I wanted to touch it one last time.

Touch her one last time.

I didn't touch her though. No, not last night.

Last night I did what I knew I had to do, and as the candle by her bed burned low, I lit the dozen others that she had in her room.

With each match I struck, with each wick I lit, the room grew brighter, washing away the shadows that concealed me.

It didn't matter though, for after tonight I would never come back here.

Never see this perfect place—this perfect child—this perfect family—again.

When all the candles were blazing, I turned to look one last time on the girl.

She was smiling, content in her sleep.

Did dreams of Christmas morning dance in her head?

I shall never know.

As I stood near the door, a slight breeze came through the window I had opened only a moment before.

A breeze that moved the light lace curtain just close enough to the flame of one of the candles so that it caught.

Caught, as my breath caught in my throat.

The flame on the curtain seemed to die away in an instant, fading to nothing but a glowing ember, but then another gust of air came through the window, and the fading ember leaped back to life.

Flames climbed up the lace toward the ceiling like a great glittering spider racing up its web. A second later, the flames had jumped the gap to the curtain on the other side of the window.

Now the wallpaper was beginning to burn, and I knew it was time for me to go.

I beheld the face of the girl one more time.

"It's all right," I whispered. "We'll be together again someday soon."

I know she heard me, for I saw a smile cross her lips.

I turned away and left before she could awaken.

As I think about it now, I know it wasn't that I didn't want her to awaken and see me—or see what I had done—that made me leave so quickly.

No, it was something else.

I simply didn't want to hear her scream.

IF YOU'VE ENJOYED THIS NOVEL
BY JOHN SAUL, LISTEN TO OTHERS
BY THIS *NEW YORK TIMES*
BESTSELLING AUTHOR.

JOHN SAUL'S **Black Creek Crossing,
Midnight Voices, Manhattan Hunt Club,** and
Nightshade are all available on audio
wherever books are sold.

"[Saul is] one of America's favorite fright
writers."—*Fort Worth Star-Telegram*

BLACK CREEK CROSSING
PERFORMANCE BY LEE MERIWETHER
0-7393-0937-4, $25.00/$38.00C
(ABRIDGED ON CASSETTE)

MANHATTAN HUNT CLUB
PERFORMANCE BY LEE MERIWETHER
0-553-52806-8, $25.95/$38.95C
(ABRIDGED ON CASSETTE)
0-553-71441-4, $29.95/$44.95C
(ABRIDGED ON CD)

MIDNIGHT VOICES
PERFORMANCE BY LEE MERIWETHER
0-553-71345-0, $25.00/$38.00C
(ABRIDGED ON CASSETTE)

NIGHTSHADE
PERFORMANCE BY LEE MERIWETHER
0-553-52733-9, $25.00/$38.00C
(ABRIDGED ON CASSETTE)

RANDOM HOUSE
AUDIO

For more information about his titles and other audiobooks
available from Random House, visit www.randomhouse.com/audio.